NOTICE: This book is licensed to Duplication or distribution by e-r printout or by other means to a person other than the original recipient is a violation of international copyright law.

© 2023 Charlotte Langtree. All rights reserved. No part of this publication may be reproduced, stored in a retrieval system, or transmitted in any form or by any means, electronic, mechanical, photocopying, recording or otherwise, without either the prior written permission of the publisher or a license permitting restricted copying in the United Kingdom issued by the Copyright Licensing Agency Ltd, 90 Tottenham Court Road, London W1P 9HE.

Published by Clarendon House Publications
76 Coal Pit Lane, Sheffield, England

Published in Sheffield 2023

ISBN #: 9798385612086

Fractured:
Tales of Flame and Fury

A Fantasy Collection by
Charlotte Langtree

To Alison,

I can't say thank you enough. Your support has been a lifeline.

Happy reading!

Charlotte Langtree

CLARENDON HOUSE PUBLICATIONS
www.clarendonhousebooks.com

For Edith,
my star, my sunshine,
who fills my world with love and light.

ACKNOWLEDGEMENTS

Seeing my own book published is the fulfilment of a lifelong dream. I am so grateful to everyone who has encouraged and supported me on the journey to making it happen.

To my publisher, Grant Hudson, and all the readers who voted for me to win the Great Clarendon House Writing Challenge 2021: Thank you. This means the world to me.

To my friends and beta readers, V.H. Stone and Geraldine Borella, who read each word of this book many times over: Without you, this would not have been possible. You helped to make my words shine.

Fractured: Tales of Flame & Fury is, above all, a book about love, and I would not have been able to write it without the love of my family. To everyone who raised me: Thank you for teaching me about real magic, for sharing all the eclectic wonders of your worlds, and for your unwavering, unconditional love throughout.

To my husband, Alex, who patiently suffers the chaos and unpredictability of being married to a writer: You're one of the good ones, my love. You push me to believe in myself, support me in all things, and you're always ready to research when I throw crazy questions your way.

And to my daughter, who is everything: This is for you. Forever, for always, little one. I love you so much I could pop.

CONTENTS

Drummer Girl	11
The Falar Path	43
Once a Queen	85
The Changeling's Sword	131
Cwenhild	161
Wind-Dancer	223
The Sleeping God	297
Him, Her & Lavender Lylah	325

Drummer Girl

NOW

The silence is heavy, oppressive, like the hand of death.

In the moon-shadowed gloaming, soldiers wait for the signal. Some of them will die; this inescapable fact sits in their guts as they study each other's faces. Which of their friends will be buried in makeshift graves in a foreign land? Who will take the news of their death to children, spouses, or parents? Whose mother's heart will break like the body of her child, pierced as surely as with a rusted blade in the hand of a Galamar warrior?

Asralyn Gydeon fears her own heart will burst free of her chest; it beats loud and fast, like the snare drum she plays when they march. The tide is going out. Soon, she will make herself a target. She is small, but she knows the arrows will still find her body; she knows their tips will slide as easily through her flesh as anyone else's.

Her comrades watch her. They are hidden well, but moonlight glints off the eyes focused on her position. The soldiers are spread out, already in place to defend, to protect, to fulfil their duty. The lone mage, hair as silver as the bright crescent hanging above, stands alone, preparing her spells and rituals. Asralyn can't see the Sebenian refugees and the remaining nurses but prays they are safe within the crumbling walls of Cybenis Abbey.

A lone gull screams into the darkness. Asralyn gasps; her breath is warm on the fingers she holds close to her mouth. It won't be long now. Death draws near.

She hopes he has a gentle touch.

THEN

Rat-a-tat-tat.

The drumsticks almost slipped from Asralyn's fingers; sweat dripped from every pore. They marched beneath a hot Sebenian sun, bodies slick with perspiration and lips drier than the Oganwi desert. She maintained the beat through sheer strength of will.

Rat-a-tat-tat.

Her nose itched like the devil, but she daren't scratch it. Missing a beat was a disciplinary offence; she already had one mark against her name and couldn't afford another. She sighed. Long marches gave her too much time to think. *What am I even doing here?* They didn't want her. She'd had to fight to get in, fight for every progression. Too short, they said. Too quiet. Too *nice* to be a soldier.

Asralyn almost snorted. Instead, she wrinkled her nose to bring relief to that bloody incessant itch. She knew what the real problem was, of course. Despite being ruled by a queen, the good old boys of the Tottenic army didn't want a woman in their ranks. The only other women on this mission with her were a handful of nurses and the mage.

Anger rising, she banged the drum a little harder than intended. She winced and reined herself in. *Don't be a fool, Asra. Focus.*

Rat-a-tat-tat.

Night would fall soon, and they'd make camp. If all went well, they'd reach the meeting point tomorrow. Asralyn wanted to be excited; she'd spent her life dreaming of adventure, longing to see distant shores. Now she was here, all she saw was the hazy shimmer of heat rising from flat ground and the sideways glances of her fellow soldiers waiting to see when she'd fail.

Keeping her eyes peeled for Galamar warriors, she marched on. It was unlikely they'd meet the enemy this far north. The Galamar had been gaining ground from the south, creeping through Sebeny like a colony of ants; they took what they wanted and, where one fell, there were always more to fill the gap. But, for now, reports said they remained in the Pomath region.

The itch returned and Asralyn held back a sigh.

NOW

There!

The tide is out. Waves splash over the walkway usually hidden by the sea, but the Galamar are done waiting. The path is clear; they make their move. Moonlight glints off the edges of their infamous serrated blades.

At the top of the tower in the centre of the courtyard, Asralyn is ready. Lifting the horn to her lips, she blows. A long note rings out, clear as a bell. Her comrades know the enemy approaches.

The first arrow grazes her ear. The Galamar do not appreciate their arrival being announced so loudly.

Still, Asra plays. Six short blasts to indicate numbers, one for each ten enemy warriors she counts; the Tottenic soldiers are outnumbered.

The walkway is wide. Galamar men rush across it, wasting no time. Rocks surround the abbey, protruding from the water like the eyes of alligators hiding in the depths, waiting for their chance to feed. Asralyn spots a small boat navigating the obstacles; it lands safely on the east side. Now, the enemy can attack from two directions. She plays the preplanned tune to warn her comrades.

An arrow rushes past her left arm, so close she feels the air move.

She keeps moving, watching the attack unfold and playing her music as long as she can.

The Galamar will not miss for long.

THEN

"This is not what I signed up for," Sister Dawla grumbled, her face red with temper and the flickering light of their campfire.

Asralyn focused on replacing the lace on her boot and listened to the conversation unfolding between the women.

Sister Nariya tutted. "You think any of us bloody signed up for this? We were all told it was a simple run. Escort a few refugees back into Tottenia, back home for harvest... Pfft. Lying bastards, the lot of them!"

"They'll chase us now, for sure," Sister Ruith said. "It's one thing to sneak off with a couple of ministers, but they'll never let us take the fucking queen of Sebeny out of the country!"

Asralyn glanced towards the larger campfire several feet away; no doubt the men were having a similar conversation. None of them had known they would be escorting Queen Imelyei to relative safety in Tottenia. The Galamar would not let that slide.

"We're all dead." Sister Dawla rested her head in her hands. "The best we can hope for is a decent compensation package for our families."

Something stirred the air beside Asralyn. She reached for the hilt of her sword.

"They are not wrong, Drummer Girl." Librith settled onto the log, her gaze fixed on the nurses.

Asralyn forced her muscles to relax. "Maybe so, Mage, but we're not dead yet."

The mage chuckled; the sound was like pond reeds rustling in the breeze, low and dry. "I am sure the Galamar will rectify that soon enough."

"You're a cheerful companion."

"I am a realist," Librith said. "We will be lucky if any of us live to tell this tale."

Carrying out one last check of her equipment before she settled for the night, Asralyn studied the older woman from the corner of her eye. The mage's youthful face was betrayed by the aged silver of her hair, but it was her eyes that lingered; the steel of her gaze was sharper than any blade. "Isn't that why we brought you along?"

The laughter faded from Librith's face. "I am powerful, Asralyn, but even I have limits. The Galamar... They are something else, entirely. We need an army of mages to defeat them."

Asralyn swallowed the lump in her throat. Dug her nails into the soft palms of her hands. "What can we do?"

"Pray."

NOW

The Galamar have reached the abbey. They climb the walls, sharp daggers gripped in their teeth, moving with unnatural ease. Asralyn has heard of their battle haze; the concoctions of drugs they take before a fight leaves them stronger, fearless, and crazed.

Storing her bugle, she picks up her drum. Her comrades know the enemy is here; she can give them no more warnings. But she can stir their blood; fill their hearts with patriotism; sound the call to greater glory. They will die with honour.

Her eyes are wet. The spray from the sea sticks to her hair and presses against her lips with a salty kiss. In the silence of waiting, the rhythmic sway of the water is a lullaby calling her to eternal sleep. She bites her lip until she tastes blood, and spits it to the wind; she will go out with a bang.

Bang.

The drum beat breaks the quiet like a sudden scream. She keeps moving, waiting for the next arrow to strike, waiting for the first cry to pierce the night.

Bang. Bang.

She picks up the pace, steady beat interspersed with rolling thunder. Even now, there is something about the booming music of a drum that lifts her spirits. She hopes it will do the same for her comrades. Prays it will cast fear into the heart of her enemy.

Bang. Bang. Bang.

That one was louder. Why? Asralyn glances to her left. Sees Librith flashing a pearly grin; the mage knows what Asra is trying to do and has amplified the sound. Her lips narrowed into a thin line, Asralyn plays on. *Fight!* She urges them on in her mind. *Fight like the devil, and send those bastards to hell!*

She watches as the Galamar reach the top of the wall and launch themselves over the other side, using hooks and ropes to slow their descent. The Tottenic soldiers are ready. Swords clash in the darkness, steel ringing on steel as shadows mute the blood and gore spilling from fallen friends. Nothing can mute the screams.

Asralyn weeps as she plays.

THEN

Biting the inside of her cheek, Asralyn tried to resist the urge to turn around to see if they were being followed. Librith had been sensing the Galamar for two days and it was only a matter of time before they caught up; it was easier to move at speed when you didn't care how many mounts you killed on the journey.

Three days. Three more days until they reached the coast and boarded the boat that should be waiting for them. If they made it that far, they would be safe for a while. She held on to that thought as she marched. The alternative didn't bear thinking about.

"What's got into you?"

Asralyn spared a glance for the soldier marching next to her but didn't miss a beat. "What?"

"You look glum," Drummer Blayney said. "Someone forget your birthday or something?"

"Yeah." She rolled her eyes. "The Galamar are on our tail and you think I'm worried about my birthday."

Blayney shrugged. "We'll deal with them when they come. No point borrowing trouble."

Ignoring him, she focused on the young queen of Sebeny, riding side-saddle between two nurses and her own two maids, and surrounded by a contingent of armed soldiers. It had surprised her that Queen Imelyei was still a child, not even twelve summers old. Knowing that, it made sense that they were taking her to Tottenia. Their countries had a strong alliance and Tottenia could protect the child-queen until she came of age and could lead her own uprising. Asralyn wouldn't be at all surprised if marriage was on the cards between Imelyei and the Tottenic prince. Queen Leysia's second child, Prince Hughen, was only a year or so older than Imelyei; the union would be beneficial for both lands.

But for that to happen, they had to make it home. Asralyn's gut wasn't convinced they would get that far.

Ahead, Librith straightened in her saddle. "Galamar!"

Asralyn glanced back to the hill they had just ridden down. At its crest, a cloud of dust stained the air as Galamar hooves churned the earth. They rode like the wind, racing down the hill with no care for their horses.

She missed a beat. Forced herself to release the breath she held. Fought against the urge to drop her drumsticks and run.

The column protecting young Queen Imelyei galloped ahead, while the foot soldiers moved into formation to tackle the Galamar army. Asralyn and the other drummers stayed at the back, switching seamlessly from the marching cadence to the formidable Tottenic war song.

The Galamar did not stop. They charged straight into the ranks of Tottenic soldiers, cutting them down with serrated swords, spraying them with blood spatter and gore. Men and horses screamed. Blades clashed. Bodies fell.

The stench of sweat mingled with the metallic zest of blood; the air was so thick with it, Asralyn could almost taste it. She gagged, her eyes stinging and her tongue recoiling. Torn between joining the fight, running away, or following orders, she gave in to duty and beat her drum louder. The other drummers around her, led by Drum Major Navarez, made sure their beat remained steadier than their hands.

Fierce and fast, the fighting was hard to follow; Asralyn struggled to understand who was winning. Shadows flitted between bodies; it must have been a trick of the light, but she froze in horror. When she glimpsed a Galamar face, she recoiled at the sight of black orbs rolling in a sea of curdled milk. She knew that battle could confuse the mind. Knew that some people struggled to process what they saw in wartime and that their minds made things up to fill the gaps. But this... It was too real. There was something wrong with them, something unnatural.

From the back of the Galamar surge, a rain of arrows cut through the air. On her right, a startled gurgle rolled out like the long, last note of a bugle; turning, she watched Blayney fall, his eyes wide open to stare death in the face. A small wail escaped her lips before she cut it off.

And then Librith was there, silver hair gleaming like the Galamar blades as her fury burned brighter than the sun. The old woman pushed her horse into the fray, lashing about with a glowing whip that seemed to be made of sunlight itself; it burned and lacerated and cauterised as it sliced through limbs like a knife through soft butter.

"Drohilh isustor!" she called out in the old language. *Fall back!*

Asralyn gasped as the mage's eyes burned with the white-hot rage of stars, and clouds danced across the sun. The wind howled, kicking up swirls of dust and dirt. Librith reached her arm skywards and opened her fist. Thunder crashed; lightning flashed. Within seconds, a storm raged: a writhing, whirling, thrashing deluge of blinding intensity. It was impossible to see anything beyond an inch or two.

More accustomed to wet weather, the Tottenic soldiers gained a slight advantage; their boots were firmer on the slick ground, their grips tighter on their swords. They pushed back against the Galamar until they could safely withdraw, and then they fled.

"Retreat!" the Galamar captain roared against the storm.

Asralyn slipped and slid in the sudden mud as she followed Drum Major Navarez along the road. She wanted to cry, but thoughts of Blayney's body lying abandoned in the downpour spurred her on. He'd had a wife, and a young son; someone had to tell them he'd died a hero.

She wondered if someone would tell her family the same. No. Back there, in the melee of guts and glory, she'd been a frightened child, longing for someone to save her. Die a hero? She was a coward. They'd all been right; she didn't belong here.

The rain concealing her tears, Asralyn pushed on, her heart as heavy as her aching limbs.

NOW

All is chaos.

This is their darkest hour; death lives in the shadows. Men fall, their bodies strewn across the courtyard, painting the stones with their blood. Asralyn cannot tell which bodies are Tottenic and which are Galamar. Still banging her drum, she hopes Librith will rise to the occasion, golden whip decimating their enemy as it did once before. But she knows better; the mage is weary, her magic exhausted by the relentless battles on their journey here, her body close to giving in and giving out. No, magic will not save them this time.

She wonders what will. What can? Her mind draws a blank.

"Surrender the queen and we will let you live!" The Galamar captain bellows his ultimatum into the night.

Captain Doonan doesn't bother to reply. At least, Asralyn hopes that's his strategy; she is scared he may already be dead.

For a brief moment, the moon peeks out from behind a cloud, and the world beneath Asralyn's tower is revealed in a series of silver montages, bright and surreal against the crescendo of earsplitting screams. She peeps over the wall, and then ducks to avoid the arrow that narrowly misses her head.

Fear grips her like a vice. What should she do?

Risking one more glance, she sees a pile of men lying in a crumpled heap over the stone well. A small pocket of Galamar creeps across the courtyard, edging closer to the crumbling walls of the hall where the young queen hides.

Asralyn looks around, hoping someone else has spotted the danger. But the Tottenic soldiers are fighting for their lives. Librith holds a small Galamar army at bay in the east corner, the strain clear on her aged face. There is no one else to defend Imelyei.

Her breath is loud in her ears, her heart frantic in her chest. She lets the drum hang from the strap on her shoulders, the sticks secured at her waist. She crawls to the top of the spiral staircase just in time to see a shadow climbing higher. Her trembling hand reaches for the sword she has yet to use.

He sees her. Smirks, like a tiger cornering its prey. And reaches out.

THEN

Nightmares plagued Asralyn's sleep that night: dark dreams of demons slaughtering her friends. She woke sweating, a scream caught on her lips. In the next bed, Librith tossed and turned in her sleep, whimpering at unseen foes.

"I guess I'm not the only one struggling to sleep." Sister Dawla sat cross-legged on top of her blanket, her head in her hands and, when she looked up, a haunted look in her eyes.

Asralyn nodded. She rubbed the sleep from her eyes and stared at her hands, wondering if what she remembered could possibly be true. The shadows flitting between Galamar warriors… Surely that had just been her panicked mind misinterpreting the horrors her eyes beheld? And the black orbs of their eyes…

She shuddered. There was something unnatural about them. The ease with which they'd swept through Sebeny had shaken an entire continent; perhaps they'd had more help than people realised.

"Dawla," she began, the words catching in her throat. She coughed and tried again. "Dawla, what are they?"

The sister sighed. "Monsters, Asra. Whether of the human kind or something more, they're monsters. I've never seen anyone take such glee in ending life."

"I wish I'd stayed home."

Stirring from sleep, Librith snorted. "I wish you'd stayed in bed. Some people are trying to sleep here."

Heat crept up her cheeks. "Sorry."

The old mage kicked her blanket off and moved to sit on the edge of her bed. Her silver hair spiked in every direction, wild as her spirit. She narrowed her eyes at Asralyn. "Come on. If we're up, we might as well enjoy the moon."

Asralyn reluctantly followed Librith out of their tent. They walked a few paces away from where others were sleeping, tipping their heads to acknowledge the soldiers keeping guard. The stars were bright, the air crisp and clear; crickets chirped in the long grass. It felt a long way from the battlefield.

"What you did out there…" Asralyn blew air out through her teeth. "You saved all our lives."

The lines around the mage's mouth deepened. "Used too much, though. They're stronger than they should be. More dangerous. I don't know if I'll have the strength to do it again."

"Don't tell me that."

"You want me to lie? We're up the creek out here, girl. Never should've come this far with so few men. But we're here now, and all we can do is fight the fuckers all the way home."

The words, and the vehemence behind them, surprised a laugh out of Asralyn. "That's your best advice?"

"Better than lying back and taking it."

She blinked to ease the sting in her eyes. Listened to the crickets. Tried to let the moon's serenity soak into her skin. After a moment, she turned back to Librith. "Teach me."

Librith emitted a bark of laughter. "Teach you? I can't teach a frog how to be a phoenix. You haven't got the slightest bit of magic in you, girl. I'm a mage, not a miracle worker."

That stung, too. "I meant the fighting, not the magic. The courage, the confidence, the savagery. I want to go home; I need to toughen up."

The pearly grin flashed again. "Now, that's a different story."

NOW

Asralyn's gaze flits between the Galamar warrior's sword and his savage smile. The black orbs of his eyes watch her greedily. She scrambles back into the corner. Her mind churns. Her heart races. She shakes her head, which only seems to widen his grin.

He climbs the last step and towers above her, all broad shoulders and bulging muscles. She takes in details as if time has slowed and she is studying him through a pane of glass. He is clean-shaven but for a neat moustache, curled at each end. A silver scar runs across his chin, accentuating the squareness of his jaw. His clothes are black. His shoes are scuffed.

She watches those shoes as they stride close enough to touch.

Drawing back, recoiling from his ill intent, she wills her body to seep through the cold stone pressed against her shoulders.

The gull shrieks again and the sound startles her voice from its cage. "No!"

He laughs then, the razor-blade rumble grating against her skin. He lifts his serrated sword and prepares to swing.

Asralyn flinches and her knee knocks against her drum. *Bang!* Her heart echoes the beat; her mind continues the martial cadence. Moving in time with the rhythm rolling through her head, she rolls away from the downward strike of his sword. Uses the momentum to leap to her feet. Grabs the drum and raises it like a shield, just in time to catch the blade thrusting towards her chest.

Taken aback by the sword tip poking through the drum mere inches from her chest, she grits her teeth and turns the drum, twisting the weapon along with it. Surprisingly, it works: the Galamar warrior loses his sword as she twists it out of his grip. The drum is done for, but it died a good death. Grabbing her own blade, she screams as she shoves it into her enemy's throat, catching him in that moment of shock as he wonders how a mere girl has disarmed him.

Blood sprays. The warrior gurgles. Asralyn gags then vomits on the shoes now pointing to the sky. *Can't see the scuff now,* she thinks, lost in shock.

She narrows her eyes at the sword wedged in the Galamar's neck. Debates with herself for a fraction of a second. *No.* Trembling, she pulls the serrated blade from the remains of her drum instead.

Her shock is shattered by a scream and she remembers the Galamar men moving toward the young queen. She straightens her back, tightens her grip, and takes the stairs two at a time on her way down. The soldiers always told her the first kill was the hardest; she was about to put that to the test.

THEN

"Get up, girl!" Librith yelled. "What do they teach you in basic training these days?

Asralyn rolled to her feet with a wince; she'd definitely have bruises in the morning.

They'd made camp as the sun set, grabbed a quick bite to eat, and then Librith had dragged her away from the others. The old woman had pushed on until she'd found a small mound of uneven grass next to a stream. Then, the sticks had come out. It had only degenerated from there.

"Let me try again," she said.

"Try harder."

Wielding a stick like a Galamar sword, Librith launched an attack that sent Asralyn scrambling backwards. Barely managing to block the blows, Asra struggled to defend herself. She looked for an opening. Winced at the impact on her arms. Lost ground under the onslaught. And stumbled over a rock hidden in a tuft of grass.

She fell with the grace of a duck in a mudslide, legs in the air, arms flailing as she tried to catch herself. The splash as she hit the water was deafening. Sinking under, she pushed back to the surface, coughing and spluttering as she spat out dirty liquid.

Librith doubled over with laughter, clutching her stomach and rubbing her eyes. "You looked like an upended turtle!"

Asralyn fought the sting of tears. The urge to crawl into her bed and never leave was strong. But memories of black orbs where eyes should have been lingered, there behind closed lids every time she blinked. She didn't have the luxury to rely on others to save her. Not anymore.

Standing, she pushed wet hair off her face and breathed out through gritted teeth. She climbed the bank, shook herself off, and picked up the stick she'd dropped on the way down. Readying her stance, she looked up and met the mage's gaze. "Again."

NOW

Madness surrounds her. Men groan at her feet, Tottenic and Galamar alike, each clutching spilt guts or lying in bright pools of blood; some stare with eyes that will never see again. Her stomach churns but Asralyn hardens herself to it all. She picks her way past the fallen, ducking and hiding behind crumbling stones to avoid catching the attention of those still living.

All around, pockets of fighting rage on. Her comrades fight like devils, but she sees the Galamar steadily gaining ground. Is this it, then? Is this their last stand, their final page in the history books?

In the doorway to the crumbling hall of Cybenis Abbey, Librith now stands with her lightning whip, holding a dozen men at bay. The mage is the only one who stands between the Galamar and the queen of Sebeny. Even she, powerful as she is, cannot withstand the onslaught forever.

Asralyn moves as fast as she dares, scurrying between groups of clashing swords, leaping over piles of bodies strewn across the ground like autumn leaves, fallen from a tree at the height of their glory. She desperately wishes someone else will come to her aid but even the other drummers are engaged in the battle.

She darts past Drum Major Navarez, who stares down two opponents with a bored expression; they do not make music and he has no time for such good-for-nothings. She wants to smile until she slips on gore and faces the grim reality of death, falling atop the body of glassy-eyed Sergeant Greven. He was bright once, quick to laugh: a true gentle giant. Memory flashes; he held her when her grandfather died, dried her tears, listened to her stories and her grief. Now she will grieve for him.

As she raises a hand to wipe the tears from her eyes, the bloody stains on her skin disgust her. She recoils and blinks instead. There is no time to sit with grief. Back on her feet, she dances out of the reach of a pale Gamalar hand and, on instinct, slices her sword through his knees. It is sharper than she expects, sliding deep into muscle before it meets resistance. The man screams. *Did he kill Greven?* She kicks him over and finishes the job.

It's definitely easier.

THEN

"What are you doing?"
Asralyn shrugged. "Just whittling. Passes the time."

"What is it?"

She turned, expecting to see one of the nurses, and nicked herself when she saw Queen Imelyei warming her hands by the fire. "Your Majesty! What are you doing here?"

The young queen offered a wan smile. "It is hard to sit still," she said in accented Tottenic. "They killed my father. Threatened me. Now, I worry for my people."

Asralyn took in the shadows beneath the queen's eyes and the sallow shade of her skin. It was easy to forget her age from a distance; up close, she seemed even younger than her years. "You couldn't stay, Your Majesty. They would kill you, and then who would be left to fight them?"

"I know. But sometimes running away feels like the wrong thing to do."

Asralyn nodded, turning the half-carved soldier over in her hands. Maybe she'd add a drum. "You need to keep busy. Keep your mind off it. When... When we reach Tottenia, you'll be in a better position to make plans for Sebeny."

"Of course." Queen Imelyei took a step closer, the folds of her blue gown rustling as she walked. "May I see?"

Asra handed the unfinished soldier over and wondered if she'd get in trouble for talking to the child-queen. Should she have curtsied or something? She swallowed. "It's not finished yet."

"It's beautiful."

"You're welcome to have a go." Asralyn took a small branch of silver birch from beside her pack, rooted around until she found a spare whittling knife, and handed both to Imelyei. "Start small and simple."

"Thank you."

They sat next to each other on a fallen tree close to the campfire. Asralyn spent a few minutes showing the queen how to get started with her piece of wood, peeling the bark and holding the blade pointed away from her body, and then they settled into a comfortable silence. The crackling of the flames, the croaking of crickets, and the soft scrape of metal on wood were a balm. Asralyn relaxed her muscles as she carved, releasing tension with each slice.

After a while, Queen Imelyei took a deep breath. "The others all tell me what I want to hear. Treat me like a child."

"Oh?"

"They say we will make it to Tottenia. That the Galamar pose no threat to me now we are so close to the sea. We will reach the boats tomorrow."

Asralyn deftly sliced the tiniest sliver of wood from her carving and admired the detail she'd added to the snare drum carried by her wooden soldier. "Yes. We won't need to make camp again."

"But will we make it? I don't want to leave Sebeny, but I have a terrible feeling I'll not live to see another shore."

Clearing her throat, Asralyn averted her gaze and focused on the largest log burning in the fire. "I should lie. Tell you everything will be fine."

"Why?"

"Because you are a child."

Imelyei lifted her chin. "I am a queen."

She nodded her acknowledgement. "I don't know if we'll make it. I hope we do. I know my comrades will fight to the death to get you safely out of Sebeny."

"But you cannot tell me we won't be killed first."

"I won't make a promise I can't keep."

"I respect that," Queen Imelyei said. "What promise will you make?"

Asralyn met the child-queen's gaze. "I promise to do everything in my power to keep you alive."

"That will be enough, my friend." The queen squeezed Asra's hand. "That will be enough."

NOW

Asralyn's throat burns as she drags ragged breaths in through her mouth. She pushes herself harder, moves faster; Librith's attacks are weakening and the mage will not last much longer without help.

There are only five men charging the doorway now, but they are vicious and cruel. One more falls as she watches. Asra's heart leaps until she sees Librith stumble, an arrow protruding from the old woman's shoulder. Still, Librith fights; she lashes out with whip and sword, her lips moving silently in an ancient chant.

Asralyn winces at the stitch beneath her ribs. She slows for the briefest second, then forces herself on.

There is so much screaming it takes her a moment to pick out Imelyei's voice.

Her vision blurs as sweat drips from her brow. Asra blinks to clear the oxygen-deprived haze over her eyes. Her chest tightens. Librith is nowhere to be seen. Three men storm the doorway, serrated swords held at the ready.

Only seconds behind them, she barrels through the crumbling stone frame with no plan, no thought of how she will stop the Galamar warriors. She only knows she has to get there in time; she will not let the child-queen die.

"Imelyei!" she yells, regretting it as soon as the sound leaves her lips.

Two of the men turn to her, while the other keeps his weapon trained on Imelyei and the other women. Asra scans the room quickly, taking in the crumpled body of the queen's older maid and Librith's bloodied form thrown aside like a ragdoll; only the rise and fall of the arrows in the mage's shoulder tells Asra she is still alive.

She focuses on the warriors. Swallows at the sight of their sharp, serrated blades. Tries to remember Librith's training, despite the slight tremble in her hand.

Confidence, she recalls, hearing the old woman's voice in her head. *Act confident and that's half the battle.*

She pushes her shoulders back and loosens her stance. Taking a deep breath, she raises her eyes to meet the Galamars' gaze.

It takes everything she has not to scream.

It's obvious which man is the leader; the darkness is complete in his eyes, with tendrils of oily black shadow snaking through the veins on his face. He laughs at her fear, and wisps of dark smoke escape the thin walls of his lips.

She takes a small step back and curses herself for it.

He laughs even more.

Furrowing her brow, gripping the hilt of the sword as if it can save her, Asra juts her chin out. "Jyahgen, I assume?" Everyone knows his name; it is the first time she's said it aloud. She looks him up and down, assessing him like a cut of meat, bluffing for all she's worth.

He leers. "It goes all the way down, little soldier. Do you wish to inspect that, too?"

She hates herself for the blush that creeps into her cheeks.

All three men laugh again. Asra's mind races. Can she defeat three of them?

And then Imelyei evens the odds.

Taking advantage of the distraction of their laughter, Imelyei lunges at the Galamar closest to her and stabs her whittling knife, until then concealed in her dress, deep into his ear. The child-queen grunts with effort as she uses her whole body to push the blade deeper into the man's skull. Blood trickles from his ear, dripping down his neck and staining the edges of his tunic. Imelyei pulls the blade free. The warrior blinks once, drops to his knees, and doesn't get up.

For a moment, a shocked silence hangs like a shroud over their crumbling corner of the abbey.

Then Jyahgen roars. "I'll kill you, you little bitch!"

Both remaining men reach for the queen, who cowers back from their rage. Asra leaps without thinking, whipping her sword across the back of the younger man's legs. He cries out and stumbles forward.

Jyahgen rounds on her. He swings his blade faster than magic, knocking her own weapon from her hands with the sudden fury of his blow. She yelps. Ducks to the side. Trips over the maid's body and lands on her knees in a stagnant pool of sticky blood. Gagging, she climbs to her feet just in time to dodge the sword swung at her head. When she dodges again, she bumps into Imelyei. The child-queen's shadowed eyes are bright with unshed tears.

"Stay behind me," Asra says, though she wonders if she will be anything more than another body in Jyahgen's path to regicide.

She lifts her fists. Almost laughs at the ridiculousness of fighting a sword with her hands.

Jyahgen flashes that wolfish smile. "I'm going to enjoy making you scream."

THEN

The Galamar had tried stealth later that night, sending a handful of warriors to kill the queen in her sleep.

Librith was ready for them, as always. Asralyn wanted to smile at the memory of the shock on their faces, fixed even in death. But there was no reason to smile now; the boat was not there.

"Where is it?" Sister Ruith asked. "Why isn't it here?"

Rumours spilt down the line, of shipwrecks and pirates and Galamar treachery, but in truth, nobody knew why the ship was not waiting for them. Asralyn hoped it was simply delayed and would arrive at any moment.

While the higher-ups discussed plans and possible problems, Queen Imelyei summoned her new friend. Surrounded by maids and guards, Asralyn sat with the child-queen on the soft sand, enjoying the heat of the sun on her face and the cool of the golden grains beneath her fingers. Above, the sky was a perfect cornflower blue. In the distance, she spotted what looked to be a floating castle; she'd seen it on their way to Sebeny, but still had no idea how it had been built in the middle of the sea.

"What is that place?" Asra asked the queen.

Imelyei glanced up from the bird she was whittling and smiled. "Cybenis Abbey. The oldest building in Sebeny. It was occupied for almost eight-hundred years, though it has been empty for two centuries now. I was hoping to appoint caretakers but the war has ended any hope of that."

Asralyn studied the dilapidated building. "Does magic keep it afloat?"

The queen chuckled. "No. It's on an island. There is a walkway, but it's only accessible at low tide."

"Clever." Asra nodded her approval.

"What are you working on?"

"Hmm?" She looked up from her work. "Oh, it's nothing much. Just an old drumstick. I had the idea of carving tiny images along a pair of sticks to commemorate the trip. Probably a silly idea, but it passes the time."

"It's not silly at all. What a great way to remember it all!"

Asralyn ducked her head. "How's the bird going?"

Imelyei sighed. "It looked better in my head."

"That happens to all of us as we're learning."

The tide was on its way out but the sound of the sea rolling against the shore lulled Asra. Breathing in the fresh salt tang, she closed her eyes for a moment, resting her blade against the end of the drumstick as she soaked it all up; she might never venture so far from Tottenia again.

And then the drumbeat broke the quiet.

Asra jumped. Her knife sliced the end of the drumstick, shearing the tip clean off and leaving a sharp point, like the tip of an arrow. She cursed.

The drum continued.

"Lusonne!" she said.

Imelyei raised an eyebrow.

"He went with two of the soldiers to keep watch." She put the knife away quickly and slipped the broken drumstick into a sheath on her belt. "This is a warning. The Galamar are here."

As the two women shared a worried glance, the drumbeat came to a sudden stop.

NOW

Jyahgen is on more than the normal Galamar battle-drug concoction, that much is clear. The black rage of his eyes is a darkness so deep it is an abyss. His fists smoke with inky shadows and his teeth are sharpened to points. Horror creeps through Asralyn's flesh; a screaming, seeping, saccharine surge of adrenaline accelerates her heartbeat. She is weaponless. Powerless.

Behind her, the child-queen recoils from the face of her own death. Across the room, the mage lies unconscious, floating in the bliss of oblivion. Asra wishes she didn't know what was coming.

Jyahgen spots the bugle and drumsticks at her waist and the insignia on her lapels. "A drummer girl?" He laughs. "Should be good for a quick bang, then."

She shudders. Grabs the first thing she comes to; it's the flint she carries in her pocket. It makes a good projectile, swift and unexpected. Her aim is true. The flint strikes Jyahgen on his forehead. A small sliver of blood drips onto his left eyebrow.

He snarls, more annoyed than hurt.

Still, she is proud that she struck him.

He raises his sword.

Asra's mind scrambles. "Do you really need that to fight an unarmed girl? You're more of a coward than I thought."

"I don't need it." He looks at the sword. "But I like the way it slides through guts."

Swallowing her fear, she tries not to react when Imelyei touches her waist. Asra reaches back to take what the child-queen offers. As her hand closes around cold metal, she settles; it is the whittling knife she gave Imelyei on the journey. No match for a Galamar blade, but better than her bare fists. She lifts it and chooses to ignore his laughter.

When he lunges, almost lazily, she tries to use what Librith taught her. Block. Attack at the same time. Let no opportunity pass by. She dodges the thrust of his sword by spinning her body forward and to the right, slipping past his guard. Her knife leaves the faintest scratch on his forearm as she dances out of his reach.

Jyahgen swings again, then lashes out with his foot in a powerful arc; his boot kicks her hand and knocks the whittling knife from her grip.

Stumbling backwards, she almost trips over a broken stone fallen from the wall. She rights herself and realises she has nowhere left to run; she is cornered. Her mouth is dry. She is cold, as though ice runs through her veins.

Does dying hurt? She reaches for her waist, hoping to find something she can use as a weapon. As Jyahgen stalks closer, she wraps her fingers around a drumstick and pulls it from her belt. It won't be enough but a morbid certainty floods her body; she will die making music.

Jyahgen raises his right hand with the sword clutched tightly in his grip. He swings it down towards her neck.

Asra knows she will be cut. Sliced like jerky, ready to be salted. But, by god, she will cut him, too.

One technique from basic training rings in her mind. She moves the tiniest fraction to her right and raises her left arm in a straight line above her head, angled slightly forward. As he swings, she steps into him, feeling the scrape along her arm as the sword slides down it. Blood soaks her sleeve but she is alive.

In the same movement, she raises the drumstick with her right hand. Her heart beats so hard and fast she wonders if it will break free of her ribs. A giddy elation fills her body; the drumstick she has grabbed is the broken one with the arrow-sharp tip. Grinning like a madman, she shoves it deep into Jyahgen's left eye and pushes with all her might. It slides through more easily than she expects, meeting only slight resistance.

He jerks back, dragging his serrated sword along her ribs and squeezing her shoulder with his other hand. Agony screams through her flesh.

She keeps pushing until he lets go of both her arm and the sword. The blade clatters to the stone floor. For good measure, she knees him in the balls; the sadistic bastard deserves all the pain he gets.

He looks at her with his one good eye, black orb swirling with a burning rage. Shadows leech from his skin; long tendrils of inky darkness seep into the air in all directions. Asralyn lets go of the drumstick and scrambles back out of their reach. What is happening?

Jyahgen reaches out one more time as the black fades from his eye to reveal a plain brown iris. There is something there, something almost pleading, as the man within comes back to himself at last. Horror grows, awakens, and then dies as Jyahgen topples to the ground, cold as the stone beneath him. The shadows dart through the air and out of the crumbling doorway.

There is silence again. It is shocked, light, hopeful. It is over.

Adrenaline fades and pain hits with the suddenness of crashing cymbals. Blood is dripping from her arm and side. The room tilts. Queasy and scared, she sinks to her knees and looks through blurred vision at the people surrounding her.

Queen Imelyei, pale and shaking, reaches her first. "You did it."

"What?"

"Look!" The child-queen points through the doorway. Outside, swords clatter to the floor as hordes of Galamar warriors throw their weapons to the ground, suddenly released from the darkness that had captivated them.

Asralyn smiles. Pain fades. Her vision narrows into a bright tunnel and sweet music rings in her ears. She's going home.

LATER

Home.

Asralyn recalls a time she thought she'd never see it again. The small cottage hasn't changed in all the years she's been gone, and there is comfort in that. Roses frame the path leading to the front door, painted a cheery yellow to emulate the sun. Smoke billows from the chimney and the sweet scent of homemade pie drifts from the window. She smiles.

The door opens before she reaches it, and three pairs of arms fight to draw her in; her mother wins, holding her close while her father and younger brother grab her arms and weep.

"You're home," Omoriel Gydeon sobs into her daughter's hair. "They said you were in Sebeny. We thought we'd lost you."

Asralyn pulls back. "I'm home to stay, Mama."

Warmth seeps through her chest. Yes, she's home. An honourable discharge. The friendship and gratitude of two queens. She rubs her fingers against the side of the broken drumstick at her waist, recalling the red-brown stains soaked into her carvings: a souvenir of her first and last adventure. She is exactly where she wants to be.

"I'm home."

The Falar Path

Where am I?

Consciousness ebbed like the tide and she grabbed at it, fighting against a darkness she might never come back from. She forced her eyes open. Winced at the bright light dappling through the leaves. Rode out the wave of nausea that followed.

Leaves? The thought jarred, but trying to catch the loose thread of uncertainty was like trying to catch a dragon with a butterfly net.

Something rustled in the bush. She flinched and immediately regretted it as a kaleidoscope of pain ricocheted through her body. What in Dorov's name had happened to her? When a rabbit hopped out of the foliage, she breathed a sigh of relief. She couldn't run right now if she tried.

She groaned; her voice was hoarse, gravelly, strange to her ears. With more effort than she'd have liked, she pushed herself up to her knees, crawled to an ancient pine a mere foot away, and leaned back against the trunk. Her ears rang. Her vision narrowed. She toppled to the side like a felled tree.

The next time she came to, teeth chattering, skin icy to the touch, night had fallen and a spider had woven a delicate web across her nose. She brushed it away. Blinked. Looked up and wondered who had hidden the stars.

A forest. She took in the trees, the damp carpet of leaves, and the canopy above her head, barely visible in the dark of night. *Why am I in a forest?*

A twig snapped. She pushed the pain aside and reached for the knife in her boot.

They were good; the twig was their only mistake. But she was better. There were three of them, boots soft on the forest floor. They moved as a unit, fanning out at equal distances to block her escape. She inhaled through her teeth, ignoring the sharp pain as she climbed to her feet, forcing her body to move with an ease she didn't feel.

She waited until they were within five feet before she spoke. "It's not polite to sneak up on people."

The silence lingered like an unwelcome guest.

"At least introduce yourselves before I kill you."

A rumble of laughter was followed by the whisper of a sword sliding back into its sheath. A man stepped forward into a sliver of moonlight dancing between the leaves. At first glance, his face was forgettable: the face of a man she might have met in a tavern, or traded wares with at the market, or crossed swords with in a back alley. High cheekbones sat beside a nose that had been broken more than once over the years. Brown hair fell to his shoulders, ragged and unkempt; the lower part of his face was half-hidden beneath a moustache and beard. Then he smiled, and it was as though the sun rose with the curve of his mouth.

He arched one eyebrow. "You're so certain you could defeat me?"

"Yes. Your two friends, too."

"How -" He cleared his throat. "Three against one seems a little uneven."

She flashed her teeth. "Doesn't seem fair, does it? You can still back out, you know. Go for reinforcements."

"Oh, I like you!" His laughter boomed like a drum. "I'll be sorry to kill you, but I will if I have to."

"I won't take it personally if you don't. I would like to know why you're creeping up on me with swords drawn, though. Is it a crime to spend a night in the forest now?"

"You can't possibly think I'd believe that you don't know where you are." He held a hand up to keep the other men back when they approached.

She bit the inside of her cheek. *I should know where I am.* But every time she tried to reach for the memory, pain stabbed inside her head like a well-armed battalion.

"You really don't know?"

She shook her head.

"How is it possible for a woman like you, a woman who can pinpoint three enemies stealing through their own land and face them down with no trace of fear, to enter *Fal Dianuil* and not know it?"

She faltered then, and her face gave it away: the stark white of her eyes, the ashen tint of her skin, ghostlike in the silver shadows. Curses fell from her lips in a language she couldn't place yet understood perfectly.

The man moved his hand to his sword hilt once again, his eyes narrowed and his mouth drawn. "And now you stand before me speaking *Ithronin* as if it was your native tongue. I must ask: who are you?"

Who am I? She met his gaze as the bell rang in her ears again. Opened her mouth to answer. Stammered as the name refused to come. *Who am I?* "I don't know."

This time, when darkness came with creeping fingers, it was a blessing.

***

Ssendorin slammed his fist into the trunk of the acacia tree. Splinters flew, mingling with the blood from his torn knuckles; the pain in his heart stabbed deeper.

"Where is she?" he roared. "Where is my wife?"

Around him, the six soldiers of his unit searched the valley, eyes sharp and their swords sharper.

"I do not mean to belittle your grief, my friend," Kraestoff said, "but there is more at stake here than your wife."

Ssendorin's hand moved swifter than his thoughts, grabbing his old friend around the throat. "Seertha is your friend, too!"

"Seertha was meant to be protecting the princess. Use your head, Ssendorin! If Seertha is gone, it can only mean one thing."

He wanted to squeeze. To force his anger through trembling fingers and crush the words from Kraestoff's throat. With a strength he hadn't known he possessed, he let go instead, turning to rest his forehead against the cool wood of the acacia. "If Tsolir has them, we are all done for."

"Not yet, Ssen. Look at the valley."

Ssendorin sucked a ragged breath into his lungs and forced himself to look at the carnage painting the valley floor red. Bodies lay strewn in a circle around the epicentre of the battle, an almost even mix of Tsolir's Greycoats and soldiers of the Rondian Guard. In the circular patch of flattened grass in the middle, two pairs of footprints told their own story.

"The Guard were outnumbered," he said. "They formed a protective circle around Princess Alithis and Seertha."

Kraestoff nodded. "I imagine Seertha knew they couldn't win."

"She knew." Ssendorin took the flash of grief and locked it in a box in his mind. "She'd have searched for escape routes. Tried to find a way out."

"There was no way out."

"No. But…" He narrowed his eyes at the thin trail of blood leading away from the circle. "Someone was dragged."

The two men moved closer. Inspected the flattened grass where boot-heels had dragged across the ground. Frowned at the thin line of blood following the same path. A few feet away, Ssendorin crouched low and ran his fingers through the grass. When he lifted his hand, something gleamed in his palm.

"What is it?"

Ssendorin closed his fist. Bowed his head. "The princess's brooch. Tsolir has her now."

Kraestoff breathed in. Then out. "We don't have long. They took Alithis sometime this morning; we have maybe a week before they get what they want and kill her."

"How can you be so sure they'll get what they want?"

"No one can hold out under torture forever, Ssen. Alithis is trained for this, but even she will break eventually. When she does, we're all doomed."

Rising to his feet, Ssen turned back to the small circle where his wife's footprints marked the ground. "And what of Seertha?"

"Her prints never move from here, but there is no body." Kraestoff swallowed. "Perhaps she took the *falar* path."

They looked to the sky. Pressed two fingers against their hearts in the age-old sign of warding.

"We will pray for her, my friend."

Ssendorin placed his hand against Seertha's footprint and closed his eyes. "She is my soul, Kraestoff. I cannot leave her."

"I know." He squeezed Ssen's shoulder. "But Seertha understood duty better than any of us. The princess needs you now."

***

"I don't understand. How can you not know who you are?"

She pressed her fingers against the bridge of her nose. Pain stabbed with each effort to remember. "I don't know. It's just not there."

The aches in her body had eased, though she was still unsure if she could stand unaided. A thick fog blanketed her mind, leaving her woozy and unsure of herself. Would she ever remember?

The man with the memorable smile folded his arms across his chest, frowning now. "My name is Romond, son of Rolan, Prince of *Fal Dianuil* and Protector of the Forest."

"That's a lot of titles." She peered at him through narrowed eyes, trying to lessen the ache in her head.

"It's a lot of responsibility. Which includes keeping people out of the forest. How did you get here?"

She thought about it. Shrugged.

"Where did you come from?"

Another shrug.

"Do you know anything?" He clenched his jaw.

She considered his question, surprised at the thoughts that sprang to mind. "I know how to kill a man in countless ways. I know how to take on multiple opponents and walk away without a scratch. I've tested it out and I can speak with reasonable fluency in seven languages, identify every poisonous plant within this forest, and read the ground with more accuracy than your best tracker. What I cannot do is give you my name; I wish I could."

Romond looked her up and down. "You are a mystery. The question is, what am I going to do with you?"

Returning his gaze, she pursed her lips and ran her eyes lower. "I can think of a few things."

To her surprise, Romond's mouth twitched. She willed it to blossom into that same bright smile he'd shared outside but was left disappointed.

"Listen." She sat up straighter. "I want answers just as much as you do. There has to be a clue. Something to show how I got here. I didn't just appear in the middle of the forest!"

"You're not a Greycoat, that much I know. But that doesn't mean you're a friend. There are many who seek to enter *Fal Dianuil* and discover the secrets hidden within."

Exasperated, she looked down at her hands. What kind of hands were they? Her fingers were long and slender, like the Himboran musicians in the north, but calluses marked the tips and the hardened skin of her palms. She lacked the fine webbing of the water-bound Degrisi, had no blue tinge to suggest Cymorish ancestry, and still retained the tips of her fingers on her left hand so was unlikely to be an inmate of the infamous Western Keep. Pulling the plait forward from behind her neck, she saw fine black strands with no trace of the typical Lojiese white-gold locks. Where did that leave her?

She examined her clothes next: a simple black tunic and leggings cinched at the waist with a deep green sash. Running her fingers along the sash, she considered the smooth softness of the silk and the width of the cut. Earrings dangled from her lobes; she removed one and saw a simple gold acorn. A glance down at her chest told her the earrings matched the necklace hanging beneath her bodice. Nothing special. Nothing identifiable.

"I'm wearing Rondian clothing. Perhaps I'm from there?"

"How do you know that?" Romond ran a hand through his hair. "How can the same person identify the origin of a simple cloth and behave like a trained assassin? You do not add up... Dorov's sake, I have to call you something."

She arched her brow. "Careful."

His lips twitched again. "Juni. We found you beside a juniper thriving amongst the pine trees. I'll call you Juni."

She considered it. Rolled it around her tongue and let it settle like a cloak, ill-fitting but snug against her shoulders. It wasn't quite right but it would do until her memories returned. "Juni. I like it."

Someone knocked on the door. Romond left the room for a moment, then returned with a grim expression on his face.

"What is it?" Juni asked.

"Out of nowhere, you appear in our forest. Then I receive word that Tsolir's Greycoats are gathering along our southern border." Romond paced the room, the crease in his brow deepening. "You are connected to this, somehow. I can't decide if you're telling the truth or if you're here to cause trouble."

She closed her eyes. "I wish I knew. I don't think I'm here to cause trouble. I don't feel like I am. But I don't know why I'm here. I don't know anything."

"I have to go but I can't leave you here. I have to keep an eye on you."

"Go where?"

He didn't answer. Instead, he moved closer, closer still, until his body brushed against hers. She stepped back and then cursed herself for the involuntary reaction. Her breath hitched.

"What are you doing?"

Romond leaned in, letting his breath warm her ear. "If I find out you're lying to me, you'll wish you never entered my forest."

Amused now, she tilted her head to meet his gaze. "Are you trying to scare me?"

"Not at all." He let the smile free and, while she was distracted, slipped a length of rope around her wrists and pulled it tight. "Just a friendly warning. For now, Juni, I'm keeping you close enough to watch."

She looked down at the rope. Calculated at least four different ways she could escape from it. Chose to play along while it suited her. She smiled back at him. "Well, this could be interesting."

Shaking his head, even as the smile still tugged at his lips, Romond led her from the building to a pair of waiting horses.

***

Ssendorin stood from studying the ground and let his eyes roam across the distant hills. "They're heading north, Kraes."

"Only two reasons I can think of for that." Kraestoff shifted in his saddle. The shadows beneath his eyes added years to his face. "He could be trying to form an alliance with the Cymorish."

"No." Ssen shook his head. "Even Tsolir isn't foolish enough to think they'd join with him. He must know, even if he conquered their land, the Cymorish would fade into the hills and eat his army in small bites."

"I assume you are speaking figuratively, Ssen?"

He shrugged. "Who can tell? Nothing they do surprises me anymore."

"So he will not go to Cymorn."

"No. I have no doubt Tsolir is travelling to *Fal Dianuil*. He has long suspected the seed is hidden there."

"Is it?"

"It could be. The royals have told no one where they hid it." Ssen took a steadying breath, very aware of the box he had locked in his mind. Even her name was safe inside it now. "Regardless, there are things in *Fal Dianuil* no sane man would risk. If Tsolir takes the forest, the rest of us will not be long for this world."

"Have you been there, my friend?"

"Once." He shuddered and his face paled. "On the outskirts, many years ago. I would not venture there willingly."

Kraestoff cast a pitying glance towards his friend. "You may have to. We must stop Tsolir. Save the princess."

At what cost? Ssen forced the thought from his mind. He knew the answer; they would save the princess at any cost. He prayed the price wasn't too high.

***

Somewhere in the northern reaches, leading his army - figuratively speaking, of course - through the sodden moorlands of Mithombryge, Tsolir lost his temper.

"Why is it taking so long?"

The men around him trembled. One took a small step back; his eyes widened and his mouth parted mere seconds before Tsolir brought lightning from the clear sky to pierce the young man's heart.

"I expected to reach *Fal Dianuil* two days ago," he snarled.

"My lord," General Hawson cleared his throat, "the men cannot travel as fast in the heavy rain, and the mudslide added further delay. Rest assured, the troops sent earlier have already reached the forest and are preparing for your arrival."

Not for the first time, Tsolir cursed the wizards who'd bound him in this rotting flesh, his power so diminished he couldn't even transport his army. Anger surged through him at the memory of his children's betrayal; how dare they turn against him when he had given them life and power beyond mortal imagining? Centuries later, the treachery still burned deep in his soul.

Oh, he longed for the good old days, when he reigned with an iron fist, worshipped and feared by all. In the beginning, false gods had laid claim to his title, bandying their meagre powers about, building temples and selecting priestesses from virginal wells. His lesson had been swift and pointed. The memory brought a smile to his face; the flesh of other gods, even false ones, had been sweet nectar in his mouth - their powers even sweeter as they added to his own considerable potency. Gods dead, temples burned, priestesses deflowered - people shouted his name to the heavens by the time he was done.

Tsolir was the *only* god; all pretenders had fallen beneath his wrath.

And then his scattered children, sons and daughters of those former priestesses, had banded together to lessen him.

Remembering, he clenched his fist and a nearby tree splintered into tiny fragments.

They had paid dearly for their treachery, but he still struggled with the humiliation and the diminishment of human flesh. When he reclaimed his true form, the entire world would make recompense for his suffering.

A muffled noise drew his attention back to the present and he turned, irked by the interruption. Annoyance quickly turned to amusement.

"You are infinitely entertaining, Princess." He flashed his teeth as she finished strangling one of his soldiers. "I seem to recall your hands being tied behind your back, yet somehow you have them in front of you and around my servant's neck."

She'd probably have snarled at him if she wasn't gagged. Still, her eyes shot daggers - at least, the one that wasn't swollen shut.

"In four days you have picked off seventeen... No, eighteen of my men. I am beginning to see why the royal family keeps you well hidden."

Her dark hair was a wild tangle of knots and weeds, and grime was smeared across her face and clothes. The left side of her face was a rainbow of bruises. Blood crusted under her nose. Still, she lifted her chin in defiance and kicked out at another soldier who tried to restrain her.

"I could put you in a ring and sell tickets," Tsolir said in admiration. "But we have places to be so I'm going to have to ask you to settle down."

She turned to run. With a sigh, he waved his hand and transported her to sit in front of him on his horse; it took more effort than he cared to admit, but the delicious gasp that escaped her throat was worth it. He wrapped an arm around her waist like a vice, enjoyed the way her body stiffened and tried to pull away from him, and spurred his mount into an easy trot.

Tsolir grinned. *At least I'm not bored anymore.*

***

Juni walked behind Romond, debating whether she'd had enough of being led around at the end of a rope. Four days. She'd followed him around for four days, while his people stared at her and whispered. It was humiliating. She pressed her tongue to the roof of her mouth and placed her feet with a heavy carelessness, snapping twigs and crunching leaves to get her point across.

"Do you *have* to do that?" Romond asked.

"No," Juni said. "But I *want* to."

He made a noise low in his throat, almost a growl. "You're lucky we're nowhere near the border or the Greycoats would have an arrow in you between one step and the next."

"If we were that close to them, I wouldn't still be letting you lead me around like a dog."

He stopped. Turned to her. Met her gaze. "A dog? *Letting* me?"

She stepped closer. "I could have freed my hands within thirty seconds of you tying them but I'm trying to cooperate. There is a limit to my good behaviour, Romond."

"I think I'd like to see what happens when you reach that limit."

He flashed that smile again and her eyes were drawn to his lips. "Are you trying to distract me?"

"Perhaps." He leaned in, moving his mouth closer to hers. "Is it working?"

She tilted her chin. Rested her hands against his chest. Grabbed the front of his tunic and pulled him down. "Not in the slightest," she said as she kissed him.

Someone cleared their throat. "Sir!"

With a sigh, Romond pulled away. "Yes?"

"Sir, there's news from the south. You're needed back at camp." The young soldier blushed a warm red and averted his gaze as he spoke.

"Thank you, Majret. I'll be there shortly."

Majret nodded and departed, leaving them alone once again.

Romond ran a hand through his unkempt hair, adding to the dishevelment. "I wish I could trust you, Juni. If we knew who you were…"

"I know." She'd had glimpses of memory, often accompanied by monstrous headaches, but nothing that had cleared up the mystery of who she was: a flash of riding a horse, hair blowing back in the wind; scanning a crowd for signs of danger; sparring with another woman in a cobbled courtyard, thriving on the adrenaline spurred by the friendly fight. "I know I'm on your side, but I understand that you can't be sure without proof."

She followed him through the trees, quieter this time and blanketed with a bitter melancholy. *Who am I? What if I am a danger to Romond and the forest? Why can't I remember?* She pulled her cloak tighter around her shoulders and forced herself to focus on her surroundings.

Be alert. The voice sounded in her mind: a snippet of memory, almost too small to catch hold of. *Be aware. It may save your life one day.*

Ahead, almost perfectly camouflaged in a dense thicket, four men waited for them. Three she recognised; they were Romond's soldiers, well-trained and loyal. The other man didn't look familiar.

He spotted Romond and saluted. "Your Highness."

"What news, Jon?"

"Sir. Tsolir will reach the forest's edge by tomorrow afternoon. Our men have spotted the rest of his army marching through Paridian pass. And Sir, Tsolir has Rondia's princess with him. The Guard sent word by messenger pigeon that Alithis was taken several days ago; they should arrive the day after Tsolir."

Juni studied the man's face as he spoke. His brow was lined with crevices, made deeper by the tightening of his face as he frowned. Black hair was speckled with grey and heavy shadows weighed beneath tired eyes. When he spoke of the princess, a vein bulged at his temple. *He's worried*, she thought. *Alithis*. She rolled the name around in her mind but nothing stirred.

Mid-sentence, Jon broke off and stared at Juni.

She flexed her hands, testing the strength of the ropes, and shrugged; she could still fight if need be. "Is there a problem?"

"Ma'am." Jon looked her up and down. "You're wearing the clothes of the princess's personal guard."

"What?" She looked down at herself.

Jon shared a glance with Romond. "Sir, when the princess was taken, one of her guards vanished. The Rondian Guard sent men out to find her while they follow the princess."

"You think Juni is this guard?" Romond laughed. "She has been here for four days already. How could she arrive here so soon before Tsolir?"

Memory hammered against Juni's brain. External noises were muffled as she struggled to keep hold of the sounds and images racing inside her mind. The whistle of swords flying through the air and the heavy clang of metal clashing. The shouts of men bellowing for their surrender. *Who were they? What did they want?* A body pressed against her back - another woman, sword in hand. The copper tang of blood permeated her mouth.

"Juni!"

She came back to herself with a jolt. Romond gripped her upper arms, his face close to hers.

"What happened?" he asked.

"I…" She shook her head. "A memory. I think. Of when they took the princess."

"How could you remember that?"

Swallowing the fear lodged in her throat, she raised her eyes to meet his. "Because I was there. I don't know how, but I was there."

Jon cleared his throat. "They're saying she took the *falar* path."

Romond abruptly let her go. He dropped the rope to the ground and stepped back. "No one has taken that path in over a hundred years. How can it be?"

"I don't know." She blinked the tears from her eyes. "I don't remember."

"I am not surprised. The *falar* path was created by the wizards of old, safe only for them. I had heard there may be a small few who'd survived to pass their blood down, but I had no idea..." He took a breath and ran a hand across his face. "I thought the *falar* path was lost to us. Lost to time. Do you have any idea what this means?"

She shook her head again. "I still don't know who I am, Romond. I don't know what anything means."

"Your blood is more diluted. Less of Tsolir's magic runs through your veins. It is a wonder your brain isn't totally scrambled after navigating that path. Legend says even the old ones often struggled with it."

"I..." Her mind latched on to one thing. "I'm descended from that monster?"

Romond sighed. "You must be. Only those of his blood can open the portal to the *falar* path."

A seeping cold settled over her body, sinking deep into her bones until she shivered beneath the dappled sun. Something about their words seemed so wrong. Descended from that madman? She shuddered, looking at the lines on her palms as if they could tell her the secrets she longed to know. She had walked the *falar* path and lost her memories along the way - what else had happened on that forbidden road? Her mind raced with questions, and one screamed louder than them all: *What am I?*

***

"Where is the seed?"

The princess flinched from the expected blow, though she couldn't go far with her arms tied to the tent pole above her head.

Tsolir paused to enjoy his handiwork. Naked and exposed, she was a shell of the woman he'd taken from Rondia only days before. The paleness of her skin was marred with lines in bright red and deep brown, the old and new blood combining in rivers between the curves of her breasts and down the legs she was so fond of kicking with. Perfect circles of seared flesh dotted sensitive areas where he'd burned her with the tip of his finger, the lightning sizzling out in controlled bursts at his pleasure.

And oh, it was a pleasure; her whimpers and screams were ecstasies to him. The bulge of his erection tempted him to ignore his resolution not to lie with fertile women. A cruel smile curved across his lips; if he killed her once he was done with her, there'd be no chance of her bearing another brat who could try to ruin him.

Still, she had to give him the seed first. Once he knew where it was, nothing could stop him. Yes, once she'd given him her seed, he'd give her his. He flashed his teeth and forced a kiss on her lips. When she bit, it only stirred him more.

"Where is the seed, Princess?" He ran a finger across her ribs, relishing the way her eyes flashed and her teeth ground together as he charred the soft flesh of her stomach. He bent and licked a trail of fresh blood from her chest. "This doesn't have to be so unpleasant for you. Just tell me where it is."

Her whole body shuddered. "I'll die before I tell you anything!"

About to try a sweeter persuasion, he paused at the sudden scream from the camp outside. He sighed. "They can't do anything without supervision, you know. Children, all of them. But don't worry; I'll be back to continue our conversation shortly, my dear. Try not to miss me too much."

She spat at him, meeting his gaze despite the fear sweating out of every pore.

Chuckling, Tsolir strode from the tent and walked straight into chaos.

Men scurried like ants, erecting hasty defences as arrows rained from above. Dead bodies, shafts protruding from chests and limbs, were dotted between the tents. At the eastern edge of the camp, a small fire raged; one soldier screamed as flames engulfed him.

Tsolir let the fury fill him until his body expanded to twice its size. Spotting a handful of archers hidden among the trees, he opened his mouth and roared his wrath into the air; the impact of his voice hit the archers like a godly fist. Blood streamed from their orifices as they screamed, clutched their faces, and dropped dead to rot amongst the mulch on the forest floor.

And so it begins. Tsolir let the battle-fury stir his blood. He had come to fight, and these heretics would soon learn the error of their ways. He raised his fist and the sky crackled in response. Today, he would remind the crawling ants of this land who their god was.

***

"Give me the seed and I may let you live," Tsolir bellowed, his voice lashing like a whip through *Fal Dianuil*.

Creatures small and large scrambled deeper into the forest as the leaves shook on the trees. Romond gritted his teeth against the force of it as every man looked to him for direction.

He looked back at them: proud, unflinching, Prince and Protector bearing the mantle of his responsibility. "We knew this day was coming, my friends. Long has Tsolir coveted what he thinks lies in this forest. We do not have his seed, but he will come anyway. He will come with his Greycoats and his magic and his blood-soaked blades. But we will show him our teeth! We will show him the truth of *Fal Dianuil!*"

Silent only to avoid announcing their presence, each man lifted his fist to his chest and bowed his head to Romond.

Juni ran her tongue along her teeth as she considered his words. "The seed isn't here?"

He shook his head. "It never was. I have no idea what the Rondian royals did with it, but it was never in *Fal Dianuil.*"

"Then what are you protecting?"

"There are more things in this forest than anyone knows, Juni. Things Tsolir could twist to his power. Things he could hurt. He has been told the seed isn't here but he chooses not to believe it. Regardless, we must stop him."

An older man stood to attention. "Your orders, Sir?"

"You know the plan," Romond said. "This is what we've been preparing for. Trigger the alert."

Juni watched with curiosity as the man nodded and pulled something from his belt. Instead of the horn she expected, he held out a wooden amulet shaped in a perfect circle; flecks of gold swirled among the inner rings. He held the amulet up against the trunk of the nearest pine, pressing the swirling gold against its bark.

From out of nowhere, a breeze stirred the leaves and tugged at the ends of Juni's hair. A heaviness weighed in the air, the pressure building into a sense of expectation; something was happening.

"What-" Juni began to speak.

Romond silenced her with a look.

The man stepped back from the tree, his head still bowed. The air stilled.

And the tree breathed, its gentle inhale a mere whisper among the silent leaves. *We will spread the word,* a sibilant voice whispered, *as agreed long ago. Root to root, this will be done. We will do what we can to fight this coming evil.*

"My thanks." Romond dropped to one knee. "I will uphold my promise to you, *Fal Dianuil*. I will protect you to my last breath."

You are worthy of your name, Romond, son of Rolan. We will not forget.

Juni sank to the ground, a tightness building in her chest. *Fal Dianuil* was alive but, even more shocking, somehow she had known that already. Memory hit, hard and fast: lessons learned at her mother's knee; a trip through whispering pines in her youth, the trees towering above her eight-year-old body; a pact bound in blood.

Her name wasn't Juni. She remembered now. She opened her mouth, called for Romond, and reeled back with horror as an arrow pierced his shoulder. "Romond!"

***

Ssendorin ignored the relentless aching of his muscles and pushed on, guided by moonbeams and the knowledge that time was running out.

Was the princess still alive? Was - He cut the thought off; thinking of her would cripple him. No, he needed to stay sharp, strong, unassailable. By morning, he would have answers.

Leading his men through the darkness, he focused his senses and remained alert for danger. Kraestoff had fallen back to hurry the Rondian army, but Ssen knew they would not arrive in time. If the princess had any hope, it was up to him and his half dozen elite warriors. This was what they trained for, what they lived for. And what they may yet die for.

But if *she* was truly gone, then what reason did he have to live?

He swallowed the lump in his throat. Paused to take a swig from his water pouch. They had travelled for two days now without sleep, knowing time was something the princess didn't have. His men were weary.

He held up a hand and pressed his ear to the ground. Vibrations travelled through the earth, but he could not make sense of them. "Something is happening," he said.

"What?" one of the men asked.

He shrugged. "We're close, and it sounds like trouble. Be ready for anything."

They pressed on, leading their horses between trees and shadows as they neared the boundary of *Fal Dianuil*. In the witching hour, all should have been quiet. At the foot of a hill, they heard the first screams.

Ssen gestured to his men and they raced up the hill, taking the last few feet on their bellies to avoid being seen. At the crest, they peered over into the valley that held the entrance to *Fal Dianuil*. A large camp spread across the valley floor, tents pitched atop the grass and fires burning at regular intervals. The line of trees marking the edge of the forest seemed close together, stretching their already imposing height in a warning to any foolish enough to venture through.

Ssen narrowed his eyes. He had lost count of how many years had passed since he'd dipped a toe into that sacred wood, but his memory remained true; there was something different about it now. Something dark and ominous. Something threatening. Goosebumps rose on his arms, and the fine hairs stood upright.

As they watched, several men in the camp fell beneath a rain of arrows. In retaliation, a giant of a man lifted a torch from a campfire and set it against the base of the nearest tree. An inhuman scream pierced the air as the flames licked at the tree's trunk.

"Tsolir!" Ssen hissed.

Just behind the line of trees, shadowy figures darted through the darkness where no one else could see them. One raced into the camp, ran his knife across the throat of an old Greycoat, and vanished back into the forest before anyone noticed. Several more did the same, picking off their enemy one at a time; it barely made a dint on the number of Greycoats in the camp.

Cursing beneath his breath, Ssen saw Tsolir's men organise themselves into groups, readying themselves for another attack. Whoever protected the forest would be dead within minutes if they could do no better than dancing on the outskirts! Still, that was not his job. He had one task; rescue the princess. He raised a hand, about to signal to his men, and a ghostly figure caught his eye.

She walked out of the largest tent, her bare skin a beacon in the darkness of the early hour. Glancing around to be sure she wasn't spotted in the chaos, she nodded at the sight of smoke pouring from the open doorway of the canvas structure.

What did she do? Ssen wondered. He was too far away to recognise who she was, but she seemed familiar; it had to be the princess. When the moon emerged from behind a cloud and something silver glinted in the woman's hand, he knew it was time to move. What was she thinking? She was going to get herself killed!

He gave the signal and his men oozed into the darkness, inky as the shadows. He moved too, keeping his eye on the princess as he descended the steep hill. She slunk through the camp, driving her knife into every Greycoat she found. The soldiers already in formation had no inkling she was there, their concentration firmly on the threat coming from the forest, but several men remained behind, guarding the camp or preparing for a more covert assault on *Fal Dianuil*. She killed them all, a stealthy assassin soul-bound to the old moon-goddess who'd heeded their calls before Tsolir cast his darkness over the world.

Ssen raced as fast as he dared, certain she would be caught before he reached her. At one point, his gut churned as three men surprised her beside a small campfire. They drew their blades and attacked from three directions; Ssen had dark visions of returning the princess's body skewered like a roasted boar. He almost tripped when she lashed out with blade and feet, moving like the wind in a series of attacks even his trained eye could barely follow. Within seconds, all three men lay dead at her feet, having made not a sound as they breathed their last.

Who taught her how to do that?

He had no time to wonder. Nearing the camp, he threw himself to the ground as a large explosion buffeted the valley and a sheet of fire sizzled above his head. What, in Dorov's name, had just happened? Lifting his head cautiously, he saw one of his men dead a few feet away, his head blackened and charred like a burnt steak. His stomach roiled. He forced himself to breathe through the sickly sweet stench and crawled on his stomach until he moved inside the Greycoat's camp.

He glanced at the line of trees; the front row was tinged black from the flames but he could see no damage beyond that. Several battalions of Greycoats held their now-singed shields aloft to protect themselves from another volley of arrows. The giant man he'd seen earlier flicked the arrows away like they were flies, all the while shouting curses at *Fal Dianuil*. Tsolir! It had to be.

Ssen may never know exactly what had happened, but he guessed Tsolir had tried to burn the forest down, not knowing that its magic would reflect the flames back away from the trees.

The princess!

Had she been burned? He lifted himself into a crouch and ran, risking being seen despite staying low to the ground. He had to find her.

He prayed as he ran, though he knew no one listened. Tsolir had made sure no god could save them now. Rage spurring him on, Ssen raced through the burning camp to find the princess.

***

"The trees are tiring," Romond said, his voice hoarse from shouting. He leaned against a pine and winced as he moved his bandaged shoulder. "It won't be long before Tsolir breaks through."

"What can we do, Sir?"

The prince's mouth was a thin line cutting through the grime and dirt on his face. "We welcome him in."

"Sir?"

"Tsolir has no knowledge of this place. He doesn't know to watch out for the sting of the *veniko*, or to stay clear of the *papari* lair. He won't recognise the signs of the sinking bogs or tune out the call of the *huldra*. He can search for that damned seed all he likes but all he will find here is death for him and his men."

"So we just let him in?"

Romond nodded. "Let him in, but stay close. Take every opportunity to thin his ranks or steer him into danger. We can still win this."

Juni blinked as she took in his words, reacting a moment too late as if something stopped the sound from reaching her ears. It was as though she sat inside a bubble and watched everything unfold from a great distance. The scratch of the bark against her back held her attention as much as the angry bellows emanating from beyond the forest. Why were they here again? She contemplated that as someone grabbed her hand and led her through the trees. She wondered where they were going but couldn't summon up the energy to ask.

"What's wrong with you?" Romond asked.

She blinked. Wrong? With her? She thought about it and shrugged, content to follow him wherever he led. He had a nice smile, she remembered. A smile that stirred the butterflies in her stomach.

She'd been trying to tell him something. What was it? She frowned as pain stabbed between her ears. It was something important. But then the arrow had lodged in his shoulder and she'd thought he was dead. She glanced at the bandage that now crossed his chest and shoulder. Oh yes, someone had dragged him to safety. Her, too.

Then what?

Something had hit her head! Dorov, it hurt. It was like tiny men mined inside her brain with pickaxes. She tried to tug at the thread again. What did she need to tell him? But the comfort of his hand in hers was too distracting, and it was easier to just let him pull her along.

Maybe she'd remember when they stopped.

***

Ssen picked up his pace as the woman slipped into the forest; he could lose her in a heartbeat if she ventured far enough into *Fal Dianuil*. Steeling himself to face one of the few things that scared him, he followed her into the shadows and prayed.

He narrowed his eyes, forcing himself to focus in the sudden gloom after the brightness of raging fire back in Tsolir's camp. Where was she?

There! A ghostly figure was locked in a killing dance beneath the goddess-moon, silver glinting off skin and sword as the beams cast mottled light though the canopy. Blood spilled once more, though none of it was hers. Ssen knew Alithis had trained with Seertha and the other guards, but the way she moved... The way she took life as easily, as calmly, as she took breath...

But she was hurt. He could see it now he was closer. It was in the way she danced so lightly on her feet, as if each press of sole against the ground brought suffering, and in the stiffness of her spine, the way she twisted and turned with such painful caution. He caught glimpses of dark marks marring her naked form. What had that bastard done to her? His gut clenched as he thought of what Seertha had done to try to save Alithis, and of what the queen would say when he returned her daughter in such bad condition. Perhaps it would be even worse for him when Her Majesty discovered the princess had rescued herself before Ssen had arrived.

He would not fail her again.

As he spurred himself forward, the princess moved again. Even though her last opponent lay dead on the forest floor, she jerked to one side and then the other, her arms raised in defence and her back to Ssen. He paused, unable to comprehend what she was fighting.

Until he spotted the gnarled tree roots coiled around her ankles and creeping higher towards her neck.

"Princess!" He called her name and slid the knife from his belt, sawing and slicing the tangled roots.

When she cried out, his throat tightened and tears pricked at his eyes. In desperation, he sawed faster. Prayed. Begged. Promised to worship any god who came to help.

And the sound of Tsolir's cutting laughter stabbed at his heart.

***

Tsolir wasn't sure whether to laugh or kill somebody.

He'd finally fought his way into this forsaken forest and the first thing he found was that bloody princess tangled in the foliage. How had she escaped his tent? And who was the scruffy soldier pawing at her?

When tree roots moved to clutch at his skin, he understood. And laughed. So the forest was alive - and thought it could stand against a god? With a careless flick of his hand, he burned the roots to a crisp and relished the inhuman screams reverberating through the trees.

"It will take more than that to stop a god!" he bellowed.

He turned back to the princess - she would not escape him again - and frowned as she vanished behind a thicket, free of the roots that had entangled her and closely followed by the soldier. She'd been entertaining for a while, but her constant mutiny grew tiresome. He'd fuck her, force the whereabouts of the seed from her dying lips, and throw her body to the vulture-worms. Perhaps the queen of Rondia would be more willing to bow to him once he'd shown her what happened to those who disobeyed.

Plan firm in his mind, he left his men to fight the forest and strode confidently after the princess. She knew where the seed was, and she would lead him to it. One way or another.

***

Juni crouched behind a thick pine, watching with growing horror as half a dozen Greycoats sank into the bog they'd inadvertently walked into. Like quicksand, it dragged them down, screaming and struggling against the unstoppable pull. When they were finally submerged, the quiet stillness of the clearing was almost too much to bear.

His expression grim, Romond rose to his feet and nodded to his men. "The forest is slowing them. Splitting them up, sending them in circles. Steering them to danger."

"Will it be enough, Sir?"

"For the Greycoats… Yes. For Tsolir…" He shrugged. "He was a god once. I don't know how to stop a god, my friend. But I will die to protect *Fal Dianuil*."

"Sir, where is your father? He could help!"

"He is on his way but will not arrive in time, I'm afraid. When he travelled to forge an alliance with Lothroan, we could not have foreseen this."

"What can we do?"

Juni moved to join the conversation. The niggle that had been pulling at her mind since their flight through the forest had grown stronger. Pushing through the headache stabbing behind her eyes, she pressed her fingers to the bridge of her nose and swore.

All the men looked at her.

"Romond," she said. "I have to tell you something."

His eyes darkened. "That sounds ominous."

"It's about my name. It's not Juni." She clutched the sash at her waist.

"I know that." He sighed and ran a hand through his hair. "We know you're not Juni. Can't this wait?"

"No! It's important, Romond. I…" She winced as the pain intensified. Breathing deeply, she kept digging at the thread of information buried in her mind. "I knew it. Before the arrow hit you, I started to remember. And now it's gone again but I know it's important."

"It's likely you're the missing guard. Your name doesn't matter right now."

"But it does! Don't you see? There's something… Something else going on here."

Heavy breathing and careless footsteps sounded nearby. They drew their swords and listened. When two figures burst into the clearing, Juni froze. She knew their faces! The woman, naked and covered in blood, clutched her weapon like a cornered animal. Behind her, an armed man reached for her arm.

Still, another sound followed them; something else was coming.

All through the forest, men screamed and blades clashed and wild animals scurried and scattered in squealing chaos. But in the clearing, a pregnant silence stilled the air. At the same moment, the soldier collapsed to his knees before the woman, tears streaming through the dirt on his face, and a giant figure broke through the foliage, his eyes blazing fire and a cruel smirk twisting perfect lips.

"Tsolir!" Romond readied his blade.

And Juni, though she was not Juni, whispered, "I remember."

The two women met each other's gaze as Tsolir reached out for his escaped princess.

The soldier threw himself between them. "I will not let you touch her, you bastard!"

And one voice, certain now of who she was, thundered, "Stop!"

All turned to her, even the once-powerful god poised with one hand set to crush the soldier.

Romond kept his eye on their enemy as he asked, "Juni?"

"My name is Alithis," she said, standing straighter. "Princess of Rondia."

Mouths gaped and eyes widened.

Tsolir clenched both fists; the air around him heated by several degrees. "Then who," he seethed, "is that?"

Jaw clenched, standing tall despite her bloodied, naked body, the other woman pulled the broken fragments of herself back together, refusing to be cowed by the monster she'd been lying to. "My name is Seertha. I told you you'd get nothing from me."

At her side, Ssendorin wept openly, pain and grief and relief cracking open the box he'd kept so carefully locked inside his mind. He gripped her hand like a lifeline.

"You let me believe you were the princess," Tsolir growled. "You wasted a week of my time."

Seertha forced her mouth to twist into a smile, unfamiliar and unnatural after her ordeal. Her lips cracked and bled. A gap showed where he'd torn a tooth from her gums. Still, she smiled. "How does it feel to have been fooled by a mere human? A woman?"

Time seemed to slow as he absorbed her words. And when he erupted, his rage boiled over like magma breaking free of the earth. The heat emanating from his body simmered in the air, making it harder to breathe. Behind him, an older tree caught fire and its neighbours drew back from the flames licking at their trunks. The god raised his arms and called black clouds overhead; lightning flashed and crackled through the gaps in the canopy and thunder rolled like a drumbeat.

"I will have the seed!" He roared and lashed out with a lightning bolt moulded into the shape of a sword.

Romond dived to intercept, meeting Tsolir's crackling blade with his own. The god laughed as power surged through their weapons into Romond's body and the brave prince fell to the ground, jerking and shaking as if in the grip of death.

The prince's men rushed in, attacking the god on all sides. Tsolir swung with fist and sword. Bodies flew. Backs broke against immovable trunks. Death carpeted the forest floor, blood seeping into the mulch.

Alithis, Seertha, and Ssendorin stood between Romond and Tsolir, forming a line to stand against the murderous god. Their hearts were heavy and their guts churned, but their hands remained steady on the hilts of their weapons.

Tsolir, towering above their mortal bodies, brought rain down from the clouds and transformed it into droplets of fire that singed their skin. He squeezed his thumb and index finger together while looking at Ssendorin, and the guardsman dropped to his knees gasping for breath.

Ssen clawed at the ground. Pulled at the tunic against his throat. Turned wide eyes to his wife.

The women attacked as one. They spun to each side, swinging their blades. Tsolir, caught in the middle, followed Alithis; he blocked the slice of her sword and bellowed his anger as Seertha dug her weapon into the back of his knee. He swung back. Threw his fist out. Sent the bloodied woman flying across the clearing. Distracted, Tsolir let go of the power crushing Ssen's throat, and the soldier crawled to his wife, gasping for each breath.

Alone, Alithis faltered. How could she defeat a god, even one with his strength bound? He would take the seed and - No! She could not let him! If he had the seed, he would be freed from his curse. No one would be able to stand against him.

"Give me the seed," Tsolir repeated, stalking closer.

He took a deep breath and blew; the force knocked Alithis from her feet. Her sword tumbled from her hands as she hit the ground, winded from the impact. She scrambled back. Her nails dug into the dirt. Her mother's voice whispered in her memory.

Protect it at all cost, Alithis. Anything would be better than Tsolir getting his hands on the seed.

Hands shaking, she yanked the golden acorn from her left ear. A simple twist opened the hidden compartment and a tiny seed fell into her palm. It looked like any other: small, brown, fragile. She looked up at the approaching god.

Tsolir's eyes flashed with desire. "The seed! Give it to me!"

He reached out. Alithis scrambled back again, barely avoiding his grasping hand. Panic tightened her chest. Had she made a mistake? Played right into his hands? He reached again and she recoiled. Dropped the seed. Fumbled in the grass to find it again. His fingers grazed her boot. She kicked out and he laughed, grabbing her leg and dragging her closer to him. She clutched the seed tight. Lifted her hands to her mouth.

And swallowed it whole.

She retched and fought to keep it down. Shivered as a strange seeping cold settled inside her bones. Her vision bloomed into a burst of white light until she could see nothing else. Lost in sensation, she didn't see or hear the fallen god lifting up her body.

"Worthless bitch!" Tsolir bellowed. "I'll tear you apart to get it back!"

In the back of her mind, she was aware of Seertha, Ssen, and a still-shaking Romond attacking the god with desperate fury. But her body spoke, and Alithis could only listen.

The seed burned her with an icy kiss, working its way down her throat and settling in her stomach. In her core. Warmth radiated then, soothing the searing freeze. It extended beyond her body, bursting free of every pore until her skin glowed and her eyes shone. Her mind raced deep inside the forest, connected with every plant, every tree, every root buried beneath the rich soil. She awed at it, caressed it, and it purred with pleasure, her wilful servant, her loyal subject, her loving child. All nature was hers to control. To nurture. To protect.

As Tsolir spat fire and strained to tear her body apart, Alithis was reborn with the power of life blossoming within. She knew now. She knew why it was important to nourish the soil, to encourage the crops to grow, to leave fields fallow and rotate livestock. She knew why each animal mattered, how they maintained the balance of all things, and the ways in which death gave life.

And she knew how to stop the erstwhile god.

Her body screamed as he stretched her beyond what she could bear. Pushing past it, she focused on the world without and the power within. Dug deep to find her strength. And called the roots and the branches to do her bidding.

Forcing Tsolir back with her light, Alithis pulled branches forward to gather around his arms and bind him in position. He fought against it. Roared and railed and writhed, promising retribution for their sins. She urged the roots to wind around his legs, securing him to the ground. And, when he was still and subdued, the fire fading from his eyes, she encouraged them to grow.

"The world is not made to be dominated, Tsolir," she told him. "You were made to serve it. When you forgot that, you lost yourself."

He opened his mouth to reply but she gave him no chance. Within seconds, roots twined around his entire body and face, thickening until they coalesced into rough bark, strong and sturdy. Branches sprouted, reaching for the sky. Tsolir's muffled screams faded until silence blanketed the clearing once more. A few seconds later, a red-bellied bullfinch flew onto an upper branch and let out a melancholy whistle.

***

Medals gleamed on the left breasts of Seertha and Ssendorin's uniforms as they rode their horses at a walk through *Fal Dianuil* a few weeks later. They would have dismounted sooner but Seertha's body was still healing and Ssen could not bear to see the pain etched on his wife's face when she moved. It was difficult enough watching her suffer the nightmares that often woke her with a scream. Still, he had her back, when he'd thought he'd never see her again. Holding her in his arms was a heaven he would never take for granted.

Ahead of them, beside the Tsolir-tree now guarded by towering pines, Romond and Alithis stood hand-in-hand. When the friends met, they greeted each other with hugs and warm smiles.

"They look good on you," Alithis said, nodding at the medals.

"We are honoured, Your Highness," Ssen replied when Seertha remained quiet. "Thank you."

With a soft sigh, Alithis lifted a finger to her friend's chin. "Seertha. A simple sorry or thank you doesn't seem enough for what you did for me. For what you still suffer for it."

Seertha looked down. "I did my duty."

"You did more than that, my friend," Romond said. "When they came for her, you took her place. You opened the door to the *falar* path, pushed her through it, and paid dearly for your bravery. You are a hero across the land, Seertha. Honoured in Rondia. A legend in your own time. And in *Fal Dianuil*, you are beloved, for you saved Alithis so that I might love her. You have my gratitude, my respect, and my eternal friendship."

Seertha's eyes shone as Ssen put his arm around her shoulders. "I'm glad your memory has fully returned, Alithis. I'm sorry; I didn't know that would happen when I sent you through the portal."

"How could you have known? No one in living memory has travelled that path."

"I hate that having this power means I'm descended from him." Her face darkened.

"Understandable. But you survived him. Escaped from him. Defeated him. Your strength, your power, is all your own, Seertha. Look at it this way; you're descended from him, but you're also descended from the people who took his godhood from him."

She nodded. "What will happen now?"

Romond laid a hand on the tree. Its bark was darker than the others. "My family will continue to protect the forest and to guard this tree. We don't know if any of his power or his evil remains within, but we will always be ready."

"And we will marry," Alithis added, heat creeping up her cheeks. "Quite soon."

Seertha and Ssen grinned, perhaps the first genuine smile they'd shared since Tsolir had taken her. "That's wonderful news! But why the rush?"

The princess looked down at her stomach and cradled it with her hands. "I am one with life, but apparently even I can be surprised by the gifts of nature. We had already decided to marry before this news. Now, we'll move the ceremony so we can unite our houses and tie my magic to the magic of the forest."

Grinning like a fool, Romond said, "It's almost as if nature has a plan for us."

"Let's celebrate." Ssen shook the prince's hand.

"Music to my ears!"

They walked from the clearing together, turning their backs on Tsolir and the darkness that had plagued their world for so long. Their conversation looked to the future; to new life; to joy and love and all things good.

Nature had found its balance.

***

In the dark of night, a small figure flitted between the trees: a child, no more than ten years old. He approached the Tsolir-tree with caution, pacing each footstep to ensure no sound escaped the clearing. As soon as he was close enough, he placed one hand on the rough bark and studied the tree. He gave a small shake of his head.

A few seconds later, birds and insects scattered from the clearing as darkness wrapped around it like a cloak. A little mouse, not fast enough to outrace the onyx blanket, squeaked and trembled behind a tuft of grass. Between one blink and the next, the darkness lifted and the forest returned to normal. The animals came back. The birds settled in their nests. And the little mouse scurried back into its hole.

And if the Tsolir-tree was darker, blackened in death, no one was there to notice. The sun rose, the birds sang, and life continued.

Once a Queen

"Stay with me."

The voice seemed far away, muffled as if it travelled through water. Lilise fought to hold on to it. Her eyes were heavy; she forced them open and recoiled from the sudden brightness of flickering candlelight. The room was smoky. Scents of cedarwood and lavender swirled in the air.

"Don't leave me, Mother."

That voice again! She clung to it, called to bend to its will. Urging her eyes to open one more time, she latched on to the blurred face peering down at her, catching vague impressions of grey hair, deep lines, and pleading blue eyes. It took all her strength, but she raised one hand to his face and pushed a single word through her parched throat.

"Love."

The warmth of his tears soaked into her skin but she did not feel it. Spent, her arm dropped and her eyes closed for the last time.

A low voice intoned, "The Queen is dead. Long live the King."

***

She woke beside a river. The water was so calm it was almost still. Yet, she could not see beneath the surface; its inky depths held many secrets. The ground she lay on was cold and rocky, stones digging deep into her aged flesh. Above her head, there was nothing but black sky. A wave of dizziness rolled over her and she drew her knees up to her chest.

"Speak your name," a deep voice boomed.

She jumped, opening her eyes to see a large skiff bobbing on the water, manned by a cloaked man carrying a long pole half-submerged. Calm acceptance filled her body. "I'm dead, aren't I?"

"Speak your name."

"Queen Lilise of Caeredene." She lifted her chin. Tried to meet his gaze but couldn't see anything inside the dark shadows of his hood.

He lifted a skeletal hand, palm up. "Ninety-two summers. A family grieves. A nation mourns. Lives taken and lives saved. The balance lies in your favour. What do you offer?"

His words made it all real. The weight of her years pressed down on aching bones, and memories, good and bad, danced in her mind. She wiped a tear from her cheek and held her head high. Reaching into her pocket, she found the coin her son had buried her with. She offered it to the ferryman and dropped it into his open palm. "My toll."

He turned and gestured to the empty boat. As she boarded, a cold fog rolled in, coating the surface of the water in ethereal silver. Lilise shivered, longing for the cosy chair and the warm fireplace in her chambers. *No point looking back*, she told herself. But, oh, it hurt to imagine her son weeping over her grave. She allowed herself one glance back at the shore as the ferryman pushed his pole to move them out onto the river.

"I would have stayed if I could," she whispered.

***

"She would have stayed if she could."

Newly-crowned King Aethius nodded his acknowledgement. "I know, Ungar."

The aide sighed as Aethius paced the room. "Forgive me for speaking so bluntly, Sir, but your mourning period may have to be cut short. The nations are unsettled. Tensions rise. There is already talk of disunification. Meanwhile, the Gevorians gather outside our borders, their numbers increasing like rabbits. The people look to you, Your Majesty."

"And I looked to my mother!" He slammed his fist down on the table, lines deepening in his brow. "I am an old man, Ungar. Past my prime. And still, I am lost without her."

"She was an extraordinary woman," Ungar spoke from his heart. He reached out to place a hand on the king's shoulder. "She taught you well."

Aethius took a shaky breath. "Call a meeting. Tell them we need to coordinate our defences against the Gevorians. Tell them anything; just get them here. I will rise to the occasion, my friend. Duty first."

"Very good, Sir." Ungar turned to the door before he allowed his lips to curve in a small smile. The first steps were often the hardest.

***

The ferryman did not speak. He guided the boat with small movements of the pole, his eyes always focused on something unseen through the creeping fog. If he breathed, even that made no noise. The gentle ripples of water stirred by the motion of the skiff were the only sounds to penetrate the eerie hush of the darkness surrounding them.

Lilise pulled her cloak tighter around her shoulders and searched the gloom for signs of… anything. Her chest felt heavy. Was Aethius alright without her? Sixty-eight years she'd been there for him; her passing would weigh on his heart. She clutched the necklace around her throat, a simple pearl he'd given her when he returned from war in Daesih. She would not wish away his life but it helped to know they would one day meet again in the meadows of Elubrette, as she would soon be reunited with her beloved Harald.

Her attention drifted, as did the boat. They stopped often, gathering other souls from rocks and beaches and small islands. After a while, Lilise gave up wondering how big the river was or how long they would travel. She remained seated in the bow, chin high and eyes forward; there was no point in looking back.

A sudden roar reverberated through the darkness. Lilise had no time to react before something rammed the boat. The vessel lurched. Frightened souls screamed. The ferryman lifted his pole from the water. And Lilise tumbled over the side, gasping as she hit the ice-cold water and sank beneath its grasping stillness.

Her ears rang. She held her breath as her legs tangled in her skirts. Which way was up? Desperate, she focused on a faint pinprick of light and pushed her body towards it. She surfaced briefly, coughing and spluttering before she was pulled under once more. Her mind struggled to process what she'd seen.

The ferryman's feet kicked in the air, someone's pale hands around his throat. Grey souls faded into the darkness, screams unheard. And wood splintered in every direction.

She sank under again and swallowed water. Surfacing once more, she flinched as a pale head turned towards her, attracted by the splash of water. Her heart thundered in her ears. Her chest burned. A strange certainty settled in her bones; if those eyes met hers, she would find no passage to Elubrette.

Taking a quick breath, she forced herself back under the water and let herself sink into the stillness, praying no ripple would give her away. The silver fog rolled back over the space where she had been. She felt his presence as he passed over the river. Her skin crawled at his nearness. Her lungs burned and spots danced behind her eyelids. What would happen if she *died* here? Would her soul vanish, never to join her loved ones in the sacred meadows? Fear gripped her.

She waited as long as she could before bursting to the surface and taking deep, gulping breaths. The man was gone. So was everything else. All that remained were several shattered pieces of wood floating atop the river; of the ferryman and his passengers, there was no sign they had ever existed.

There was no land in sight. Reaching for a larger plank, her fingers slipped off the edge and she dipped beneath the surface for a moment, swallowing another mouthful of dark water before she bobbed back up to clutch the wood. The water made her throat tingle, then her stomach, until she was filled with a throbbing pressure.

Lilise clung to the plank in disbelief. Death was supposed to bring peace. What had happened here? She shivered as the fog rolled around her and the river's flow swept her along. Her bones ached and she longed for sleep but thoughts of those pale hands kept her awake. Who was that man? *What* was he? No one should have been able to kill the ferryman. And what would happen now to all the souls searching for Elubrette? With no passage to the sacred meadows, they would be lost forever.

Aethius! If her son could find no passage to Elubrette, she would never be reunited with him. Many other families would suffer the same cruel fate. Something had to be done! Though her eyes were wet, she lifted her head and watched for any sign of land. Minutes passed like hours before she finally laid eyes on a small island. Ignoring the weariness of her muscles and the fog encroaching on her brain, she moved her legs and swam like the competitive girl she'd once been, fighting against the current until her tired arms clutched tufts of grass and her fingers sank into the soil.

She dragged herself up and crawled until she was free of the river, that strange pressure still throbbing inside her chest. Had she swallowed too much water? The Xhiel was not a normal river; who knew what she had imbibed with her dunking? Exhausted, she let her head rest on the grass and closed her eyes, unaware of the silver fog creeping ever closer.

***

"Why have you called us here?"

Aethius narrowed his gaze at the snarling governor of Norvina. What was his name? *Borlias.* "What a pleasure to see you again, Governor Borlias. I failed to see you at my mother's funeral."

Borlias averted his gaze. "Ah, my condolences, Your Majesty, and my deepest apologies. My daughter had Yagas Fever and I did not want to risk bringing it to court. I sent a message."

"Of course," Aethius agreed smoothly. "My daughter Cybelle often speaks of your Jasmora. I hope she has fully recovered." He didn't feel the need to clarify in what way Cybelle spoke of the high-strung young woman.

"She is much better, thank you. A lingering weakness in her legs, but that is all."

"I'm glad to hear it, Borlias." He patted the man on his shoulder and pointedly turned away to address the governess of Asturim. "Melindria. How are you, my friend?"

Melindria managed to keep a straight face. "Better than the poor beggars howling at our borders, Aethius. There is something wrong with them; I just can't place my finger on it."

"That's one of the reasons I brought you all here," Aethius said.

"Good," Finton, Governor of Dwen, boomed. "Lilise said she had a plan for dealing with the Gevorians. I thought I might have to take matters into my own hands when she died."

Tactful as ever, Aethius mused. "Thank you for the confidence, Finton." He gestured to the seats around the circular table, and to the plates laden with food. "Shall we?"

They talked as they ate. Aethius allowed them the time to catch up on more trivial matters. Melindria spoke of the success of her flagship university, soon to be accessible to all who wished to learn, regardless of wealth. Finton beamed as he told tales of his new grandson and his prizewinning horses. Quieter than the others, Borlias sipped his wine and helped himself to generous lashings of roast goose and gravy. As the conversation wound down, Melindria placed her fingers on the back of Aethius' hand.

"We all miss your mother, Aethius," she said. "This must be very difficult for you but it's a comfort to know the kingdom is in safe hands."

He blinked. Smiled. "Thank you, Melindria."

Borlias cleared his throat. "I agree, Your Majesty. It is a good idea to discuss a united approach to dealing with the Gevorians. Just last week, an outlying village was raided. It's increasingly difficult to repel an invading force with no barriers to hold them back and no way to predict where they might strike next."

"What was Lilise's plan?" Finton asked, grease from the goose dripping down his chin.

Aethius took a deep breath and was interrupted by a sharp knock at the door. "Yes?"

A young woman wearing the uniform of an army captain marched in and saluted. Several medals decorated her chest.

Aethius smiled. "Governors, you remember Cybelle."

"This is your daughter?" Melindria lifted a hand to her breast. "She was but knee-high the last time I saw her. You let her in the army, Aethius? Really?"

He chuckled at the slight arching of his daughter's brow. "All members of our family must serve. It is our duty."

"Surely just the boys."

"My mother spent six years in the army before she became queen, Melindria. Cybelle follows in her footsteps."

"Looks like her, too," Finton commented, grabbing a handful of olives.

Cybelle coughed. "If I may, Father?"

"What is it, Cybelle?"

"I've just received word that a large group of Gevorians have made it across the swamplands into Asturim. They're heading towards Morimbra." She stood with her hands clasped behind her back and her eyes focused straight ahead.

Melindria pushed her chair back and rose to her feet. "No. How did they survive the swamplands? What do they want?" She turned to Aethius. "We have to do something!"

The King thought of his mother: strong, decisive, proactive. He looked at his daughter. "Captain. Ready the army. We leave at dawn."

Cybelle saluted, turned on her heels, and left the room.

"Governors," Aethius continued, "send messengers immediately."

"Are we all to march to Morimbra?" Borlias asked.

Aethius shook his head. "We don't know if the Gevorians plan on attacking elsewhere. The last thing we ought to do is move all our soldiers to the southern tip of Asturim, leaving the other nations undefended."

Melindria narrowed her eyes. "My people need help."

"And they will get it." He spoke as he scribbled a note onto parchment and passed it to Ungar. "This is why Caeredene exists, my friends. None of us are alone in times of need. That also means we cannot act alone. We must show a united front to our enemies."

Borlias snorted. "Your mother liked to bandy that thought around, too. Let's see how you handle this problem, Your Majesty."

Aethius rose to his full height. "Do not cause me any more problems, Borlias, or you will be blessed with personal experience in how I deal with them."

The governor bowed his head. "Of course, Your Majesty. I am not here to cause problems, merely to represent the interests of Norvina."

"You have your orders," Aethius said. "All of you are to return to your own nations and guard your own borders until given further instructions. I will investigate and deal with the Gevorians in Asturim. But be prepared to answer my call, Governors. You are still bound to Caeredene and, if you want my support, then you will offer yours in return."

Finton and Borlias bowed and Melindria curtsied before all took their leave. When Aethius and Ungar were alone once more, the king took a long drink of wine.

"You handled them well, Sir," Ungar offered.

"Did I?" He shook his head. "I am not so sure, Ungar. I wish my mother was here."

Ungar didn't speak the words in his heart. *We all do.*

***

The fog blanketed her. Caressed her, like a parent soothing a child. Lilise leaned into its comfort for a moment before memory hit in waves. The pale man! She looked around the small island. Where was she? Silver fog trailed atop the grass as far as she could see, blurring the line between water and land. She felt no breeze but it danced around her, ethereal tendrils chilling her skin. Was it connected to the pale man? She scrambled back and it followed.

She swallowed the fear wedged like a lump in her throat. She had been threatened, attacked, and insulted by darker things than fog in her time. She was a queen, after all, and she would not be cowed. "What are you?"

The fog paused. Pulled back. Coalesced into a silver orb that twisted and swirled until it mutated into the shape of a human face.

Lilise reached for a sword that was no longer there. *They didn't bury it with me.*

"Lilise of Caeredene," the face said.

Warmth blossomed in her chest. Filled with sudden certainty, she closed her eyes and prostrated herself before him. "Arig!"

"Yes." The face grew a body and limbs, all made of the same swirling mist. "Rise before your god, Lilise of Caeredene. You are worthy."

She did as he bade her, forcing her trembling legs to hold her weight.

"You are lost, child. I saw what Sohta did. The ferryman. The other souls. I saw you hiding from him."

Lilise gasped. The pale man had been Sohta? Words tumbled from her mouth as her mind raced and she forgot whose presence she was in. "How was he able to do that? I thought Sohta could not leave Karalus, just as you could not leave Elubrette."

She stopped herself. Looked at the misty figure of her god and the emptiness of the small island she'd found.

"This is not Elubrette," she said. "Yet you are here."

Arig nodded. "Sohta has broken the terms of our agreement. After all these years, he has chosen a more destructive path. I am bound to Elubrette, but Sohta's betrayal allows me to reach further beyond the sacred meadows than I have in millennia. There are consequences to his actions."

Feeling every bit of her old age, Lilise sat on the ground and allowed herself a moment of self-pity. "Consequences? Sohta is bound to watch over the souls of the wicked in Karalus, is he not? Can he not simply be sent back?"

The swirling god laughed, though there was no humour in his voice. "I'm afraid it's not that simple. My brother is not a child to be spanked and sent to his room. His power matches mine. If I followed him on this path, our meeting and inevitable battle could destroy the world."

"But..." She rubbed her arms with her hands and wished Harald was there to hold her. "I don't understand. What is he doing? He killed the ferryman. He... I don't know what he did to the other souls in the boat."

"He consumed them," Arig said, turning his gaze to the river.

"He... He what?"

"It is possible for us to absorb the essence of a soul and use it to bolster our powers, but doing so wipes that soul from existence. They will never journey to Elubrette. Never reunite with their loved ones. Never know the peace of life after death." He sighed. "When we came here, with no memory of anything that came before, we swore to protect our people. Promised we would never take a soul that way. But something dark has festered within Sohta. Long has he sought dominion over me. He is my twin, the other half of my own soul. Yet, he despises me, for I am everything that he is not. I foolishly thought he would be content within his own domain. Instead, he has been building his strength and waiting for the right opportunity. Now, he moves to destroy me."

Lilise looked up sharply. "You can stop him."

Arig's silence hit her like a fist.

"You have to stop him," she repeated. "Is he going to attack every soul trying to reach Elubrette? What will happen without the ferryman? How will we ever reach the meadows?"

"You cannot. Those already in Elubrette are safe from Sohta; I can protect them. But beyond my meadows, Sohta is stronger than me. I cannot risk leaving the souls there unprotected."

Lilise's hands shook. She wouldn't see Harald? Her parents? What would happen when Aethius passed? She pushed her chin forward. As queen, she had problem-solved for decades; she wasn't about to stop now. "Unacceptable. There must be something we can do. Could I go back? Try to keep the souls from leaving the world until Sohta is stopped?"

Arig's foggy eyes hazed even further, as if his focus was elsewhere. "Your world is not safe from Sohta. He is already preventing souls from crossing over. Forcing them to stay in empty vessels now controlled by him."

"You can't just leave people to face him alone!" She took a step closer to him, fists clenched, then remembered who she was speaking to. "I mean... What does he want?"

"Dominion. Over life, the afterlife, and over me." Arig offered her his hand. "You survived your encounter with him, Lilise of Caeredene. I have not the strength to stop him, but I have enough to carry you home to Elubrette. Come with me now, before Sohta returns."

She looked at his hand. Gazed out over the river. She longed to be with Harald again. To see her father's smile and find comfort in her mother's arms. Reaching out to Arig, she paused. "No."

"No?"

She shook her head. "I can't hide while my people suffer."

"You will be happy in Elubrette. Pain will not touch you."

"Happy?" This time, she didn't care that she was talking to a god. "How could any mother be happy knowing what fate awaited her children? Knowing she would never see them again? Not even Elubrette could take that pain away."

She turned back to the water, peering through the gloom for inspiration, and so didn't see the small smile curving on the silver god's misty face.

"Send me back to them," she said. When she received no reply, she spun to glare at him. "Please!"

"And what can one old woman with no body to return to do against a god?" He tilted his head as he waited for her answer.

She clenched her jaw. "Try. Which is more than you're doing. Send me back!"

Arig's face transformed as his smile widened. "Ah, Lilise. In nine decades of life, you passed every test placed before you, and now you do it again. A father does not have favourites, but I am exceptionally proud of you, my child."

"Test?" Her fists clenched again.

His form swelled until it doubled in size. The grey glow of his body intensified and a bright silver light bathed everywhere within sight. The river gleamed in his magnificence. "I was not fast enough to stop Sohta but, when I sensed a soul remained here, I had to come. I wanted to bring you back to Elubrette, to save just one more from my brother's evil plans. But when I saw it was you, hope flared within me. I wondered. Could Queen Lilise of Caeredene serve her god one last time? Would she be willing to risk her eternity for those she left behind? My child, your loyalty is legendary and you do not disappoint. With your help, there is yet hope. Will you have faith in me once more, my child?"

Warmed by the radiance of his love, Lilise closed her eyes and basked in it. After a moment, she sank to one knee, ignoring the creaks and aches of her old bones. She bowed her head. Clasped a fisted hand to her heart. And gave her word. "I will."

***

They'd ridden for days. Aethius would never admit it, but his body was too old for anything other than comfortable cushions and soft beds. Every inch of him ached, and he daren't dismount in front of his soldiers lest they see him fall to the ground when his stiff legs refused to cooperate.

Cybelle and her soldiers, the Eighth Division, would be in Morimbra already. They should have arrived the day before; he wondered what they had found. The king in him hoped she had engaged the enemy to protect the people; the father in him prayed the enemy was long gone. Either way, he would find out once they made it across the river and rounded the Morimbran foothills. The water was low this time of year, especially at the ford. His horse picked its way carefully across the rocky river bed, the current rising only to its knees. Soldiers rode ahead, behind, and on either side, protecting their king; Aethius felt like a fool. Maybe he should have listened to Ungar and stayed behind, but he didn't want his people to think they had a weak leader. The monarch had to set the example.

As they proceeded into the foothills, a sharp cry rang out from ahead. Aethius reached for his sword a fraction later than his men did.

"Your Majesty! Gevorians in the valley! The Eighth has engaged them."

Cybelle! "Help them!" Aethius drove his heels into his horse's sides.

Commanders bellowed orders. Hooves thundered on soft ground. And a thousand swords whispered as they were freed from leather sheaths.

The soldiers charged around the corner and galloped into the fray without hesitation. Aethius moved to follow and was held back by a blockade of a dozen men.

"Let me pass," he demanded.

"I'm sorry, Your Majesty," one man said. "Lord Ungar said we're not to allow both royals into battle at the same time. Caeredene can't afford to lose both of you."

"I can't afford to lose my daughter," he snarled, but stilled his horse and watched the battle unfold. Where was she? He scanned the tangled mass of bodies, searching for the red-plumed helmet indicating her rank. There!

Cybelle fought in the centre of the melee, battling two opponents at once. It was hard to see what was going on; the Gevorians looked no different to the Caeredenians except for the white gleam of their armour, which soon looked the same blood-red as that of their enemy. Aethius clenched his fists as he watched his daughter. She fought like her grandmother; pride filled him in equal measure with fear. His mother had taught all of them how to fight but the lessons had stuck far more with Cybelle than they ever had with him. Dancing between her opponent's blades, she swung low and sliced one man's hamstring, spun, and followed through by bringing it back up to skewer the second. Without pause, she moved on to the next bodies in the crowd.

Grief churned in Aethius' gut as he viewed the carnage. So much blood! He'd never had the stomach for battle. Never understood why some people lived for the thrill of it. To his mind, there was always a better alternative. Still, his mother had taught him to take a stand against bullies. These Gevorians had attacked the Caeredene people, invaded their land, and put their union at risk. If they wanted a fight, they would get one.

Yet each blow pounded against his heart. Each spray of bright blood brought fresh tears to his eyes. And the thud-thud-thud of falling bodies resounded like death-drums in the grim silence of his mind.

"No!"

He turned sharply, spying a young woman weeping several feet away.

"Please, stop!" she cried. "This isn't necessary. Please!"

Aethius gestured for her to be brought to him and the guards complied after checking her for weapons. When she was closer, he realised she was younger than he'd first thought, no more than twelve years of age. "What's your name, child?"

She sniffed. "Kezra."

"Are you from Morimbra, Kezra?"

"Sometimes." She wiped the back of her hand across her nose and looked away. "My mother was Morimbran. My father is Gevorian."

Aethius leaned back in his saddle. "I was not aware the two peoples intermingled."

"Morimbra is on the outskirts of Asturim, Your Majesty. We're closer to the outlying villages of Gevoria than we are to the capital of our own nation. Trade has flourished here for many years."

He glanced at the nearest soldier. "Melindria has told me nothing of this."

Kezra shrugged. "Governess Melindria issued a decree to stop trading with them a year ago, but both sides would starve without that business."

"So why are the Gevorians invading?" He narrowed his eyes. None of this made sense.

"They're not," she said, "but Governess Melindria wouldn't listen. She pulled the villagers out and sent her troops in. None of them speak Gevorian and they're not listening! Please, Your Majesty! You have to stop this. They're going to kill my papa!"

Aethius' mind raced. Melindria had known about the Gevorians before Cybelle's message back in Caeredene! What was she playing at? "But why are the Gevorians fighting? This doesn't make any sense."

Kezra wrung her hands, glancing between the battle and the king. "We weren't here to fight! We came for refuge, Your Majesty. For help, for sanctuary, for safe-haven! We came to escape death, not to court it!"

A heaviness settled on his shoulders. He looked beyond the battle, to the edges of the swamplands the Gevorians had braved to make it here. "Refuge from what?"

The girl shuddered. She too turned her eyes towards the swamps. "From the Soulless."

***

Her hands glowed. Lilise turned them over, mesmerised by the faint sheen emanating from her skin. Before Arig had returned to Elubrette, he'd sent her on her way with a small gift and words of warning. She must be careful. Although she now carried a smidgeon of Arig's power, it wasn't nearly enough to match Sohta's. If she fought him, her soul would be lost forever. Instead, she must somehow keep Sohta occupied in the world of the living while Arig sought to diminish his brother's strength in the afterworld.

But the gift - aside from a taste of his magic - left her stunned.

Age fell from her like leaves from a tree, the years dropping one by one as she watched colours bloom on her body, the gold of her hair complemented by the red blush in her cheeks. Strength returned to her muscles; her biceps and stomach were toned and defined once more. And the pain she had lived with for thirty years was cut from her, a dead branch removed from the healthy whole. She felt twenty years old again - vibrant, strong, energised in a way she had forgotten was even possible.

Laughter bubbled in her throat. Youth truly was wasted on the young.

She navigated her own boat now, one Arig had pulled together from the scattered pieces of the ferryman's broken skiff. She used the pole to move upstream, searching for the door to where she needed to be. It had taken her some time to get used to it. At first, the visions at each piece of land were alarming. The rocky mound on the left showed a group of men creeping through a forest thick with vines, their spears held low and their voices guttural and strange to her ear. On the right, a sandy beach held a shining doorway to a crowded castle, grey as the clouds hovering above its turrets.

She moved on, fascinated by the doorways into other people's lives: barons and beggars, knights and knaves, saviours and sinners. They walked, ate, slept, and worried about their children. Most tried to be good; all made mistakes. And, if Sohta could be stopped, all would end up sharing a boat along the Xhiel to Elubrette. Death truly was a great equaliser.

Further along, she almost missed the grassy bank tucked around a meander in the river. Edging past it, she stopped, pulled by something she couldn't name. It tugged at her until she used the pole to push her boat to the shore. The doorway gleamed golden in the gloom.

Only the ferryman can see the doorways, Arig had said. *And only the ferryman can go back through one, though he never has.*

The image blurred. Lilise narrowed her eyes, struggling to separate the small shapes she saw within, struggling to understand what she was seeing. She blinked to clear her vision. Was that Aethius?

No! As her mind made sense of the picture, she pulled back and held a hand to her mouth. Caeredenians and Gevorians killed each other in a large field, staining the grass red beneath the carpet of bodies. The forked tree! She knew that tree; it grew just outside of Morimbra. What, in Arig's name, were they doing? Before Lilise died, the governors had made several complaints about the Gevorians gathering at their borders, but she had always managed to calm them with logic. She never thought the Gevorians were there with malintent - and, now she knew the truth, she couldn't comprehend what had happened since her passing.

With a speed her renewed youth afforded her, she moored the boat and climbed the bank to the doorway. Even Cybelle was there, fighting with every technique Lilise had taught her. And Aethius, astride his mount atop a nearby hill, lifted a horn to his lips. Lilise growled her frustration. Were they all so caught up in their petty disagreement that they couldn't see the danger creeping at their backs? Even now, she saw the dark shapes shambling out of the swamplands; Sohta had wasted no time in accelerating his plan. She had to do something!

Her hand reached for the hilt of the sword Arig had gifted her. Taking a deep breath, she stepped through the doorway and back into the world of the living.

***

Cybelle kicked a yellow-bearded man away from her, spun her sword in a one-handed grip, and froze as her father's horn sounded at the same time as a blinding light exploded through the centre of the melee. Soldiers on both sides stopped fighting, unable to see their own hands in front of their faces. The sudden silence left a ringing in Cybelle's ears. She gripped the hilt of her sword tighter and waited.

"Stop fighting!" a voice bellowed.

Cybelle gasped. She knew that voice. It had comforted her when her mother died, soothed her when she couldn't sleep, and cheered her on through all her training. "Grandmother?"

The light faded, revealing a young woman wielding a glowing sword; a strange gleam emanated from her skin. There was something familiar about the way she lifted her chin and the steely glint of her eyes.

"That's Queen Lilise!" one of the older soldiers cried out and pointed to her. "But she's... young again!"

Eyes wide, Cybelle walked closer to her grandmother. Was it really her? The pain of her loss still cut like a knife. How was this possible? The gathered soldiers backed away, battle forgotten as they gaped at the vision of their erstwhile queen. Even the Gevorians watched with a mix of fear and awe.

Thundering hooves broke her concentration; she glanced back and saw her father driving his horse downhill to the spectre of her grandmother. They reached her at the same time; three generations of Caeredene royalty held hands in the centre of that bloodied field and wept.

"Mother?" Aethius sobbed. "Is it really you?"

Lilise cupped his face with her hand. "Yes, my son. It's me."

"But you died. You died, and you're young again."

She nodded. "And I am still dead. But there are forces at work, both in the afterlife and here, that you must be told about. We have much to discuss."

Cybelle, still dazed, dropped her sword and flung her arms around her grandmother's neck. Clinging to her like a child, she relished the warmth of their embrace and breathed in the familiar scent of lime and rose blossom. "What happened to you, Grandmother?"

"My Cybelle," Lilise said, kissing the top of her granddaughter's head. "I would hold you for eternity if I could, my love. But danger lies at our backs. Even explanations will have to wait, I'm afraid. They're already here."

"Who?" Cybelle asked.

Aethius looked towards the swamplands. "The Soulless," he said. He turned to his mother. "I know, Mother. I found out just as you arrived."

Lilise clasped his hand. She closed her eyes for a moment and the bright glow returned. Casting her voice over the crowd, she said, "Caeredenians and Gevorians, your war ends here. You were never enemies! The Gevorians came seeking refuge from the Soulless. Instead of fighting your neighbours, Caeredenians, you should have taken them in and learned from them. You should have been preparing yourselves for the real fight. That fight is now upon us, and there is no time to ready yourselves. The Soulless are here. Pick up your swords and fight side by side now, lest all of you fall prey to the eternal wastelands of Sohta and his spreading darkness."

The Gevorians moved straight away, turning their weapons towards the swamplands and the shambling bodies moving ever closer.

"Look!" a young Caeredenian yelled and pointed at the grey-skinned creatures. "What are they?"

"Questions later," Lilise said firmly. "Right now, fight as if your children's lives depend on it; they do. This enemy is fearless; tireless; they do not feel pain. They will keep coming until their plague is spread across the whole world. Stop them!"

Cybelle looked over her grandmother's shoulder and recoiled. They came in their thousands, far outnumbering the already-depleted Gevorian and Caeredenian forces. Their skin was ashen and loose, hanging off them like snakeskin being sloughed, and their eyes were unfocused white orbs. Moving with a strange shambling gait, they shuffled and lurched until they reached the first of the warriors.

"Don't let them get hold of you!" Lilise warned.

Leading their defence, the glowing queen charged into the front line of the Soulless, her shining sword dancing through the air. She moved with the grace of youth, the strength of practice, and the wisdom of age; dozens fell beneath her blade. With a united roar, Caeredenian and Gevorian soldiers rallied at her side, pushing themselves to the limit as if they hadn't just been fighting each other only moments before. Aethius, horn replaced with royal sword, fought back to back with his mother in the midst of the melee.

Cybelle drew on every ounce of her strength to make her way to her family. She gave herself over to the battle fury her hotheaded mother had been famous for and fought like she was possessed. She'd lost her grandmother once and she wasn't about to let it happen again. Pushing through the horde, she chopped and stabbed and severed any limb that reached for her. Hearing a gut-wrenching scream, she caught a glimpse of one of her men sinking beneath the wave of Soulless, his cry cut short as blood-curdling growls and sucking noises pierced the air. Swallowing the bile in her throat, she took her revenge in blood.

Pressed against her grandmother on one side and her father on the other, Cybelle heard the faint whisper on the wind.

Lilise, you are needed elsewhere. The voice swirled around their ears, teasing the strands of hair at their brows. *Come now!*

"Who is that?" Cybelle cried.

"Arig." Her mouth a thin line, Lilise decapitated one of the Soulless with a vicious swing. "Hold them off, my darlings," she said. "I promise you'll see me again."

***

The journey back to the afterworld was disjointing, a blur of shape and colour and the incongruous scent of fresh flowers. Lilise returned to her skiff on the Xhiel to find Arig waiting for her, his swirling form oozing from the fog blanketing the river. With a wave of his hand, he moved the boat across the surface until they reached a sandy bay.

Lilise noticed the pointed turrets beyond the portal. "You're sure about this?"

"Yes," Arig said. "Sohta could not have done what he has in the world of the living without help. This is where he got that help."

"Our families have been friends and allies for generations." She sighed. "Yet I can understand his choice. I will deal with him, but what of Sohta?"

Arig moved his silver body into a sitting position, his legs crossed and his head bowed as if in meditation. "Humanity does not remember, but Sohta and I were one once."

"Brothers. Twin brothers. Yes."

"More than that. We are like twins now but back then, before the Unknowing, we were one soul. After, when we woke with no memory of before, that was the only thing we knew; what once was one became two. Sohta was filled with darkness, and I with light."

Stepping onto the bay, Lilise paused. "You were never meant to be separate."

"Exactly. To stop him now, I must find a way to merge his soul with mine once more. I do not know if it is possible."

"You still love him."

He looked up, surprised. "Of course. He is my brother. The other half of my soul. For all his faults, he is a part of me."

She tilted her head. "In all my years as queen, I found the best way to settle disputes was with compassion. Perhaps you need to find a way to welcome him home."

"Alas, he now plagues the world of the living while I must stay close to Elubrette."

"Then we must find a way to bring him home," she said with a smile.

The lurch as she stepped from bay to battlements made her stumble. She righted herself quickly and strode across the familiar stones, down the spiral staircase, and through drafty corridors until she reached his chambers. At this time of day, she doubted he'd be anywhere else. She weighed up her options and then pushed the door open without knocking.

He jumped to his feet, hand reaching for the hilt of his sword. His hair was a mess, strands flying in every direction. Dark shadows bruised the skin beneath his eyes. A young woman sat listlessly in an armchair by the empty fireplace; she didn't stir at Lilise's entrance.

"Borlias." Lilise took in his appearance and sighed.

"Who are you? How did you get in here?"

"Look closer," she said. "Your father would have known me. Although, if he were here, we would not be in this predicament, would we? Governor Borleroy would never have betrayed his kingdom."

He blinked. Flinched. Dropped back into his chair, his whole body shaking. "Your Majesty? But... you're dead!"

"Indeed! And, even in death, I'm still forced to clean up your mess. Really, Borlias. Why didn't you come to me? I would have helped."

When he spoke again, it was in a weak and reedy voice. "How could you have helped? Jasmora was dying. She -" He lifted a hand to his cheek to wipe the tears away.

Lilise steeled her heart, though sympathy washed over her in a wave. "Jasmora never recovered from the Yagas fever, did she?"

He shook his head. His eyes glazed over, his mind elsewhere. "She was so sick. Fever wracked her body yet she shivered with the chills. She couldn't draw enough breath in, constantly fighting for it. That gasping, wheezing, rattling sound haunts my nightmares. She was pale as death, and I knew he was coming for her. My child. My Jasmora."

She sat beside him and placed a hand atop his. "What happened?"

"I thought all hope was lost. I took my knife, ready to press it into my heart, and waited for her to pass so I could follow."

"Oh, Borlias. No parent should go through that."

"She breathed out; it was a long, wheezing breath. I was so sure it was her last. But something happened. Everything seemed to freeze in that moment. I held her hand; it was still warm, still soft against mine. And then I heard his voice."

Lilise sat up straighter. "Whose voice?"

"At first, I believed it was Arig. I believed my prayers had been answered and he had come to take me with her." Borlias pleaded with his eyes. "He said he could save her. Bring her back. I just had to do one thing in return."

"What did you have to do, Borlias?"

He swallowed. "Give him a replacement."

"A life for a life." She took a breath to calm the sickness and disgust rolling through her body. She'd watched this man grow from a child. Read stories to him when she'd visited Norvina. Attended his wedding and sent gifts for the birth of his daughter. "You really thought Arig would ask you to take a life?"

"That's just it. I didn't think; not at first. I just wanted Jasmora to be alright."

"And when you took that life? Did you still believe it then?"

He cast his gaze down. "No. I convinced myself it was Arig, that I was only doing what my god requested. But deep down I knew. I knew it was wrong. I was just too far gone to care."

Her heart heavy, Lilise held a hand out to the woman in the armchair. The Yagas fever had ravaged her body so much that Lilise hadn't recognised her at first. Scars marred her face and arms. Her skin was ashen and her hair dull and lifeless. She made no movement other than an occasional slow blink. Lilise asked, "Was it worth it?"

His eyes were red and puffy. "I... I should have just died with her. That would have been better than this. To be together in Elubrette... Please, Your Majesty! Is it real? Tell me it's real."

"It's real, Borlias. Elubrette is real. But you took lives. You murdered people. How many, Borlias? How many people did you kill so Jasmora could live like this?"

"I thought it would only be the one, you see. But he held it over me. Threatened to take her soul if I stopped helping him. I had to give him more and more until I lost count."

"How did you get away with it without anybody noticing?"

He wrung his hands together. "It was easy at first. When I started killing more, I travelled and took people from different places so no one noticed a pattern. I transported the bodies beyond our borders. I didn't care what he did with them after that."

Lilise gripped his hand tighter, a seeping horror chilling her to the bone. "You created the Soulless! You killed them so he could absorb their souls, and then he used their empty husks to create an unstoppable army. Do you have any idea what you've done? Do you understand who you've been working for? You may have ruined us all, Borlias!"

"I'm sorry." His shoulders slumped. "I pray Arig will forgive me, but Sohta took ownership of my soul the day he laid claim to Jasmora's. If I stop helping him, she will go to Karalus."

She stood abruptly and paced the room. "He's taking everyone's souls now, Borlias. Absorbing some for power. Sending others to Karalus for whatever dark purpose he has in mind. There will be no Elubrette for anyone if we don't stop him."

"How?"

She looked to the ceiling and ran her hands across her face. "We have to find him first. Where is he?"

Borlias shrugged. "The last time he demanded a life, he told me it was time to reap the benefits of his labour."

"Reap the benefits?" She gasped. "Morimbra!"

Grabbing his arm, she yanked him from the chair and dragged him back to the battlements to find the portal only she could see. He pulled against her and several guards moved to intervene.

"Stay back!" she boomed, her voice reverberating between the stones. She felt the power of her voice tingle along her spine and was satisfied when the guards did as they were told.

"Where are you taking me?" Borlias asked.

She gripped him tighter and launched him over the edge of the battlements. "To clean your mess up," she snarled as she followed him through the gleaming doorway.

***

The melee had moved several feet by the time she returned, though it still raged around a sea of bloodied bodies. Standing a short distance away, she gave Borlias only a handful of seconds to indulge in his quivering and wailing;

the journey between worlds had not been easy for a man who was not yet dead.

Still gripping the sobbing man's arm, Lilise scanned the battlefield to get her bearings. Aethius and Cybelle were separated now, but both still fought for their lives. *Thank Arig!* The bodies littering the field seemed to be around two-thirds Soulless, with the remaining corpses a mixture of Caeredenian and Gevorian. A number of familiar faces rested between blades of grass, their eyes open and unseeing.

"Was it worth this, Borlias? All this death? How many parents have lost their children here?"

He whimpered and pointed a trembling finger to the edge of the field where a pale figure drifted. Sohta! He moved closer, stopping only to study each corpse along the way and to rip their souls from their newly dead bodies. Each time he absorbed a soul, his wraithlike body shuddered with pleasure and the strange shadow surrounding him grew darker, stronger. His long fingers curled and unfurled convulsively.

"Sohta," Lilise breathed his name. "He's getting stronger."

Raising his pale hands, the dark god lifted the bodies from the ground and stood them back on their feet. As one, they moved to rejoin the fight, eyes and mouths gaping as the empty shells lurched into battle.

"He's making more of them!"

Borlias threw himself to the ground and vomited. "He cannot be stopped. He will just make more and more until we all belong to him. Don't you see? If we surrender, maybe _"

"No." She cut him off. "I will surrender nothing."

But how could she stop him? She pulled Borlias back to his feet, rolling her eyes as he recoiled from the glowing sheen of her skin. *Of course!* She threw Borlias forward.

"Call your master," she said, drawing her sword.

He cowered, refusing to meet her gaze.

"I won't waste time with you anymore." Kicking him out of the way, she strode towards the battle. *If you want something done right, always do it yourself.* "Sohta!"

The god paused. Sniffed the air. Spun on his heels with a wide, thin-lipped grin. In the blink of an eye, he moved three feet closer, gliding across the blood-soaked ground.

"Call them off."

He spoke with slow deliberation, and an oozing cold swept the field. "You are not supposed to be in this world."

Lilise shrugged despite the ice creeping down her spine. "You killed the ferryman, Sohta. Didn't leave me with many places to go."

His eyes lit up. "I thought someone else was there. You were in the water? How delightful! Your soul is brighter than the others. More powerful. Will you taste of the Xhiel, I wonder?"

"I won't taste very nice," she assured him. "Bitter. Sour. A little salty." She tightened her mouth and arched one brow, showing him the face that had always cowed people into submission.

Still smiling, he glanced back to the melee as the shrieks and groans intensified. Lilise edged closer, panic fluttering in her chest; Aethius and Cybelle had been separated. Her son struggled against dozens of enemies and her granddaughter was nowhere in sight. The Gevorian chief swung his battleaxe into a grey head before the Soulless man could bite Aethius. The two of them blocked and dodged and decapitated, but the Soulless kept coming.

And there was Cybelle! The red plume was long gone from her helmet. Blood trailed down one arm, and her breath came in ragged pants. She bared her teeth in a growling grimace and dashed forward, always on the offensive - just as Lilise had taught her.

Pride and fear and love swam through Lilise's body.

Sohta smirked. "She is your blood. She bears your eyes, your mouth, your fighting stance. She matters to you?"

Her breath caught in her throat. "Stay away from her."

A sly shadow passed across his eyes. With a nod of his head, he apparated to where Cybelle was. The Soulless recoiled from his presence and turned their attention elsewhere. Cybelle looked the pale god up and down, tightened her grip on her sword, and spat at his feet. Sohta reached out with long fingers.

"No!" Lilise bellowed her rage and charged towards her granddaughter. She would not allow it to end this way. "Cybelle!"

Grateful for her younger body, she ploughed through masses of the Soulless, pushing and cutting and kicking bodies out of her way. The strange sensation she'd felt after climbing from the Xhiel resurfaced within her chest, throbbing and pulsating with a building pressure. Her mind calculated as she ran, and dread struck like a sword to the gut; she wouldn't make it in time.

Cybelle swung her blade at Sohta's outstretched hand; it sailed through his flesh as if he wasn't there, leaving no mark, no scratch, no sign she'd attacked him. He laughed: that cold, seeping, abrasive laugh that shivered through people's veins like liquid ice. Amused, he moved closer until his fingertips almost brushed her cheek and Cybelle stumbled backwards, eyes wide and heart racing.

Lilise knew if he touched Cybelle, her granddaughter would die.

And then Aethius was there, shoving his daughter aside and standing between her and the danger, as any parent would for their child.

Lilise fought to reach him. Her own child, full-grown and white-haired, but still her baby. She dug deep for every ounce of strength, every burst of speed, every scrap of stamina.

But Sohta was inexorable. His fingers stroked the skin on the back of Aethius' hand and a faint hiss sizzled in the air. Aethius sucked a breath in. Stiffened. Dropped to his knees.

"Aethius!" Lilise screamed.

She got to him as he toppled forward; she caught his body and lowered him gently to the ground, turning him so she could see his vacant eyes. Pain hit so hard, so fast, she couldn't breathe. Silent tears streamed down her cheeks as she stroked his hair, his face, his arm, and got no response.

"Aethius," she said, her voice breaking along with her heart.

Sohta held his hand out towards Aethius' corpse. A bright light grew in Aethius' chest until it seeped beyond his flesh, casting a glowing replica of his body.

"Ah, there's something electrifying about a pointless death," Sohta said, sucking Aethius' light closer to his mouth.

Lilise's horror grew as her son's soul was stripped from his corpse. Acting on instinct, she leapt to her feet and reached for his soul's glowing arm. "You will not have him, Sohta!"

When she touched Aethius' soul, something flared inside her own body: something warm and fierce and tingling through her blood. Aethius froze in place, tugged between his mother and the pale god.

Lines appeared on Sohta's brow. "How is it possible?"

"How is what possible?" Lilise held up a hand to warn Cybelle to stay back, far away from Sohta's deathly reach.

"I am calling his soul. You cannot stop it. Yet, you are."

She gritted her teeth. "He is my son. You will not have him."

With a roar, she yanked Aethius away and dived in front of him, pressing the tip of her sword against Sohta's chest. Her son's soul wavered before returning to hover above his body.

"Go home, Sohta. Go back to Karalus and leave us in peace."

Shadows passed over his eyes. "I have spent enough years hiding in that barren place. No more! I will take what my brother has kept from me. No mortal can stop me."

Lilise tightened her grip on the hilt. "I will stop you. I made a promise to protect my people; to serve them my whole life. You should have killed me in the river; you'll regret that before I'm through." She flicked her wrist and grazed his arm with the edge of her blade. A thick, golden ichor oozed tiny droplets from the wound.

Sohta flinched. Ran his finger along the cut and stared at the small amount of blood he gathered. He clenched his fist and pinned Lilise with his gaze. "What are you?"

"I am a queen."

"No. What happened to you in the Xhiel? Did you swallow its water?"

She nodded. "More than once. Three times, in fact. I almost drowned in it hiding from you."

His pale face turned ashen. "Three times. It cannot be. No. I will destroy you. I will take the soul of everyone you love. I will ravage this world and all of your people. And I will take their souls to Karalus. Elubrette will never be seen again!"

Pain surged inside Lilise until she felt nothing else. She could contain it no longer; she had to move or die. She had no more words; no more tears; only a sword to speak her grief and her anguish. She used it. Years of study and practice and muscle memory rose to the fore and she gave herself to it.

Sohta drew a thin sword from his sleeve and blocked her blow. They swung and parried, lunged and stabbed, clashed and countered as soldiers and Soulless fought around them. Breaking apart, breath heavy and swords held low, they circled each other. Sohta's teeth flashed in a snarl.

"You should not be able to fight me like this," he said. "Even with the Xhiel, with Arig's blessings - how do you stand against a god?"

Lilise met his gaze. "Because I stand for *something*."

He was furious, feral, frenzied. Losing the calm façade, he pounced like a tiger and Lilise barely managed to dance back beyond the reach of his rapier. All around her, bodies fell, cut down like wheat in a field. Screams of the wounded and dying competed with the snarls and grunts of the Soulless. Cybelle appeared beside her, and Lilise yelled for her to stay back.

Everything weighed on her, the pressure building until she wanted to scream. Sohta. The Soulless. Her son lying lifeless on the blood-soaked ground. Her mind grasped at ideas, considering and discarding them in seconds. What could she do? Arig hadn't come through yet. How could she stop a god? How could she save a world of people when she couldn't even save her son? Sohta wanted Aethius' soul and she -

Sohta wants Aethius' soul.

The burning spark of an idea drifted in the periphery of her thoughts and she grasped it like a lifeline. Keeping a close eye on Sohta, she checked where the doorway was and edged closer to it, still circling and making sure he followed.

"Come to me, Aethius!" she called to her son. He did as she asked, leaving his body behind and staying clear of Sohta. She taunted the pale god, "You want our souls?"

"I will have them."

He lunged at her and she sidestepped into the portal, pulling Aethius with her. Sohta paused, torn between following them or leading the Soulless to victory.

"Borlias!" he bellowed to the cowering governor. "Control the Soulless. Kill the woman. If you fail me, your daughter's soul will be lost to you forever."

Borlias drew his sword even as he wept. "Yes, Master."

Liilse snapped. She shouted through the doorway, "Borlias, if you touch my granddaughter I will cut off whatever balls you have left and feed them to you!"

Cybelle, still guarding her father's body from the Soulless but unable to see his soul watching her with such sorrow, called several soldiers to her side to keep him safe while she faced Borlias. "It's alright, Grandmother. I can handle this weasel."

Pride. Love. It filled her. Gave her strength. "If you want us, Sohta," she said, smirking, "come and get us."

And she dived back into the river Xhiel, dragging Aethius with her, down below the silver fog and deep beneath the surface. If its water had gifted her with something that took her beyond mere mortal, perhaps it could do the same for her son.

***

Cybelle left her soldiers to watch her father's body, trusted the Gevorian and Caeredenian forces to handle the Soulless, and focused on Governor Borlias, a man she'd once trusted like an uncle.

"Why'd you do it, Borlias?" she asked, more to distract him than because she really wanted to know. It didn't matter why he'd done it; he was still a traitor.

Borlias made a weak attempt to cut her arm with his sword and she dodged easily. "I had no choice," he said. "Jasmora was dying."

"And now my father is dead." She lashed out like a whip, slicing her blade across his cheek and leaving a thin trail of blood.

"I'm sorry for that, Cybelle; your father was a good man." He thrust firmly, remembering his own skill with a sword, and she parried. "But there is no pain worse than losing a child. You must understand."

"I do understand," she said. "But I do not forgive, and nor would Jasmora. She wouldn't have wanted this Borlias. No one could want this."

Done with talking, she slid closer to him, putting him on the defensive. Their swords clashed time and again. His made a fine whistle as it glided through the air; hers was of better quality, as was her swordsmanship. He fought well, she gave him that. Against most other opponents, he would have been victorious. But she had been trained by Queen Lilise of Caeredene, and none had ever bettered her.

Taking her time, making sure she made no mistakes, Cybelle slipped past his guard and thrust her weapon deep into his gut.

His eyes widened. His grip loosened and his sword dropped to the ground. A groaning gurgle escaped his lips as she leaned in and whispered into his ear.

"I hope Sohta takes your soul, Borlias. You deserve no better than the fate you thrust on so many of your people. You die a traitor."

His lips opened and closed, and opened again. His fading eyes sought hers. "Please..."

She shook her head. "You betrayed your daughter, your people, your king… and now your queen. I waste no more time on you."

She stepped away, kicked his body off her sword, turned her back on him. And walked away with tears weaving lines on her cheeks as his frenzied sobs faded and died.

***

Sohta was looking for them.

Lilise knew they couldn't stay submerged forever. Even dead, they could not survive that. As her lungs burned, she dragged Aethius back to the surface and prayed. She had promised she would bring Sohta to Arig; now she could only hope Arig would be there to save them.

"Lilise!" Sohta bellowed, his oozing voice reverberating through the cavernous space.

Aethius clung to her arm. "Mother, I don't know how much longer I can swim."

"Keep going," she snapped. "You have no choice."

They swam until they reached the same shore where she'd met Arig, and crawled onto the grassy mounds, exhausted and gasping for breath. The swirling fog stayed atop the water; there was no sign of their god, but Sohta's voice grew ever nearer.

Every muscle trembled, but she forced herself to her feet and slid her sword from its scabbard once more.

"Stand up, Aethius," she said.

He groaned.

"Stand up! If we are to die, we die on our feet."

He did as she demanded, drawing his own weapon and standing at her side. "Yes, Mother."

She sniffed. "I'm proud of you, son. Whatever happens next, remember that. And know I love you."

Cruel laughter scratched at their ears. "Isn't that sweet," Sohta said, appearing in front of them, his long fingers clasped in front of his chest.

Lilise steeled herself and whispered, "Where are you, Arig?"

I'm here!

The silver fog, silent and unnoticed, already swirled around Sohta's legs. In the blink of an eye, it moved higher, coiling misty tendrils around the pale god's body. Sohta had time to glance down, eyes wide, before Arig's cloudy shape hardened into a muscled figure and tackled his brother to the ground.

Lilise and Aethius dived out of the way of the feuding brothers, watching as grey mist and black shadow roiled and writhed, changing from one form to another, coalescing into human shape one moment and dispersing into hazy nothingness the next. The two gods never separated, staying clasped together even as they rolled into the suddenly rough waters of the Xhiel and disappeared beneath its surface.

"What's happening?" Aethius asked.

Lilise sought out their shape beneath the water. It struck her that they had become so merged together she could no longer separate them with her eyes. "I don't know."

With a bellowing roar, they resurfaced, splashing water across the small island. Their battle tore rock from the walls, gouged holes in the land, and created waterspouts that spiralled dangerously around the cavern. Lilise and Aethius backed further away until they had nowhere left to go.

"Why, brother?" Arig yelled, pain emanating from each word.

Sohta hissed. "Why? Because you spend your years relaxing in a meadow with happy people while I wither away in a wasteland with the scum of the earth! Don't you think that would be enough to sour any soul, *brother*? I can't bear it anymore! The screaming, the whining, the... the loneliness! No. You do not get to take all the good and hide it away in Elubrette. I am taking my share now."

The silence was sudden.

Arig pulled away from the fight with his brother and a tearing sound pierced the air. The two gods faced each other across the small island, both panting for breath, both scarred and battered from their struggle.

Eventually, Arig took the first step. "You were never meant to be alone, my brother."

"Then why was I?"

"No more." Arig held his hand out. "I hear you, Sohta. I see your pain. Come back to me now. Let us be one again."

Sohta took his brother's hand. Leaned in to embrace him. And plunged a knife deep into his heart.

Arig's face filled with pain. "Why?"

"It is too late to go back, brother. I forge my own path now."

Lilise raced to her god, but Arig raised his hand to hold her back, still clutching his traitorous brother in his arms. With a sigh, he swirled the mist into his own silver knife and struck Sohta with it, wounding him in the same fatal place.

The two gods fell apart, each clutching their chests, each spitting gold ichor from their mouths. Arig looked to Lilise.

"The time of gods is over, Lilise of Caeredene."

Lilise sank to her knees, her world shaken. "What will we do?"

He smiled, and gold poured from his lips. "Perhaps it was always meant to be this way. Look at what the Xhiel has done for you, faithful Lilise. Your heart is true. Your line is steadfast. Start a new tradition, a new way of serving in the afterlife. You will be fine…" His breath hitched. "Without me."

"No." She clutched Aethius' hand, lost for the first time in her life. "No."

"Brother!" Sohta crawled across the island to Arig, paying no heed to the mortals in his way.

The two gods reached each other, golden tears dripping from their eyes. They fell into each other's arms.

"Hush, Sohta," Arig said. "We will be together again now."

Lying side by side, holding tight to one another, they closed their eyes and breathed their last. Fading into mist, their two bodies swirled together until they became one once more. The stones wailed their grief; the grass bowed in sorrow. The mist seeped towards the Xhiel and brightened, paused for a brief moment, and drifted up into the cavernous dark above.

Lilise buried her face in the grass and wept.

"Mother." Aethius put a hand on her shoulder.

She looked up. "What will we do without our god, Aethius?"

He drew her into his arms and held her close. "Did you know that you're glowing?"

***

She wanted to grieve. Wanted to shriek and wail and reproach, and beg some higher power to return. But the gods were gone and there was no one else to fix things. So Lilise did what she had always done; she stood for her people.

There was no boat anymore, no ferryman to take them to Elubrette. But something Arig had said stuck in Lilise's mind; what if this was how it was meant to be all along? With that in mind, she waited with Aethius on the island where the gods had died, and they learned how to reach their senses out to each portal, how to know when new souls arrived. Aethius, too, had drunk of the Xhiel, and this would be their new normal.

They guided each soul to swim to Elubrette, save the small few who did not deserve its blessings; those they held out of the water, building a new boat to transport them straight to Karalus for penance.

They often looked in on Cybelle, watching her blossom as Queen of Caeredene. She did them proud, uniting the nations and ushering in an era of peace for her people. One of her first decisions as monarch was finding more honourable governors to replace the traitorous Borlias and selfish Melindria. Once that was done, she built statues in the capital to honour her father and grandmother, heroes of the Soulless War. And she led by example, priding fairness and compassion and duty above all. When she fell in love and grew heavy with child, Lilise and Aethius watched from afar, grateful for the blessing of family and the genetic heirloom apparent in each baby's cornflower eyes.

And, when the time was right, Lilise left Aethius to his work, finally retiring from her several lifetimes of service so she could be reunited with her beloved Harald. She knew, one day, her son would join her, and each generation of her family would take their turns as monarch and ferryman before finding their own peace in Elubrette.

Perhaps one day the gods would return but, until then, the world was safe in Lilise's hands.

The Changeling's Sword

Word had already spread that the crop was thin this year. Heavy rains flooded the soil and accidents plagued the farmers; some said a curse had befallen them since the men turned away a traveller in need. Charms hung from doors to ward off bad luck and townsfolk left small offerings at the edge of the wood, but still the women and bairns went hungry.

Hungrier than the men, at any rate. The men had to be fed to work the land; never mind the women labouring at home or bearing the weight of new life in their wombs. Only last week, Orla Doonan lost her babe after fainting from hunger; she was a shell of a woman now, mourning her world.

Still, the men toiled beneath the sun, taking pride in their mastery of nature's rolling curves, as easy as their dominance over their wives' wasting husks of flesh. They would never admit that nature had turned against them and their arrogance.

A bad day of farming meant only one thing to Maebh Brock: pain.

Aye, she'd been a young fool when she'd eloped with Fergal Brock with the simple goal of escaping her father; from the frying pan into the fire, as they say. Fergal had a wide smile and an easy laugh, all charm and swagger and boyish grace. She'd fallen hard; landed harder, when the heavy days led to heavy liquor and heavy fists.

Rubbing the purple bruise fading on her left wrist, Maebh watched as Fergal stumbled along the dirt path outside their small cottage. In the darkening light, shadows lingered on his face, framing the rage in his eyes. How had she ever thought him handsome? A wild boar had more sweetness than him.

A shudder ran down her spine.

Her footsteps were close to silent as she retreated to her bed. She would pretend to be asleep, knowing all the while it would make no difference if Fergal came for her.

***

The sun rose, but Maebh's head took a little more convincing to lift from her pillow. Pain stabbed at her neck and between her ears, insistent as a screaming banshee; her eyes throbbed and protested when she tried to peep through the swelling. She took small breaths, torn between the need for air and the desire to stem the sharp stab of her broken ribs.

'Twasn't the first time Fergal had treated her so; her body would heal, she knew. Eventually.

She winced at the sound of a muffled thump from downstairs. Fergal never woke before her; he'd be angry she didn't have his breakfast on the table.

Moving as fast as she was able, Maebh hurried out of bed and rushed to get dressed.

His back was to her when she entered the small kitchen. The dark curl of hair at the nape of his neck had once stirred her heart; now her chest pounded for a different reason. The muscles in his shoulders tensed at her footsteps. Without a word, she busied herself with making porridge and tea, and caught the faint trace of memory as she tipped a smidgen of nutmeg in, just like her ma once had; it warmed her, despite everything.

She placed the food before him, and he smiled. Maebh's eyes widened; her body tensed.

She swallowed her fear. "Good mornin', Fergal."

"Aye, 'tis a fine morning, isn't it?" He looked at her and pushed his chair away from the table with a loud scrape of wood on stone. "Your face!"

Maebh averted her gaze and flinched when his hand brushed her cheek. He pulled his hand back. Stepped away and lowered his eyes. Surprise stirred the butterflies in her stomach.

Fergal returned to his seat and ate his breakfast in silence. When the bowl was empty, he nodded in her direction. *"Go raibh maith agat."*

"You-" She gaped. Fergal never said thank you; he'd rather go to bed with a hot poker than show appreciation for a woman.

Maebh's mind raced. He surely looked like her husband, but there was a marked difference, a quiet stillness the restless Fergal could never exude. 'Twas almost as if… Nay, she was being fanciful. The beating must have rattled her brain. And yet, this man was nothing like the monster who'd come to her bed the previous night. It couldn't be true, could it?

A sudden certainty settled in her gut like a weighted hook; shock, followed by fear, and then an overwhelming sense of relief.

"You're not Fergal," she said, as sure of it as she was that the sun would rise each dawn.

He bit the inside of his cheek, tried to protest.

Maebh shook her head, one hand on her hip. "I know my husband. You look like him, but you're not him. He'd have smacked me silly as soon as I was late down the stairs."

The man, whoever he was, straightened his shoulders and arched one eyebrow. "Then he was never worthy of you."

Heat spread across her cheeks. "I've heard the stories. You're a changeling, aren't you?"

He nodded and offered his hand. "My name is Cian Mac Diarmuid. It's a pleasure to meet you, Maebh Brock."

As she shook his hand, struggling to ignore the flutter of excitement in her chest, Maebh recalled her grandmother's tales around the fire when she was but a child; tales of young ones taken in the night, replaced with one of the fair folk from beneath the hills. Of course, time had moved on since then. The fae shared the world with humans now, though they still kept mostly to themselves. Why would a changeling take Fergal's place?

"Why are you here, Cian Mac Diarmuid?" she asked.

His reply was quick and easy. "To study. The fae have limited understanding of humans; if we're to live in harmony, we need to learn more about you. How do you live? What brings you joy? What makes you get up in the morning? We want to know you so we can live beside you."

The snort that escaped her would never have found freedom in the presence of the real Fergal. "By kidnapping us? Most humans would be a mite angry about that."

There was magic in his voice; it wrapped around her like the shawl her mama had once swaddled her in, lulling her into a sense of comfort and safety. "My apologies, Maebh Brock. I'll leave immediately and return your husband to you."

His words hit her like a fist. "No! Please. I... Please, don't send him back."

Cian narrowed his eyes as he reached out to touch her face again. "He did this?"

She looked away. "Aye. 'Tis not the worst he's done to me."

He turned, stalked to the window, and glanced out at the drizzle of rain watering the grass. Maebh saw small details now, differences she hadn't noticed before, or maybe he wasn't bothering to hide them as much now she already knew. He was slightly taller than Fergal, a little broader in the shoulder. Fergal wore his confidence like an ill-fitting suit, uncomfortable and worn for show. But Cian carried his confidence as though it were part of his skin, his mouth curved in one corner and his hands clasped behind his back.

But the biggest difference was in the eyes. Both sets were blue, but where Fergal's flashed with rage and the desire to destroy, Cian's were as deep and steady as the sky. She didn't know Cian, but something in her knew she was safer with him than her husband.

She took a breath. Reached into the cupboard for the moonshine Fergal always stashed there. Took a long drink.

"Stay, Cian Mac Diarmuid," she said, wiping her hand across her mouth and taking another swig. "Stay, and you'll have my gratitude."

Slowly, his skin shifted and sparkled until she had to look away, like when the sun shone too brightly between drifting puff clouds. White spots danced behind her eyes and, when she looked again, a different man stood before her; only the eyes remained the same. Cian's body was larger, as if it had unfolded from the trappings of human form. His hair was longer and framed a face that could have been cast in marble. The fullness of his lips curved into a half smile as she gaped at him.

His gaze was piercing. "I'll stay."

***

They fell into an easy rhythm; mornings were for gentle conversation around the breakfast table before Cian left to work the fields, and they spent evenings strolling beneath the stars or talking around a warm fire as they learned each other's secrets. Whenever they were alone, Cian wore his own form, casting Fergal aside like an ugly coat.

Maebh was wary of him at first, flinching when he moved too fast and watching him with narrowed eyes. She knew he worked around her, slowing his steps and sharing his wide smile at every opportunity. Aye, he gentled her like a wild mare, whispering softness in that lilting voice until she could no longer resist his efforts; some days it galled her how easy she was to win.

On her birthday, he gave her a piece of wood he'd whittled into a miniature version of herself, hair blowing in the wind and a mysterious half-smile on her face. She snorted at the fanciful image.

"Is that how you see me?"

Cian nodded. "Beautiful, free, and a little wild."

She pushed back the tears that crept to her eyes. Swallowed the lump in her throat. "Thank you."

He nodded again before returning to his chores. When she was sure he wasn't looking, Maebh took the gift to her room and placed it on the windowsill, looking out onto the rainswept hills. She took a breath. Let the tears fall. Smiled through them.

It was the sweetest gift she'd ever received, and she knew she'd treasure it for life.

Still, it wasn't always easy. As the days grew shorter, so did Maebh's temper, something she'd inherited from her fire-haired mother. After years of holding it in for fear of Fergal's blunt retaliation, she found it hard to pick her moments. She could admit to herself, in the silence of her own thoughts, that she may on occasion sound like a screeching fishwife. Several times, Cian's arched brow or clenched jaw was her only warning before he abruptly left the room.

They were different, and it showed.

Maebh grew up on hearty stews and filling roasts, but Cian refused to eat meat. What else was she supposed to cook? Sure, she couldn't fill a grown man with nothing but vegetables. Especially when the crops were sparse. Ignoring her objections, he took her out onto the hills and showed her how to find more food that was safe to eat, taught her how to make plentiful meals with her harvest; she'd never seen a man prepare a meal, and she gaped as he deftly diced carrots and wild garlic as if he'd done it a hundred times before.

And who'd have thought that one of the fae would snore like a drunken sailor? He laughed when she complained one morning, bleary-eyed and short-tempered. Infuriating man.

When telling old folktales, they argued about the accuracy of each version; was the faerie maiden a villain or a victim? Oh, the man was exasperating and exhilarating in equal measure, and Maebh couldn't catch her balance. One thing was for sure; she felt more alive with Cian than she ever had with her monster of a husband.

He loved music and sang with a voice so beautiful it haunted her dreams. She'd enjoyed dancing once, before the world had crushed her dreams; he gave that back to her, swinging her around the room with a merriment so real and so complete, she couldn't fight it if she'd wanted to. They danced often after that first time, and each dance spun her closer to his light.

As time passed, Maebh's bruises faded. Her ribs healed, scars paled, and the shadows disappeared from her eyes. Like a cautious bud opening beneath the first kiss of the sun, she bloomed in Cian's company.

And their first kiss, when it surprised them both three months after his arrival, was an awakening.

Their neighbours spoke in awe of the change in Fergal and put it down to a good crop and the love of a good woman. Maebh blushed at the thought of how true that was; she loved Cian, God help her. Was she to be a fool for love again? Frowning, she gave herself a stern talking-to in the small mirror she kept in her room. She'd tried love once, and it had beaten the romance out of her.

Still, his gentle nature eroded her resolve.

One evening, as they shared wine beside the crackling hearth, she caught his gaze and held it. She swallowed her nerves, forcing them past the lump in her throat, clinging to the memory of the passionate, daring girl she'd been before her ill-fated marriage. She took his hand. Licked her dry lips. Shuffled closer.

Cian raised one eyebrow. His eyes never left hers.

Maebh took a deep breath and dived. "I love you, Cian Mac Diarmuid."

"I love you, too," he whispered, no hesitation, hand stroking her cheek. He glanced away. "But you are not mine to love."

Her back stiffened. "Fergal?"

"You married him."

Maebh snarled. "He lost any right to me the first time he raised his fist. Don't you dare say I belong to him! If you send that bastard back to me, I'll skewer him like the pig he is. My heart is mine and I choose to give it to you."

It took her a moment to realise the soft noise she heard was a chuckle escaping from his lips.

She laughed with him, the sound as free as a bird in flight, and a weight lifted from her chest.

"It's your heart," Cian agreed, pulling her into his arms, "and I shall treasure it for eternity."

***

The seasons turned like the wheels on an old carriage; rickety, a little askew, but steady enough to get them through.

Winter was mild, apart from one particularly icy day when the wood ran low and they found other, more interesting ways to keep warm. Spring arrived somewhat hesitantly, heralded with heavy downpours and flash storms that watered Maebh's poor vegetable garden a little too vigorously. It brought with it the joys of bright wildflowers blanketing the meadows, spritely lambs bounding in every farmer's field, and, unexpectedly, the certainty of new life blooming within Maebh's womb.

She found him in the barn, calming an expectant ewe. "Cian?"

He looked up, a streak of blood on his arm. "The lamb will be here soon."

Maebh glanced at the ewe's wide eyes, taking in the largeness of her belly and the frantic sounds of distress. She swallowed hard.

"The miracle of birth is a double-edged sword for the poor mother," he said, gently rubbing the sheep's back and comforting her with his voice.

She snorted. "Aye, and isn't that always the way for us women? I hope you'll be this attentive when it's my turn."

He turned sharply. His brow arched. The ewe bleated her objection.

"Aye, I'm with child," Maebh said, riding out the waves of giddiness as she spoke the words aloud for the first time. "You're going to be a father."

Joy lit up his face. He caressed her stomach with wonder and awe, then pulled her tight against his chest, spinning her through the air as wild laughter escaped his lips. In the next moment, shadows gathered in his eyes.

"Maebh."

"What's wrong? I thought you'd be happy."

He shook his head. "I'm happy, *mo ghrá*, but they won't be."

Mo ghrá. Her heart leapt. *My love*. "Who?"

"The other fae. It's forbidden to mate with humans. If they find out..." His face paled.

Maebh swallowed her immediate response. "Then we can't let them find out. Why would they? You don't have to go back. No one needs to know you're not Fergal."

Drawing her into his arms, he pressed a gentle kiss against her brow and ran his hand over her hair.

She clutched her stomach. "I can't lose either of you."

His warm voice hushed against her ear, but he made no promises.

***

The next morning, Cian woke her early, a dark look in his eye. Downstairs, he cleared a large space by pushing the furniture aside.

Maebh blinked, sleep still clinging to her eyes. Irritation niggled. "What's going on?"

When he pressed the hilt of a sword into her hand, she gasped.

It was lighter than it looked. An intricate pattern coiled around the cross-guard and a single crystal nestled in the pommel. There was a darkness to it. A potent rush of pain and beauty and grief and power, all rolled into a sharp, whistling melody that seeped into her ears. It filled her heart with blood and fire.

"What is this?" she breathed.

"It is *Scáth Dorcha*. The Dark Shadow. It's been in my family for generations and triumphed over all enemies."

She swallowed. "Why is it here?"

"I'm going to teach you to fight, *mo ghrá*. You are my wife in every way that matters, and the mother of my child; I'll not leave you unable to defend yourself."

With the sword whispering in her mind, she raised the blade and admired the gleam of firelight on its edge; it was almost seductive. She had never held a sword before, but it felt natural in her hand. Strength filled her; confidence flowed through her blood. She'd been a victim for long enough: never again.

Over the days and weeks that followed, Maebh trained hard, careful only of the babe growing inside her. She trained religiously, waking early each grey morning to face her demons. She trained to kill and knew she would do anything to protect what was hers.

And all the while, *Scáth Dorcha* cast its tendrils deep into her soul.

***

When their daughter was born one wet autumn morning, screaming her objection to her sudden arrival, their world seemed complete.

"What shall we call her?" Maebh asked as she cradled her sweet child, her eyes leaking fresh tears of joy.

Cian placed a hand on the baby's head. "Aoife. After my grandmother, who would've blessed our love despite what the other fae thought."

She swallowed the lump in her throat. "A strong name for a strong girl."

Sleep called, and they all settled to rest, with Aoife swaddled in a soft blanket knitted by her mother.

The days that followed were sweet and simple, with Maebh's time taken up with her daughter. It warmed her to see the bond between Cian and Aoife, especially when the baby slept so peacefully on her father's chest. The soft snuffle of both their snores as Maebh darned clothes or knitted small shoes was the loveliest lullaby, her irritation at his nocturnal noises long since forgotten.

And then, seemingly in the blink of an eye, Aoife turned one.

They celebrated with freshly baked cake. Cian pulled out a lute he'd carved over the summer and plucked the strings as he sang a merry tune for his girls to dance to.

When the door blew open, wild winds howling through the sudden stillness of the room, he threw the lute down and jumped to his feet. Maebh grabbed Aoife and pulled her back behind her father.

Six figures entered, each more coldly beautiful than the last, until they filled the small space with the weight of their presence. The temperature dropped. Maebh shivered and held Aoife closer.

"Cian Mac Diarmuid," the leader said.

Cian locked eyes with him, fists clenched. "Eoghan. Why are you here?"

"You know why we're here. The rules cannot be broken, brother. Come with us."

"And if I don't?"

Eoghan's expression didn't change. "We'll take you by force. Fae cannot be with human; Queen Ríoghna will decide your punishment."

For a moment, rage flashed in Cian's eyes. He took a breath and lowered his shoulders. *"Briseadh agus brú ort*, Eoghan. I'll go with you if you promise to leave the humans in peace; this isn't their doing."

Maebh's heart clenched. She shouted her objection at the same time as Aoife's sweet voice called out.

"Dada?"

Eoghan and the other fae turned to stare at the child, their eyes narrowed. A single moment of silence dragged out like the last exhalation of a dead man. Then they all moved at once. The six fae strode towards Aoife; Cian dived to intercept, rolling his body into their feet and sending three falling to the floor.

Maebh pushed her child against the wall, stepped forward, and raised her fists. Her muscles clenched as memory took over, recalling months of intensive training with her love; she would not let them touch her daughter. A deep rage filled her; a rage like nothing she had ever felt before.

"You'll be turning around now," she said, forcing her voice not to shake. "Forgetting you ever saw us here."

They moved closer, eyes flat and hard.

Panic tore at her chest.

There was an explosion of movement. Fists pounded against flesh. Boots ground against bone. Guttural screams resounded in the small space.

Maebh lost herself in the struggle. Half of her mind lingered with Aoife, her heart wincing at the sound of her child's fearful cries. The other half flashed between opponents; she grunted in pain, tasted blood, pushed the sting of sweat from her eyes.

She knew how to take a punch; Fergal had been good for that, at least. They came relentlessly, and she dodged and blocked, bringing her elbows up to protect her head. Cian's training rushed through her, and she used everything she had; when an arm wrapped around her throat, she bit until she tasted blood and chewed on sinew. She was not afraid to aim low. She brought her knee up into the groin of one fae and, as he doubled over, lifted the same knee to his face with all her strength.

Still, they came.

Across the room, Cian fought like a demon. Already, two opponents lay unconscious at his feet.

But it was not enough.

Gasping through the pain, Maebh crumpled to the floor. Curled into a foetal position as boots kicked at her head. Tears tracked through the blood streaming down her face. She tried to crawl to her screaming daughter, reached out with everything she had left, and wailed at the horror reflected in her child's face. When the last boot pounded on her skull, the darkness was swift and all-consuming.

***

Maebh knew before she opened her eyes they were gone.

The fae had taken her sweet child and the man she loved. She was alone in a sticky pool of her own blood. Every inch of her body throbbed and ached, though no pain could be worse than that in her heart.

She missed Cian, feared for him, but losing Aoife left a gaping hole, a raw wound salted with every breath. Despite everything, she had failed to protect her daughter. She didn't know how long she drifted in and out of consciousness before one thought settled in her mind: *Scáth Dorcha*.

Cian had shown her where he had hidden the sword; she doubted the fae would have thought to take it. Her pulse raced as she recalled the seductive whisper of the blade. It called to her now, as if knowing its name rolled through her mind. She crawled to the fireplace. Clung to the stones to pull herself to her feet. The embers had long since died and the stones inside the hearth were cool to the touch as she reached in and pulled three loose ones out. Behind them, wrapped in a silk cloth created by fae weavers and designed to protect the contents from extremes of any temperature, was *Scáth Dorcha*.

Her hands trembled until she held the hilt. Then an eerie calm settled over her.

Yes, its voice whispered in her mind. An image flashed behind her lids: a crimson rain drenching the land. *Yes*.

Maebh gripped the sword tighter. "I'm coming, Aoife. I'll make the bastards pay."

Behind her, the scrape of the wooden door on the stone floor broke the silence. Maebh turned as if in a dream. She should have been surprised to see Fergal's large frame filling the doorway, but she wasn't; this was the day for all bad things. He'd lost weight but made up for it with his rage. His ruddy cheeks puffed out with each breath and a large blue vein throbbed at his temple.

"I saw everything you did," he snarled, stepping closer. "Every time you let that pig stick you. Whore! You'll pay for all of it."

Unexpectedly, she laughed, the sound rolling like sharp pins into Fergal's sensitive skin. "You fool, Fergal. Do you think I care about you and your temper? There is far worse pain out there than what you can dole out, you worthless swine. Go on with you. I've got more important things to attend to than you."

Fergal roared and rushed at her.

Time slowed. Maebh raised *Scáth Dorcha*. A curious detachment blanketed her mind.

When Fergal stopped mid-lunge, with *Scáth Dorcha* buried to the hilt in his heaving chest, the silver blade sang its glory, and Maebh's heart soared.

More, the sibilant voice demanded.

"Yes." Maebh kicked her dead husband off the sword and felt nothing. "There will be more."

***

Maebh came back to herself at the side of the road.

For all she knew, weeks, even months, could have passed while she lost herself in the bloody haze of *Scáth Dorcha's* rage. She had no idea how many days it had been since she left home in search of Cian and Aoife. Thunder crashed overhead, matching the pounding in her head.

Around her, crumpled in red-stained heaps, the bodies of several fae lay where they fell, shocked eyes frozen in vacant death-stares beneath the cold, uncaring night sky.

Maebh felt no remorse. They had served their purpose; she now knew how to enter the realm of the fae, hidden inside the ancient mounds dotting the wild moors. Several fae dwelt among the humans in towns and villages, but she knew her loves would not be there. Nay, she would have to venture deep into their darkness to find Cian and Aoife.

She walked through the shadows, hiding from the glimmers of moonlight above. She'd needed to rest at first, but the longer she held Cian's cursed blade, the more she shunned earthly needs; food and sleep were for the weak. Only the blood of her enemies nourished her now. The more she drew, the more the sword called for, until she felt as though they swam in rivers of it.

Dawn planted soft pink kisses on the land as she crested a hill and saw the sign she was looking for; a large mound guarded by a pair of sturdy oak trees, branches intertwining above. *Talamh Ceilte*; the Hidden Land.

Maebh reached the trees and said, "*Oscail.*"

The grassy mound shimmered, and an ancient door appeared before her. It opened at her touch, swinging ponderously towards her. *Scáth Dorcha* sang in her hand.

A pair of startled violet eyes shone from the darkness behind the door. Maebh needed no light to see; the fire of *Scáth Dorcha's* bloodlust was bright enough. There was little sound as the greedy blade sliced through the young fae's chest.

She stepped inside, gasping at the sudden chill that rushed through her veins as she entered the Land of Faerie. She was not meant to be there. Goosebumps rose on her arms. A tingle spread across the back of her neck. It wanted her gone; she could feel its ill-intent prickling at her skin.

She smiled; let them come. She was lost already, her child taken and at someone else's mercy. Weeks had passed in a blur of blood and pain until encroaching numbness brought blessed relief. Aye, she welcomed the fight; all that was left to her now was vengeance.

Huge trees towered into a sky so dark she could see no stars. They lined either side of a narrow path, winding through a thick fog that oozed like ghostly fingers sneaking between the shadows. A faint light came from glowing orbs hovering above her head every few feet along the way. She would have thought it pretty once, back when pretty mattered.

Maebh walked on, *Scáth Dorcha* ready in her hand. Sharp twigs reached out to scratch her as she passed; rocks appeared beneath her feet.

"I'll leave," Maebh said aloud, "if you give my daughter back."

The wind picked up and the leaves hissed their disdain.

She shrugged, not willing to waste more breath. She would follow the path and, eventually, she would find more fae blood to shed. One of them would take her to Aoife.

It took her almost an hour to realise the forest was sending her in circles.

"Ach! Morida's curse upon you!" Kicking at the dirt, she turned and screamed into the night. A weariness settled in her heart until *Scáth Dorcha*'s voice whispered in her mind.

Tear it all down, the sword suggested.

The surge of adrenaline jolted her back to the moment. *Scáth Dorcha*'s insatiable savagery seeped into her soul until she craved it as much as she needed her next breath. In a wide arc, she swung the blade against the branches. Bark flew through the air. Leaves pooled on the dirt like green blood. The rustling whisper that had followed her from the entrance grew louder until it turned into a high-pitched scream so powerful it made her nose bleed.

Breathless with the rush of destruction, Maebh hacked and cut and sliced with irreverent glee.

They had destroyed her world; now she would destroy theirs.

As the trees recoiled, several fae surrounded her, sharp arrows pointed at her chest.

Maebh laughed. "Took you long enough."

A male fae with long dark hair stepped forward. "How did you get here, human?"

"Let myself in." She shrugged. "Give me my family and I'll leave again."

Scáth Dorcha twitched in her hand. *Kill them*, it said. *Take what you want.*

She gripped the hilt tighter. Rolled onto the balls of her feet. Flashed her teeth at the watching men.

"I'm sorry," the male fae spoke again. "You cannot leave here alive."

Somewhere deep inside, a spark of fear lit Maebh's soul; if they wanted to kill her merely for being human, what had they done to Aoife? The flare of panic consumed her until *Scáth Dorcha* blanketed her with its rage. She surrendered to it.

Arrows flew. Whistled as they zoomed past her ears. Landed with a loud thwack in the trunks of nearby trees. Maebh ducked and dived, tucked and turned. She raced for the closest fae, blocking one arrow with her blade. *Scáth Dorcha* sang as she swung it towards his head. It sliced cleanly through his skull. She turned away before he fell. Several others rushed at her, their own blades drawn. They moved with the swift agility only the fae possessed. Graceful as dancers, they waged battle like they sang poetry: beautiful, potent, deadly.

Without Cian's sword, Maebh knew she'd have died several times over. As she gave herself over to the bloodlust, a fog settled in her mind. Everything was hazy, shadows of darkness and light, and deep crimson, dancing at the edges of her vision. She moved like a puppet, strings pulled by some unseen force. Stab, slice, swing. A kick here, an elbow there. Block, punch, dodge. Seconds passed like years as her mind strove to keep up.

And then it was over.

The fae lay in pieces on the ground, floating in pools of their own blood. One was still alive, despite the gaping wound in his gut. His breath hitched as he watched her come closer.

"Will the forest let me through now?" she asked.

He looked away. "Aye."

Something about the profile of his face caused her to pause. In the growing shadows, with the light falling just so, he reminded her of her older brother, Enda. They'd been close once, Maebh recalled, as she fought her way out of the mist in her mind.

"The path will lead you to them now," the young fae said, his voice faint. "But there will be more waiting for you when you get there."

Aye, she'd expected as much. She caught his eye. "They took my child. Left me no choice. I'm sorry."

His mouth gaped at her words. A wave of pain hit and he groaned. "Grant me the mercy of death," he begged.

Maebh nodded. Rose to her feet. Swung her blade.

When she turned to follow the road, it opened before her. She scrubbed at the silvery tears tracking paths through the dirt on her face. Overwhelmed, she let herself sink into the heady nothingness of *Scáth Dorcha's* seductive control; the sword would do what needed to be done.

Her awareness faded in and out as she walked. There were flashes of thick branches recoiling from the gleaming edge of her blade, and glimpses of bright eyes peering out from the foliage. She had no idea how much time passed before she arrived in a large clearing shaped in a perfect circle, with the treeline edged by a rainbow of rose bushes in full bloom.

Dozens of fae gathered in a semi-circle facing her. Their leader was a tall woman with riotous black curls pulled back to highlight the jewels decorating her pointed ears, and a sharp nose that dominated her face. Maebh couldn't say that she was beautiful, but there was something striking about her, something that briefly pulled Maebh from the fog she was drowning in. She became more aware of her surroundings and her gaze found a face she recognised; Eoghan stood at the front of a group of warriors with their swords at the ready.

"You!" She stepped forward. Paused when she noticed the arrows aimed at her heart.

One side of Eoghan's mouth tipped up in a smirk.

"Where are they?" Maebh demanded.

"Somewhere you'll never find them," he replied, his lilting voice so similar and yet so different to Cian's warm drawl.

Scáth Dorcha snarled through Maebh's lips, rising with the flare of her anger.

"I promise you: I'll keep spilling precious fae blood until I have my family back," she hissed.

The sharp-nosed woman raised one hand in the air, and everyone froze; even the animals in the forest seemed to hold their breath to wait for the music of her voice.

"Who is this woman?" Her words were songs that sent thrills down even the most unfeeling spines. For a moment, Maebh swam back up through the fog and gaped at the mass of curls framing gleaming golden eyes, and at the sensuous way the folds of her gown clung to each curve of her body.

Eoghan's top lip curled back. "She's the human whore Cian dallied with."

The woman's face tightened. "Have you been spending so much time with humans you now speak with such vulgar language, Eoghan?"

Heat spread across his cheeks and he cast his eyes down. "I beg your forgiveness, Queen Ríoghna."

The Queen glided across the grass, her head tilted to one side as she studied Maebh. "How did one human woman enter our realm and kill several of our strongest warriors?"

Maebh shrugged. "Do you have children?"

Ríoghna nodded once.

"What would you do if someone took them?"

"I would tear the world down," Ríoghna admitted, tipping her head to acknowledge Maebh's words. Her eyes lighted on Maebh's sword, hanging close against the side of her leg. "I know that sword."

Scáth Dorcha stirred.

"That blade should not be in human hands," Ríoghna said. "It is dangerous even for the fae; only our magic allows us some level of control over it. Legend says a cursed soul inhabits it. Broken, weakened, but still capable of great evil. It lusts for power, for blood, and grows stronger with each life taken. Stronger and harder to control."

A sibilant voice hissed through the clearing. *I was not made to be controlled.*

Maebh forced herself to stay afloat despite the seductive voice trying to pull her under. She watched Ríoghna. Studied the flawless features of her face and the timeless wisdom of her eyes. Maybe, just maybe, this woman could be reasoned with.

"I want my baby back."

Ríoghna's mouth tilted. "Our laws forbid relations between humans and fae."

Maebh opened her mouth to speak but Ríoghna silenced her with a gesture.

"But our laws are centuries old, and time has moved on without them. Perhaps, if we are to find a way to live in harmony, we must-"

No!

Maebh screamed. *Scáth Dorcha* battered her with its will. The pain blinded her. Sweat dripped onto her face. She fought to rise above it, to release her grip on the sword, but the darkness consumed her. She sunk deeper into the mire. Choked on a miasma of hatred and bloody desire. In horror, she watched as she raised the blade and rushed at the nearest group of fae.

The queen arched her back and dived out of harm's reach, landing on her feet like a cat. Many others did the same, but some were not so lucky. An inhuman strength filled Maebh's body. She contorted into positions no woman should reach. And the blood flowed like wine, dripping crimson rivers of life to stain the carpet of soft grass with death. Voices screamed and feet pounded the earth as they ran to escape. Limbs flew. Blood gushed. Bodies fell. And deep inside, lost in the dark forest of her own mind, Maebh wept.

Sharp steel clashed against *Scáth Dorcha*. Ríoghna's golden gown flared around her, contrasting the silver of her blade. The guards cleared a space around them.

"What do you want, *Scáth Dorcha*?" the queen asked.

To kill, the sword hissed through Maebh's mouth.

In a sudden, darting move, Maebh knocked aside Ríoghna's weapon and levelled *Scáth Dorcha* at her chest. The rush of bloodlust boiled in her veins. Saliva flooded her mouth. The beat of her heart pounded in her head and her breath rang in her ears.

"Maebh!"

She froze. That voice… She knew that voice.

Kill her!

"Maebh, please."

She struggled to swim back to the surface of herself. *Scáth Dorcha* pushed her down, crushed her beneath its countless centuries of hate and rage.

But Maebh had been crushed before. And, by God, she knew how to rise from each punch. She clung to thoughts of Aoife's sweet smile and Cian's strong hands. Remembered her mother's voice urging her on through all things. Wept as she recalled her daughter's tears the day Eoghan took her.

And forced her way through the heavy cloud of dark desires.

She gasped, still fighting against the sword she couldn't release.

"Maebh?"

"Cian?" She blinked. Saw his handsome face a few feet away from her, and a small figure clutched in his arms.

Scáth Dorcha thundered inside her head, attacking her with pain and grief and rage unlike anything she'd ever felt. She screamed. The sword shook in her hands. It rose, then fell, then rose again as she battled for control.

"Cian, I can't stop it!" she cried. "How do I stop it?"

"Hold on to my voice," he pleaded. "Come back to us, Maebh. Come home."

Tears blurred her vision. She ground her teeth together. Tried to force her feet to sink into the dirt. Still, the fury fought its way to the fore. "They took you! They took my baby!"

"I know, *mo ghrá*. They were wrong. Queen Ríoghna is letting us go, letting us live in peace."

"You're lying!"

"No." Ríoghna's voice rang through the clearing. "This is a new age, an age where fae must live alongside humans. Our old laws must change. I had already granted their freedom before you arrived here."

Maebh dug deep. Grunted through the pain. "Cian, help me!"

I control you. The sword snarled in her mind. *You will give me blood.*

She looked up at her family. Her whole body yearned for them.

Aoife reached out with one small hand. "Mama?"

The word stabbed deep into Maebh's heart. She roared as she pushed through the pain. Climbed back to her feet. Her hands shook. Each finger pressed so tightly against the hilt, her knuckles were white. The blade rose higher. *Scáth Dorcha* laughed. Maebh took a deep breath.

The bastard thought it had won, thought it had conquered her will. But Maebh's mother hadn't raised a weak fool, and she hadn't been through hell and back to be beaten by a sodding piece of metal. Aye, and if Fergal's fists hadn't beaten her down, this bloodthirsty toy surely couldn't.

"To hell with you!" She forced the words out through gritted teeth and threw the blade with every ounce of strength she possessed.

As soon as it left her hand, the rush of release left her weak at the knees. She fell to the ground, watching the blade in the grass, inanimate now and rendered harmless. How could a strip of metal forged by man cause so much suffering?

Cian ran to her, grabbed her in his arms, stroked her hair with one gentle hand. Aoife's cheek pressed against hers. Their tears mingled on her skin.

Maebh laughed and cried as she held her family close.

"Is it over?" she asked when she'd caught her breath.

"It's over," Cian said, pressing his forehead to hers. "I'm so sorry; I'd no idea what *Scáth Dorcha* was capable of. I should never have left it with you."

She bit the edge of her lip, weighed down by the horror of what she had done under the sword's influence. "What will happen to it now?"

Queen Ríoghna picked up the blade and dropped it into a sack held by Eoghan. "We will destroy it," she said. "I'm sorry, Cian. I know it's been in your family for generations, but we cannot risk this happening again."

He nodded. "I don't care about a sword. I have my family back; I have all I need."

Ríoghna gestured with her hand and Eoghan passed the sack to an older man with white hair and black eyes. The man bowed his head and disappeared into the forest.

Maebh's heart settled as she kissed the man she knew would be her husband. Aoife wriggled her way between them and placed a hand on each parent's cheek. Maebh felt love wrap around her like the blanket her mother once made; love that wouldn't fade in any season. She was home now, safe in their arms.

Aye, that was all she needed.

Cwenhild

The fire called to her. It flickered and danced, like the naked warriors circling around it, harking to the steady beat of the *symbel* drums. Sweat dripped from the dancers' bodies, smudging the intricate blue patterns painted onto their skin. Around them, the drummers joined their voices with the swell of the music, building to a crescendo, a mighty battle to appease the bloodthirst of the war god Isoden.

Cwenhild picked up the traditional fire chains her mother had given her, made from rare iron by a master smith. They had short wicks attached, and well-oiled balls on the ends. In silence, she dipped the balls in the fire and enjoyed the way her blood stirred as they caught alight. With practised swings, she spun the chains in increasingly faster circles, crossing her body and painting fire in the air in time to the measured beat. The tribe's children watched her performance with rapt eyes, drawn by the danger, the complexity, and the brightness of the flames.

She'd been told the men watched for other reasons. Perhaps it was the way her hair matched the blaze of the fire or the way the woad-blue markings on her pale naked body accentuated her warrior's figure. Either way, she scorned them. Cwenhild had eyes for one man only, and she knew he never watched her dance.

Bitterness fuelling the flame, she emphasised every movement with aggression, confidence, and a reminder to any who thought her a challenge; her name was feared across the realm.

The drumbeat quickened. Pressure squeezed the air. Something was coming.

She watched the fire they danced around, her gaze drawn to the pale blue in its centre. Warm mead sat heavy in her stomach and made her head spin, her ears ring. There was something... A hazy image hidden in the fire's core. What was it trying to show her? Still spinning the fiery chains, she glanced around to see if any others noticed the message concealed within the blaze.

Fræda, the druidic dream-walker of the Demovantes tribe, sat cross-legged on the grass, closer to the fire than any other. The flames licked her aged skin and the mask on her face, part wolf and part dragon, gleamed in the orange light. Singing in low, husky tones, she barked out words in the old language and drank deeply from the *symbel vessel*, a special cup made from the severed skull of a great enemy. Cwenhild was sickened and intrigued by the cup in equal measure. It was said to be a connection to the world of the dead, a way to make their secret knowledge spill into the minds of those who drank from it.

When Fræda threw her head back, all noise ceased and all heads turned to watch.

"Darkness is coming," she said in a voice deeper than her own, its baritone growl rumbling in her throat. "The raven speaks. A friend who is not a friend. An enemy who is not an enemy."

Cwenhild hissed to silence the murmurs of the other tribesmen. She kept the chains spinning rhythmically, knowing Fræda had more to say.

"They come for our heart!" The druid jolted, her chest pushing forward and her shoulders back. "The dragon! His mouth opens and he eats... I see the stone circle. Heed the past, Demovantes! The time of testing begins."

With a gurgle, she fell back in a faint and all fire went out, including Cwenhild's chains, leaving the tribe in sudden darkness.

But an image burned behind Cwenhild's closed lids; the last shape of the flames before all light extinguished. A dragon. Wings spread in flight. Claws curving sharply. He rose, burning like embers, and his breath rained fire on all.

***

Cwenhild couldn't stop thinking about Fræda's *symbel* vision and the image in the flames. What did it mean? Ravens spoke prophecy; she knew better than to ignore its warning. Walking among her people the following day, she found herself looking at familiar faces and wondering if they would turn out to be the *friend who is not a friend*. And the dragon... She shuddered. Dragons had long been gone from the world, but even their names were powerful. To dream of one, especially one feeding, was a bad omen indeed.

Frustrated with her thoughts, she found a tree stump and sat on it to sharpen her sword. Like the fire chains, it had also belonged to her mother, Cweneth. Made from cast bronze with a hammered edge, the blade was long and leaf-shaped, with a bone handle that, according to tribal legend, had once been part of her grandmother. Cwenhild often prayed to Isoden that she would prove to be half the warrior her maternal ancestors had been.

A child's laughter drew her attention and she turned to watch the chief's youngest son chasing a wolf pup across the meadow. The pup tumbled into a basket of wool, getting tangled in the yarn, and the women at the loom shook their fists in mock anger as the boy grabbed his four-legged companion and raced away.

When she saw Fræda crossing the meadow towards her, Cwenhild sighed. The sense of peace she'd felt evaporated. When the druid sought you out, there would be trouble for somebody. Putting her blade back into its scabbard, she rose to greet the old woman, careful to show the proper respect; Fræda's position within the tribe was higher than that of the chief himself.

"Cwenhild," Fræda said.

She bowed her head. Opened her mouth to respond. And the deep boom of the carnyx shattered the quiet.

The horn player blew one long note followed by three short, lower ones. Loud enough to carry throughout the settlement, the pattern of notes was more than music. It was a warning; the enemy invaded.

The weavers grabbed the children and ran for the trees. Fræda left as quietly as she'd arrived; druids never fought in battle. Eyes scanning for danger, Cwenhild redrew her sword. Irritation boiled in her blood; the blade she'd just sharpened was about to be dulled again. Who was it? Who dared to attack the Demovantes on their own soil? Whoever it was would pay dearly for their arrogance.

She saw a flash of red and recognised the shield of the Calurii, a neighbouring tribe they often traded with. What were they thinking? Years of peace thrown away in an instant.

Still, she bared her teeth as her blood stirred. Threw her head back and let loose an ululating war cry to strike fear into their traitorous hearts. Around the settlement, other voices joined hers, roaring above the clash of swords and the thud of blades hitting shields. Screams of the dying added to the carnage. The tang of blood tainted the air.

When one of the Calurii skewered a Demovantes lad, no more than twelve summers of age, it fanned the flames of her rage. She snarled. Ran towards the enemy. Howled like the wolves she'd played with as a child. Her bronze sword danced — an extension of her body. She spun. Stabbed. Twisted. Thrust. Sliced, severed, and sundered. And when a sea of death lay all around her, bodies bent and broken like flowers crushed beneath careless feet, she stalked to the single survivor and laughed.

"Make it quick," he begged as he sank to his knees.

Cwenhild looked down at his braided beard, the markings of a seasoned warrior. "You expect mercy when you invaded our home?"

He shook his head. "We did not want to attack Demovantes. Many spoke against it and were punished by the druid. Our chief said we must do as he commands."

"But why?" She snarled the words through clenched teeth. "We had peace. Why have the Calurii betrayed that?"

His face paled and his limbs trembled. His voice, when he answered, was barely louder than the breeze ruffling his hair. "It's killing us. We've tried to fight it. Tried to send it back. But it's stronger than you could ever imagine. Our best warriors slain. Children torn to pieces. Huts and bodies burned beyond recognition. Wouldn't you try to run? Try to find another home away from such a monster? The advisor -"

"What are you talking about? What is this beast?" She kept her gaze focused on her captive as a small crowd gathered behind him to listen to his words.

"The Ancient One," he said, his nostrils flaring as he met Cwenhild's gaze. "He has risen from the sea. The dragon will kill us all."

Dragon? Cwenhild's breath caught in her throat. Fræda always said there were no coincidences. "If there truly is a dragon, we should be working together."

"I -" Blood poured from his mouth. The tip of a sword poked from his chest. His eyes met hers one last time before he toppled into the dirt.

Cwenhild raised her own sword and glared at the people standing behind the Calurii's body. "Which of you gutless pigs interfered with my kill?"

Several familiar faces looked down at the ground, while others glanced towards a fair-haired and beardless man in the centre of the group. Cwenhild studied him, taking in the pristine white of his robe and the calculating sharpness of his eyes. When he lifted his gaze to meet hers, a chill ran down her spine.

"Who are you?" she demanded.

He smiled. "My apologies, my lady. I thought the villain was going to kill you."

"I'm not your lady," she said. "And I will kill *you* if you don't tell me your name."

"Oh, you can't do that, I'm afraid. I'm a guest of your chief." He brushed a nonexistent speck of dirt from his robe. "My name is Vitus. It's a pleasure to meet you."

She stepped closer until she looked up at his hooked nose. "If you interfere with my kill again, even the chief won't be able to save you."

"Ah." Vitus sniffed. "We'll see."

Cwenhild watched as he walked away, escorted by a handful of women and children. The others seemed charmed by him, hanging on his every word and treating him with a respect usually reserved for druids. She narrowed her eyes. Where had he come from? Why had he killed the Calurii warrior? The man had been on his knees, answering every question Cwenhild threw at him; there had been no need for Vitus to kill him. The chill in her spine increased to an icy tingle. He brought danger to the Demovantes; she felt it in her bones.

The unsettling worry stayed with her as she helped to dig a dozen graves along the edges of their settlement. Her tribe worked tirelessly and in silence, as was their custom; once the funeral rites began, speech was akin to dishonour. Only when the last of the fallen Demovantes had been placed in the earth, their heads facing the sacred *menhir*, could the living speak again. Sweat dripped from Cwenhild's brow; she wiped it with her arm and patted the dirt down atop the last grave. She couldn't see the *menhir* from where she stood but she knew where it was; they all did. Turning to look in its direction, she closed her eyes and pictured the circle of standing stones, tall and proud against the backdrop of white-tipped peaks.

Isoden, guide them to the next life.

Soft footsteps drew her back. "Fræda."

"You have honoured them, Cwenhild," the druid said, leaning on a staff and following Cwenhild's gaze towards the *menhir*. "Tonight, we will celebrate their lives. When tomorrow dawns, we must speak."

"Of course." She bowed her head.

"Come to the *menhir* at first light. Visions plague me, Cwenhild. And every one of them shows me your face."

***

Mead still warmed Cwenhild's belly as she approached the *menhir*. The sun just kissed the tops of the stones, blessing them with its warmth and promise. She should be elated; the Demovantes had triumphed over the Calurii, the fallen had moved on to their next lives, and she had been summoned by the druid - there was no higher honour than to be vision-called! Why, then, did nerves twist inside her gut like a bloated, maggot-infested corpse?

Fræda waited in the centre of the *menhir*, beside the sacred oak tree, leaning heavily on her staff and pulling her cloak close around her body. "Cwenhild."

"You wished to see me, Fræda."

"Yes. Danger threatens, Cwenhild. My visions grow darker and more frequent." She sighed and waved her arm towards the mountains. "Look at the world. So much beauty. So much life. Yet, my mind's eye shows it all bathed in shadow, crumbling beneath the weight of whatever is to come. How do I stop it?"

Unsure how to respond, Cwenhild held her tongue.

"Still, I have mothers coming to me, complaining that their children are missing. How does it connect? The bones tell me it does but the visions reveal nothing." Fræda made a low noise in the back of her throat, frustration and anger tightening her mouth.

Cwenhild narrowed her eyes. "How many children?"

"Six, so far. I believe they are alive but I cannot prove it. We Demovantes can win any battle, but cannot keep track of our own children!"

"You wish me to find them?" Cwenhild straightened her shoulders.

"If only it were that simple," Fræda said. "There is still the matter of the dragon to discuss. If that man told the truth, the Calurii were so frightened of this beast, they betrayed one of their oldest alliances to escape it. Is it truly a dragon? Think of the magic his coming will bring to the world, Cwenhild!"

Her chest tingled with excitement. A dragon!

Fræda continued, "And think of the destruction just one of his breaths could wreak. Many problems plague our tribe right now. Not least of which is that fawning outsider."

Cwenhild wrinkled her nose. "Vitus."

"There is something about him…" Fræda's mouth curved down in disgust. "I do not trust his intentions. Where did he come from? How does he know the chief, and why are they on such good terms that Edwulf would ignore my advice?"

Eyes widening, Cwenhild stepped closer and glanced around to make sure no one was listening. "What are you saying?"

Fræda walked to one of the stones and placed a wrinkled hand against it. She breathed deeply and a sense of calm washed over her. "I see the lines connecting it all: bright, filled with power, and so tangled I cannot unravel how they meet. There is a link; Isoden has shown me this. Something joins it all. The dragon, the missing children, this dark presence, Vitus' questionable arrival, and the Fwenha." She opened her eyes and fixed her gaze on Cwenhild. "And you."

Cwenhild blinked. Chose to ignore the comment about herself. "The Fwenha?" What did the Fwenha have to do with anything? As the largest tribe in the north, everyone had heard of them; their warriors were renowned for being fearless and quick to anger. The Demovantes rarely interacted with them.

"They are..." Fræda sighed. "Expanding."

"Expanding?"

"So far, the Epidae, the Selgoli, and the Votadones have been conquered. The Fwenha march north, taking land, killing men. It seems nothing will stop them."

A deep cold ran through her veins. If Fræda was right, only one tribe remained between the Fwenha and the Demovantes. "How do you know this?"

"The raven told me."

Sudden screams pierced the stillness of the morning. Cwenhild drew her sword and raced down the hill, away from the *menhir*. This was her land, the land of her ancestors, and it spoke within her blood; she knew where the scream had come from. Knowing Fræda would follow, she pushed herself to move faster. The screams continued, growing louder as she neared their source.

In a small glade just within the boundary of the trees, several women cowered against each other, their arms up to protect their heads and their faces turned away. Two had fainted and lay still on the ground. Cwenhild gripped the hilt of her sword and searched the glade with her eyes. Something dark flickered at the edge of her vision. She spun just in time to avoid being skewered by the horns of a beast the likes of which she had never seen before. Flexing her knees, she focused her breathing and met the monster's amber gaze.

It was as tall as she was, but walked on all fours with thudding paws the size of her head. Sharp horns protruded from its scalp. Spikes ran along its back, and its black fur was matted and stained with dried blood.

Isoden, guide my hand!

Edging through the glade until she planted herself between the beast and the women, Cwenhild listened to its ragged breathing; when it sped up, she lunged forward, preempting its attack. Her blade sliced through the flesh of its right front leg and it howled in pain. Black blood seeped from the wound. She longed for a spear to keep her out of its reach, but her sword would have to do. She raised the weapon, knowing she could be facing her death.

And then Fræda was there.

Pale as the spirit of an ancestor, the druid drove her staff into the beast's side. "Be gone, Shifter!"

Something passed between them. A roar. A whimper. Unseen magic, buoyed by strength of will. Fræda thrust her staff once more and the beast curled in on itself. The air shimmered. Between one blink and the next, the beast was gone, and a small bird flew from the glade in silence.

Deprived of the fight her adrenaline surge called for, Cwenhild paced the glade and checked on the women, who sobbed and shook and prayed to Isoden.

"What was that?" she asked.

Fræda sucked her cheeks in and spat on the ground. "A Shifter. An old spirit. A trickster and a charlatan. Isoden, curse him!"

"I don't understand." Shifters were stories told to frighten children, weren't they?

"Neither do I," Fræda said. "He has no business here. I must be told immediately if he returns so I can drive him out."

A small-boned woman cleared her throat. "Druid Fræda?"

"Yes?"

"We've seen him before. In different shapes, each more unbelievable than the last."

The druid clicked her tongue. "When did these sightings start?"

She thought about it for a moment. "When the moon was full."

The moon is almost full again, Cwenhild thought. *Why have we not been told about this?*

"Why was I not informed?" Fræda snarled.

The woman flinched. "We told the chief. He said we were drunk or crazy, and if we bothered him again we'd have to pay a body fine."

A storm raged in Fræda's eyes. "He said that? The chief himself?"

"Well, he passed the message through his advisor."

"Vitus." The druid clenched her staff. "He dares usurp the rights of a druid? We shall see about that."

Leading the way through the forest, Fræda set a brisk pace and didn't look back. Cwenhild followed a few paces behind, enjoying listening to Fræda's grumblings about wearing the upstart's head at her belt.

They found the chief outside his roundhouse, talking with his son, Lyulf. Cwenhild paused, staying back while Fræda strode to within inches of the chief and jabbed a wrinkled finger in his face. Chief Edwulf leaned back, his brow furrowed.

"What are you doing, Fræda?" he asked.

The old druid straightened herself to her full height and pinned him with her gaze. "Where is that snake, Vitus?"

"Gone," Edwulf said. "He left at first light. Why?"

Lyulf edged closer to Cwenhild. His lips curved into a smile as they watched his father argue with Fræda.

"Do you think we should leave them to it?" he asked, leaning down to whisper in her ear.

Cwenhild swallowed. "Perhaps. I would like to know what happened with Vitus, though."

"I convinced him to leave."

She looked at him, felt the heat creeping up her cheeks, and looked away. "Why?"

His face darkened. "Because I do not trust him. I don't know what hold he has over my father, but there is something not right about that man."

Cwenhild watched Fræda and Edwulf move inside his circular dwelling to continue their argument. The chief's face was bright red and his shoulders were hunched. "I agree. Vitus is dangerous and I'm glad he's gone. If he returns, I'd be glad to skewer him for you."

Lyulf threw an arm across her shoulders and grinned. "You're a good friend, Cwen."

Distracted by his smile, it took a moment for his words to sink in. *A good friend*. With a snort, she shrugged his arm off, ignoring the rush she felt as his hand brushed against her skin. "Don't block my sword arm."

He held his hands up. "I could use some practice. Join me for training?"

She gaped at him as memories of the last time they'd trained together flooded her body. The thrill of holding his ice-blue gaze. The rush of excitement as they matched swords and strength. And the gut-wrenching disappointment when he'd thanked her for the chance to improve his skills, patted her on the back, and left to share mead with the admiring women who'd watched him with adoring eyes.

"Cwen?"

She gritted her teeth. "I have to go."

Without further words, she turned on her heels and strode back through the forest, feeling Lyulf's gaze burning into her back until she was out of sight.

***

"Move faster, girl!"

Cwenhild grunted with effort as she listened to Fræda's instructions and pushed her tired legs into a sprint. Diving into a roll, she grabbed the staff from the ground and brought it back up with her, lithely regaining her feet. She spun, clutched the staff in two hands, bent her knees, and dropped into a fighting stance.

"Better," Fræda said. "Good. You need to make sure you can fight even if you lose your sword."

Her breathing heavy, Cwenhild only nodded in response. They'd been training since the first hints of light had kissed the *menhir*. Fræda passed her a waterskin and she drank deeply.

"Isoden has not blessed me with another vision," the druid said with a sigh. "But you are a part of this, Cwenhild. Your face has played a part in every vision I've had since the equinox. You must be ready for whatever threat you are to face."

"I am always ready," she replied when she'd caught her breath.

Fræda nodded. "Then, I hope you're ready for the gift I'm about to give you."

Cwenhild watched with wide eyes as the old druid crouched to light a fire within a small circle of stones in the centre of the *menhir*. "What are you doing? I thought we couldn't light fires in the *menhir*!"

"You can't," Fræda said with a smirk. "But I am a druid and I control the flames. Within this sacred space, I light the sacred flame and give the sacred gift, blessed by the ancestors. Very few even know of its existence."

As the blaze grew, Fræda took a waterskin from her belt and passed it over. Cwenhild took it, her brow arched.

"Drink," the druid demanded. "Drink it all."

One did not argue with a druid; Cwenhild did as she was told, swigging from the skin until it was empty. The liquid burned her throat and warmed her gullet. Her eyes watered. She coughed. Spluttered. Blinked as the ground seemed to shift beneath her feet. "What, in Isoden's name, was in that drink?"

Fræda cackled. "The good stuff."

Everything tilted to the left. With some effort, Cwenhild righted herself. Sweat dripped from her body as Fræda guided her closer to the fire. Between one blink and the next, a measured drumbeat started up, matching the rhythm of her heart. She turned to the druid and recoiled from the half-wolf, half-dragon creature dancing in the centre of her vision.

Fræda's deep voice faded in and out, whispers and shouts chanted in the old tongue.

Before she knew what was happening, Cwenhild found herself stumbling into the fire, which roared to twice her height and danced around her woad-painted flesh. She recoiled. Cried out. Threw her arms in front of her face and prayed to Isoden.

The drumbeat intensified. Her breath, ragged and desperate, thundered in her ears. Heat licked her body. Beyond the flames, the wolf-dragon danced around the blaze, still chanting.

She tried to scream and paused when she realised she was able to inhale without choking on smoke and heat. Straightening her body, she blinked. Held her hands out in front of her. Watched as the flames rolled around her skin but left no mark. Caused no pain. She felt the heat, but as if it was at a distance instead of burning around her. She breathed deeply. Turned to gaze through the flames and marvel that she could keep her eyes open, unaffected by the fire.

Her racing heart calmed. The deep chanting ceased, and the wolf-dragon faded into the grey shadows between night and day. Cwenhild opened her palms and reached for the flames; fire leapt into her open hands. With some concentration, she moulded it into two spheres that writhed and flickered like angry stars. Feeling playful, she tossed them in the air and caught them again when they fell. She surprised herself when a burst of laughter escaped her lips. Bringing her hands together, she pushed the spheres into each other and stretched the shape out into the semblance of a sword. Nudging it with her mind, she tweaked the shape, created a hilt, and wielded it in a steady hand. The sword blazed with the fury of a thousand suns. She lifted it. Took a few practised swings. Grinned at the featherlight weight of it gliding through the heat-hazed air.

Gradually, the heat of the blaze seared away the drunken daze of Fræda's potent brew. Sober once more, Cwenhild stepped out of the fire and into the blanketing darkness of the new night. Although she left the flames behind, she knew they burned inside her, ready to answer her call.

"The ancestors have blessed you," the druid said as she stepped from behind one of the larger standing stones, still leaning heavily on her staff.

"You could have warned me," Cwenhild said. She arched a brow but could not control the twitch of her lips.

Fræda grinned. "Where's the fun in that?"

Cwen tipped her head in acknowledgement. "What next, Fræda? What do I do with this power?"

"That has not been revealed to me yet." The old woman closed her eyes and turned her face to the stars. "But, when it is, you will be ready now. When the call comes, you will know."

***

In the days that followed, Cwenhild struggled to go about her daily life, knowing what blazed inside her and imagining what she may need to do with such power. When leading training exercises, she found her mind wandering to thoughts of the dragon. At mealtimes, she ate in a daze and finished her food without being aware of a single bite touching her lips. At the next *symbel* gathering, she was drawn to the bonfire and had to concentrate to keep herself from walking into the flames.

One evening, as she followed the stream that wound through their settlement and allowed her thoughts to follow a similar meandering path, the sudden crack of twigs crunching underfoot had her reaching for her sword. Twilight shadows blurred the edges of the trees and made it harder to distinguish between objects, but this was her land;

it had nourished her from birth, her blood had soaked into its heart, and her roots lay deep within the valley. Breathing deeply, she wrinkled her nose and turned to the south, her back to the water.

"Vitus."

The hook-nosed man sauntered from behind a tree and smoothed the folds of his robe. "Cwenhild. What a pleasure to find you here."

She snorted. "What do you want?"

"I'm just out for a stroll, my dear. What could I possibly want?"

"Let me rephrase. Why are you back on Demovantes land?"

He flashed a smile he clearly thought was charming. "I've just shared supper with Edwulf. I often take a stroll after supper; it helps me sleep well."

Cwenhild rolled her tongue across her teeth as she debated how much trouble she might be in if she just skewered the outsider while no one was watching. "I don't trust you, Vitus."

He sniffed. "I'm sure you'll get over it once you get to know me. Perhaps you could join me for my walk."

She started to shake her head, then thought better of it. Did she really want him walking around Demovantes land without supervision? With a heavy sigh, she resheathed her sword. "Fine."

"Lovely." He set off back the way she had come, following the stream towards the main group of homesteads. "It's a pleasant evening, I must say. Even more so with such beautiful company."

Her flesh crawled. "Flattering me will get you nowhere. I still don't trust you."

"That is a shame." He cast her a sideways glance as he picked his way over a fallen branch. "We could go far, you and I. Literally and figuratively speaking. You should give it some thought."

Coming to a halt, she pinned him with a sharp gaze. The thought of doing anything with that slime-eel of a man made her shudder. "No."

Anger flashed behind his eyes. "You shouldn't be so dismissive, Cwenhild. My friendship could be very beneficial to you."

She stood her ground as he moved closer to her, watching his eyes for any sign he was about to attack. She was a Demovantes, a seasoned warrior, blessed with the gift of the ancestors, but something about him made her hackles rise. When he was a foot away, she moved her hand to the hilt of her sword and raised one eyebrow in challenge.

To her surprise, he laughed. "I wouldn't need force to take you, foolish girl. Women fall at my feet."

"Not me."

He leaned in, and she drew her sword, letting the slow rub of bronze on leather whisper war into the stillness.

"You should leave now," she told him.

He held her gaze for a moment. Searched her eyes for something... she didn't know what. "Suit yourself," he said.

He turned to walk away. Spun back with the speed of a striking wolf. Brought a hand to his lips and blew a cloud of strange blue dust into her face. Coughing and spluttering, she stepped towards him, weapon raised, and lunged for his throat. Between one blink and the next, he was gone.

Cwenhild stumbled. Where was he? No man could just vanish into thin air! The blue dust coated her face, filled her nostrils, and stuck to her eyeballs. Blinking furiously, she retched and tried to brush it away. Her vision reeled in and out of focus, and everything she saw was tinged with that same deep blue. She forced air into her lungs; the sound thundered in her ears.

Above her head, a measured beat soared across the treetops. A rush of air stirred the ends of her hair. She looked up, a sense of dread lodged in her gut. Something green filled the sky. It hovered between Cwenhild and the moon, blocking all light save the dappled, shimmering glow that seeped around its scaled edges.

Its immense body tapered into a long, barbed tail. Slanted golden eyes nestled on either side of a reptilian face. Wide wings the colour of seafoam held the beast aloft as it breathed small tendrils of bright fire into the dark night.

Cwenhild fell to the ground. Scrambled back on hands and feet. Gasped when the creature turned its monstrous head towards her.

The dragon opened its mouth, revealing gleaming, pointed teeth. It roared, and sheets of fire rained down from the sky. With a thrust of its wings, it dived towards her, reaching out with sharp claws. The trees trembled. The air shimmered. And Cwenhild screamed. Lifting an arm to protect her head, she braced for the impact of teeth and talons on her fragile bones.

"Cwenhild!"

She jumped. Cautiously opened her eyes and looked around. The dragon was gone, and so was the moon. Bright sunlight filled the clearing. Somehow, she was lying on the mossy ground, her booted feet resting in the trickling stream. An acrid taste lingered on her tongue, and a throbbing pain in her head.

"What, in Isoden's name, are you doing?" Fræda used the end of her staff to poke Cwenhild's ribs.

Cwen groaned. "Fræda?"

"We've been searching for you all morning." The druid's face was red and her brow furrowed.

"Vitus." She swallowed the bile in her throat. "He did something. Threw something in my face. I... Fræda, the dragon! I saw him!"

Fræda's expression hardened. She pressed her hand to Cwenhild's forehead. "I should have known that fawning sycophant was up to no good." Muttering under her breath, she took the waterskin from her belt and dropped a powdery mixture into it. She swilled it around until it dissolved, and then passed the skin to Cwenhild. "This will help."

Cwen drank, gagged on the foul-tasting brew, and forced it down her throat. Within seconds, the haze cleared from her head. "I'll kill the bastard!"

"You might have some help with that," the druid said. "A lot has happened this morning. I do want to hear more about the dragon you saw, but it will have to wait. Eight of our own are missing and I suspect Vitus had something to do with it."

She dug her fingers into the earth. "What?"

"They're gone, Cwenhild. Even Edwulf. No one knows where. They were all just gone when we woke."

The chief was gone? She bit the insides of her cheeks and tasted blood. The dragon had come to her. The tribe was fractured, the chief missing, and its people vanished. The fire stirred within her blood.

"It's time," Fræda said.

"I know."

***

One night. That's all she had left before she had to leave. It was time to find her courage.

The bonfire had dwindled to embers. Most of her clansmen had retired to their beds - or someone else's. Taking a large swig of mead for confidence, she strode across the clearing to where Lyulf chatted with one of his younger brothers. He smiled when he saw her approach, the corners of his eyes creasing and his jaw softening, and the butterflies started up in her stomach again.

"Cwen," he said with a wide grin.

She dug her nails into the palm of her hand. "I need to talk to you."

He waited.

"Alone."

"Of course." He patted his brother on the back and moved to Cwnehild's side. "We'll go to my house."

She followed him, as she would have anywhere, conscious of the curious stares at their back and the brush of his arm against her side as they walked. Within minutes, they reached his roundhouse and went inside. It was on the smaller side as he lived alone, but the wattle and daub structure was the same as every other dwelling, the inner walls lime-washed to add the illusion of light. In the centre of the space was a fireplace; Lyulf made short work of rubbing sticks together to start a small fire. Tendrils of smoke drifted through the room.

Lyulf sat close to the fire on a large pile of furs. He moved to one side and gestured for her to join him. "What do you need to talk about, Cwen? Is it the dragon? The missing people?" He grimaced. "I pray to Isoden that my father will be found safe. I am not ready to be chief."

"You never know," she said, nudging his ribs with her elbow. "The tribe might not vote for you."

He blinked. Guffawed with laughter and threw a mock frown her way. "You always have known how to cheer me up, Cwen."

She held her hands out to the fire. "I leave at first light, Lyulf."

"I know. I don't fully know why, but I understand the druid is sending you on this quest. Are you nervous?"

"No." She shook her head. "If I die, I will do so with honour, and I will join my mother and grandmother in the next life. I have lived well enough to earn that. No, I have no fear of death."

He looked away. "Then you have more courage than I."

She shuffled a little closer. Laid a hand on his arm and waited until he turned his face back to hers. "There is something I fear. That's what I wish to talk to you about."

"What is it?" He leaned in closer.

She felt his breath on her face. "I…"

"Yes?"

She almost turned away. Almost gave in to fear. But something in his gaze held her there; something hopeful, expectant, full of promise. Could it be? She swallowed hard and blurted out her words. "I fear leaving without telling you that I like you."

"I like you, too."

"As more than a friend."

His mouth parted slightly. "You do?"

Heat crept up her cheeks. She seriously considered falling on her own sword. How could she have thought he might feel the same? In all their years of friendship, he would have spoken sooner if he felt the way she did. She pulled back. Started climbing to her feet. "I'm sorry. I didn't want to leave without… I shouldn't have said anything. I –"

He quietened her with a finger to her lips. Grabbed her hands and gently tugged her back onto the furs. "We are both fools."

"What?" She tugged her hand away and wiped her cheeks with the back of it.

"How long?"

"What?" She frowned as she repeated herself.

"How long have you felt this way?"

She shrugged. "As long as I can remember."

"Cwen!" He groaned. Moved his hands to cup her cheeks. Pressed his brow against hers. "Why didn't you say something? No, I can't say that. Oh, why didn't *I* say something? I could kick myself. All these years, Cwen!"

Her brain stumbled as she tried to follow his words. "What?"

"We are a pair of fools."

"You –"

This time he silenced her with a kiss. A deep, yearning kiss that seeped into her very soul. He ran his hands up her arms, pulled her close against his body, and whispered her name against her lips. Cwenhild lost herself in his kiss. It was everything she'd dreamed of; everything she'd yearned for since they'd been young warriors learning to fight at each other's side. For a brief moment, she wondered if she was still hallucinating, still under the influence of Vitus' potent powder.

But every detail was so real. His lips were soft and tasted of the mead he'd supped by the bonfire. The heat from the fire warmed their skin as they lay on the furs. The crackle of the flames melded with their ragged gasps. His hands, gentle and firm, were lined with calluses from hard work; he used them well, strumming her body like a lyre until he stirred the fire within her and she throbbed with need.

"Lyulf." She breathed his name.

And when he sank into her, their bodies joining as one, she lost herself in his arms.

***

"Are you ready?" Fræda asked when she heard Cwenhild's approach at first light.

Cwen cleared her throat.

The old druid turned. Raised a brow at the sight of Cwenhild and Lyulf holding hands. Smirked as she looked them up and down. "Well, it's about time."

Cwenhild blushed. "I'm almost ready, Fræda. There's just one thing I'd like your help with before I leave."

"He can't go with you, child. He's needed here, and the ancestors did not show me his face. This is a journey you must take alone."

"I know." She squeezed Lyulf's hand. "We wish to be handfasted."

Fræda pursed her lips. "That's a serious commitment. It will bind you even while you're apart from each other."

"We've lost enough time," Lyulf said. "I don't want to be parted from Cwenhild. Not now. But I have to accept it."

"I feel the same," Cwenhild continued. "Fræda, we both know that I might not return from this quest. If Lyulf and I never have the chance to live together, at least I will have died handfasted to the man I love."

"So be it." She nodded once, then beamed at them as she pulled a short rope from the sack at her feet. "It's good that I came prepared."

Cwenhild gaped. "How did you know?"

"I didn't. Not for sure. But you two have been casting love-eyes at each other for years. When you disappeared from the bonfire last night, I had an inkling this might happen."

As the sun crept higher in the horizon and kissed the *menhir* stones, Cwenhild and Lyulf stood before the druid and vowed to belong to each other for a year and a day. Lyulf held his arms out, palms up, and Cwen rested hers on top of his, palms down. In silence, Fræda took the rope and wound it around their wrists. She tied the knot, binding them together, and pressed two fingers to each of their brows.

"The blessing of the birds and the beasts I give to you. The blessing of the water and the weeds. May your love blossom like wildflowers: strong in adversity, determined through difficulty, growing and changing with the needs of the season. A year and a day," the druid said. "Until then, you are committed to each other. After that time, you must decide whether to part ways or join souls. May Isoden keep your love safe in his heart."

***

Lyulf rode with Cwen until they reached the edge of Demovantes land, keeping their horses at a brisk trot. Her heart grew heavier with each step. They had only just discovered their love; she wasn't ready to leave him.

"I wish I could go with you," Lyulf said.

"I wish I could stay." She sighed. "But I am called by Fræda's visions and I cannot ignore that."

"You wouldn't be Cwenhild if you could ignore it." He smiled, but it didn't reach his eyes. "Come home to me, please."

She straightened her spine. "I am a warrior of the Demovantes. Daughter of Cweneth; granddaughter of Cwenfreda. If any can survive this, it is I."

He leaned across the gap between their mounts, brushed the hair from her face and pressed a kiss to her brow, another to her lips. She tasted the salt of his tears.

"If Isoden wills it, I will return. After a year and a day, if I am not home, then know that I love you and I will see you in the next life." She kissed him then, long and deep, imprinting him on her memory. When the nights were cold and the days laced with death, she knew she would draw on his love for strength. "Goodbye, Lyulf."

Isoden, why does it hurt so much to ride away? Cwenhild kept her back to the sun and nudged her horse into a slow walk. When she passed the painted staff, decorated with feathers and bones, that marked the boundary of Demovantes land, she looked over her shoulder. Once; that was all she'd allow herself. Blinking away the tears, she focused on the way forward and rode until darkness fell; she wrapped herself in it like a babe in a blanket and wished it was Lyulf's arms.

Several days passed in a landscape of rolling hills, long grass, and the wind howling through each valley. Cwenhild rode from sunrise to sunset, guiding her mount at a steady pace to keep him strong and eating as she rode. Twice a day she stopped to let the horse drink from fresh streams and munch on grass. When the sun sank beneath the horizon, she found secluded places to rest and replenish. Occasionally, she hunted for meat and started a small fire to cook on. Other nights, she foraged and ate from the land.

And all the while, something tugged at the edges of her consciousness. A seeping, sibilant whisper calling her name. Drawing her towards the Calurii settlement and the sea beyond. It was easy to ignore, at first. But the closer she got, the stronger the voice became until it roared in her mind and kept her from sleep. Each night, she dreamed of the emerald-scaled dragon with seafoam wings.

After three days, she sensed danger at her back, dismounted, and pressed her ear to the ground; riders approached. She guided her horse into a large thicket, brushed their tracks from the ground, and hid; who knew what trouble she might find?

Within minutes, four riders turned the corner and came into view. They were outsiders, she noted, wearing long robes like Vitus, and leather sandals on their feet. They rode on saddles and used reins that pulled at their horses' mouths. Cwenhild sneered. Where was the bond with their mount? The Demovantes would be shamed and ostracised if they rode with anything more than a soft blanket on their horse's back.

Where had they come from? For months now, they had heard rumours of more outsiders travelling from across the sea. Sometimes she dreamed of strange lands and wild customs, but she had no desire to visit them and she distrusted their intentions here.

She narrowed her eyes. Between their horses, a group of six natives walked in a line, tied together with one long rope: three women, two men, and a child of no more than six summers. Disgust curdled in her throat; so, that's what the outsiders wanted - able bodies for their cursed slave trade! As she watched, one of the robed men lashed a whip at the slaves, who cowered from its bite.

"Move faster," the slaver demanded, lashing the whip once more. It grazed a woman's arm and left a trail of blood on her clothing.

Cwenhild had seen enough. These people may not be Demovantes, but they were of the same land, and no outsider had the right to treat them like cattle. With no time to apply woad or strip to her skin, she pressed two fingers into the dirt and wiped the mud across her face. She drew her sword. Rose to her feet. Bellowed her warcry into the wind. And charged.

Their horses reared; three of the four men fell from their saddles and landed on their backs in the grass. The fourth clutched his reins, eyes wide and mouth agape. Cwenhild tackled him first. Before he could react, she reached up and pulled him from his mount; the horse immediately ran off. The others got to their feet and drew weapons. One pointed his sword at the slaves while the other three focused on Cwenhild.

She grinned. Held her sword ready. Flexed her knees.

A grey-haired man said something in a foreign tongue, casting a disgusted look at his colleagues. They snickered, nodding in agreement.

"Let the slaves go and I'll let you live," Cwen said, not really caring whether they understood her or not.

The tall, wiry outsider lunged at her with the point of his blade; she blocked it easily, spinning her sword with enough force to twist the weapon from his grip. As it clattered to the floor, she simultaneously swung her blade at the grey-haired man and kicked the tall one in the gut. He crumpled, gasping and moaning. The third man joined the fray.

The fire stirred in Cwenhild's chest but she held it at bay; these fools were not worthy of that power. Her sword flashing with lightning speed, she gave the outsiders a taste of the savagery they often accused her people of. Within minutes, the three men lay dead at her feet. She turned to the fourth. Raised her bloody sword and screamed as she stepped towards him. And laughed when he dropped his weapon and ran.

The slaves watched her warily. Now she had the chance to look closer, she could see they were Calurii; the leather bands around their wrists marked them as such.

"Demovantes." A golden-haired, golden-eyed woman nodded at Cwenhild. "Our thanks."

Cwen nodded in return. She used her sword to cut the ropes binding them. "Our people were friends once."

"We heard what happened. It was not our choice. We had already run from the dragon by the time our chief ordered the attack on your land. We ran to the Demovantes, but these bastards caught us first. They killed my son."

"I'm sorry about your son. You are not my enemy." Cwenhild spat on the nearest body. "These men are our enemies. We should be uniting against them."

"Agreed. But I fear that will never happen. We are divided. Mistrustful. And the Calurii have scattered from the dragon that rises from the sea."

"I'm headed for Calurii land now. Our druid has seen the dragon in her dreams and sent me to face it."

"I will pray for you."

Cwen cleaned her blade on the grass. She glanced at her fallen enemies and considered taking their heads but decided against it; these men were of no value, even in death. "Would you like to travel with me?"

The woman shook her head, and the others all cried out against it. "We have no wish to see the dragon again. Do you think your chief would welcome us if we followed our original path to the Demovantes?"

"Yes." She decided not to tell them about the missing chief; they would find out soon enough, and Lyulf would welcome them in the meantime. "I suggest you take the outsiders' horses; you'll get there faster."

"Thank you." The woman picked up her child and held him close. "We will not forget what you have done for us. We owe you a debt."

Cwenhild waited until the Calurii gathered the horses and set off back towards Demovantes land. Once they were out of sight, she mounted her own horse and resumed her journey west. She knew it should take no more than two more nights to reach her destination. Nerves mixed with anticipation in her gut. Would bards sing of her deeds one day? Or would she become nothing more than a snack for a hungry dragon? Only time would tell.

***

That night, as she sat by a small fire and picked the bones of the rabbit she'd caught, Lyulf walked out of the darkness.

She jumped to her feet. Ran to him and threw her arms around his neck. "What are you doing here?"

He took her arms and pushed her away from him. "Bringing you back. You shouldn't be here, Cwenhild. Why are you wasting time on this foolish errand when your people need you back home? More of us go missing every day and you are off gallivanting on some foolhardy quest for a dragon! Of all things! You know they've been extinct for centuries."

Cwen blinked. His tone was cold; she'd never heard him speak like that to her before. "You can't mean that, Lyulf. You know Fræda sent me. You know the ancestors spoke to her."

Red crept up his neck and into his cheeks. "Are you questioning me? With my father missing, I am the chief of our tribe. How dare you disobey an order!"

"What?" She took another step away from him. What had happened to make him behave like this? She clenched her fists. "I don't know what's going on with you, but you know Fræda has more power than you. She is a druid and I obey her in all things."

His jaw tightened. "I will take you back by force if I have to."

Cwen backed away as he reached out to grab her. He missed her arm and caught her wrist instead. Scared by the unfamiliar rage on his face, she pulled her arm back and then pushed it forward again, swift and sudden. The change of direction threw him; she thrust the heel of her hand into his nose and blood streamed over his mouth. Keeping her momentum, she used her other hand to hold his elbow, while he still gripped her wrist. She pushed the elbow up and then down, twisting his arm until the movement forced him to drop to his knees. He grimaced. Let out a small yelp. She pushed harder and shoved him face-first into the dirt. Still holding his arm, locking it into place so he couldn't move, she added a little more pressure and listened as a whimper escaped his throat.

A cold certainty settled in her bones; this was not her Lyulf. Holding him in place with one hand, she lifted her other palm and called the fire; a blazing orb leapt out of her skin and lit up the darkness. "I don't know who you are, but I know you're not who you're pretending to be. He would never behave like this."

The man who was not Lyulf started to laugh. Quiet at first, but it soon grew to a loud guffaw. It was a rasping, grating, dissonant laugh with a sharpness and a cruelty that sent shivers down her spine. "You're not as besotted as I thought," he said.

She moved the fire-orb closer to his face, which distorted beneath its light. His features shifted, revealing thin lips, slanted ears, and hollow cheeks. Alabaster skin was framed by hair as black as the raven's wing. "Who are you?"

He grinned, flashing pointed teeth, and vanished between one blink and the next. Cwen stumbled as the pressure of holding his arm disappeared. The flame in her hand extinguished and she dropped to her knees, feeling a wave of coldness wash over her skin.

Although she tried to rest, sleep eluded her after that meeting. She rose before dawn and resumed her journey before the birds began their song. She travelled for four days, with the dragon's voice increasingly pressing in her mind, before she realised she was going in circles. As she passed the same oak tree for the third time, she veered towards it, dismounted, and knelt before its wide trunk. Sweat dripped down her back. Small stones dug into her knees. Hunger gnawed at her stomach. She pressed her palms to the bark.

"Sacred oak," she began. "Ancient ancestor. Gateway to the spirit world. I beg your help."

A faint breeze stirred the leaves above her head.

"I am lost. I travel west; I walk away from the sun and yet I turn in circles. Something is stopping me from moving on."

Silence greeted her.

She dragged the dagger from her thigh, sliced it across her left palm, and pressed the wound to the base of the tree. "My blood: as sacrifice, as promise, and as proof; I am Demovantes, daughter of Cweneth, granddaughter of Cwenfreda."

Cwenhild watched as the blood soaked into the bark and the wound on her hand knitted itself back together. She said nothing, knowing it was not her time to speak.

A voice danced through the leaves. *Daughter. Granddaughter. Cwenhild of Demovantes. We hear you and we answer.*

Her cheeks were wet but she dared not move to dry them. Those voices lived in her earliest memories: the gentle love of her mother and the pride of her grandmother.

Danger follows you, Cwenhild. There is one who is not as he seems, who wears many shapes and faces. A trickster, a shifter, a twister of words and deeds. He seeks to stop you from reaching the coast and keep you distracted while he weaves his web of lies and treachery.

Her mouth narrowed into a thin line. "Who is he?"

He is known by many names. You have known him as Vitus and as the horned beast in the forest.

Cwen spat on the ground to her left. "That slimy bastard. I knew there was something wrong with him."

Do not underestimate him! He does not seek to kill you yet. He chooses no sides but his own, does as he pleases regardless of others, and, above all, thrives on the chaos he causes. When it suits him, he will send you to the next life with as little care as if he were pulling a blade of grass from the dirt. He is strong, Cwenhild. Stronger than you can imagine. The blood of the gods runs through his veins.

"He is a god?" She thought of Lyulf and wondered if she'd ever see him again; how could she defeat a god?

His name is Dægar. Beware his trickery. The roots of his mischief are deep and tangled; even we cannot see the whole of what he plans.

"What should I do?"

Stay the course. Complete the quest Fræda has sent you on. Be true to yourself, your tribe, your power; only in the light of truth will Dægar's wickedness be known.

Cwenhild hesitated a moment. "If the dragon kills me –"

We will see you again in the next life, child. We are with you, always; you are made of us, mother to daughter, through countless years. Goodbye, Cwenhild, until we meet again.

They were gone. She felt their absence in every part of her body, and it left a gaping hole she knew would never heal. Still, they had given her what she needed. Turning back to her horse, she mounted up, faced westwards, and raised one arm in the air. She called on the sacred power Fræda and the ancestors had blessed her with and gasped at the sudden thrill as fire roared to life in her hand. Holding it aloft like a torch, even in the bright sunlight, she looked ahead and saw the path she must follow. She shifted her weight forward and the horse set off at a brisk trot.

Before long, the ground seemed to shift, guiding her off course and to the left. She held the flame higher and the illusion faded until she could see both paths and knew which to take. She rode like that through the night, worried that Dægar might trick her if she stopped to sleep. When she almost drifted off in her saddle, her horse whinnied with alarm and she forced herself to focus on the way ahead. Sometimes, she sang to herself to keep herself awake - loud, defiant songs of heroic deeds and courageous ancestors.

And somewhere at the back of her mind, she heard another voice, deep and resonant, calling her name.

Come to me, Cwenhild. Seek the sea and the shore, and the secret shadows. Dive down into the darkest depths; burn with the blood and the breath, and the beauty of becoming. Yes, Cwenhild. Come, and we will test your mettle.

Sleep-deprived, half-starved, and tormented with waking dreams and trickery, Cwenhild whispered, "Yes."

***

The blackbirds sang to her as she approached the sea, the first rays of daylight barely kissing the craggy hilltop overlooking the coast. A blanketing fog rolled across the land until she could see nothing below her mount's neck. The horse let out a long, high-pitched whinny and refused to walk any further. In a daze, Cwenhild dismounted and waded through the mist to the rocky peak; one misstep and she would fall to the crashing waves below.

As she reached the edge, something rose from beneath the precipice, hovering on immense wings the colour of seafoam.

Each movement of those great wings stirred the air and lifted Cwenhild's braids.

Cwenhild of the Demovantes!

His voice thundered in her mind. She lifted her foot to step again and jolted back when a roar erupted from behind her. She turned. Drew a sharp breath in through her open mouth.

A second dragon, identical to the first, flattened large swathes of grass as it landed on the hilltop. *Don't listen to the trickster*, it said within her mind.

She swung her gaze back and forth, searching for any difference, looking for a sign to tell her which was the real dragon and which was Dægar in disguise. They were indistinguishable from pointed teeth to barbed tails, bright scales glimmering in the sunlit fog. Frozen in place, she wondered if she'd survive battling both of them.

Seasoned warriors had fallen beneath the dragon's wrath; grown men had run screaming from its fiery breath. A whole tribe had been chased away from their settlement in fear of its rising.

And yet...

In all the days his voice had whispered within her mind, he'd never spoken of fighting her. Fræda had sent her to face the beast but she'd never told her to kill it. What if something more was happening here? Something greater, deeper, *older* than the instinct to war against anything different? Could this be a chance to change fate?

A sudden calm descended on her. She reached for the fire within her belly, the sacred flame of the Demovantes, and called it to rise. It roared to life, a raging inferno encasing her in its blue-white blaze, colouring her vision with its heat and haze. The dragon hovering above the sea seemed to grin in appreciation and threw a quick blast of flaming breath to add to her bonfire. Tipping its head, he allowed himself to sink back down to the water.

The dragon on the grass, however, recoiled from her light. She took a step closer to it and watched as its immense form shifted and folded in on itself. When the movement stopped, she once again saw that same alabaster face that had surprised her on her journey to the coast.

"Dægar," she called him by name.

He climbed to his feet. His nostrils flared and his hollow cheeks puffed in and out as he fought to steady his breathing. "Do what you will, little fool. You're too late to stop me, anyway."

He reached for her, as he had once before, but she danced beyond his grasp. Spun on her heels. And ran towards the precipice.

With a graceful leap, she dived over the edge, arms stretched out to her sides, blazing like a falling star. The wind buffeted her and roared in her ears. Her stomach rolled in giddy waves. The salt tang of the sea drifted up in welcome.

As she fell towards the water, towards the dragon waiting in its depths, countless ancestors reached through time to roar his name in her mind: *Merehwit*.

I'm coming, Merehwit.

And he rose from the depths to break her fall, catching her on seafoam wings and carrying her on his strong back. They climbed higher, breaking through the clouds, and she saw the trickster god had vanished. But she could not wonder where he'd gone; sensations rippled through her like waves in a storm. She clung to Merehwit as they soared through the sky. An immediate connection raced through them: body, mind, and soul merging, melding as if they were made for one another.

In an instant, centuries of knowledge rushed into Cwenhild's thoughts. Ancient history came to her memory like she'd lived it yesterday. The dragons had been Isoden's finest creation, fierce and beautiful in equal measure, protectors of mankind since the dawn of time. In her mind's eye, she watched as those dragons bonded with the people they cared for, as they learned to live in harmony, in a kind of symbiosis that blessed the world with comfort and peace. Tribes formed around specific dragons but all were friends and allies.

Years passed in seconds. As the world progressed, small groups of people broke away from the dragons and turned to dark magic. One of these women seduced the son of Isoden, and Dægar was born from their union, his birth rending his mother's body so badly she could not survive.

Atop Merehwit's back, Cwenhild gasped. The wind blew the tears from her cheeks as, in the vision, Dægar's mother died in agony, his essence bringing chaos and destruction from his very first breath.

He chose that path, even then, Merehwit said through their connected minds. *He was not like other newborn babes. Old maids wept at his beauty. Battle-tested men knelt before him. From within the womb, he had the capacity to plan and scheme and choose; he wanted his mother dead so he'd be free to do as he pleased with no ties or obligations to the world. From the beginning, he fed on chaos, on confusion, on pain and grief and all the things that muddle a mind. It strengthens him as nothing else can, and he will not stop; it is like a drug, and he is drunk on its nectar.*

Still seeing Merehwit's memories behind her closed eyelids, Cwenhild recoiled as war broke out between dragons and men. Many tribes fought alongside their reptilian friends, but they were slaughtered like pigs. Dægar's dark magic drew supporters to his side. Drove a wedge between humans and dragons. The majestic beasts were hunted and killed in a sickening frenzy until the last of them retreated from the world to lick their wounds in silent defeat.

Heartbroken at the world's loss, ancient druids gathered together to weaken Dægar's power. They succeeded but at a great cost. Tribes scattered across the land, enmities formed between those who had once been friends, and an age of darkness plunged the earth into chaos. Diminished but not gone, Dægar plotted and schemed and spread havoc with his trickery, all the while building back the power he had lost.

Merehwit's rumbling voice sighed in Cwenhild's mind. *And so, here we are. We dragons always planned to return but I am the only one who has. My brethren remain hidden, unwilling to risk their lives for people who have forgotten and forsaken them.*

Why did you come back? Cwenhild asked.

Because your thoughts stirred my dreams and disturbed my slumber. When I realised it was more than a dream, I wondered... Who is this woman? Who is she that can awaken a dragon when our bond with humans has long since died? Yet, our bond was there from the start, Cwenhild. I do not claim to understand how you called to me but that is what you did. Do you feel it?

Yes. I feel it. She sank into it and it thrilled her.

Merehwit rejoiced in her excitement, rolling and diving through the clouds like a hatchling still discovering his capacity. He spread his wings as far as they would reach and stretched his limbs until they creaked. *I have been still for too long. It is good to be back!*

Cwen threw her head back and shouted her joy to the wind. They laughed together and, when Merehwit blew flames above them, she added her own stream of fire to the blaze. The power she felt within her chest seemed amplified by their connection, by the matching flame within his own immense body.

Eventually, Merehwit slowed and turned his head to look at her sitting on his back. *We must deal with Dægar before his power grows too strong. He did not anticipate my return and is not prepared for it but, if we wait too long, he will build both his army and his strength and will be unstoppable.*

Cwenhild released the breath she was holding. *Do you know where he is?*

Yes. I can sense his magic. He marches now with a tribe you call the Fwenha, stirring them to hatred, greed, and despicable acts. Many have fallen beneath their blades and their unnatural hunger.

"No!" she shouted aloud, then bit her lip as she recalled Fræda's words about the Fwenha. *Do they attack the Demovantes? Can you see that? How do you know?*

Yes. Your tribe has been pressed back to the foothills, where they guard the menhir in their last stand. The Fwenha are many and will overrun the Demovantes. As for how I know… Dragons were made to protect this land and its people, Cwenhild. We know and see it all as easily as we see what is right before our eyes.

We have to help them!

Then, let's fly.

With a burst of speed, Merehwit took them soaring through the sky, heading back towards Demovantes land. Cwenhild tried to follow the land beneath them to see how far they had to go, but the height and the motion turned her stomach and she returned her gaze to the back of his scaly head. He flew faster than she'd ever dreamed was possible, devouring miles with each ripple of his vast wings.

As they neared her land, scenes of devastation played out below. Heaps of bodies baked in the midday sun, their blood staining the ground. Crops lay trampled from a thousand hooves or razed by fire. Everywhere she looked, the earth had been churned into a muddy battlefield. Soon, agonised screams reached her ears.

We have to hurry, Merehwit!

In silent acknowledgement, he lowered his head and dived towards the hills where the *menhir* lay hidden. Figures moved through the trees as they flew overhead, men and women with sharp swords and sharper eyes. The trees opened out into the wide space around the menhir, with the snow-tipped peaks in the distance; the area was filled with Fwenha and outsiders brandishing blades and spears and two-headed axes. The Fwenha gathered in groups, pushing forward with impatience, desperate for their chance to spill blood. In the centre of the space, the outsiders waited in orderly lines, their shields forming an almost impenetrable barrier as they advanced on the depleting numbers of Demovantes and slowly nudged them further up the hill. To Cwenhild's eye, it was the high position that had allowed her tribe to survive so long. Atop the hill, around and inside the *menhir*, the Demovantes waited, defending their sacred space. A wooden contraption, manned by several of the strongest tribesmen, launched heavy rocks into the bloodthirsty horde below. It was crude but effective, flattening a dozen enemy warriors at a time. Still, it was like crushing ants; more soon came to fill the gaps.

There! Fræda's skull-topped staff stood above the group and drew Cwenhild's gaze. The druid had one hand on the tallest *menhir* stone. The part wolf, part dragon mask nestled on her face. At her side, Lyulf studied the enemy and barked orders to his people. Even from such a distance, the deep lines marring his brow were clearly visible.

We must draw Dægar out! Merehwit's voice resounded in her head.

Cwenhild looked but saw no sign of him. *How?*

With chaos. She heard the smile in his voice. *He will be drawn to it like a child to a favourite toy. Call your fire, Cwenhild. We are masters of sky, sea, and land, and these intruders will soon learn their folly!*

She reached for the blaze in her belly. Pulled on the immensity of Merehwit's flame. Roared to life like an inferno, surrounding herself and the dragon in golden heat. As Merehwit dived towards the horde, she let loose an ululating battle cry. He channelled the fire, breathing it across the gathered warriors in long swathes of burning rage. The Fwenha and the outsiders screamed as their flesh charred and sizzled. Many broke from the crowd and ran from the beast and its golden rider, wailing that the gods had come to smite them for their treachery.

After several passes with the purging fire, a rasping voice bellowed from the treeline. "You think this will stop me? Fools! I feed on chaos, and you have given me a feast!"

Dægar, astride a horse as dark as death, emerged from the forest, his alabaster face beaming as he revelled in the mayhem. The Fwenha and the outsiders parted to make a path for him, and he moved further into the open, looking up at Cwenhild and Merehwit. Distracted by the madness and the mayhem, everyone stopped fighting for a moment and watched, transfixed, as the trickster god stood in his saddle and raised his fist to the seafoam dragon and its flaming rider.

"You are too late," Dægar called out. "Too late to prevent this. I am stronger already. Your little display is all for nothing."

Cwenhild reached for Merehwit. *I don't understand what he's doing here. What does he hope to achieve?*

Nothing more than chaos, my friend. Dægar feeds on it, remember? He has incited the Fwenha to violence, playing on their greed and insecurities. The outsiders acted under his manipulation, building their trade in slaves, bringing further turmoil to the people of this land. In the guise of a friend, he has stirred distrust and disbelief against the druids, seduced loyal men from their tribes, beguiled and tricked leaders of the land into abandoning their people... All to add to the discord, the upheaval, the chaos he so desires.

We need to draw him from the crowd or we'll never get to him.

Go to the menhir, Merehwit said. *He will come to you; he won't be able to resist the chance to humiliate the one who has seen through all of his schemings.*

What about the Fwenha? And the outsiders?

He flashed his teeth. *Leave them to me.*

Merehwit soared through the sky, easily dodging arrows and rocks launched by the Fwenha. Hovering above the *menhir*, he lowered himself into the centre of the stone circle, his immense body barely fitting in the space. The Demovantes scrambled to get out of his way.

Cwenhild pressed her hand to his back. *Be safe, Merehwit.*

You too, Cwenhild. Our bond is new but I do not wish to lose it.

With some awkwardness, she slid down his side and landed on bent knees in front of Lyulf and Fræda, her hand scraping the dirt at her feet. The druid arched her brow and Cwenhild noticed raven feathers woven into her hair, black against white.

Lyulf grinned and pounded a fist against his chest. His dark hair had been washed in limewater and the shocking white strands pushed up in spikes away from his scalp. Woad-blue patterning decorated his bare skin, his muscles bulging beneath angry swirls and lines. Dirt and blood stained his body, though he appeared unharmed.

"I found the dragon," Cwenhild said, conscious of the thousands of eyes watching her.

Fræda cleared her throat. "I can see that."

Everyone looked at Merehwit, who tipped his head in greeting.

"I assume he doesn't want to eat us?" the old druid asked.

Merehwit flashed his pointed teeth and launched himself back into the sky. He flew in circles above the gathered armies, breathing fire on the Fwenha and the outsiders and leaving a barrier of flame between them and the

Demovantes. Cwenhild's tribe cheered and raised their swords to salute him. In the gaps between the fires, pockets of fighters battled in a loud melee.

"He is a friend," Cwenhild explained. "A truer one than we have ever known."

"Do you know what's going on here?" Fræda asked. "The visions have given some clarity, but many things lay mired in uncertainty."

"Yes, but there is no time for explanations. I need you to trust me."

Without waiting for their response, she started removing her clothes, letting them drop to the floor until she stood naked in the cold. As skirmishes broke out between the patches of fire, and the Demovantes fought to keep their enemy from the *menhir*, Fræda took a bowl of woad dye and held it out to Lyulf. He dipped his fingers in the paint and drew winding spirals and careful knotwork across Cwenhild's flesh He worked with haste but took care as he caressed her skin, each painted stroke arousing her further. She took the heat and channelled it into aggression; she would need it all in the coming fight.

When Lyulf was done, bright blue symbols danced on her pale skin and were accented by the fierce blaze of her hair, which hung in loose waves around her shoulders. She reached for the sword she'd discarded with her clothes and tied the scabbard around her waist.

"Wait," Fræda said, and handed her a set of fire chains. "My visions showed you using these so I brought them here in case you returned."

Cwenhild took the chains and examined them in silence. They were made of iron and were stronger than any she'd used before. At each end, the solid, oiled ball was covered with sharp spikes that would tear flesh and shatter bone. She looked at Fræda, at Lyulf, and at all her people waiting expectantly for her to save them. She swallowed the lump in her throat.

"This ends here!" she shouted. "We will wipe this evil from the land and drink the blood of our enemies ere the sun sets. Demovantes, remember who you are! Sons of Aart, who tore down the walls of the Idonii; Daughters of Eostre, who fought the monsters of Tallia! The druids themselves rose from the ranks of our tribe! Why should you fear these lesser fools? Show them how *scared* you are, Demovantes! Let them see the true face of who they battle. We are the demons they run from in their dreams, and we will bathe in their blood!"

A loud roar erupted as the people of her tribe raised their swords and their voices. One by one, the warriors who weren't already engaged in battle stripped their own clothes and wiped the woad paint across their faces. Within the *menhir*, the drummers took up a swift beat that resounded through the valley. Several men lifted carnyxes of various shapes and sizes, some with long snouts and rows of teeth, others with glowing eyes and pointed horns. The wailing harmony joined the drums in a stirring battle song. Tribal warriors lifted their shields, banging their swords against them to add to the music. Children and the elderly, treating wounded within the *menhir*, raised their voices in a chanting battlesong, building to a crescendo as every man, woman, and child faced the enemy and screamed their fury into the valley below.

Cwenhild punched her left fist into the air and all fell silent. In the valley, men quivered in their boots. The outsiders prayed to their god, many hands moving in signs of worship. She waited, making sure she had their attention. "Dægar!"

His alabaster face rose from the crowd as he made himself grow to twice his size. "You put on quite the spectacle, Cwenhild. My army is still larger than yours."

"Your army is pissing itself with fear," she retorted. "They know the Demovantes will take their heads and use them to decorate our houses!"

With a disgusted scowl, Dægar lifted his shoulders in acknowledgement. "Even a coward knows where to stick a sword to make you bleed."

"Why don't you face me yourself, and leave the cowards out of it?"

His laughter carried. "You think *you* could stand against *me*?"

"What are you scared of?" She shrugged. "If you really think I don't stand a chance against you, what do you have to lose?"

"The chaos," he said. "It would be over too quickly."

With a final laugh, he shifted into the shape of a bat, flew to the lead group of outsiders, and changed back into Vitus. Cwenhild watched as he gave instructions to the men, though she could hear nothing of what he said. Her mouth narrowed into a thin line. She needed to get him to come to her. How else could she end this?

As one, the outsiders banged their shields and then rearranged them into a forward-facing block. In unison, they shouted monosyllabic responses to commands barked out by their leader, a square-jawed man wearing a red-plumed helmet atop his head. Together, with thundering, measured steps, they marched towards the Demovantes. They found a wide patch of ground where the flames had mostly died and stepped over it at a steady pace.

Merehwit, seeing what they were doing, swooped overhead and breathed fire at their helmets. In response, they lifted their shields above their heads and formed a guard to protect them from the flames. Cwenhild was sure they still felt the heat, but their makeshift barrier worked well enough to get them through. Seeing other warriors finding points to attack, the dragon turned his attention to them.

You will have to deal with those ones, Cwenhild, he said through their shared bond.

The beginnings of an idea sparked in her mind.

"Chaos," she said.

Lyulf looked at her. "What?"

"He wants chaos. I say we give him some. It's the only thing that'll draw him to me now."

"I won't pretend to understand what you're talking about," Lyulf said, "but tell me what you need and I will see it done."

She nodded. Searched the land with her eyes. Focused on the sacred oak in the centre of the *menhir* and grinned. "I need to talk to Fræda. After that, I'll need your help to clear a path and draw Dægar in. Maximum chaos."

He pressed his fist to his chest once more.

Wary of the approaching outsiders, Cwenhild ran to Fræda. When she told the old woman what she planned, the druid flashed her teeth in a wolfish smile.

"Are you sure you're not a druid, Cwenhild?" Fræda teased. "At times, you seem to think like one."

Cwenhild wrinkled her nose. "Just be ready."

She turned back to Lyulf, who waited with a group of warriors: men and women with woad warpaint and bloodied weapons. The legion of outsiders neared the halfway point on the hillside and dozens of Demovantes had already rushed to engage them. Cwenhild counted the shields; more than twice the numbers of her small group.

She looked at her tribesmen. "Destroy them."

Their warcry thundered ahead of them as they raced down the hill to meet their enemy. Fear was gone, replaced by the thrill of the fight. Live or die, they would honour their tribe and their ancestors.

Isoden, be at our side today.

As they neared the outsiders, Cwenhild called on her flame. It came to her in a rush of power, strengthened by the bond between her and Merehwit. She reached for him and knew he was safe in the sky, raining death on their enemies. On the ground, she blazed to life, golden and glorious. The fire chains were enveloped in flames, the spiked balls blazing as she held them ready. At her side, Lyulf held his sword low and his shield close.

The crash as the two groups met was earsplitting. Shield thudded into shield with splintering force. Sword clashed against spear and dagger. Shouting voices melded into a cacophony of human pain and anger.

When the shields slipped and the outsider army saw Cwenhild aflame for the first time, they faltered.

She took advantage, throwing herself into battle with the frenzy of a berserker. She dived into the block of men, burning whoever she touched. Swung her chains in fierce circles, pulling and throwing to strike and crush and scorch. Soldiers fell beneath her fury. The solid line of men began to crumble as they faltered under her onslaught. Streaks of bright blood, none of it her own, added to the woad patterning on her skin.

Cwenhild, Lyulf, and the others pushed their enemy back down the hill until, as they reached the bottom, the last outsider fell to a Demovantes sword. On the other side of Merehwit's flame barrier, the Fwenha clutched their weapons in shaking hands. For a moment, silence blanketed the valley with an eerie calm.

"No!" Dægar bellowed. "Keep fighting!"

Above their heads, Merehwit dived and blew swathes of fire at the enemy. Several men ran screaming from the valley, abandoning their tribesmen and Dægar.

Roaring with rage, Dægar threw himself into the air. Alabaster skin shifted and changed to ruby-red scales, and immense wings sprung from his back. He soared to Merehwit's height and the two dragons, one red as fresh blood and the other the shimmering glow of seafoam, met in a clash of tooth and claw. They rolled and writhed, locked in battle beneath an angry sun. Lashing his tail, Merehwit landed a resounding blow that knocked Dægar back several feet. But the trickster god caught himself and dived back into the fight. He snapped his immense jaws and clamped his teeth down on Merehwit's neck. At the same time, he scraped his talons across the soft underside of Merehwit's belly. The seafoam dragon screamed in pain.

Merehwit! Cwenhild cried.

Summoning his energy, Merehwit writhed out of Dægar's grip and raked his own claws across the trickster's neck. Dægar howled. Spun to retaliate. But Merehwit's strength was done. Golden eyes glazed and rolled back into his head. His mouth parted and a faint drift of smoke seeped out. With a soft groan, his wings collapsed and he plummeted to the ground, tumbling through the air like a feather in a storm.

He dropped behind a snowy peak and a muffled thud reached their ears.

Cwenhild gasped. She reached out with her mind. *Merehwit? Merehwit, please!*

It might have been a trick of the eye, but all colour seemed to drain from the sky until only a blinding whiteness remained. Dægar breathed a stream of crimson fire from his ruby jaws and painted the heavens red like heart-blood.

"How could you?" she screamed at Dægar.

Turning his bloody gaze on her, he swooped down and roared, breathing tongues of flame in her direction. She leapt forward and called her own power to retaliate. Fire pushed against flame in scorching battle until Dægar craned his neck low and tried to bite Cwenhild. She lashed out with her sword, slicing it across his cheek as she threw herself out of his reach. He bellowed and recoiled, and the fire sizzled out.

A flash of silver danced in the air before he landed in front of Cwenhild in the shape of a dire wolf. A large one, three times the size of any she'd seen before. With teeth the size of her forearm. Spittle flew from his immense jaws. A cloud of shaggy silver-black fur hung from his body. He howled, and the sound clawed its way up her spine.

"This is not over." Dægar growled each word. "Your death will be slow and painful, and I will revel in it."

Her heart in her throat, Cwenhild dampened her flames and ran.

Dægar gave chase, loping after her and eating up the ground with his long stride. Lyulf and the others threw themselves in his way to slow him down, but he tossed them aside like hollow logs. Many didn't get back up.

At the peak, where the *menhir* sat like a crown on the head of Demovantes land, people scattered like leaves in the wind as they ran from Dægar. Only Fræda remained, hidden behind one of the standing stones.

Cwenhild pushed herself past the pain. Her lungs burned and her limbs ached but still she ran. She heard him behind her, barking and growling as he reached out with sharp teeth and claws. He was so close, his breath warmed her naked back.

Running inside the circle of the *menhir*, she dived into a forward roll to escape his bite and came to her feet beside the sacred oak. She stopped. Held her hands out and pressed her back against the bark.

"You have nowhere left to run, little girl," Dægar said.

Behind him, Fræda gave a small shake of her head; she needed more time.

Cwenhild filled her lungs. Called the flame. And blazed like an inferno.

"That won't help you now," Dægar said. "I can withstand any fire."

"I won't make this easy for you," she replied. "If I am to die, you go with me. I swear it on my mother's grave."

He leapt at her and she rolled to the side a moment too late. His claws gouged her outer thigh; it was painful but would not kill her yet. Using the adrenaline to dampen the pain, she jumped to her feet and swung the chains in steady circles. She kept moving, dodging his attacks, forcing him to turn to follow her.

Distracted by Cwenhild, he did not see Fræda until she jabbed her staff into his side and he howled in agony.

The druid had sharpened the tip of the staff into a point and coated it with sap from a yew tree - a poison deadly to most animals. She cackled as she danced back out of his reach.

Dægar growled and launched himself at the old woman. He backed her up against the oak tree and snarled. When Cwenhild swung her fire chains into his shoulder, he yelped and lashed out with one colossal paw to send her flying to the other side of the *menhir*.

Fræda held her staff out and gritted her teeth. "We will not give in, shifter. Whatever happens here, you will be diminished."

With a roar, he snapped his teeth around her body and gouged the flesh from her bones. Discarding her like a ragdoll, he howled his victory to the sun.

"Fræda!" Cwenhild screamed. She called the fire. Shaped it into a ball and threw it at Dægar. He yelped as she raced to the druid's side. "No!"

Broken and dying, Fræda smiled. Her teeth were stained with blood; her body was soaked in it. With a shaking hand, she scooped the blood from her chest and lifted it to the trunk of the oak, pressing it deep against the bark. "Do not mourn me, child. All miracles require a sacrifice."

Realisation dawned. Horror roiled in the pit of her stomach. Heart breaking, she threw another fireball to hold Dægar back for one more second. "Oh, Fræda. We will sing of you."

The druid clasped Cwenhild's hand. "I am proud of you, Cwenhild. I will see you in the next life."

Cwenhild wept as Fræda took her last breath.

And Dægar's laughter wheezed and rasped along her nerves.

"You bastard!" She cursed him even as grief weighed her to the ground. Her heart was so heavy she felt as if she could never stand again. When a chorus of voices whispered in her ear, she almost didn't hear it.

We are with you, Cwenhild.

Fræda. Cweneth. Cwenfreda. And so many others: Demovantes who had lived and died through untold centuries. Mothers and daughters whose love had been passed down through countless generations. Fathers and sons whose blood had spilled so their tribe could live.

We are with you.

Her back straightened. The fire came to her call. She rose to her feet like a phoenix from the ashes.

"You can join her in the next life now," Dægar said, shifting back into his own form. "Your allies are dead. You have nowhere to run. It's over."

Cwenhild met his gaze. "You're forgetting something."

He arched his brow. "What's that?"

"Where we are."

"What?" He looked around the *menhir* and scoffed. "I fail to see the relevance."

"This is the sacred land of my people. A place of worship." She looked at Fræda. "And sacrifice. A place where the gods hear our calls and answer them."

Dægar curled his lips into a sneer. "The gods? Fickle, unfaithful fools. They answer when it suits them, and have no qualms about leaving you to your fate. Besides, I am the son of a god. Do you really think they'll help you now?"

She shook her head and stepped back until the oak's bark rubbed her shoulders; it basked in her fire and did not burn. "They aren't the only ones who speak to us here, Dægar."

He stalked her, moving closer until she could smell the blood on his breath. He leaned in. Ran his tongue along her cheek. Paused and pulled back a fraction.

"You're starting to remember." Something shimmered behind her, bright enough to register even though she faced the other way. "Trees are gateways, Dægar. Guess where this one leads."

She dived to the side, dousing her flame and immediately revealing the golden light of the doorway that had opened in the trunk of the sacred oak. Dægar tried to run but his epiphany had come too late. Within the doorway, dozens of arms clamoured to reach him; dozens of faces shone with hatred and rage. Among them was Fræda, who grabbed his arm with gnarled fingers and helped pull his soul from his body and into the tree.

He screamed. Shimmered as he tried and failed to shift his shape. Horror swam behind his eyes.

"Your powers are useless here," Cwenhild told him as she watched from a distance. "Once you've been touched by the spirit world, there is no return, even for the son of a god."

"No!" He begged and wept as the spirits pulled his soul inexorably into the gateway. "Please!"

Cwenhild clenched her jaw. "You were a fool to come for us here in our sacred space. A fool to kill Fræda where her sacrifice would open this door. Did you forget that our ancestors never leave us, Dægar? That all worlds are connected by the trees that reach to the heavens and sink their roots into the earth?"

The trickster god screamed for his father as his spirit vanished into the ether. But no god replied. And in the end, Cwenhild's ancestors sent him to the next life, where his power and his magic would be stripped from him to start anew, as all things must in the circle of life.

His soulless body crumpled like parchment, and black blood oozed from every orifice.

Before the gateway closed, Fræda and her family looked out at her, hands held to their hearts.

Bloodied and bruised, physically and in her heart, Cwenhild sank to the ground and wept.

***

A black cat slipped through the shadows, twining between the stones of the *menhir*. Ignoring the sounds of battle, it moved unnoticed to the great tree, where three bodies sprawled on the ground.

One was still breathing; he wasn't interested in that. He sniffed another, a female, and turned away. No, not that one.

The final body, a man with alabaster skin, was coated in black blood. The cat's tail pointed skyward. He edged closer, making no noise in the wet grass. When he was close enough, he lowered his head and lapped at the black ichor. His amber eyes filled with an oozing blackness.

***

Silence.

No voices would be heard until the last Demovantes had been buried, their heads pointing to the *menhir*.

At Fræda's grave, Cwenhild lay bright wildflowers and several Fwenha heads. The old druid had made the ultimate sacrifice and would be honoured in death as she was in life, remembered in songs and tales as long as the Demovantes continued.

It had been an arduous task to find and bury all their dead. The toll lay heavy on her; a sadness had settled on her shoulders and would not shift.

Still, it could have been worse. She remembered lying broken on the ground after Dægar's defeat. Recalled the battle cries of the Fwenha as they took advantage of the confusion and sought to claim victory. And thanked Isoden every day for the other tribes who had arrived in the nick of time.

It seemed Lyulf had sent out messengers to all nearby tribes, warning them that the Fwenha had allied with the outsiders. His words had managed to do something that had been unheard of since the time of dragons - make the tribes fight together against a common enemy. By the end of that fateful day, the Fwenha were no more.

One more bright ray had lightened the darkness in her heart: Merehwit's voice had returned to her mind, strong and well after recovering from his wounds. They were bonded for life now, and Cwenhild had promised she would help him seek out other dragons once she had buried their dead.

Chief Edwulf and the others were still missing; Lyulf had sent men out to search for them but there had been no sign so far. Had they been sold into slavery? Slaughtered without ever stepping foot off Denovantes land? Only Daegar knew what he'd done with them.

Several feet away, Lyulf cleared his throat. "That's the last of them."

She went to him, the man she had chosen to become handfasted to, and linked her arm with his. She didn't need a year and a day to know she would choose to stay with the man who stood by her side in every way.

Visions still haunted her. Some she considered signs from Fræda, and others mere dreams brought on by the trauma. But the ravens sang of her future with this man; of her belly growing round with child; and of the peaceful reign of the Demovantes, who would lead their people into a better world.

Death had come for them all, fire had purged the land, and new life would grow from it. The cycle of life would continue; Fræda had taught her that.

Wind-Dancer

SIX

They took her in the dark. Shoved her into the back of a carriage with three other girls carrying nothing but the clothes on their backs. The orphanage had never been home but who knew where they'd end up now? Lady Arlowen had told them nothing.

"What's happening, Maeri? Where are they taking us?"

Although it was hard to see in the unlit carriage, Maerelith Doone recognised the voice of Little Roo. The girl was a year or so younger than the rest of them, but her naïveté made the difference so much more. "I don't know, Little Roo." She squeezed the younger girl's hand. "But it's okay. Maybe we'll be given a real home now. At least we're all together."

A snort penetrated the darkness: Estha Broja's trademark retort. "More likely they're selling us on the underground market."

Maeri cleared her throat. "Nah, they wouldn't have fed us so well beforehand if that's what they were going to do."

"Maybe," Estha pretended to agree. "Maybe they just wanted to be rid of us troublemakers."

"Who are you calling a troublemaker?" Lisel asked, her voice barely audible above the rumble of wheels on dirt. "I did everything they asked and they're still sending me away. Whatever the reason, we've lost another home."

"Or gained a better one," Maeri said. "Let's save judgement until we get there. In the meantime, we should get some sleep. Who knows what morning will bring?"

Estha yawned. "Aye, Maeri's right. We've been up since the crack of dawn and may well be again. *Candles out, girls.*" She mimicked Lady Arlowen's voice and snorted again.

The older girls settled down and Maeri pulled Roo into her shoulder. The rocking motion of the carriage soothed them and, before long, their soft snores gentled the heavy air. Maeri closed her eyes but sleep was elusive. Her mind racing, she mouthed a silent prayer to Avora, goddess of the lost; despite her earlier words, there was every possibility they were headed for the underground market. Lady Arlowen had no love for her charges, only the money donated for their raising.

Her stomach rolled. The things she'd heard about the underground market were enough to make anyone sick. Even girls their age, none of them older than seven, would bring a good price from the dirty old men who shopped there. If that was their destination, she would have to find a way to escape with the others. Yes, she needed to stay alert. Be on her guard. She had a feeling nothing good awaited them on this dark night.

Holding Roo close, Maeri listened to the thud of the horse's hooves and the occasional shriek of some creature in the darkness. She didn't know how long she waited for something to happen but, after a while, she too sank into a restless slumber and surrendered to dreams of rocking boats and fiery dawns. And, when she whimpered in her sleep, no one heard; no one was there to offer comfort to a young girl on a dangerous journey.

A loud bang awoke her.

Maeri looked at the faint light dappling through the cracks in the wooden carriage. *Where am I?* Her arm tingled and she looked down to see Little Roo sleeping on her shoulder; memories of the night before came flooding back.

"Wake up," she said with a hiss, jumping to her feet to face the carriage door. Muffled voices came from the other side, and the soft whinny of the horse as it greeted a familiar face. Her heart thudding, she kicked Estha's feet and nudged Lisel's shoulder. "Wake up!"

The girls jolted awake, saw the alarm on Maeri's face, and jumped to their feet. Lisel woke Little Roo and pushed the younger girl to the back, leaving the three of them to face whatever came through the door. Maeri looked for a weapon, found nothing, and took off one of her shoes to use instead.

"Maeri?" Roo's voice quivered.

"It'll be alright," she promised, praying that wasn't a lie. "Whatever happens, we'll be okay."

Estha snorted.

When the door opened, creaking outwards with a slow groan, bright sunlight shone inside. The girls recoiled from the light. Lisel gasped. Roo screamed. And Maeri threw her shoe before she could see what she threw it at. She heard it hit flesh. Winced at the ensuing yelp. Narrowed her eyes when laughter followed.

"What the fuck was that?"

A deep chuckle danced through the air. "That was a shoe, Seyer. It seems we've got a wild one inside."

"Fucking Lady Arlowen. She never tells 'em where they're going. It's no wonder they arrive in a state."

"Just wants the finder's fee, that one." He spat on the floor. "Better call one of the sisters to deal with the bairns."

Sisters? Curiosity piqued, Maeri ventured a step closer to the door. Outside, two men waited, their arms folded across their chests. One was short and stocky, with a patch over one eye and a shiny bald head. The other, tall and lanky, had a long curved nose that reminded her of a bird's beak. She lifted her chin and looked down her own nose at them, mimicking the haughty expression Lady Arlowen often directed towards her.

"Give me my shoe," she demanded.

The one named Seyer waved the offending shoe in the air. "I think I'll hang onto it until I'm sure you won't be throwing it no more. Gonna leave a shiner, that is."

She knitted her brow and pinned them with her gaze.

"Maeri." Estha put a hand on her friend's shoulder. "What do they want with us?"

About to answer, Maeri was struck speechless when a white-robed woman appeared behind the two men. A white scarf held her hair back and a pale blue sash sat on her waist. Her face was smooth and rounded. When she looked at the girls, it was with eyes the same shade as the sash.

"What's the problem, Seyer?" the woman asked in a voice as smooth as honey.

Seyer held up the shoe. "They've been sent by the *esteemed* Lady Arlowen."

The curses that fell from the woman's lips were far less than ladylike. "Someone needs to have words with that woman."

"Aye." He handed her the shoe. "Can you get them out? We've got to pick another delivery up and, if we're late, we'll lose our pay."

Maeri followed the conversation with interest. The woman didn't seem like someone who traded on the underground market. But then, she wouldn't make it obvious, would she? She held a hand back to warn the other girls to stay behind her as she edged closer to the carriage doors. The bright sunlight stabbed at her eyes and she flinched. When she'd blinked the stinging tears away, she took stock of where they were.

Wild moorlands. Moody grey skies. And a grey stone manor house with arched windows filled with stained glass. Ornate details were carved into the stone and glaring gargoyles sat atop each corner. Where were they?

The woman in the white robe waved a hand to catch Maeri's attention. "Excuse me?"

Maeri bared her teeth. "We ain't going nowhere, lady."

"My name is Sister Benedita. Where did Lady Arlowen say you were going?"

"She didn't." Maeri lifted one clenched fist. "I won't let you sell us on the underground market, no matter how fancy your name is."

Benedita pursed her lips. "Well, that explains the shoe. No, my dears. I promise we are not selling you on the underground market."

"Well, sure she's gonna say that!" Estha snorted in the back of the carriage.

"Oh, never mind." Benedita rolled her eyes and put her hands on her hips. "It'll be easier to show you."

"Show us what?" Maeri asked.

Benedita didn't reply; instead, she brought her hands together, closed her eyes, and whispered strange words under her breath. The air stirred. Blades of grass bent towards her. Seyer and his friend backed away. Within seconds, the wind raged, but only around Benedita. It swirled around her body, a column of air spinning in a contained circle. The noise was immense. The edges of the funnel pulled at everything around it: the long grass on the ground; the carriage doors, which swung wider; the hem of Maeri's skirt. Maeri scrambled back, tripped on her shoeless foot, and gaped.

The Sister smiled. Spread her arms. Rose up inside the wind funnel until she levitated five feet in the air. Using the wind to carry her voice beyond the swirling gale, she said, "Welcome to the Sisterhood of Aktai. You are family now. Sisters. Wind-Dancers."

Stubborn to the last, Maeri took off her other shoe and held it at the ready.

SIXTEEN

Maeri never could believe her luck in being sent to the Sisterhood. She spent the first year making escape plans while looking out for Estha, Lisel, and Little Roo. The three years after that, studying books and practising technique, were a kind of balancing act; realising this was her new home, she'd worked hard to prove her worth for fear of being sent away once more. Even a decade later, aged sixteen and ready for her initiation, there were times she felt like an outsider, different to the other girls and uncertain of her place in the world.

"Are you ready, Maeri?" Estha asked as she finished braiding Maeri's hair into the traditional Aktai plait.

Little Roo, reclining on Maeri's bed, sighed. "I wish I could be initiated with you all. It's not fair. We came here together; we should progress together."

"You've only another year to wait, Roo." Lisel ruffled the younger girl's hair. "Don't be in such a hurry to grow up."

Tuning them out, Maeri walked to the window and looked out at the moorlands that had become as familiar to her as her own face. She was restless, the thud of her heart loud in her ears. Her feet itched to run in the grass, barefoot as the day she'd arrived. But after ten years of being raised in the ancient order of the Wind-Dancers, she knew enough about her own feelings to understand she was nervous about the upcoming initiation. Why? It shouldn't bother her. It was only the next step, after all. Her instructors said she was as talented as any who'd gone before. Her friends assured her she had the strength to pass the test and to serve the people. Even Mother Superior Karola could not deny Maeri was an asset to the Sisterhood.

Still, she was not popular like Estha, book-smart like Lisel, or beloved like Little Roo. She was just Maeri, the girl who once threw her shoe at Sister Benedita. Fingering the grey sash at her waist, she wondered what it would feel like to wear the pale blue of the initiated.

"Why do you look so glum, Maeri?" Little Roo asked. "You should be excited."

She shrugged. "I guess I'm worried about the initiation. What if I fail?"

"Ha." Estha snorted - some things never changed. "Maeri, you know it's more for show than anything else. All the *true* Wind-Dancers are long gone and the tests have had to be simplified so we *acquired* Wind-Dancers can pass them. Why fret about it?"

"I don't know, Es." Maeri dragged her eyes from the moors. "I guess I feel like I'm wearing a mask. Like I'm not really one of you."

"Don't be daft."

Was she being silly? Maeri wasn't sure, but she forced a smile to her lips and linked arms with her friend. "We'd best get going. We don't want to be late to our own initiation."

They walked along the dark corridors in silence; even Little Roo was affected by the nervous energy surrounding them. Ten years of learning had led to this day, and the outcome meant the difference between becoming Sisters of Aktai or becoming homeless overnight.

Maeri shivered; the stones were cold beneath her feet. "Oh no!" She groaned and pulled back from her friends.

"What's wrong?" Lisel asked.

Heat crept up her cheeks. "I forgot my shoes. I'll catch up."

She ran back to her room, cursing her idiocy. How could she forget her shoes? She'd spent ten years being teased for throwing her shoes when she arrived; she couldn't walk into her initiation with bare feet!

When she'd found her shoes and pulled them onto her feet, she raced along the corridor again. Down the stairs. Through the ornate arched doorway. Into the inner sanctum. Each room was empty; everyone must already be in the Initiation Hall. Rounding a corner, she slowed when she heard people talking. She recognised the voice of Mother Superior Karola, but the other voice was definitely male; what was he doing there? Men were never allowed within the Order.

Without knowing quite why, she pressed her back against the wall and edged closer to the corner. Her stomach quivered. Her palms were sweaty. An inner voice told her to stay hidden and she felt a sinking certainty that, if she were caught, she wouldn't make it to her initiation.

"Keep your voice down," Mother Karola hissed.

"Then keep up your end of the bargain." The man spoke in a growl.

Maeri could well imagine why he was angry with Mother Karola. In all her years with the Sisterhood, she had never warmed to the Mother Superior nor felt any warmth in return. Their relationship could be summed up in three words: avoidance, disappointment, and frustration. Maeri held her breath as she listened to their conversation.

"You'll get your supply, Hosha. But don't threaten me. And don't come here again. Everything will be ruined if you're seen here."

"Midnight tomorrow," Hosha said. His voice lowered again and Maeri strained to hear. "Or your girls will pay the price."

Their footsteps receded and Maeri released her breath. What had she just heard? Horror filled her. Who was that man? What was Mother Karola supplying him with? Thoughts hurtled through her mind until she could barely grasp hold of each one. One thing was for sure: she was never supposed to hear that conversation and nothing good would happen to her if she revealed she had.

A bell tolled and she gasped - the initiation! She lifted her robe and ran until she reached the Initiation Hall, slipping inside as the bell rang for the fifth time. She had made it. She pushed the conversation from her mind and focused on what was happening in the vaulted room. The edges of the hall were lined with white-robed Sisters there to watch the initiation. A row of girls, including Estha and Lisel, faced the centre; Maeri joined them, praying no one had noticed her tardiness. At the back of the room, a small dais held three chairs, each with a blue-robed woman sitting upon it. Maeri bit her lip. Those three women held her life in their hands. They were the Magistrates who would decide whether the initiates passed or failed.

Swallowing the lump in her throat, she forced herself to focus as each girl was called to the middle of the room and subjected to three tasks. First, they had to call the wind to lift them into the air. Next, the girl whispered a pre-chosen message into the breeze she controlled and delivered that message to one of the Magistrates. If the Magistrate heard and understood the message, and it matched the pre-set message the girl had specified before the event, then she would move on to the third and final stage of the initiation. Under close supervision by their mentor, the budding Wind-Dancer would steal the air from a volunteer until that person passed out. The volunteer would then be taken away to recover while the hopeful initiate waited for a verdict.

Because of her lateness, Maeri was forced to watch all the other girls go first. She tried to steady her heart as she tapped her fingertips repeatedly against her palms. When the third girl failed the third task, a collective gasp spread among the Sisters. The poor girl sobbed as she was escorted away. Maeri reminded herself to breathe.

Lisel scraped through, passing by the skin of her teeth after an initial fumble. Estha performed as she always did - with confidence and flair. And then it was Maeri's turn. She inhaled. Filled her lungs with air. Blew it back out through clenched teeth.

They called her name. "Maerelith Doone."

Still tapping her palms, she moved into the centre of the room and tried to ignore the sea of faces staring at her. She focused on the Magistrates. Let everything else wash over her and drift away.

"Task one," the Magistrate on the right said. "You may begin."

Maeri nodded. Other Wind-Dancers liked to close their eyes to help them grasp hold of the air but she'd never understood that; she kept hers wide open. Why close your eyes to potential dangers just to feel something you already know is there and should already be able to feel? She was sure it was nothing more than a bad habit - one she would never allow herself to pick up. She held her hands low, palms up and cupped at her stomach. The wind came as soon as she called it, strands of air pulled from everywhere and everyone within the Initiation Hall. Not enough to harm anyone, but enough combined to create a swirling funnel like the one Sister Benedita had created on Maeri's first day at the Sisterhood.

It whirled around her. Caressed her skin. Teased the edges of her hair. When she was ready, she used it to lift herself up into the vaulted ceiling. She remembered the first time she'd tried, when fear had frazzled her nerves and disbelief had blocked her power. Now, it was much easier. She spun in a slow circle to demonstrate her control and then lowered herself back to the marbled floor before dismissing the wind.

Silence hung in the pause like a miasma.

"Impressive," the lead Magistrate said in a clipped voice. "I wonder if you'll find task two as easy."

It struck Maeri that, despite accomplishing what they'd asked of her, it felt like she'd made a mistake.

Preparing herself for the second task, she sized up the Magistrates and chose the one on the left, who was quieter and more rounded than the others. She lifted her hand, palm up again, to her mouth, and crooked a finger. One invisible current of air drifted to her hand. Speaking in the softest tones, she whispered her message and sent the breeze spiralling over to the Magistrate.

When the wind murmured her message, a collective gasp rose from the gathered crowd. Maeri's message was audible throughout the Hall.

I dance with the wind, she had said in her whispered message, voicing the ancient words of the true Wind-Dancers, *and it dances with me.*

Maeri swallowed. She'd never managed to make it so loud in practice. How was it possible?

The lead Magistrate furrowed her brow. "Impressive, indeed. Call your mentor for the final task, please."

Hands trembling again, Maeri turned to call Sister Benedita. The older woman joined Maeri in the middle of the room. They clasped hands and pressed their brows together in the traditional greeting.

"Hold your power back, Maeri," Benedita said so softly no one else could hear. "I beg of you. Fumble on this last task. Trust me."

Maeri sucked her cheeks in, fear clawing at her chest. Benedita's words were not to be taken lightly. Meeting her mentor's gaze, she tipped her head in agreement.

"I'm ready," she told the Magistrates.

A volunteer stepped forward, one of the initiates from the previous year; her name was Yima. Maeri sensed the air in Yima's body. It would be so easy to take it all, to keep drawing it away until there was nothing left. Even in lessons, that had always come easily to her. Yet, instinctively, she'd known not to go that far.

Remembering Benedita's warning as she faced Yima, Maeri wrinkled her forehead and bit her bottom lip. Sweat poured from her - more from nerves than effort, but no one needed to know that. In the corner of her vision, she saw Mother Karola watching with a pinched expression and knew Benedita was right.

She reached out a hand and tugged the air from Yima's lungs. It came in a trickle. Yima seemed unaffected until she clasped her throat with her hands and her face turned red. Maeri tugged a little more and Yima's chest sucked in as she struggled to breathe. Had she done enough to pass? She wasn't sure but Benedita's words crawled up her spine and she let go, stumbling back as if the task had been difficult. Yima gasped several ragged breaths and returned to her seat.

Maeri looked at the Magistrates.

The lead Magistrate wore a smirk on her aged face. "I have to say, that was disappointing after your results in the first two tasks. Still, it was a pass. Barely. Congratulations, Sister Maerelith. Welcome to the Sisterhood of Aktai. You may now wear the blue sash of a Wind-Dancer."

Cheers erupted as the eleven successful initiates joined each other on the marble floor. Surrounded by smiling faces and congratulatory handshakes, Maeri found herself looking for Sister Benedita. When their eyes met, a silent promise passed between them: later.

TWENTY-SIX

Maeri followed the lines on Sister Benedita's face with her eyes. When had her mentor developed the crow's feet to go with her almost permanent smile? Time had snuck up on her, it seemed. It had been twenty years since they'd first met and Benedita had become like a mother to Maeri; to Maeri's mind, the older woman was still as beautiful as ever.

"Ah, stop looking at me like that, Maeri." Benedita tutted.

Maeri flashed her teeth. "I haven't seen you in six months, Benedita. I have to look my fill when I'm home."

"Aye, same for me, love." Benedita wrapped an arm around Maeri's shoulders. "But you're doing good work out there. I'm proud of you."

They walked further across the moorlands, Maeri barefoot as always, until they had clear views in every direction and could be sure they were alone. The summer sun had burned away the morning's low-lying fog. Heather bloomed in bright shades of purple and mauve, and its musky scent teased their nostrils.

After a final glance to check no one was listening, Benedita said, "Have you been practising?"

"Yes." Maeri rolled her sleeve up to reveal three faint wavy lines hidden in the crook of her arm. "Look! Is this what you said it would be? Am I *true*?"

Benedita gasped as she inspected the pale blue lines. "This is exactly as it looks in the old books, Maeri. I knew it!"

She pulled her sleeve back down to hide the mark again. Nausea rolled over her in a wave as she felt the blood drain from her face. How could she be a *true* Wind-Dancer? Everything she'd been taught at the Sisterhood said they didn't exist anymore.

"I wish we knew who your parents were," Benedita said. "Perhaps one of them was *true*. Regardless, it's a miracle, Maeri. Do you know what this means?"

A cold shiver ran down her spine. "Nothing good, I'm sure."

"No." Benedita took Maeri's face in her hands. "This is everything good, my girl. Three centuries they've been gone, and the world has fallen to pieces. You could do so much good with this."

"Then why do I have to hide it?"

"Because something isn't right. You know that."

Maeri tipped her head. Benedita was right. The old books gave no explanation for the vanishing of the *true* Wind-Dancers, or why some people could *acquire* a lesser power. And she'd never forgotten that strange meeting between Mother Karola and that man, nor Benedita's hissed warning at her initiation. "Have you managed to dig anything else up about Mother Karola while I've been gone?"

"Nothing concrete," Benedita tightened her mouth. "But many things are not adding up. Where does she disappear to for days on end? Why is she so obsessed with finding more recruits when our numbers are plentiful? And I still haven't found anything to explain what happened to Kosa or Tanith."

Maeri sighed. According to Benedita, both girls had shown signs of being *true* in their initiation, just as Maeri had before she fumbled the final task. There was no way to be sure, of course. *True* power grew with time, unlike the *acquired* power that could be strengthened like one might strengthen a muscle, but would never grow beyond its original limits. Kosa had vanished before Maeri arrived at the Sisterhood, disappearing the night after her initiation. Tanith passed her initiation three years after Maeri did, but had run away a week later. At least, that's what Mother Karola told everyone. Maeri had a bad feeling about both girls.

"You must keep your mark hidden from Karola, my love." Benedita pinned her gaze to drive the point home. "Promise me you will keep your head down and stay beneath her notice."

"Of course. Anyway, I'm being sent to Sebasha in two days. It will be hard for her to notice me when I'm so far away."

Benedita blinked. "Sebasha? Why?"

"There's a dispute they need help settling."

"What's so important they need to call in a Wind-Dancer?"

She shrugged. "I guess I'll find out when I get there. The request came directly from the Chief so it must be important."

The lines in the older woman's brow grew deeper. "Be careful out there, Maeri. The betweenlands grow more dangerous with each passing year."

"I'll be careful." Maeri squeezed Benedita's hand. She'd have to be careful. The number of marauding mud-dwellers had more than tripled in the years she'd been carrying out official duties. Reports of attacks came in every day. The betweenlands had become unsafe for normal travellers; only Wind-Dancers and the desperate traversed them now. Everyone else stayed safe inside the cities dotted around the realm. "Make sure you're careful too, Benedita. I don't feel like the Sisterhood is safe anymore, either."

"I will." Benedita gestured back to the house. "Come. I'll help you pack for your trip."

Maeri missed the sun as soon as she stepped back inside. She yearned to feel the grass between her toes again, and the wind teasing her hair. But Mother Karola insisted on shoes. Besides, she still had to pack, as Benedita had reminded her. She did it quickly as it was not a task she enjoyed, and spent the next day catching up with Estha, Lisel, and Little Roo. They picnicked beneath their favourite oak tree, nibbling on bread and cheese, and sipping fresh water gathered from the stream.

"How was Hunen?" Maeri asked Lisel.

"Oh," she said with a shrug. "It was uneventful. I supervised the competition, announced the winner, and enjoyed some fine food before heading back."

Estha nudged Maeri in the ribs. "I wonder if she shared that fine food with a certain Lady Fariyaa."

Lisel's cheeks reddened and she averted her gaze. "I might have. I like her."

"As long as she treats you well, we'd love to meet her," Maeri said.

Little Roo giggled. "I'm being sent to Hunen for the harvest this year. Maybe I can say hello to her then."

Lisel's blush deepened.

"Ah, give her a break," Estha said with a grin. "Can't you see the girl's in love?"

Clearing her throat, Lisel turned to look at Maeri. "What about you? You're going to Sebasha tomorrow?"

"Yes." Maeri finished chewing her piece of cheese and took a sip of water before continuing. "Settling some sort of dispute. I don't think I know anyone in Sebasha. Do any of you?"

Estha nodded, her face drawn. "Had a cousin in Sebasha before I wound up at the orphanage. My father's sister's boy.

Couple of years older than me, I think. He likely wouldn't remember me, though. After his mum declined to take me in, I never heard from them again."

"What's his name?"

"Kam Maroya. Last I heard, he raises horses out there. Sebasha's not that big a place; you might bump into him."

Maeri smirked. "I'll pass on your regards, shall I?"

And she grinned when Estha let out her signature snort.

She was sad to say farewell to her friends and Sister Benedita again, but it was always exciting travelling to a new place. With her pack thrown over her shoulder, she called the wind and lifted herself up into it, resisting the urge to giggle. After all these years, she still loved the weightlessness of lying in the wind's embrace, cradled by it as it carried her wherever she wanted to go. It came as naturally as breathing now and she surrendered to the rush. Let herself float in the right direction until she tugged on the tails of a larger gust and spun her body into it. Finding her momentum, she twisted and turned, dived and danced between blowing breezes until the sun sank low in the sky and she was forced to stop to find a place to sleep.

The first day had been easy but Maeri would never let her guard down. Too many Wind-Dancers fell afoul of marauders when they stopped for the night. With that in mind, she settled in the curved nook of two high branches and cajoled the wind to keep her safe while she slept.

She made good time throughout the second and third days, each night finding a safe place to rest. Whenever she caught sight of marauders, she shifted currents and stayed out of their way. The scenery slipped by in a blur of green fading to a reddish brown the closer she got to her destination. On the afternoon of the fourth day, she arrived at Sebasha.

The walls were twice as high as the trees and reinforced with several layers of stone. Thick wooden gates were set into the stone and closed against the outside world. Atop the walls, several soldiers patrolled with sharp blades and ready bows. Riding the wind, Maeri sent a message on the breeze to alert them to her arrival, then soared over the wall to land in the town square.

"Welcome, Wind-Dancer," a white-haired man greeted her. He wore dark leather and carried a short blade on his belt. His brown eyes were shadowed. "I am Chief Rafayn. Thank you for coming to Sebasha."

She tipped her head. "I am happy to help, Chief Rafayn."

He led her inside one of the larger buildings, where food and drink were laid out on a table.

Rafayn gestured to the spread. "I thought you might prefer to eat while we discuss the problem."

She widened her grin and took an apple from the fruit bowl. "Thank you. Now, tell me: how can I help?"

Maeri listened as the chief explained why the town of Sebasha had requested aid from the Sisterhood of Aktai. When she'd finished the apple, she helped herself to a chicken leg and a mug of watery wine.

"Marauders raided Sebasha a week ago," Rafayn explained. "They took most of our supplies as well as three young girls. We need -"

"Hold on," she said. "I was told you needed help settling a dispute."

"We do. We can't agree on whether to go after the kidnapped girls or not."

She pinched the bridge of her nose to block the headache she knew was coming. "Your message mentioned nothing about kidnapped girls. If it had, more Dancers would have been sent, and sooner."

He spread his hands. "I can only apologise, Sister Maerelith. But we must act soon, whatever we decide to do. If we are to save those girls, I do not know how much time we have. If not, we must focus on our defences before the marauders return for more of our women."

Maeri resisted the urge to groan. "Who the fuck doesn't want to save the girls?"

His eyes widened. "Um... Some of the councilmen think it is too dangerous."

Grabbing some dried dates, she dropped her pack on a chair and paced the room. "Tell me about the girls. And about who took them."

"The girls are all fifteen. Vivoria Mygo, Carochel Keest, and Ingren Maroya."

Maeri jerked to a stop. "Maroya? Related to Kam?"

"She's Kam's little sister. Do you know the family?"

She shook her head. "No, but a friend does. Go on."

The chief sat down heavily, as if the weight of his story was crushing him. "The girls were at the market when the raid happened. They didn't manage to hide in time. The marauders just scooped them up onto the back of their horses and rode right out of town, with the girls kicking and screaming all the way. I daren't think about what might have happened to them in the week since."

"No." Maeri closed her eyes, remembering her own fear of being taken to the underground market. That fucking market still existed twenty years later and those girls were likely headed for it if they weren't there already. "Has anything been done to try to track them down?"

He refused to meet her gaze. "Kam and a handful of others left town straight away, including Vivoria's parents and Carochel's father. We've not heard from them since. You have to understand, Sister Maeri. It's my job to protect the whole town, not just the few."

She stalked closer to him, not stopping until she leaned in so close she could see every pore on his face. "Let me make something clear, Chief. You made the wrong decision. You mishandled the communication with the Sisterhood, you abandoned those girls to an unthinkable fate, and you have done nothing in the past week but wallow in your misery. You leave me in an untenable position here, Chief. I am not supposed to go after marauders on my own; it is policy to have at least a five-man team for situations like this. However, morally, I cannot leave those girls. I'm sending an immediate communication to send reinforcements. With the urgency of my message, they should make it here within three days. You will be ready for them. You will give them everything they need. Do you understand me?"

"Yes." His voice shook. "You're going out there?"

She looked down her nose at him. "Someone has to."

"I'm sorry. Please. I'm sorry."

"Tell it to the parents of those girls. Now, which way did they go?"

"East."

She looked out of the window in the direction he pointed, then realised she could see nothing but the walls of Sebasha. Grabbing her pack, she checked her weapons were secure at her waist and headed back outside. If she kept moving, maybe she could convince herself that the churning in her gut wasn't fear, that she wasn't terrified at the thought of what might happen out in the betweenlands.

You're not a little girl anymore, Maeri, she told herself. *Buck up. Those girls need you.*

Without further words, she called the wind and soared back over the wall. The girls might already be dead, but there was still a chance they were alive. There was no time to waste.

She danced with the wind, riding it eastwards until the sun began to set in a haze of mauve and fire. With no trees to rest in, she gathered shrubs for a small fire, used her flint to create a spark, and nudged the breeze to breathe life into the flames. Wrapping her cloak around her, she rested her head on more shrubs and looked up at a dark sky full of stars.

Keep me safe while I sleep, she whispered to the wind. The air tightened, wrapping around her like a gentle hug and she drifted into dreams.

Her sleep was fitful and she woke early. Disheartened by the lack of any evidence of their passing her route, Maeri asked the wind for help once more, sending breezes out in every direction to search for signs of the missing girls. While she waited for a response, she gathered her things and continued heading eastwards. She was a week behind and had little hope of finding them quickly, but she had to keep trying.

The next day, the wind tugged at her, pulling on her hair and robe until she changed her course to angle slightly south. She followed that course for two more days, turning when the wind nudged her and sleeping only when it was too dark to travel safely. As the sun reached its peak, the wind brought snippets of voices to her ears, snatches of conversation from ahead.

"We have to... girls... help..."

"I don't think..."

"... marauders... too many..."

Dancing with the currents, Maeri aimed for the voices and lowered herself down behind a group of half a dozen men and one woman. They turned with swords drawn and fear in their eyes.

Maeri lifted her hands to show them she wasn't wielding a weapon.

A red-bearded man stepped forward. "Wind-Dancer. It's about time. Could have done with you a week ago."

She acknowledged the complaint with a tilt of her head. "My apologies. I came as soon as your chief told me what had happened."

"Where are the others?"

Her mouth tightened. "Delayed. Rafayn did not tell anyone about the missing girls until I arrived in Sebasha. I sent for reinforcements but they'll be three days behind me."

He snarled. "That will be too late for our daughters."

"I know." She met his gaze. "I will do what I can alone. Are you one of the fathers?"

"Yes. I'm Wexley Mygo, Vivoria's father." He gestured to the woman. "This is my wife, Zayda. Over there are my brothers, Torence and Ricard." Lifting an arm, he pointed to the bushy-haired man next to them. "That's Carochel's father, Kon Keest."

Maeri nodded her head to each person. The other two men were younger; one was around her age, and the other looked still in his teens. "And you two?"

The older one offered his hand. "I'm Kam Maroya, Ingren's brother. This is Ingren's betrothed, Lucash Brenson."

Maeri took his hand. She would have guessed who he was even if he hadn't told her. There was one clear difference, though; his eyes were the palest green, contrasting with the darkness of his skin. She cleared her throat, realising she'd been staring for too long. "You look like Estha."

"Estha?" His jaw clenched. "What do you mean? What do you know about Estha?"

Surprised by the anger in his tone, she withdrew her hand. "Just that she's your cousin and you once played together as children."

"How would you know that?" Kam asked. "She died twenty years ago."

Maeri's mouth parted. "What? Kam, she's still alive. She's a Wind-Dancer."

Something flashed in his eyes. Disbelief. Understanding. And a sad acceptance. "My mother said she died with her parents."

"That's not true. She was orphaned. We were sent to the Sisterhood together."

"I…" He looked down at his hands. "I'd like to see her when we've got the girls back."

"I'll take you to her. For now, let's concentrate on the girls. Do you know how far ahead they are?"

Wexley held a hand out. "They can't be too far. We caught sight of them this morning before losing them by the ravine. We've been expecting to catch up with them all day."

Maeri glanced at their horses. Steam rose from their flanks as they grazed on the small patches of grass they could find.

"We had to stop to give them a rest," Wexley said, following her gaze. "If they drop on us, we'll never catch the marauders."

"Do you know it's the right group?" she asked, possible plans racing through her mind. "Did you see the girls?"

"At least one of them." He side-eyed Kon. "Looking worse for wear."

Maeri could only imagine what he meant by that. Her heart broke at the thought of what those poor girls were going through. She was supposed to wait for help. A Wind-Dancer would be a great prize for the marauders; no doubt they would brag about her capture and torture. But she couldn't live with abandoning three young women to a fate she herself was scared of. "How many men do they have?"

"More than us," Kam answered. "Maybe twenty."

She winced. She'd hoped for less. With a heavy sigh, she handed her pack to Kam. "Take this. When your horses are rested, try to catch up with me. I'll need help."

He grabbed her wrist as she turned. "I want to save my sister, but I don't want you dead. Be careful."

A thought crossed her mind. Risky. Unprecedented. But it might just work. "Kam?"

"Yes?"

"How are you with heights?"

She couldn't take them all and told them so, but she knew her own power; riding the wind was easy for her and she had no doubt she could carry another. Leaving the others with the horses and clear instructions, she called the wind. As it swirled around her, she held a hand out to Kam, trying to ignore the strange fluttering in her stomach.

"Don't let me fall," he said as he took it.

She held tight as they rose into the air. When his hand squeezed a little too hard, she squeezed back and offered him a warm smile. The wind spiralled all around them, dancing beneath their feet and holding them safely high above the ground. Conscious of the man at her side, she moved a little slower than normal, stepping between currents with care. Air rushed past their ears. Danced between their fingers.

Kam tugged on her arm and pointed to the group of riders just visible in the distance. She counted them quickly: eighteen horses. Three of them had an extra rider on the back. It had to be the girls.

"Your focus is the girls," she said to Kam. "Try to get them away from the group. I'll be able to fight them better if the girls are out of the way."

"Understood."

Biting her lip as she concentrated, she took them over the top of the riders and dropped down in front of them, startling their horses. Several reared and two men fell to the ground. Pushing gusts of wind around the riderless horses' ears, she scared them into bolting. The marauders shouted and drew their swords, charging towards Maeri and Kam. Three drew their bows and loosed arrows but Maeri pushed them back with the wind. As the rest kept charging, she lifted Kam and set him down to one side.

The front line of marauders was almost upon her. She moved her arms in the air and commanded the wind to blow sideways across their ranks. The horses squealed. Several men were lifted clean from their saddles and dumped a hundred feet away. Acting on instinct, she wrestled the wind into a whip and lashed out with it, striking the five men closest to her. She directed with her hands, created an air funnel around the fallen men, and spun them across the plain. Some didn't get up again; the others crawled on their hands and knees and vomited into the dirt.

Then, the rest were upon her.

She used the air to make herself weightless, then spun and dived and kicked in an intricate dance. Their swords sliced the air where her head had been. Barely nicked the edge of her arm. She parried with her own blade, knocking theirs aside and cutting through soft flesh with the strength of a localised gale. She tired and still they came, but she kept half an eye on Kam, waiting for the right moment to act.

Kam didn't fight like a man who raised horses. He fought like one who'd scrapped in the old arenas and faced barbarians over breakfast. His teeth were bared, his muscles taut, and his eyes focused.

The marauders carrying the girls, plus a handful more to guard them, stayed back from Maeri, and Kam went straight for them. Although they were on horseback and he fought on his feet, he killed two men with ease. A third charged towards him, spurring the horse faster. As it neared, Kam threw his pouch into the horse's face; it reared and turned to the side. Without pause, Kam grabbed the reins, parried the rider's sword, and twisted his own weapon to slice across the man's neck.

Shoving him off and stealing his horse, Kam launched a dagger and it landed between another marauder's eyes; Ingren took the man's sword, pushed him from the saddle, and took the reins. She ran her horse into another and gutted the man holding Vivoria.

Maeri grinned. Kam was more than keeping up his end. Dancing backwards on the wind, she drew the remaining marauders with her until they were separated from the girls by a least fifty feet. She pulled on the well of calm in her centre and drew a wind funnel around herself. She held it there, waiting until the men were almost close enough to skewer her with their blades. Then, she threw her arms out to knock them from their horses with the sudden gust. She hoped the horses would run but didn't have time to wait. She prayed she had the strength to do what she needed to next. She'd only ever tried it on one person before, and never with such a wide area. But what choice did she have?

Pulling her arms back in, she inhaled sharply and sucked all the air within twenty feet into the funnel. She held it there, watching as the marauders gasped and clawed at their necks. With no air to breathe, they fell to their knees and their eyes bulged.

Maeri panted. Sweat poured from her brow. Her vision blurred. The effort to hold the air was excruciating. The funnel dropped. Her toes touched the ground. The men stilled.

As she slipped from consciousness, Maeri could only hope she'd done enough.

Everything went dark. Somehow, she was still aware of the ragged sound of her own breathing. Other noises drifted to her ears: screams and clashing swords; shouted names and tearful greetings; a soft voice calling for the Wind-Dancer whose name he hadn't had a chance to learn.

She blinked. Groaned at the sudden rush of pain throughout her body. Moved her tongue against the dryness of her mouth.

"Water," she croaked. "Please."

Kam held his waterskin to her lips and she drank. When she'd had her fill, he helped her to her feet, keeping his arm around her waist to steady her. Nine solemn faces watched her. Zayda held onto a red-haired young girl who had to be Vivoria. Kon watched over a slender blonde, and Lucash stroked the hair of a girl who looked like a younger version of Estha. The other men aimed swords at a marauder kneeling on the ground; he was the only one of his crew left alive.

"What did I miss?" she asked.

Wexley tugged on his beard. "We got here just in time to see you… Lady, I've never seen anything like that in my life. I used to be in the Guard so I've spent my fair share of time with you Wind-Dancers, but I ain't never seen anything like that. You sucked the breath right from 'em!"

Maeri studied the bodies on the ground and swallowed hard. They were dead because of her. "Yeah. I've never seen anything like that before, either. First time for me too, my friend. I just wanted to save your girls."

"You did save them. We are forever in your debt." He pounded a fist against his heart. "Please, Wind-Dancer. Tell us your name so we know who we are indebted to."

"Maerelith Doone. My friends call me Maeri."

He nodded. "Thank you. After you took care of those marauders, we finished off what was left of them. We kept one alive for questioning. I think you might want to hear what he has to say."

She spared a glance for the man on his knees. He'd been roughed up; blood dripped from his nose and bruises were already appearing on his face. His hands had been tied behind his back. There was something off about him. Something that tugged at the back of her mind. He didn't have the rough-and-ready look of a marauder; didn't seem half-starved and desperate. There was plenty of meat on his bones. She looked around; the dead men were the same. She studied his face again and it struck her.

"I know you."

He said nothing, just watched her with disdainful eyes.

"Where do I know you from?" She searched her memory as she stepped closer, shaking off Kam's protective arm. When it dawned on her, she gasped. "You were there that night. With the Mother Superior."

His expression didn't change.

What was his name? *Horace? Hashim?* It was on the tip of her tongue, that night burned into her brain. That was it. "Hosha."

His eyebrows rose and his jaw dropped. "How do you know my name?"

"I saw you. Rather, I heard you. Talking with Mother Karola. You threatened her. She promised you something."

The others gathered behind her but the man gave no response. Maeri struggled to understand. Why was he here? What was his relationship with Mother Karola? Why did he take the girls from Sebasha? None of it added up. Her brow furrowed and she rolled up the sleeves of her robe.

"I want answers, Hosha," she said. "And you're going to give them to me."

"I can't." He pressed his lips together. "She'll kill me."

"I'll kill you," Maeri pointed out. "Ask yourself how you can make it hurt less."

Hosha searched the faces of everyone there and found no sympathy. "Please. I can't."

Carochel launched herself forward and slapped him across the face, leaving a deep red mark on his cheek. "I begged, too," she snarled. "I begged while you and your friends raped me over and over! You had no mercy for me then and we have none for you now. Answer her questions or I'll show you exactly how you made me feel."

Kam cried out. "They hurt you? All of you?"

Ingren nodded, refusing to meet his gaze.

Vivoria shook her head, clinging to her mother's arm. "They didn't want a redhead. They called me a witch. Said no man would touch me. But they held me down and made me watch what they did to Ingren and Caro."

Maeri felt a rage building inside her, like nothing she'd ever felt before. How could these men have been so cruel? How could they treat anyone so callously? She clenched her fists and bit the inside of her cheek. Twisting the wind with one hand, she leaned in close to Hosha's face and watched as she pulled the air from his lungs. Just enough to leave him gasping and panicked.

"How does it feel to know your life is in someone else's hands?" she asked him. "To know I could do anything I wanted and no one would stop me? I should cut your balls off and make you eat them for what you did to those girls."

Hosha clawed at his throat. He tried to speak but only a wheeze came out.

"What was that?" She released the air and gave him a moment to catch his breath. "You're ready to talk?"

"Yes. I'm sorry. Please…" he gasped, the air wheezing through his throat. "We were just following orders."

Maeri pursed her lips. "I think you'd better start from the beginning."

He coughed, spat blood, and sighed. "How far back should I go?"

"Ten years. What were you doing with Mother Karola?"

"She hired a few of us, more than ten years ago. Mud-dwellers. I can't even remember how long we've worked for her. It seems like forever. She promised us food, clean water, and… supplies of the Aktai orchid."

Maeri leaned back as the others gasped. The Aktai orchid was only grown within the Sisterhood and was forbidden everywhere else because of its powerful hallucinogenic properties. Addicts craved it. Dealers killed for it. And, for years, law agencies had wondered where the supply came from. If Hosha was telling the truth, Mother Karola was far worse than she'd ever imagined. "She supplies you with the orchid?"

"Yes. We get a delivery every six months. It's how we make our living."

"Why would she do that?" She ran a hand over her face. "What do you do in return?"

"We give her the girls."

Wexley lost control of his temper. Bellowing with rage, he grabbed Hosha's throat and squeezed. "Liar! What would a Wind-Dancer want with teenage girls? We all know you were taking them to market, you bastard!"

Maeri blew air through narrowed lips and pulled Wexley back. "Why would she need to steal girls? Any who show an aptitude are sent to her anyway. You're not making much sense, Hosha."

"You must know," he spat. "I saw what you just did. They all showed the signs, too."

The blood drained from her face and a wave of nausea rolled through her body. "*True* Wind-Dancers. You're taking them to Mother Karola. Why? How do you find them?"

Ingren snorted - a close match to her cousin's signature sound. "We're not Wind-Dancers, you fool."

Hosha ignored her, keeping his gaze on Maeri. "Karola told us the old signs to watch out for. We have people in every town. They tell us when and where to strike, who to take."

Maeri folded her arms across her chest. "If you're taking the girls for Mother Karola, why would you dare abuse them the way you have?"

He laughed then, and it sent chills down her spine. "She doesn't care what state they arrive in," he said, "as long as they're alive enough for her to kill herself."

His eyes grew distant. Rolled up until only the whites were visible. A damp patch appeared in the seat of his pants.

"No!" he screamed. "Please! I had no choice!"

His whole body spasmed. Blood poured from eyes, ears, nose, mouth. With a blood-curdling scream, he fell face-first into the dirt, kicked his legs for a moment, and then stilled.

Ingren edged closer. Nudged his body over with her toes. Gave him a solid kick in the balls. "I'm pretty sure he's dead," she said.

Maeri sat down. The others gathered around her, their silence as loud as a crowd of clamouring voices. "I can't believe it."

Kam ran a hand through grimy hair. "I don't think he was lying."

"Neither do I. That's the problem." She straightened her spine. "What killed him?"

"He was calling to someone. Begging them." He shrugged. "I don't know."

"Fuck! We have to move!" She jumped up and grabbed the reins of a dead marauder's horse. "Someone was watching!"

They moved as one, mounting their horses and racing for the line of trees just visible in the distant north. The horses ran with their necks stretched out and their ears back, sensing the panic of their riders. Maeri leaned low over her mount, holding its mane instead of the reins and urging it to go faster. Hooves thundered on the arid ground. Spittle flew from the horses' mouths.

"This way!" she cried, leading the group deep into the trees, forcing the horses to slow in the dense forest.

They kept moving, hoping to make it as far away as possible before night fell. When the setting sun dappled through the canopy of leaves, they found a clearing and set up camp for the night. They picketed the horses near a stream they could drink from. The girls and Lucash collected wood, and Kam started a small fire. Vivoria's parents caught two rabbits and a quail; Maeri foraged for nuts, berries, and edible leaves. Between them, they produced a meagre meal with just enough for everyone to share.

"Are we going to talk about what just happened?" Wexley asked.

Maeri poked the fire with a stick and said nothing; she didn't know what to say.

Zayda leaned forward. "Let me check my understanding here. The Mother Superior of the Sisterhood of Aktai, the oldest, most trusted, most honourable organisation in the world, is arranging the kidnapping of young girls who show signs of being *true* Wind-Dancers so she can... What? Kill them? Why? Not only that, but she just killed that man from a vast distance, knows that we witnessed it, and now we're on the run from everyone and everything we know because she might just kill us, too."

"Yep." Maeri ran her tongue along her teeth. "That about sums it up."

"What are we going to do?"

"Fuck knows."

Kam stood suddenly. "We have to stop her."

"And how do you propose we do that?" Maeri asked, her tone sour. Her whole life, everything she thought she knew, was all a lie.

Vivoria raised a hand. "I don't know about the rest of it, but those men took us because they thought we were *true*. What if we are? What if *you* are? We saw what you did to them. You could teach us. We could find more before she gets to them and you could teach us all. Then maybe we could fight back."

The life she'd thought she'd had was over; Maeri felt it in her bones. But something in Vivoria's words lit the spark of another life, one where she could still do something meaningful. Whatever Mother Karola was doing, she had to be stopped. Who else could do it? She met the gazes of everyone around the campfire. "It won't be easy," she said. "It won't be safe."

Carochel snapped a twig in her hands. "Safe and easy were stolen from us the minute those men took us from Sebasha."

"It won't be quick," she added.

Kam put an arm around his sister and pulled her close. "None of us want this, Maeri. I don't want my sister anywhere near danger after what she's been through. But we're in it all the same and there's no way back. I've no doubt we'd be arrested or killed as soon as we set foot back in Sebasha. As far as we know, we're the only ones who know the truth. The only ones who can possibly stop this from happening to other girls. We have no choice but to try."

"Aye." Several voices chorused their agreement.

Maeri grinned, though she felt no joy. "Well, you'd better hope we all get along. We're going to be spending a lot of time together from now on."

"I can think of worse things," Kam said with a twinkle in his eye.

She blushed, and cursed herself for it. Whatever tomorrow might bring, she knew it wouldn't be boring.

THIRTY-SIX

Maeri waited in the tree until she was sure Vivoria was alone. The young woman had changed in the decade they'd known each other; red hair had deepened to the shade of burning embers, and the lines of her face had grown harder. Nudging the air into a protective border, she lowered herself from the branch and landed on the soft grass.

"Been a while, Viv," she said.

Vivoria gave a half smile, the most she honoured anyone with since her kidnapping. "It's not easy to sneak away from Karola. She watches everyone like a hawk since Benedita defected to you and took a half dozen Wind-Dancers with her."

She couldn't resist the smirk. "That was a good day."

"Not in the Sisterhood, it wasn't." Vivoria shuddered. "It's been awful ever since. Karola would happily dine on your entrails and carry your head around on a pike."

"She's welcome to try. I'd relish the chance to face her one-to-one. I've come a long way in ten years."

"Don't underestimate her, Maeri. There's a darkness in her that runs deep. You don't know what she's capable of."

Maeri sighed. "Fair point. It never ends well if you underestimate your opponent. Didn't I teach you that, once?"

"One of many lessons I've taken to heart." Viv turned her head to the side. "I never expected to be there this long."

"Ah, I'm sorry, Viv. I didn't either. You're making the difference, though. The information you've sent us has saved so many lives. We're close; I can feel it."

"I hope so."

Maeri ran a hand through her hair. How had it been ten years already? After she'd saved the girls from the marauders, they'd lost themselves for a while. Travelled aimlessly. It had taken some time to figure out what she needed to do, but the following months had been a hard lesson in evading Karola's forces and figuring out how to fight back. When Vivoria had suggested she could join the Sisterhood and spy for them, Maeri had been reluctant to put the young girl in harm's way. But Viv made a good point; they had to do everything they could to save other *true* Wind-Dancers.

But how will you hide that you're true? Maeri remembered asking her.

I don't have the mark yet. I can hide the strength of my power. Look, we need someone on the inside. I know you have friends there, but how will you even contact them without a road in? And it has to be me. Ingren and Carochel... we can't do this to them. They need support to recover. I'm the logical choice. Young enough to be taken in, for them to think I'm still malleable. I can do this, Maeri. I have to do this.

"How are you doing, Viv?" she asked now. "Are you okay?"

"It's getting harder. How are my parents?"

"They're good. They miss you. Kellen tells everyone his big sister is a hero."

Vivoria turned away again and sniffed. "And Kam, and Yalexi?"

Warmth spread through Maeri's body as she thought about her husband and daughter. "Kam has found his calling running our home in the forest. He's a mother hen, fussing and keeping everyone safe. Yalexi already shows signs of being *true* so I train with her whenever I can." A pang of guilt pulled at her heart. "She understands Mama has to be away sometimes."

"It's getting harder on us all, isn't it?"

She nodded. "Yes. But we're so close, Viv. I just need to find out where she takes the kidnapped girls. That's the last piece of this, I'm sure."

Light flashed across Vivoria's eyes. "That's why I'm here, Maeri. I think I've found it."

Maeri grabbed her friend's hands. Her heart thundered in her ears. "Where is it?"

Viv handed her a piece of paper with a crude map drawn on it. "I think it's doable. You'll need time to plan, I know, but send word and I'll make sure others are there to witness. It's taken us too long to get to this point, Maer. Who knows what's happened to all the girls she's managed to grab? We need to end it."

"Agreed. At least we've been able to save some, too. You haven't seen how our camp has grown, Viv. We have hundreds of Wind-Dancers now. All of them girls we saved from Karola."

She offered that sad half-smile again. "Maybe one day I'll have the chance to get to know them."

"You will."

"I have to get back. I don't want anyone wondering where I've gone. Give my love to my family."

Maeri hugged the younger woman and then watched her go. Her heart felt heavy. This was not the life she would have chosen for any of them. Was it really worth it? She had to believe it was; otherwise, what were they fighting for? Feeling older than she had only moments before, she called the wind and let it cradle her as she journeyed along its currents. She'd go home, hold her daughter, and plan a rebellion.

As if in protest, her bones creaked and her body ached.

"I'm getting too old for this," she told the wind.

The wind made no response but seemed to hold her tighter until she made it back to the forest north of Berdam two days later. She longed for the comfort of Kam's arms and the sweetness of her daughter's smile. Checking the air-barrier before she neared, she made sure no one had been snooping around in her absence; the wind would tell her if they had.

"Mama!"

Maeri grinned at the freckle-faced child who raced towards her, plaited pigtails swinging as she ran. "Yalexi!" She swung her daughter into the air, soaked up the sweet giggles and beaming smile, and held her close against her heart. "Oh, I've missed you, little one."

"I've missed you too, Mama." Yalexi snuggled her face into Maeri's.

Turning, Maeri saw Kam watching from a few feet away, warmth in his eyes. Her heart fluttered and heat crept up her cheeks. After all this time, how could he still make her weak at the knees? He moved closer, never breaking eye contact. Took her face in his hands. Kissed her with a tenderness that brought tears to her eyes.

Yalexi giggled and tugged on her daddy's hair. "Mama's home," she said.

"How long for?" he asked.

And the heaviness blanketed her once more. "Not long enough."

Kam pulled his girls close. "Then we'll make the most of it."

She gave herself two days to make a plan and one to just be with her family. It wasn't enough; it could never be enough. But she found joy in it all the same. When she studied the map Vivoria had given her, her mind raced with ideas and strategies. She called others to give her advice. Measured distances. Practised different scenarios. And, in the end, went with her gut. In a week, one way or another, it would all be over.

That settled, she pushed it out of her mind and cherished every minute with Kam and Yalexi. They picnicked by a stream, chased each other through long grass, and shared stories by the campfire. Maeri spent some time teaching Yalexi to call the wind, delighting in her daughter's aptitude for it. And when Yalexi fell asleep wrapped in her mother's arms, Maeri held her close and watched the steady rise and fall of her chest.

"She understands, Maeri," Kam said.

Maeri wiped her eyes with the back of her hand. "She shouldn't have to."

"I know. But it's not your fault."

"It feels like it sometimes." She sighed. In all her years of life, in all her many travels, she'd never experienced anything as magical as holding her own child in her arms. "A mother shouldn't have to leave her child, Kam. It's not natural. It's not right."

He moved to sit beside her and threw an arm across her shoulder. "It's not," he agreed. "That's on Karola. Not you. Maeri, you're saving other mothers and daughters. Hundreds of them. Don't you see that?"

"I do. I just..." Her voice trembled. "I have to leave in the morning. All these years and it's finally coming to a head. I have to go. But what if this is the last time I can hold her, Kam? What if she has to lose her mother so that others don't?"

Kam took a deep breath. "Maerelith Doone Maroya, you listen to me now. You are coming home to us. I will not accept anything less. Understand?"

She nodded and rested her head on his shoulder. "I understand, my love. I'll do my best."

The three of them held each other all night but Maeri slept fitfully. She dreamed of Karola's sharp-angled face and a knife sliding between her ribs. She sweated and shook at the thought of leaving her family, never to return. In the morning, when pink light woke her from her nightmare, she gathered her things with trembling hands and a heavy heart. Kam watched her in silence.

Maeri kissed Yalexi's brow, took something from her pocket and wrapped it around her daughter's hands. It was a heart-shaped ruby pendant on a leather strap. "I was saving this for your birthday, little one, but..." Her breath hitched and she paused to calm it. "Always know you have my heart, darling girl. I love you forever."

With a cry, she turned to Kam and buried her face in his chest. He guided her out of the room as sobs wracked her body. Outside, the air cool and the morning fresh with possibility, he lifted her chin with his hand and kissed her firmly.

"I am proud of you, Maeri," he said, his own eyes wet. "Yours is not a life any would have chosen but for ten years you have fought for what is good and right. You have sacrificed so much more than anyone will ever know or understand. You are a hero, my love. Especially to Yalexi and me."

"I'm not a hero." She sniffed as he kissed her tears away.

"You are," he insisted. "To them as well."

She looked up and saw over a hundred women waiting for her, each one of them a Wind-Dancer she had stolen from Karola or trained herself in the past decade. Benedita stood at the front of the group, older now and lined with years, but still ready to fight for her people. Carochel and Ingren waited by her side, along with many other faces she had grown to love. Pride swelled within Maeri's chest. She had come from nothing. An orphan with no home, no roots. A traitor to the Sisterhood that had taken her in. Yet these women believed in her. Believed in everything she stood for. They were ready to fight, and possibly die, for their cause.

Pride, yes. But also responsibility. She was leading them into this fight. How many wouldn't return? Her throat tightened. Her heart thundered in her ears.

Benedita took her hand. "Breathe, Maeri. This fight belongs to all of us. It's our choice. Our duty. We fight with you but not because of you. Let it go now."

"I don't want to lose any of you," she said in ragged gasps. "You've been a mother to me, Benedita. I lost one mother; I don't want to lose another."

"Love can't ever be lost, Maeri. Even after death, love lingers within us. Don't you understand? We're made of it. Every time someone loves us, that love becomes a part of us - another stone in our architecture. There's nothing in this life or the next that can take that away. A mother's love especially. You know that."

She smiled through the tears. "Even so, try to stick around in this life, okay?"

Benedita nodded. "It's time to go now."

"I know."

Gripped with fear, and a deep sense of impending doom, she said goodbye to Kam and led her small army to the edge of their safe haven. One by one, the women called the wind and rose to travel along its currents. Maeri went first and prayed they weren't making a terrible mistake. The wind seemed restless. Uneasy. As if it waited for something.

Protect us today, old friend, she begged as she spun between gusts and swells. *When all is done, carry us safely home.*

The wind held her close.

Time passed in a blur. Day and night melded. She stopped only when she needed to eat or sleep, and never for long.

Her Wind-Dancers would arrive separately, taking different paths to avoid attention, and she needed to be there first. She had started this and she would finish it. When she soared over the moors, a twinge of longing surprised her. Did she really still miss it after all these years? It had been home, she supposed, at a time when she'd both lost and needed one. Pushing the thought aside, she journeyed on until the hills grew steeper and rockier, and the temperature plummeted as precipitously as the shale dropping from the cliffsides.

She lowered herself onto a narrow goat's path and walked the rest of the way up; she didn't know if Karola would have set defences to warn if any Wind-Dancers approached. The air was cold and her breath left silver webs in front of her face, but she hid her pack behind some rocks and proceeded without it. She wouldn't need it where she was going and, if she made it back, the pack would be there waiting.

Checking the map Vivoria had drawn, she recognised the fork in the path ahead and knew she was close. She moved in silence, her eyes and ears peeled for any sign of human life around her. The sound of falling water grew louder as she progressed. When she reached a dead end, she froze. A rock face lay ahead of her. Tall trees grew in front of it and creeping foliage climbed up the stones. A small waterfall cascaded down its left side, pooling in a basin at its foot. She looked at the map again. This was where she was supposed to wait for the others. The place Vivoria had marked as the entrance to the caverns, though not the entrance Karola used. So where was it?

Biting her lip, Maeri edged closer and walked around the basin and along the front of the wall. There was something…

She slipped between dense trees, pulled thick vines away from her face, and caught a glimpse of a narrow gap behind the waterfall.

I make no wonder this entrance is unused.

She looked around. Argued with herself. Wrinkled her nose and sighed. She should wait but wouldn't it be a good idea to check what lay inside? Doubting herself, she grabbed some pebbles and arranged a small pile into an arrow pointing the way into the cavern. If she wasn't back when the others arrived, at least they'd be able to follow her in.

Once inside, she paused to let her eyes adjust to the gloom. The temperature dropped again and she shivered. Something about the enclosed space pressed in on her, an oppressive weight stealing the breath from her lungs. The crashing of the waterfall grew fainter as she moved deeper into the cavern, but dampness was heavy in the air. Long stalactites hung from the ceiling, and elongated stalagmites grew up from the ground; she walked around them, trailing her fingers along the cold formations. She'd seen similar on her travels before but always marvelled at them; how could simple mineral deposits look so majestic?

At the back of the cavern, a dark tunnel led further into the depths of the mountain. She hesitated but something pulled her on. Stepping into the tunnel, she took a piece of chalk from her pocket and marked the wall so the others would be able to follow her path. Darkness enclosed her. A wave of fear washed over her, strong enough to make the hairs on her arms stand up. She inhaled sharply and tried not to cough as a sweet musty scent assaulted her nose and the back of her throat. Her hands shook.

There was something familiar about this place. Something that dragged at her chest and made her feel as if she waded through thick mud. Had she been here before? She walked on, pushing past the strange sense of recognition. Using the chalk to mark her way, she wove around several corners and through narrowing passageways until she had no idea where she was. Still, that odd familiarity pulled her on.

Maeri came to a cavern with two other tunnels leading away from it and walked unerringly to the right. How did she know? Unnerved and a little afraid, she slowed her pace and pressed a hand to the stone. What secrets did these tunnels hide? The sweetness of the air sharpened into a textured, smoky odour. Memory flashed behind her eyelids.

Her feet bled. The stone gouged into them but still, she ran. Mama told her to keep running until she found help.

Maeri gasped. Was the memory real? Had she run through these tunnels as a child? She knew so little of her life before the orphanage. Reluctant now, she walked on and the smokiness increased; something burned.

The smoke stung her eyes. The altar fires burned incessantly; she wasn't allowed to ask what they were burning. When she stumbled into the light, that stung more. Tears tracked down her cheeks. She blinked over and over. Peeked through slitted lids at a bright, hazy world filled with green things growing from the ground and a sky - oh, the sky! Mama had told her about that, once - so vast she felt as though she drowned in it.

Pebbles dug into her knees. When had she fallen? Pain thudded at her temple. The stench of the smoke invaded her air, hanging like a miasma of grating memory and cloying apprehension. What was burning? She had to know! Pushing herself to her feet, she followed the wall deeper into the mountain and prayed she'd make it out again.

Soon, voices carried to her ears. She slowed and moved with caution, peering around every corner before she progressed. Her heart thudded more with each step. She was torn between the panicked urge to run away and the need to find answers to what lay ahead. Hesitating, she stumbled on loose rock and held her breath to see if anyone had heard. When their conversation continued, she sighed. The others had to have arrived by now; surely they would catch up to her soon.

"Please, don't."

The voice startled Maeri. She jumped a little. Froze. Peered through the gloom and saw nothing. When she realised the voice came from around the next corner, where faint flickering lights suggested someone waited, she straightened her shoulder and reached for the hilt of her sword.

"Have mercy!" The voice cried out again, stronger this time. "She's just a child!"

"That's why I'll kill her quicker."

Maeri bit her lip. Her skin crawled at the callousness of that last voice. She glanced back, hoping reinforcements might have arrived, and saw nothing but the gaping blackness of the tunnel she'd just exited.

"No! Please, I'll do anything. Just don't hurt her." Sobs echoed off the walls. A child's frightened wail added to the volume.

A vice gripped Maeri's chest. She closed her eyes and visions danced behind her lids again.

"*I beg of you, let her go.*" Mama had never sounded so scared.

Maeri looked at the face that was her whole world. Eyes of the brightest blue swam with tears. "Mama, I'm scared."

With a defiant roar and inhuman strength, Mama strained against the chains holding her to the wall. Her lips moved and the stone seemed to crumble. She launched herself at the three robed women. Spittle flew from her mouth. Blood flew from their faces as she beat them with all the strength she could muster.

"Run, Maeri! I love you! Run!"

"Mama?"

"Run, my baby. Run until you find help. I love you!"

So she ran, and the anguished screams followed her through the dark tunnels until she hit her head on a low-hanging rock and woke to silence.

"Mama." A small noise escaped Maeri's throat. Around the corner, the woman continued to plead for her child. Past and present merged until Maeri was lost in grief and anger. She should wait for help, she knew. But she imagined being in that woman's place, begging for Yalexi's life. No. She had to do something.

Her sword slid silently from its sheath: a secret; a whisper; a promise. She probed the air so she knew what she could do with her powers. And she turned the corner.

A large cavern greeted her. The stone walls were a deep red-brown, like dried blood, and a small pool of water gathered at the opposite side. She was sickened at the sight of chains hanging from the walls, enough to hold a dozen women. Suspicious marks stained the uneven ground. Focusing on the immediate problem, she held her sword low and pinpointed the source of the voices. Two armed men and one robed woman stood with their backs to her. Before them, a naked woman clutched a small child to her chest; both were wracked with heaving sobs.

Maeri's vision blurred. The woman's face melded with her mother's and she moved without thinking. She didn't call the wind for this; she didn't need to. Her sword danced on its own. She took the woman down first; the white robe spoke of power but her blood spilled the same as everyone else's. Without pause, Maeri turned to the men and thrust her sword into the nearest one's chest. Blood spurted from his mouth as he gaped at the blade piercing his torso. The second man, bald and wiry, grabbed his weapon and charged. Maeri tried to yank her sword free but it was stuck firm between the first man's ribs. Growling her frustration, she ducked the sword aimed at her head, kicked out with her feet and knocked the bald man to the ground. His sword clattered across the stone. In one move, she rolled on top of him and pummelled his face with her fists until only a bloody mess stared back at her. He gurgled once and his eyes glazed in death.

Panting with the exertion, Maeri retrieved her sword with a little wiggle and tug, and cleaned it on the dead woman's white robe. She wiped sweat from her brow. Turned to the mother and child and noticed, for the first time, that the woman was pregnant; her belly curved with a gentle swell.

"Thank you," the woman said, her voice raspy and strained. "Thank you."

Maeri nodded. Noticing the woman's nakedness again, she grimaced. "I'm sorry. I should've saved the robe for you."

The woman spat on the Wind-Dancer's corpse. "I'll never wear a robe like that. I'd rather die."

Maeri arched her brow. "That man's clothes don't have too much blood on them. Will they do?"

"Yes." Taking the child with her, the woman stripped the bald man's clothes and put them on herself. "Who are you?"

"My name's Maeri. You?"

"Donaya. And this is my daughter, Suzyth." She glanced around the cavern, a vein pulsing at her temple. "I just... I know your name but *who are you*? I didn't think anyone knew we were here. I didn't think we'd ever be saved."

Maeri swallowed hard. "How long have you been here?"

"Suzyth was born here," Donaya said. "I've been here since I was a child myself. They took -" She heaved a breath in and let it out with a judder.

Maeri pulled the woman into her arms.

Donaya met her gaze with sorrow marring every feature. "I had three other children here. She killed them all."

As the full horror of what Donaya had experienced hit her, a searing cold blanketed Maeri's body. What was Karola doing here? Why was she keeping *true* Wind-Dancers captive in these caves? What did she gain by killing them? Her resolve hardened. Had this been her mother's fate all those years ago? She locked the thought away and ran a gentle hand over Suzyth's golden curls.

"Follow the marks on the walls," she said to Donaya. "They'll lead you outside. You should come across some other women. Other Wind-Dancers. Like me, not like Karola. They'll keep you safe."

"What about you?"

Maeri tightened her grip on her sword. "I've got a debt to settle," she said. "Are there others here?"

Donaya nodded. "Hundreds. She keeps some of us for years. Breeds us like cattle. And slaughters us like that, too. She has a few women helping her, all in those robes. And lots of men; they have no power, but they like to exert their authority in all the ways you can imagine." Her face darkened. "Karola has them impregnate us. She says everybody wins. We don't count, I guess."

"I'm sorry. I'll save the others if I can." She grabbed Donaya's arm. "When you see the Wind-Dancers, send them my way, please. I think I'll need all the help I can get."

"Aktai be with you, my friend." Donaya placed a hand on her stomach. "If this one is a girl, I'll name her Maeri."

Touched, Maeri blinked to hold the tears at bay. "I hope to see you again."

She watched as Donaya and Suzyth hurried into the tunnel, following the chalk marks she'd left on the walls. When she could no longer see them, she turned back and followed the passage Donaya had indicated, keeping her breathing steady and her sword low. Everything about the network of tunnels and caves bombarded her senses. More memories of her mother, things she hadn't remembered in thirty years, flashed through her mind and grief hit hard. How could she have forgotten? Mama had loved her fiercely. Had died to save her. Maeri's heart ached and her throat constricted. She didn't even know her mother's name.

She moved on, her chalk running low and anticipation building in her bones. She was close; she could feel it. There was a potency in the air, a sense of expectation, of waiting.

Her skin tingled. She hadn't felt the wind stir, not so deep within the belly of the mountain, but she knew the feel of a Wind-Dancer's magic.

At the back of her mind, a voice reminded her she should wait for her friends. But she was too far gone, too lost in the anger, the memories, the blazing need to finish what she'd started ten years before.

Turning a corner, the walls suddenly opened out into a cavernous space, much bigger than the one she'd found Donaya in. Startled, she ducked behind a large group of stalagmites and held her breath, praying she hadn't been noticed. And there were plenty there to notice her. The cavern was filled with white-robed Wind-Dancers, blue sashes cinched around their waists. Naked women hung in chains along the walls, the weight of their torture mapped in searing scars and multi-hued bruises. Maeri took it all in: the flickering torches lighting the space; the army of mud-dwellers gathered in pockets throughout; and the altar in the centre, looking up at the sun shining through a hole in the cave's ceiling.

Sunbeams lit up the haggard face of the woman tied to the altar. She was emaciated, the rise and fall of each breath ragged and pained. Moaning, she pulled at the ropes binding her arms and legs.

The white-robed woman beside her turned in a full circle, arms out to encompass the gathered audience. "You will learn much today, my children."

Maeri leaned forward a little too far and almost fell, catching herself at the last moment. It was Mother Karola! And she didn't look a day older than she had the last time

Maeri had seen her. Forcing herself to think before she acted, Maeri wondered if she'd be able to challenge Karola without having to deal with the numerous Wind-Dancers protecting her. Somehow, she doubted it.

"Watch, learn, and fear me!" Karola bellowed.

Her skin crawling, Maeri peered from behind the stalagmites as Karola placed a dark gem on the woman's stomach and held it there with one hand. The Mother Superior raised her other arm above her head and looked up through the hole in the ceiling. Her lips moved as she called the wind to her bidding and air rushed down into the cavern, swirling around the altar.

The woman screamed and everyone watching recoiled.

As they watched, life drained from the prone woman. Her skin shrivelled and her body shook. She opened her mouth in a silent scream and a faint swirl of black mist drifted out, dancing in the swirling wind before it settled in the dark jewel. Her body jerked. Her heels kicked on the altar. Blood trickled from her nose and ears. With one final, wailing scream, she died.

Bile surged in Maeri's throat and she forced it back before she retched on the cave floor. Several of the white-robed women wept and vomited, though the others offered them no comfort. A miasma of fear filled the cavernous space. Horrified, Maeri saw a few faces in the crowd with gazes fixed on the stone, their bodies leaning closer and their eyes hungry.

Karola lifted the jewel and nestled it into a locket around her neck. A dark wave rolled over her and she closed her eyes, her lips curving in satisfaction. A small moan escaped her throat. When the wave passed, her skin was a little smoother, her eyes brighter. "I cannot describe how good that feels," she said.

A shaky voice called out, "Did you take her power?"

"Oh, yes." Karola flashed her teeth in the semblance of a smile. "Every last drop. Imagine the power I contain now, my children. I've lost count of the souls I've fed upon."

A small woman pushed to the front. Maeri gasped. Estha!

"Why are you telling us this?" Estha demanded. "Why are you doing it? We're supposed to help people. Be a force for good in the world. This is wrong!"

Oh, Estha. Panic filled Maeri's body. It felt so good to see her friend again after so long, but not here. Only danger lay here. She wished Estha had joined Benedita's defection, but understood that the Sisterhood had given Estha a home and family when she had none; how could she leave that? Still, that path had led her here. *Don't make yourself stand out here, Estha, please! Be safe!* She wondered if Lisel and Little Roo were there too.

Karola turned her dark gaze on Estha. "Do you think I care about wrong or right? I am beyond all that and you would do well to remember it." She waved a hand and a dozen armed mud-dwellers stepped closer to Estha. "I'm telling you all about this because I'm offering an opportunity. I've bided my time for centuries."

A gasp rolled through the crowd.

"That's right. Centuries!" Karola sneered. "I've watched countless Wind-Dancers age and die while I've grown stronger and more powerful than you could ever imagine."

"That's not possible," another familiar face, Yima, spoke up. "How could you have been Mother Superior for centuries and nobody realised it?"

"Think, you fool. Can anyone remember who was Mother Superior before me?" She pointed to the oldest person in the cave, a woman so frail she looked to be made of paper. "Do you remember?"

The old woman frowned and shook her head.

"My power has kept you all from thinking about it. The wind has many secrets none of you will ever uncover. A little sliver of it can steal your memories. A whispered command can make it silence your probing thoughts. You are all mine. Your bodies, minds, souls belong to me."

The Wind-Dancers looked around at each other, muffled murmurs spreading amongst them. Some shook their heads or shrugged their shoulders. Others bit their lips. Wrung their hands together. Backed towards the nearest tunnel. And a few stood straighter, half-smiles blooming on their eager faces.

"Who are they?" one of the interested Wind-Dancers asked. "How do you choose whose powers to take?"

Karola grinned again. "Good question. I take the powers of *true* Wind-Dancers." She paused to let her words take effect.

The murmur rose to shouts and gasps.

"But they died out," Yima protested.

"Only because I killed them to near extinction." Karola smirked, her face filled with glee. "They're not all dead. The truth is, *true* Wind-Dancers can be born at any time and into any family. They crop up all the time. But I have men watching for them and, as soon as they show signs of power, I have them brought here. People blame marauders, grieve, and move on. They don't question it beyond that."

"And the women here?"

The Mother Superior shrugged. "I kill them or breed them. Carefully managed, of course, to ensure I have enough to feed my powers but not so many they could rise against me."

"Breed them?" Cries rang out as good people were sickened at the thought.

Karola gestured to the mud-dwellers. "Men have some uses."

Tears streamed from Maeri's eyes as everything clicked into place. Decades of questions, of dark thoughts, of pieces not quite fitting together, had led to this moment of grim discovery. She had been born here. A product of her mother's captivity and rape. A pawn in Karola's sick game. All those lives taken, souls destroyed, children orphaned or killed... All for the sake of one woman's immortality and power? Dear goddess, nothing was worth the price that had been paid.

"You're sick!" Estha exclaimed, her fists clenched. "Vile! How could you do this? Do you think we're going to stand back and allow you to continue?"

Karola lashed out without warning, the wind ready at her command. Knocking Estha to her knees, she held the younger woman's throat in a fist of air and squeezed. "This is where the opportunity comes. I've waited long enough. The Sisterhood of Aktai is over; I'm starting my own sisterhood. I will be honoured. Worshipped! And I think I know enough about you all to have an idea of who will choose to join me and who will die to boost the powers of those at my side."

"No," Estha choked out. "Wind-Dancers are good people. We won't join you. You're wrong."

"Am I?" Karola released her hold on Estha and held an arm out to her left. "Let's see. If any of you would like to join me, take your place. If you'd prefer to die, stay where you are."

At first, there was no movement, and Maeri felt a surge of hope. Her sisters understood it was wrong for one person to hold so much power. Wrong to commit such evil to gain it. She started to rise, certain she'd have an army at her back.

Then Little Roo pushed her way to the front and walked to Karola's side.

No! Roo! Maeri fell back as if she'd been punched in the chest. Images of the little girl who'd followed them around, who'd clung to Maeri's arm when she was scared, flashed in her mind.

"I knew you'd be the first," Karola said with obvious pride. "My protegee."

Roo bowed her head. "Of course, Mother. I owe you everything."

The others moved one by one at first until, in a sudden surge, dozens of women crossed an invisible line and joined Karola. Some strode with glee, others with their head down and their feet slow, fear oozing from every movement. But in the end, only a handful remained on the other side, chins held high and eyes sparking defiance; Estha and Lisel were among them.

Roo took a step towards her oldest friends. "Don't be foolish. Come with me."

"No, Roo." Lisel shook her head. "I couldn't live with myself. Can you?"

"Why are you doing this?" Estha asked. "You know it's wrong, Roo. She's hurting people. Killing them. Maeri was right about her and we should have listened."

Roo met their gazes, hers empty and emotionless. "You've made your choice. So be it."

And the child they'd loved, the woman they'd grown with, reached out her arm, revealing a bracelet with a small black gem on it, just like the one wielded by Mother Karola. Estha and Lisel backed away. They called the wind and started to lift themselves up, but Roo was too fast. With power stronger than it should have been, she knocked Lisel down, pulled Estha back and grabbed her by the throat. Estha kicked and fought. Tried to cajole the wind to help her. But Roo held on until Estha's skin shrivelled and she screamed in pain. The black smoke drifted from her mouth.

"Estha!" Maeri cried, unable to hold back. Diving from her hiding place, she pushed beyond her limits to race to her friend's aid. Their eyes met and Estha's hand reached out. "Estha!"

"Maeri," Estha breathed her name, and in that one breath conveyed her love, her friendship, her allegiance. It was the last word she spoke.

"No!" Maeri screamed again as Estha's body dropped to the floor and Roo shuddered with the boost of power. Fuelled with a burning rage, she kicked at the back of Roo's knees, spun, and kicked her head as she fell. Roo fell face-first beside Estha, dazed but still alive. "What did you do, Roo?" Maeri wept. "What did you do?"

A slow clap reverberated through the cavern. "I was wondering when you'd get here, Maerelith," Karola said. "It's been a while."

Realisation dawned through the overwhelming grief. "You knew I was coming?"

"Of course. Why do you think we're all here? I thought I'd roll out the welcome wagon for such an old friend."

Vivoria! Had Karola killed her? Or had she followed Roo's dark path? Through the haze of loss, Maeri saw a handful of guards drag a prisoner out of a tunnel. Vivoria. They threw her to the ground, where she cowered and refused to look up. Blood stained her white robe and stuck to clumps of her fiery hair. "Let her go."

"Oh, but she's one of my favourite toys," Karola said. "I knew she'd help bring you to me, even if she did so unknowingly."

Maeri trembled. Her world was upended again. A friend dead. A betrayal that shook her to the core. Death waiting for her and many others. A thought surfaced through the murky haze. "You killed my mother."

Karola blinked. Tilted her head. "I've killed a lot of people. Who was your mother?"

Salt in the wound. She had no name to give. Maeri ground her teeth together. "I was born here. My mother died helping me escape."

"Impossible!" The Mother Superior's mouth parted in surprise. "Only one child escaped from here and my men told me she drowned fleeing the caves."

"I guess they lied." *Hit a mark there,* she thought.

Karola waved a hand and Maeri found herself surrounded by mud-dwellers and white-robed Wind-Dancers. Karola stepped closer.

"You remember," Maeri said. "I can see it in your face."

"She was in chains, but she still took out half a dozen of my men and another Wind-Dancer." Grudging respect tinged her tone. "She had a child. A girl. Begged for her life. I walked away. A half hour later, the child was gone."

"What did you do?"

"What did I do?" Surprise flashed across her features. "I killed her."

She'd known it already, but the words still stung.

Lost in the memory, Karola smiled. "I took her power. The strongest I've ever tasted. Sabrielle."

"What?"

"Her name was Sabrielle." Karola knitted her brow. "You're her daughter? I need to have words with those men. You should never have been allowed to escape. It explains a lot, though."

"Sabrielle." Maeri soaked it in. Her mother was Sabrielle. And she'd loved her.

"I knew it was a mistake breeding her. She was powerful but it would have been safer to kill her and have done with it. I'll not make the same mistake with you and your rescued dogs."

In the corner of her eye, Maeri saw Lisel cradling Estha's head in her lap. "I'm not a child anymore, Karola. You won't find it easy to kill me."

Karola's lips twisted into a smirk. "And, *true* or not, you won't find it easy to use your magic in a place with no wind."

"You have no idea, do you?" Maeri said with a cold laugh. "No idea what it means to be *true*. Every scrap of power you have is stolen. It fights your control with every use. I don't *need* the wind, Karola. I *make* the wind."

She raised her sword at the same time as she pulled air down through the hole in the cave ceiling. Karola countered, calling the wind to herself. A wall of air hung between them as they fought for control. All around them, the other Wind-Dancers battled with each other, and with the mud-dwellers armed with swords and axes. Maeri's heart sank; they were vastly outnumbered.

Dread blanketed her as she focused on maintaining her concentration. The sounds of fighting pulled at her soul but she kept her gaze fixed on Karola's dark eyes.

Feet thundered on stone. Defiant roars reverberated off the cave walls. And Maeri's Wind-Dancers rushed from the chalk-marked tunnel into the fray. They took the others by surprise and used every dirty trick Maeri had taught them to whittle enemy numbers down while they had them at a disadvantage. Pride surged. She beamed at Karola.

"She didn't say you had that many," Karola snarled and glanced at Vivoria, who'd struggled to her feet and stolen a mud-dweller's sword.

Maeri shrugged. "You're not the only one who can keep secrets."

The cavern filled with stolen gusts of air, the ragged gasps of those whose breath was taken away, and the frenzied clash of steel on steel. Maeri struggled with Karola, both of them pushing against the wall of wind thrown up between them; when it was released, the impact would kill whoever it hit first. Trying to break the stalemate, Maeri changed the direction of the force and thrust the wind back up through the hole; caught in the gust, Karola's followed the same path. Maeri raised her sword and rushed at Karola, using the distraction to her advantage. Unprepared, Karola drew her sword and blocked the assault with a clumsy swing of her own; the force knocked her back several steps. The Mother Superior pulled on the wind, throwing sharp gusts out to make Maeri stumble and struggle, but Maeri focused her aggression into a narrow point and kept pushing forward, hacking and thrusting with every scrappy sword-fighting technique she'd learned during ten years on the run.

When her sword pierced the soft flesh of Karola's abdomen, they were both as startled as each other.

"No," Karola whispered as blood trickled around the blade.

Pulling the sword free, Maeri raised her arms to land a final, fatal blow, only to be blocked by Little Roo with a whip of wind and the edge of her own blade.

"Roo!" Maeri hissed, watching with frustration as Karola stumbled back out of her reach.

"I won't let you kill her."

"How could you, Roo?" Maeri asked, swinging her sword to test the younger woman's reflexes.

Roo blocked and tried to call the wind but failed; too many were trying to use it. "I want to live," she said. "Karola taught me how to make sure I do."

"By killing your friends?" She struck. One, two, three.

Roo parried. "Estha made her choice. Looks like you've made yours, too."

Maeri studied Roo. She'd changed. The softness of her face was replaced with sharp lines and angles. The friendly warmth that had always been in her eyes had faded to a cold emptiness. Where had her friend gone? "As have you, Roo. You've been a sister to me my whole life. I don't want to kill you."

"Then don't."

Roo lunged again. Maeri easily danced out of her reach and flicked her sword to cut a gash in her friend's shoulder.

"Fuck you!" Roo said. "You've always been such a show-off, Maeri. But I'm stronger now."

Insight cleared the haze in her mind. Roo had killed before; she was sure of it. "How long and how many?"

"What?" Roo blinked. The distraction cost her as Maeri twisted her blade past Roo's defences and cut the sash from her waist.

"How long have you been killing for Karola? How many *true* Wind-Dancers have you killed?"

Light on her feet, Little Roo skipped to the side and nicked Maeri's thigh with her blade. "Oh. Years." She smirked. "It started before you went into hiding. And how many? I've lost count."

Sorrow. Anger. Grief. Hatred. A maelstrom of emotions hit like a barrage of fists. Roo took the opportunity to knock Maeri's sword from her hands and laughed as she pointed her own blade at Maeri's throat.

"You always underestimated me, Maeri."

"No." She shook her head. "I loved you. Until today. I don't know what happened to you, Little Roo. You're a monster."

Her face dropped for a second, revealing the lost little girl behind, the orphan who'd always longed for a mother.

"We were your family, Roo. Me. Lisel. Estha. And you killed her."

The mask went back up. "I'll kill you, too."

Driven by pain and desperation, Maeri pulled on all the air she could reach. Moulded it into a fist. And thrust it through Roo's chest.

The gaping wound left a hole through to the other side. Blood splattered everyone in a five-foot radius. For a brief moment, Roo met Maeri's eyes. Confusion. Disbelief. Sorrow. All flitted across her features before her face relaxed and her dead body fell to the ground, finally at peace.

Maeri vomited. Wailed in grief. She'd loved Roo. She'd *killed* Roo. How could she live with that? Hearing an unnatural groan, she turned back to the corpse and cursed.

Karola, clutching the wound on her stomach, fell next to Roo's body and pressed the dark jewel against it.

"Get away from her!" Maeri shouted.

But she was too late. Freshly dead, the magic coursed from Roo's body into Karola's and the Mother Superior's flesh healed in an instant as she soaked the power in. She wasted no time in getting back to her feet and attacking those around her.

Maeri recoiled from the slew of dead bodies littering the cave floor. Many were white-robed, but just as many wore stained tunics and well-worn boots. Her friends held their own against the other Wind-Dancers and the mud-dwellers; she'd trained them well. But Mother Karola was a force of nature, lashing out with immense power and leaving only death and devastation in her wake. She had to do something!

Forcing her way to Vivoria, she dispatched the redhead's opponents and said, "Take a couple of others and free the other *true* Wind-Dancers. They might be able to help us."

Vivoria nodded. "Stay safe."

Trusting her to get the job done, Maeri turned back to the melee. Karola had worked her way back to the altar, leaving a trail of bodies behind her. Surrounded by smaller pockets of fighting, she faced off against four women Maeri knew well: Benedita, Lisel, Ingren, and Carochel. The four fanned out around the Mother Superior, combining their magic to try to hold her at bay. But it wasn't enough. Maeri raced to them, praying she'd make it in time, but Karola forced her power through the barrier and sucked the air around her. Benedita and the others gasped for breath, fighting to move forward and kill the old witch.

Maeri knew they weren't strong enough. Karola had been hoarding her power for too long. Was so steeped in evil, she believed herself invincible.

Laughing with glee, the Mother Superior reached the closest woman and pressed the dark gem to her head. Carochel jerked. Gagged. Shriveled into a shell of her former self. The others tried to reach her. Benedita crawled along the ground, slowing with each second she fought for breath. But she was too late; they all were.

"Damn you, Karola!" Maeri bellowed.

Drunk on power, Karola climbed on top of the altar and reached her arms up above her head. She clenched her fists and pulled air into the cavern so fast it was like a whirlwind, the roar vibrating through the room and throwing Wind-Dancers away from each other. The wind spread, knocking people off their feet, leaving them gasping for breath. Several passed out.

Leaning into the gale, Maeri tried to pull some of the wind behind her to help push her forward; she had to reach Karola before anyone else died! A strong gust knocked the sword from her hand and sent it flying across the cavern. With no weapon, no control of the magic in the cave, and no plan in mind, she still fought against the bitter wind.

What could she use? What could she get to? She looked around. Fallen weapons lay beside fallen bodies, but they were too far to reach. Her pockets were empty. She brushed her shoes against the ground, hoping to find a loose rock, but even they had been blown away by Karola's gale.

Benedita and the others were close to death. All around, Maeri's friends lay dead or dying on the cold stone floor, fighting against a power they had no hope of defeating. It would be so easy to give in. To relax into the wind and let it end everything.

But her mother's face filled her mind, proud and fierce; she hadn't given in. Yalexi followed, her eyes pleading: *Come home, Mama.* Maeri sobbed. There had to be something she could fight with!

The shoe!

The beginnings of an idea formed. Karola was keeping everything away, making sure no weapon could touch her.

But maybe she wouldn't notice something a little smaller, a little less obvious. It was worth a try.

With Karola's attention elsewhere, Maeri slipped one shoe off her foot and held it in front of her. How could she get it past the wind?

Of course! Karola controlled the wind but had no affinity for it. Maeri loved it, became a part of it, danced with it like an old friend; it would aid her if she only asked. Channelling the little strength she had left, she whispered to the air pounding her face. The gale hitched, as if taking a sudden breath, and curved around her to caress her cheeks on its way past instead of trying to blow straight through her. She kept whispering. Slowly, the air manoeuvred itself until a gap appeared, a break in the wind, clearing space in a long line from Karola to Maeri. Caught in the toxic rush of power and destruction, Karola didn't notice; her eyes were closed and her mouth curved in a euphoric smile.

Maeri narrowed her eyes, judging the distance and the gap. Recalling the moment she'd arrived at the Sisterhood all those years ago, she pulled back her arm, took aim, and threw the shoe in a direct line towards the woman who'd been at the heart of every problem in Maeri's life.

The heel of the shoe hit Karola's forehead with a satisfying thump. Eyes rolling back in her head, the Mother Superior stumbled forward and fell from the altar, landing on her hands and knees. The wind dropped so fast, the sudden lack of sound was deafening. Fighting resumed. Benedita and the others took deep, gasping breaths to ease their burning lungs. And Maeri rushed to Mother Karola's side.

Dazed and confused, Karola lifted a hand to the angry red mark on her head. Maeri wished for a sword and started to look for one when she noticed small tendrils of air weaving in and out of Karola's body. Had she seen those before? She didn't think so. Glancing around, she saw fainter ones, and significantly fewer of them, floating around the other Wind-Dancers. Maybe it had something to do with so many Wind-Dancers being gathered together, so much power concentrated in one space, and the impossible potency of Karola's stolen magic. Intrigued and wary, Maeri edged closer. She sensed the magic oozing from each pale thread. Curiosity drove her to tug at one of them and she flinched when it wove around her arm and sank beneath her skin. Had she just taken some of Karola's power? She took another, and another until her body tingled and her hair started to float off her shoulders.

Feeling the loss, Karola shuddered and looked up at Maeri. "What are you doing?"

Maeri opened her palms towards the Mother Superior's body and the threads rushed to her as if they longed to be free of Karola.

"No!" Karola snarled and jumped to her feet. "It's not possible!"

She tore the locket from her chest and pulled the dark jewel out of it. Holding it against her skin boosted her power. Standing straighter, she sucked the air from Maeri's body with a suddenness that buckled her knees.

Muscle memory directed Maeri's arm and she landed a strong right hook on Karola's jaw. The older woman stumbled back before righting herself.

"Damn you!" Karola pressed the stone against Maeri's chest. "I'll take it all back and more. You'll be nothing more than a shrivelled husk, just like your mother!"

Stars danced before her eyes. Her lungs burned. The sounds of fighting were muffled. *What's the point in fighting? She's too strong. Too powerful.* Thoughts pummelled her. The loss of her mother. Marauders taking young girls. Blood on her hands when she'd killed Roo. Was everything darkness? Maybe the stain of evil ran too deep within humans. Even her own good intentions had led to death and pain.

Karola's face was all she saw now. The gleaming eyes. Teeth bared in a smirking grimace.

She closed her eyes. Would that be the last thing Yalexi saw, too?

"Maeri!" Benedita's voice cut through the fog. "Fight, Maeri! Please!"

Her mother's voice all those years ago. *I love you.*

Kam's words before she left. *You are coming home to us. I will not accept anything less.*

Yalexi's arms wrapped around her neck, love in every word, every gesture. *Mama!*

Maeri's womb clenched. Her heart thundered. Eyes opened.

She threw her arms wide and called the wind, begging it to help her draw Karola's power inside herself. It came to her, sucking each thread to her chest. The magic swam towards her, straining to be free of the woman who'd stolen it, who'd stolen so many lives.

Karola fought like a demon, her arms moving frantically as she tried to pull it all back. In the chaos, the black stone fell to the ground. But Maeri saw it. As the last of the threads danced beneath Maeri's skin, she lifted her foot, the one still wearing a shoe, and stamped hard.

The jewel broke to pieces beneath her heel. She stamped again, grinding it into the stone beneath.

Karola screeched and clawed at Maeri's skin, gouging deep gashes into her flesh. "No! Come back!"

Maeri stepped back, the power tingling through her body. A strange detachment blanketed her as she watched Karola wither and shrivel, her skin drying and wrinkling and falling in soft folds from her body. Her eyes bulged and bones protruded. Dark tendrils drifted from her, sinking into the crushed pieces of the jewel. With one final scream, her entire being disintegrated into dust as the stolen centuries caught up with her.

Maeri kicked the dust and the broken gem aside, not caring where the shattered pieces landed, not seeing the figure who gathered them all up in the folds of her robe.

Exhausted beyond measure, Maeri sat down, leaned her back against the side of the altar, and let sleep take her.

FORTY-SIX

The statue in the centre of the orchid garden of the Sisterhood of Aktai gleamed in the midday sun. A group of enterprising young novices had taken it upon themselves to clean it. Maeri had to praise them, but she'd been more than happy with the marbled replica of herself being hidden beneath a few years of dirt. When she'd taken over leadership of the Sisterhood, the Wind-Dancers had surprised her with it. Said she was a hero.

She scoffed. Then and now. She wasn't a hero. She'd done what she had to do and lived with the consequences of it. Little Roo's face had plagued her nightmares for the past decade.

Turning from the statue, she smiled at the three children tending flowers with Kam by their side. He was older now; they both were. Grey kissed his temples and new lines mapped his face. Even so, the butterflies still fluttered in her stomach and his smile still made her weak at the knees. Yalexi was almost grown now, a powerful Wind-Dancer in her own right, and filled with a courage that amazed Maeri every day. Beside her, eight-year-old Sabrielle and six-year-old Estha watched everything she did; they'd idolised her from the second they were born.

Ah, her world was filled with love, and every day she wondered if she deserved it. Darkness had been her focus for so long, it was hard to accept the peace and comfort of a normal life. But she soaked it all in like morning sunshine, bringing the light back to her heart.

Ten years had brought many changes. *True* Wind-Dancers had returned in abundance. The marauders and mud-dwellers had, somewhat reluctantly, been reintegrated into society and the world had opened up again. No more isolated towns afraid to venture onto the road. Trade flourished. Ideas were shared. Neighbouring villages extended friendship and aid.

Of course, bad things still happened. People were still people, after all. Bad choices were made. Mistakes happened.

But, together, they strove to rise above it. To breathe through anger and frustration, and let the breeze take it away. To rise above it all and dance with the wind.

The Sleeping God

Sabine's feet stung as though stabbed by a thousand needles with each step.

How long had she been climbing? It seemed a lifetime had passed since she'd left the world burning at the foot of this godforsaken mountain. Her mind flashed to Ezran; he'd sent her alone, insisting he had to stay to help. Would she ever see him again?

A tear escaped and froze on her cheek. The cold was like nothing she'd felt before, bitter and biting. At her back, her sleeping babe remained silent, wrapped in layers of blankets and secured in a soft sling. Sabine prayed they would survive the journey.

She looked up. The snow-topped peak of Mount Manotse towered above the clouds like an angry god, the white blanket a gleaming halo in the high midday sun. There was nothing inviting about it, nothing to reassure her there would be a safe haven when she reached the summit. Ezran had been convinced this was the only path to salvation. Sabine wasn't so sure. It was fine for him to believe in a sleeping god when it didn't matter, but if Girathos was real, where was he? Where was their god when they needed him?

Still, he was their last hope.

With a heavy sigh, she took the next step, forcing her feet to move through the thick snow. Each step was a slog, her boots sinking deeper the higher she climbed. She wondered whether it would be worse to die in fire or ice.

"Keep moving, Sabine," she whispered.

The howling wind stole her words, swirling them around the craggy mountainside and burying them deep inside snowbanks and overhanging cornices. She ploughed on. Going back meant certain death; at least Manotse's peak offered an uncertain one.

As she shivered in her tent after dark, clutching baby Runa close to her chest, Sabine was grateful Manotse wasn't one of the higher mountains Sterland was famed for. Why a god would choose to live atop a peak of smaller stature she didn't know, and couldn't begin to guess. Who knew why gods did the things they did? If she were all-powerful, she'd live somewhere that touched the clouds, or kissed the ocean: somewhere she'd see beauty and magic every day. But then, if she were a god, she wouldn't abandon her people for countless centuries.

Anger kept her warm that night. Seething bitterness stirred her blood as she cradled her child close and fell asleep to the lullaby of the blizzard singing outside her tent.

***

A week.

That's how long it took Sabine to climb to the top.

A week of bone-deep cold, of fear burning in her gut, of desperation pushing her on. More than once, she came close to giving in, to sinking down into the soft snow and snuggling into the sweet serenity of sleep, her daughter safe in her arms. Oblivion grew more appealing the higher she climbed.

But Runa whimpered, or cried, or gurgled in her sleep, and Sabine knew she could not quit.

Even though Ezran was likely dead by now, along with everyone she loved. Everyone she knew.

Maybe everyone.

Was she the last one left alive? The thought plagued her. Ate at her soul. What she'd left behind… How could anyone survive that? It was nightmarish. Awful and agonising. It was the end of days.

Her heart hitched. She forced the thought away. Kept her head down and watched her feet defeat the mountain one step at a time.

When her toes bumped against a marble pillar, it took her a moment to realise she'd made it.

The snow fell thick and heavy at Manotse's peak. It danced through the air, fast and free, like swarming locusts searching for food. Sabine tasted it. Inhaled it. Choked on the clawing cold flakes assaulting her face. At her back, Runa wailed, the sound difficult to distinguish from the weeping of the wind.

She reached a hand out. Lost sight of it mere inches from her face. And gasped with relief when her fingers rubbed across smooth marble. She'd made it. Girathos' Temple lay before her, a pearlescent paradise hidden behind white mist and swirling snow. Inching through the blizzard, she kept her hand on the stone and followed it until she found a door set back in the wall. She pulled on the handle; it opened with surprising ease and she stumbled inside, inhaling sharply at the sudden change in temperature.

A wall of heat hit her like a fist. She slammed the door shut behind her and paused to remove several layers of clothing from both herself and Runa. The baby gurgled and smiled, stretching her arms out as soon as she was free of the sling.

"We made it, Runa," Sabine cooed, pressing kisses to her daughter's nose. "It's real."

She basked in the heat as her eyes travelled the open space. A large part of her had believed she'd never find the temple, that it was nothing more than a tale spun by fanciful storytellers beside a warm hearth. But here she was, footsteps echoing on hard marble, awed by the play of torchlight over nacreous walls.

She paused. "Why are the torches lit?"

Was someone there? Clutching Runa tighter, she edged around the room, searching for signs of life. If the stories were real, no one had stepped foot inside Girathos' Temple for centuries. There was no reason for the torches to be lit, no logical explanation for why they were.

"Hello?" she called out and her own voice echoed back.

Satisfied that the rest of the room was empty, she turned to the large dais at the back. The platform was several steps above the floor and half as wide as the temple itself. Sabine lifted a foot onto the bottom step and then pulled back; both sides of the stairs were lined with treasure. Blood-red rubies lay with polished diamonds and sapphires brighter than the summer sky. Gold chains and gleaming diadems sat regally beside piles of coins in every shade of metal. Sabine took a closer look at the coins; she recognised them from books on ancient history she'd studied as a child. Who had left such riches in an abandoned temple? The token she'd brought paled in comparison; had she wasted her time?

She exhaled. Hugged her daughter close. Straightened her shoulders and climbed to the top of the dais. In the centre, a stone altar dominated the space. It was covered with a red cloth and surrounded by bouquets of fresh flowers, roses and freesias and lilies blooming as if they were planted in fertile soil in the lowlands rather than sitting in vases at the top of Mount Manotse.

Sabine narrowed her eyes. "This is ridiculous." She looked at her baby. "Am I hallucinating?"

Runa looked back with blueberry eyes and reached out to tug on her mother's nose.

"We're here now," she muttered, "even if here is only in my mind. Might as well give it a shot."

She inched closer. Took in the stony statue reclining atop the altar. Girathos was handsome, at least when cast in marble, she thought. Or maybe the sculptor had just had a good imagination. Who knew what a god might actually look like? Would he really have such a long nose, such sharp angles to his cheekbones?

Ezran's face flashed into her mind again; the corners of her mouth turned up at the same time as tears rolled down her cheeks. Her husband had a kind face; she'd fallen in love with the gentleness of his smile, the warmth of his eyes. But he'd made her promise to use the token wisely. Kissed her fiercely, vowed his undying love, even as he'd said goodbye.

With one hand, she reached into the pouch at her waist and took out a small brown bag. She placed it on the statue's chest and stepped back.

Sabine knelt on the cold floor, cradling Runa in one arm and reaching to the top of the altar with the other. Her fingers found the cold stone hand of Girathos' statue and she gripped it like a vice. Her chest tightened.

"Great Girathos," she began. A voice at the back of her mind told her she was being a fool; she shoved it away, too tired to care. When there was nothing left to try, the impossible was worth a shot. "Great Girathos, please hear me. I supplicate myself before you. Bring a priceless offering to appease you. I beg of you: we need your help. Your people need your help. Please, my god. Please wake up."

Silence. Heavy as the sky. She waited. Waited some more. The stillness taunted her. Rubbed salt in every wound. Was it all for nothing?

She screamed, and the sound reverberated through the room, casting a thousand screams back at her.

Runa cried. Weeping now, Sabine cradled her child against her chest and hummed a soft lullaby: the same lullaby Sabine's mother had once sung to her, and her mother to her, for countless generations. She tasted the salt of her tears as she sang. One more treasure that would be lost to the flood, the flames, the falling stars.

Would there be anything after? Some other existence where she could hold her child and soothe her with a song?

Her breath hitched. She fought to hold the sobs at bay.

"I'm so sorry," she whispered against her daughter's fine gold hair. "I'm so sorry I can't save you. My baby. My baby. I love you. I love you, sweet girl. I love you."

The dam broke in her chest and she wailed at the cold marble, the cold world, the cold god ignoring her pleas.

"You are no god!" she snarled at the statue. Snatched back the pouch, though it would do her no good in this life. "You bastard! What kind of god are you that you ignore your people when they cry for your help? I hope you are dead and burning in hell, like the hell you have condemned us to!"

Broken and spent, she sat with her back against the altar. She opened the front of her dress and helped Runa latch on to her breast. Runa watched her with deep blueberry eyes as she nursed, small hands kneading as she made low growling noises in the back of her throat. Sabine let herself sink into the familiar comfort, the immeasurable bond, and love surged like a tsunami.

In the end, at least they were together.

***

When Sabine heard stone grinding and small rocks tumbling to the ground, she closed her eyes then forced them open again and stared at her daughter's perfect sleeping face. The sleeping god was nothing more than a story. The earth was breaking, even atop Mount Manotse; death's fingers reached ever closer. It was time, and she would spend her last moments looking at love.

Something moved behind her. The noise reverberated through the temple and she braced for blocks of marble falling from above. But nothing came. After a moment, she relaxed her muscles and dared to lift her head.

"You make a lot of noise."

Sabine screamed, Runa wailed, and the echoes screeched from wall to wall until the no-longer-sleeping god winced.

"Is that really necessary?"

"You..." Sabine swallowed the fear in her throat. "You're... Oh my..."

"God? Yes." He yawned and stretched as the last of the stone veneer sloughed from his skin. "And you'd better have a very good reason for disturbing me."

She backed up. Swallowed the sharp words on the tip of her tongue. He was tall, handsome, with defined muscles and broad shoulders, but all of that was to be expected of a god. What was unexpected was the glazed look in his eyes and the mild slur of his speech. Sabine tightened her jaw.

"Are you intoxicated?"

Girathos shrugged. "Not nearly enough, my dear. Did you bring wine?"

Air hissed through her teeth as she inhaled sharply. "Do you have any idea what's going on in the world while you're sleeping centuries away in a drunken stupor?"

That infuriating shrug again. "World's managed perfectly fine without me before and I'm sure it will again. Wine? Or maybe trevezion powder? I'll accept honeyed loqaia in a pinch."

Sabine's blood boiled. She rose to her full height, fury making her forget who she spoke to, and pinned Girathos with her gaze as she cradled Runa to her shoulder. "You are indeed the god of revelry and idleness! Are the old stories true then? Of drunken orgies and wild frivolity? Of glutting yourself on fatted boars and rich honey cakes while the masses starved? Of year-long slumbers that seeped into mortal blood and caused whole villages to miss their harvest or sleep through months of their lives?"

"Probably." He pursed his lips. "Most likely, in fact. Ah, those were the good old days."

The pouch left her hand before she knew what she was doing. Her aim was true and it struck Girathos squarely between his eyes, then bounced back and fell to the floor with a heavy clang. The god looked from the pouch to Sabine and back again, his eyes narrowed and one hand clenched into a fist.

For a long moment, she could hear her heart beating.

Then Runa giggled.

Girathos sighed. Shook his head. Reached into thin air and pulled out a large bottle of golden liquid. He took a long swig. Then another. "I'm sensing some anger in you."

"You-"

He cut her off. Bent down to pick up the pouch, and emptied the contents into his hand. His brow arched. "I know what this is."

"I know it's not enough." The fight left her and her shoulders slumped. "But it's everything we had."

"No." Girathos looked down at the white orb resting in his palm. He dropped the pouch and ran his other hand over the top of the jewel. When he removed his hand, the orb glowed with the light of a thousand torches, its brightness muted only by the cupped barrier of his fingers.

Sabine gasped. "How did you do that?"

"Do you not know what you brought me?"

She shook her head. "It's the jewel from the king's sceptre. When the castle fell, Ezran took it to bring to you. He hoped it would be enough to trade for your help. I don't know why he had such faith in you."

"This is more than just a jewel, my dear." Girathos tilted one side of his mouth into a definite smirk. "This is a fallen star. One of the Bright Ones. Lost so long ago that even my memory does not remember their tale. Do you know how much power this holds?"

"No." She sniffed. Pushed the hair back from her brow with one hand. Met his gaze again. "Is it enough to save the world?"

***

Sabine soon learned that Girathos had an uncanny knack for steering a conversation away from unpleasant topics. When she spoke about the world beneath the mountain, he offered her wine and reminisced about a woman he'd liaised with in Lower Ibalt. She waved an arm in the air to demonstrate the rocks falling from the sky and he clicked his fingers to recreate a kingly feast he'd enjoyed with his acolytes several centuries before. At her mention of wars and murders and societal collapse, Girathos sang a bawdy sea shanty he'd learned from a notorious pirate.

Frustration fizzled in her throat until her anger erupted like the volcano that had threatened her cousin's village the year before. She grabbed the front of his shirt in one tight fist and shook him into silence. "Is it any wonder humans act like idiots when their god is no better? Listen to me, you bloody incompetent fool! The world is dying. People are dying. If you want anyone left to worship you, do something instead of sleeping through the end of everything. I see laziness, selfishness, ignorance, and sheer stupid bloody-mindedness in the people around me. Human flaws! How can we be any better when you, our god, embody all those failings? Do something. Please!"

Girathos dropped his shoulders and let his gaze drift to the left. "Human flaws. Yes. You're right, of course. But, you see, it's easier."

"Easier?"

"Easier to push all the bad things out of your mind." He waved his hand and two cosy chairs appeared around a low table filled with fresh fruit and goblets of wine, with a flickering candle set in the centre. He sat in one chair. Tapped the other for her to join him. "Easier to sink into pleasure, into sleep, into nothingness, than to face the reality that some things are too broken to fix."

Sabine puffed air into her cheeks and blew it out slowly. She sank into the empty chair and rearranged Runa to sleep comfortably in her left arm. All that way. She'd climbed a fucking mountain with an infant. Left the world burning at its foot. Said goodbye to her husband through a wall of flames. All that just to find a depressed god.

She popped a grape in her mouth. Chewed. Poured herself some wine and took a long drink.

"This is the quietest you've been since you arrived here and disturbed my sleep," Girathos said.

She looked at him. "It wasn't easy for me to get here. To leave my loved ones behind, knowing they could be dead before I found you. If I ever did. It wasn't easy for me to place my faith in a god I wasn't sure even existed."

"You weren't sure I existed?" He sipped his wine. Rolled it around his tongue. "How long have I been asleep?"

"Nobody knows really. Several centuries, at least. There's some debate over whether the stories are truth or fiction."

"Maybe that's for the best." He shrugged. "Maybe it's only right that I should fade into the realm of stories. I did little good worth remembering here."

She slammed her drink down a little harder than she intended, splashing water onto the table. "Maybe now is your chance to do something worth writing a story about."

"Why?"

Sabine blinked. "Why? Because people are dying. The world is dying. Floods have taken half the land, even though there's not enough water left to drink; fires ravage the rest. Great rocks are falling from the sky, leaving craters larger than this mountain. Men are warring with each other over silly spats: this land is mine; you looked at my wife; your grandfather insulted my great-aunt fifty years ago. Need I go on? Everything is falling apart!"

"And what out of any of that is worth saving?" He met her gaze. Forced her to hold it. "Why should I intervene to rescue a species so inherently destructive? Surely the world would be better off without them?"

"I..." She swallowed hard. Thought about the evil she'd seen. Was he right? Were they unworthy of being saved? No. "You're wrong. You're not seeing the full picture. Yes, there is darkness in humanity, but there is also light. Love. Kindness. Compassion. I know it's gone wrong somewhere along the way, but all that goodness is still there beneath the grime."

"That's an awful lot of grime, my dear."

With another wave of his hand, he cleared the table and placed the fallen star in the centre of it. He held both palms over the glowing orb, closed his eyes, and shuddered as he inhaled a tiny sliver of its essence.

"It's been so long." He sniffed and his pupils narrowed to pinpoints.

Sabine tucked her sleeping child closer into her chest and shuffled to the edge of her seat.

"I may be able to prove my point." Girathos leaned over the star again, and then sat back as the white aura pulsed and grew. Tiny pinpricks of light danced like fireflies within the glow, spreading through the air in front of Sabine and the god, until they coalesced to create a single clear image.

"My home!" Sabine reached for the image. Pulled her hand back. "When is this? It can't be now; the flames reached that part of town a week before I left."

"It's an image from last year. Watch."

She did just that. Watched as the image focused on a frail old man walking with a stick. "Ezran carved that for old Gilbur. He was so happy with it, but we haven't seen him in months."

"Watch," he repeated.

A young man rounded the corner in the image. Tipped his hat and offered to help Gilbur across the cobbles. "That's my neighbour's son, Dex. He's a good - Oh!"

She recoiled as the image filled with blood. Dex rained heavy fists upon poor Gilbur until the old man collapsed to the ground. Dex's face twisted into something almost unrecognisable; this was not the lad she knew. Screams and grunts of pain only widened his smile. There was a cruelness in the shine of his eyes, a nastiness she'd never seen before. Once Gilbur was dead, Dex rummaged through his pockets and took his coin purse. Then, he dragged the body through back alleys to the lake, weighted it down with rocks, and rolled it into the deepest part of the water.

Sabine retched. "This… This isn't real. Why did you make it show that?"

Girathos laughed, but there was no humour in the sound. "I'm afraid it's very real, my dear. Humans are so good at lying. Experts, really, at painting over the darkness with pretty words and a charming smile. Beneath it, their souls are bitter and depraved."

"That's why we haven't seen Gilbur… Ezran went out looking for him." She looked at the now-faded image of Dex smirking beside the lake and wiped the wetness from her cheeks. "How could he do that?"

"Bitter and depraved." Girathos shrugged.

"Not everyone." Sabine straightened her spine. "Please. You need to see what's happening now. See how hard people are fighting to save each other."

He finished his goblet of wine. Went to pour more. Reconsidered and drank from the bottle instead. "I'll look. But only because you threw a star at me."

Raising a hand to the glowing star again, he exhaled slowly before leaning back. The image above the orb swirled and danced, rearranging the incandescent flickers of light into a crystal-clear picture of a small town in a valley below a sleeping volcano. As they watched, the ground began to shake. Small tremors at first, followed by a larger quake that shook the town like the hand of god scolding recalcitrant children. Suitably chastised, the townsfolk crept from their homes and worked together to clear up the mess of fallen buildings and broken bodies.

"See how they help each other," Sabine said.

She fell silent again as pumice rain fell from the sky. People cowered from it, hiding in their homes until it dawned on them that nothing good could come from gods casting the first stone. Panicked and desperate, many fled. Some stayed to help others, of course. Some stayed to pack up their belongings before hitting the road. And some stayed to loot what was left behind.

One man picked his way through the rubble after most people had left. He moved with purpose, heading unerringly towards a small house with a garden now buried in layers of chipped stone. Inside, a young woman wept at the bedside of her father; the glazed emptiness in the man's eyes suggested he'd died sometime in the night. When she saw the intruder, she gasped.

"Who are you?"

In the temple, Sabine's heart sank; she knew what was coming. Didn't all women have a story to tell about men doing terrible things?

And in the image, fear came true. The man forced himself on the young woman, sobs and screams unheeded in the barren shell of what had once been home. She fought back;

he broke her leg and held his hands around her throat. When he left, she was still alive. But she couldn't walk. The poor girl lay in a pool of her own blood, beside her father's body, until the pyroclastic flow spewed from the volcano and burned her suffering away.

***

Sabine only half watched as the star jumped from one scene to the next, revealing the devastation plaguing the world below Mount Manotse. Girathos finished one bottle and started on another, his face rotating through various stages of shock and horror and grief.

The world burned. Drowned. Shrivelled in droughts. Shattered beneath rocks falling from space. Bathed in blood spilt by angry men. Tears fell from the sky and fell from the eyes of a god no longer sleeping through the pain.

"You see the suffering," Sabine said in a weary voice.

"Yes. I see the suffering mankind has brought to this world. Where have all the plants and animals gone? Hardly any of the ones I remember still brighten this place. Trees felled, land dug up for shiny stones, the sky poisoned by your smoke and sludge. You bring death and then beg me to save you from it? The world will heal itself once you are all gone."

She flinched from the blow of his words.

"For every opportunity to show the *humanity* of men," Girathos continued, "I see shining examples of misogyny, bigotry, and a callous disregard for nature. There is no balance, no symbiosis, no harmony in your way of life."

The god rose to his feet and paced the length of the room, muttering in a language Sabine didn't recognise. His eyes glowed the same colour as the fallen star. His words lashed like a whip. She remained seated, nursing her daughter; what else could she do?

"You're right," she agreed, her voice no louder than a whisper.

He heard. Stopped his raging and met her gaze.

"You're right. About everything you just said. As a species, everything we do is wrong. Maybe the world would be better off without us; I can understand why you'd think that. But…"

"But?"

She waved towards the star. "You're missing it."

"Missing what?"

"The good." She pleaded with her eyes. "I promise you, it's there. A lot of the bad we do is done in ignorance, and when we know better we try to do better. Most people don't want to hurt anyone. They want to live in peace and comfort with their families. Some of that bad comes from hunger or abuse or fear. The adult who loots a burning building was once a child whose mother died because they couldn't afford to keep themselves warm. The man who hits his wife and son was beaten by his own father until he learned that men rule with their fists - and I'm not excusing it; wrong is wrong. I'm just saying it's not always as clear-cut as you think. Find the good and you'll see what I mean."

"No amount of good can outweigh what I've seen today."

"I know. But you have to see that the good in us is worth saving. Please."

He turned his back on her. "I wouldn't even know where to start looking."

Inspiration struck, swift as an arrow. Sabine's eyes lit up. "There's a group of women in the next town over from mine. The forest burned down. They've spent every day since planting more trees and helping injured animals. They hold meetings to tell people how important plants and animals are. How they deserve life just as much as we do. They gather donations and funnel that money back into what they do."

Girathos aimed a hand at the star and watched as the image showed several white-haired ladies tending to wounded animals, patching them up with love and care. The lines of his mouth tightened. "They died a month ago when the river broke its bank."

Sadness washed over her. "My sister! Look at my sister. She runs a home for orphaned or abandoned children. Raises them like her own. She'll be protecting them even now, I know it."

He looked again. The picture changed.

"That's the orphanage."

Sabine watched with growing horror as a fire raged through the corridors, shattering windows and ravaging all within. Children dressed in nightclothes ran from the building, while others, unable to move, screamed from their beds. Sabine's sister, hair wild from sleep, gathered two infants in her arms and passed them through a window to safety. The flames raged closer but she ran back for more, handing another two children to waiting arms, then another two.

"Get out, Liren!" a voice called.

Liren paused. Hesitated. Then ran back into the burning room to gather more children in her blistered arms. She screamed, and the sound seemed to last an eternity. Sabine's sister never emerged from the fire.

"No!" Sabine wailed. "Liren. Please tell me that's not true. That it hasn't happened yet. That I can still save her. Please!"

Girathos wrapped her in godly arms and stroked her hair as she wept into his shoulder. "I'm sorry. Your sister was one of the good ones." His eyes hazed as if he was looking far away. "I think I had a sister once."

"Liren. Her name was Liren." She burned him with her gaze. "She was worth saving."

Between them, Runa squirmed. Girathos stepped back and patted her on the head like a dog. The baby reached for him.

"She likes you." Sabine wiped her nose with the back of her hand, knowing she'd never be able to wipe away the grief piercing her heart. "I have no idea why."

Runa reached for him again, this time with an accompanying squeal.

"What does she want?" Girathos asked.

"You. She wants you to hold her."

He shuddered. "No, I -"

Sabine deposited the baby in his arms, making sure he held her correctly. "Treat her like she's more precious than that star and you won't be far off. Hurt her and I don't care if you're a god or a worm; I'll crush you."

He gulped. "This... I... Gods don't really have any experience with babies. We tend to be born full-grown from a star or maybe the ocean."

She ignored him. "Show me Ezran, please. Wait! Is he alive?"

Girathos closed his eyes and nodded. "He's alive, but barely. His spirit lingers in the space between life and death."

The room tilted for a moment. She reached out. Clutched the back of the chair until she was sure she wasn't going to pass out. "Show me."

The scene changed. Cold this time. The ice-white frost of the mountain, and a single flickering light within a cave. Ezran lay beneath a blanket close to the small fire. The sheen of fever coated his brow and his eyelids danced as delirium directed his dreams. He moaned softly. A child, no more than eight years old, wiped a damp cloth over his forehead.

"Will he be okay, Mama?"

"I don't know, sweetheart."

"But he saved us."

"I know. We'll do our best for him, love, but it's out of our hands now."

The image faded and Sabine sank back into her chair. At her back, Girathos bounced Runa on his hip, laughing as she tugged at his eyebrows.

"Will he live?" Her lip quivered as she echoed the child's sentiment.

"I don't know."

She sucked a ragged breath into her lungs. "What happened to him?"

"He evacuated the town in time. Saved hundreds of lives. That mother... Her husband died in the first quake. She went into labour during the last quake, right before the town fell. She would've died, along with her children. Ezran went back for them. Carried them all to safety. But the tremors were too strong. They knocked him over. Buried him in rock. One crushed his leg. The mother and her children dragged him to the cave at the foot of this mountain and they've been taking care of him there, but infection set in three days ago."

"Please, Girathos. Ezran is a good man. Please save him."

Girathos picked up the star, his pupils dilating as soon as he touched it. Runa reached for it, her fingers grazing the orb as Girathos put it in his pocket; she squealed and her eyes flashed white as the mountaintop. "As a good man, surely he would understand the need to sacrifice a little good to eradicate a lot of bad?"

Her tears all spent, Sabine lowered her head to her hands. "I should never have come here."

"You got to meet a god. Not everyone can lay claim to that."

Her gaze skewered him.

Clearing his throat, Girathos smiled at Runa. "And I got to hold a baby. Yes, I did." The baby talk surprised them all, but Runa waved her arms and chattered back. "I've never done that before. Sabine, you gave me a true gift. A gift greater than any fallen star. Are all babies like this?"

Weary, aching, in heart as well as body, she lifted her head. "Like what? They're all different."

He lifted Runa in the air and spun her around. "So… pure, so innocent. So full of joy. Watching the world weighed me down with sadness, but it's impossible to stay sad around her. She… She makes me smile! She makes a god, who lost interest in life long ago, smile!"

And Sabine smiled then, through it all. "Yes, they're all like that. Babies are the best of us. Bundles of possibility before the hard and the sad and the painful carve it all away. We do our best to shield them from it. To raise them better, to raise them to create better."

"How do you know if it's working?"

"You don't. Not really. You watch them grow like wildflowers, watering them with everything they need, everything you want for them. Some become weeds, planted in the wrong place, taking from others. But some... They bloom in the hardest of places, bringing brightness and colour to barren land."

He held Runa against his chest, mesmerised as the baby placed one chubby hand on each of his cheeks and grabbed the skin until he winced. She pulled him closer. Gnawed with slobbery gums on the end of his nose. And enchanted him with her blueberry gaze.

"There is a universe in her eyes." Girathos exhaled slowly.

Sabine stood. "You see it, too?"

"I see it." His voice was soft. Reverent. "I see it now."

She gasped, and it echoed like a god's whisper.

"A daughter." Tears glistened on his cheeks. "I had a daughter once. A long time ago. I... How could I forget her?"

Sabine laid a hand on his arm. She opened her mouth to speak. And the sky fell.

***

"What's happening?" she screamed, grabbing Runa back and cowering from the marble rain.

Girathos' mouth narrowed into a thin line. "The earth has reached its end. She can take no more. Even Mount Manotse is falling now as the earth shakes herself free of the human blight."

Fragments of the ancient temple crashed down around them. A small chip of marble flew off a larger piece and grazed Sabine's forehead; blood trickled into her eyes and she blinked it away. The thunderous boom of falling marble drowned out Runa's frightened screams, but Sabine felt them deep in her bones. Her child was in danger and she was powerless to help.

Screaming over the noise, she grabbed Girathos' shirt and yanked him closer. "Do something!"

He wrapped his arms around her and Runa, sheltering them with his body. "Humans are not worth saving," he said.

"No! I -"

He pressed a finger to her lips. Pinned her gaze. "But you are, Sabine. The love you have for your fellow man, for Ezran and for Runa... The sorrow you feel for all the horrors of the world... You and your daughter crashed into my temple, disturbed my sleep, dared to insult a god. And you brought the light back into my life. Don't you see? The light that had been gone for so long. You brought back the memories of my daughter."

"I don't understand."

He smiled, and it took her breath away. "I don't want to hide anymore. Not in food, not in drink, not in sleep. Life is filled with good and bad, and the scales tip every day, but the good is worth saving. I believed that once, I think. I believe it now. The good is worth saving. You and Runa are worth saving."

He took the fallen star from his pocket, wrapping his fingers around it until it glowed brighter than its sisters in the night sky. Blinding white light filled what remained of the temple. Filled Girathos' body until it oozed from every pore. The tremors ceased and silence blanketed the thunder of falling debris.

"Isn't it too late?" Sabine asked.

Girathos cupped her face in one iridescent palm. "It's never too late."

He pressed his lips to her forehead and a star exploded in her mind. She gasped as the world before her eyes vanished and she floated in the darkness of space. Seeing a light, she willed herself towards it and rolled formlessly through bright rings. Dove through the atmosphere of burning planets. Skipped away from the edges of the dark nothing and watched the birth and death of stars that lived before she was born.

"This is my gift to you," Girathos spoke inside her mind. "Knowledge. Understanding. A smidgeon of power. Be the change, Sabine; be the better. I know you'll do a better job than I ever could."

She came back to herself in a sudden rush, gasping and clinging to Girathos' arms to hold herself upright. "What was that?"

"Me passing the mantle." His smile was bittersweet.

He pulled back from her then. Lifted the star to his chest and held it over his heart. It throbbed brighter, faster. Expanded and contracted in the blink of an eye. Sank into his chest as he absorbed the star, consuming its power to strengthen his own.

Shielding Runa's face against her chest, Sabine grabbed Girathos' hand and squeezed. "What did you do?"

"Even a god can't save a dying planet, Sabine. I needed some help."

"Help?"

His pupils dilated and he flashed his teeth in a wolfish grin. "I need to undo the damage. Wipe it all clean to give you a shot at that second chance. That's going to take everything I have and then some, my dear."

Her eyes shone.

"It's okay. For the best, really. I've lost too much of myself along the way and I'm not sure I want to sleep through it all anymore. I've always wanted to go out with a bang."

He turned away, then paused as Runa's small fingers dug into his arm.

"What is it, little one?"

Blueberry eyes looked deep into his own. With a warm smile, she leaned forward and kissed his cheek.

He beamed. "I'll save the world for you."

"Thank you, Girathos," Sabine spoke through her tears.

"I'd close your eyes for this bit."

The sleeping god, now wide awake and facing the dawn of a bright new day, walked to the doors of his temple and threw them open. A storm raged outside but he calmed it with a whisper. He held his arms up, turned his face to the sky, and closed his eyes as his body slowly disintegrated into gleaming particles that drifted on the wind. A silent thunderclap buffeted the mountaintop. Girathos' light contracted, then shot outwards in every direction until it bathed the damaged world in the cleansing selflessness of his sacrifice.

Sabine flinched from the burning light, her eyes squeezing shut until the glow faded and the world dulled once more.

She looked back at where Girathos had made his final stand. The last traces of his body floated up towards the sun; as they drifted beyond the open doorway, they hung in the air and then pulled back, disappearing into the shadows of the temple.

Girathos was gone.

***

In the three days it took Sabine to descend Mount Manotse, she discovered a new bounce to her step, a level of energy she hadn't possessed since childhood. She moved faster, tired infrequently, and needed little to eat. Runa seemed similarly affected. Whatever gifts Girathos had given to them, Sabine was grateful.

The world was refreshed, too. Colours were brighter, from the verdant grass and blooming flowers to the unrepentant blue of the sky. At night, millions more stars twinkled in the darkness. Sabine looked at them and remembered.

As she reached the foothills, Runa gurgled and cooed merrily about all she could see. Sabine's heart fluttered between joy and fear, wondering what she would find in the world below the mountain. Girathos had saved humanity, but what of individual people? Her sister was gone, and that grief would always live with her. Was Ezran gone, too?

Her feet were steady on the uneven path. Her stomach less so. She turned a corner heading into the lower valley and gasped.

The meadow teemed with people.

They watched her descend and an excited murmur spread through the crowd. People stopped what they were doing. Surged forward to meet her as she stepped into the valley. Some dropped to their knees and wept.

"What's going on?" Sabine wove through the kneeling bodies, a little unnerved by the gleaming reverence in their eyes and the way they reached out to touch her skirts as she passed. Familiar faces called her name and she nodded her head in acknowledgement. Smiled at them, though it didn't reach her eyes.

A figure emerged from the crowd. Tall. Broad. Hair a little longer than she remembered. Face a little sharper. A limp, though he walked with a cane across the springy grass. He smiled and the sun rose.

"Ezran."

He ran to her. Wrapped her in his arms. Runa, too. "Sabine. Runa. You did it, my love. You did it."

Her cheeks were wet as she rose on tiptoes to press a kiss to his lips. Her eyes glowed, perhaps a little whiter than they had before.

"What's this?" He cupped her cheek, fascinated by the iridescent gleam.

She placed her hand over his. "A second chance."

Him, Her & Lavender Lylah

HIM

The pain. It lives in him now, clawing at his heart, rending his skin from the inside out. He knows he is... broken. Fractured. Fragments of memory swim through the fog in his mind, drowning in the murky depths before he can pull them to the surface. Even his own name is lost to him. How long has it been since he'd known it?

Standing from the bench, he downs the last of his drink and throws a coin on the table before leaving the tavern. The night is cold but he doesn't feel it; he knows by the way his breath mists in the air before his face. At one side of the building, an old beggar woman cowers in the dirt. At the other, Fall-Down Ferd heaves his guts into the alley.

He scoffs. Even the old drunk has a name - at least, he will remember it by morning.

The loss of his name bothers him more than he cares to admit. He's found another, of course. It wasn't his first and won't be the last. Stolen from the tinker he met and killed on the road last week. The pang of regret surprises him; the blood he's spilt over the years will never wash from his hands. Why, then, does this one trouble him?

Sleep, he decides. That's what he needs. Maybe then he'll begin to understand why he feels like he's been cut apart and stitched back together by a blind dog. Although his limbs ache and his eyes feel like they're filled with grit, his mind tugs and twists at the loose strands of memory, prodding them like a tongue poking at a sore tooth. What do they mean? Are they memories, or dreams?

Walking past the docks, he growls and kicks at a small cat that gets in his way; it runs away in a streak of ginger, yowling in protest.

The moon casts little light across the cobbled road. He wrinkles his nose at the lingering stench of fish and adds speed to his steps.

"Where are you going in such a hurry?" a voice purrs from the darkness.

He almost ignores it, but the husky sweetness overrides his better judgement. Stopping in his tracks, he leers at the streetwalker who leans against the tilting wall of a rundown hovel.

The woman pouts and leans forward to flash a glimpse of cleavage. "I could help you do something else in a hurry if you like."

Frustration builds within him. He could visit the underground clubs and pick a fight, he supposes. Or he could find his release in a different way. Without speaking, he steps to the woman and pulls her into his arms. She smells of roses and sweat and wears heavy makeup that doesn't quite cover the purpling bruise on her cheek. He kisses her, pressing her body back against the wall.

"Oh!" she gasps. "We usually take it inside."

"I'll take you wherever I want," he says, biting her lip in warning.

He buries himself in her, venting the anger and bitterness that has grown within him. When he's finished, he drops her like a sack of potatoes and continues on his way.

"You're supposed to pay!" she yells after him, tears evident in her voice. "You bastard! You're supposed to pay!"

HER

White horses rode in the seafoam as the boat cut a path through the water. She watched from the portside, the hood of her cloak pulled tight around her face as the rain and the seaspray dampened her clothes. It was a clear night and the stars glittered like gods swimming in a vast ocean.

She should be pleased. After all this time, she finally had a place to focus her search. Anticipation tingled in her blood but a heavy melancholy weighed on her heart. What would it mean if she found him?

The roar and crash of the waves soothed her, as did the stillness of the sky. Peace could always be found somewhere.

"You'll catch a cold out here."

She turned. Smiled. "Good evening, Artur. Or is it closer to morning now? I'm not sure."

Artur settled the hat more firmly on his head and cleared his throat.

"Is something bothering you?" She looked at his grizzled beard, in need of a good trim, and the shadows beneath his eyes. The last time she'd seen him, he'd been full in the flush of youth, emotions high from his first captaincy. More and more these days, she noticed the toll time had taken on her friends.

"You know I'd do anything for you. I... I owe you everything." He swallowed hard. "Are you sure you want to land in Stalinoc?"

She squeezed his arm. "I'm sure, my friend."

"But it's a nest of vipers. I wouldn't feel right letting you walk off this ship and into that cesspit."

"Letting me?" She arched one eyebrow but smiled to soften the blow. "I will be fine, Artur. Would you cross me?"

He gulped. Shook his head.

"And neither will they. Besides, there are people I need to find. At least one of them is there." She returned her gaze to the horizon, watching for the thin strip of land that would tell her they neared their destination.

LAVENDER LYLAH

The tavern was busy. Good. Lylah added a little extra bounce to her step as she delivered tankards of ale to the table in the back corner. Cheers and winks and lewd suggestions greeted her. She spent a few minutes flirting, managed to wrangle a handful of coins out of the drunken fools, and sauntered back to the bar with her empty tray. Wiping the sweat from her brow, she called to the innkeeper, "I'm taking a break."

Heading into the back room, she rubbed her lower back and sighed. She was getting too old for this.

"Back hurting again, Mother?"

Lylah wrinkled her nose in a mock frown at her daughter. "Maybe."

"You know you don't have to work here anymore."

"I know, Freesia." Gods, who'd have thought she'd end up with such a smart kid? "But it brings a little more money in, doesn't it? Helps pay for your fancy education."

Freesia pushed her spectacles up her nose and brushed strands of wheat-coloured hair behind her ears. With a sigh, she manoeuvred her wheelchair out from behind the table where her books were strewn haphazardly. "Mother, your artwork has brought in enough to educate me three times over. And to pay for all my medical expenses. I don't understand why you insist on hiding your success and working in this... dump."

"Because..." Lylah took two apples from the pocket of her dress and passed one to her daughter. "Because people treat you differently when they think you have money, sweetheart. I don't want to lose friends over it. I don't want to lose who I am."

"At least consider sticking to serving drinks and not offering any... extras."

"I have! I haven't offered extras in months." She studied her daughter. The wheat-gold hair and high cheekbones. The different coloured eyes: one blue and one green. The head that was much too sensible for a mere fourteen-year-old. "Freesia, I know I haven't been the best mother, but I have done *my* best to give you what you needed. Maybe I've had to make some questionable choices but at least they were mine to make. I've done everything on my terms, found a way to provide for the *only* thing that matters to me - that's you, if you hadn't gathered - and built a life that I can be proud of. I have no regrets, baby girl. None."

Freesia sniffed. "You could at least make them stop calling you Lavender Lylah. Everyone still talks about that, and they don't care if I'm listening."

Lylah sucked her cheeks in. "Heads will roll," she promised. When Freesia laughed, she knew things were alright between them. "How are your studies going?"

"Good. Did you know that human bodies have two hundred and six bones?" The teenager's face lit up as she spoke. She grabbed one of her books and pointed out a diagram of a skeleton. "Twenty-six of them are in the foot!"

About to reply, though she struggled to think of what to say, Lylah was interrupted when the door swung open and a younger woman ran into the room. "Dulcie? What's wrong?"

Dulcie gasped as she bent over double and fought for breath. Her cheeks were red as tomatoes. "Ran here… Had to tell you… Beckah… Dead…"

"What? Beckah's dead? What happened?"

The younger girl wiped tears from her eyes. "They say she went crazy and killed a trick. Beat him with a chair or something. Then threw herself out of the window."

"She wouldn't do that." Lylah shook her head.

"I know. But that's what they're saying. Mishel told me there was a bruise on Beckah's cheek, though. And cuts on her knees. Like someone roughed her up. Mishel found her. She said Beckah smelled of rotting flesh and her eyes were all black." On the last words, Dulcie sank into Lylah's arms and sobbed on her shoulder.

Freesia cast a wide-eyed glance at her mother and Lylah shook her head. "I'm going to get Dulcie home. Go to the boat and wait for me please, Freesia. I won't be long."

For once, Freesia did as she'd been asked, gathering her books and wheeling herself out of the room. At one time, Lylah would have worried how her daughter would manage on the cobbled street between the tavern and her houseboat, but their neighbours had pitched in to flatten the path. She hadn't mentioned it to Freesia but that was another reason she wouldn't leave the area; they were a family here, and families looked out for one another.

The innkeeper, Pyeter, was included in that. When he heard what had happened, he had no problem releasing Lylah from her chores. She helped Dulcie home, wiping the younger girl's eyes with her handkerchief and making sure she had a stiff drink in her hand. Within the hour, she was at her houseboat enjoying a cup of hot tea with Freesia.

"Is Dulcie okay?"

Lylah shook her head. "She will be. It's always hard to lose someone, and she was particularly close with Beckah."

"I'm sorry, Mother. I know you were fond of Beckah, too."

Lylah kissed her daughter's brow. "You have a good heart, Freesia. Guard it well."

Freesia snorted. "I'm going to bed. I assume Tonald is coming over?"

The heat creeping up Lylah's cheeks surprised her; surely she was too old for schoolgirl blushes. "Maybe."

"Goodnight, Mother."

Lylah sipped her tea and waited, knowing her daughter was right. Tonald would come; he always did on a Tuesday. Sometimes she wondered why she kept seeing him. He'd disappear for days on end. Never told her what he did for a living. But there was something so gentle about his manner.

Something soft and good. He treated her like a princess. The only gift he'd ever given her was a spray of lavender picked from the hills because he knew it was her favourite, but he showered her with small acts of kindness. She thought she could fall in love with him if she let herself.

Calling herself a fool, she cleaned the teapot and heard his knock on the door - always four raps, *rat-a-tat-tat*, like a drumbeat. She let him in, catching a brief glimpse of the darkness outside, and of the old beggar woman singing softly of the silver sea.

HIM

He wipes the blood from his knuckles. Drinks from the waterskin at his hip and then tips some onto the grazes. He doesn't need to do it this way, he's realised. Memories have started to fill in like pieces of a puzzle. Many pieces are missing, but he's able to form enough of a picture to know that power still runs through his veins. He could beat the woman with his strength of will alone. But there is something satisfying about feeling the crack of her bones beneath his hands, or the gush of blood over his fingers as he slices and cuts.

He turns back. Scowls at the cowering, whimpering mess on the floor.

"Please," the woman begs. Her voice is ragged. Splintered.

He studies her. A wolf observing a rabbit. Her pain means nothing to him beyond what it makes her say. And she will speak. She will spill more than her blood. "Where is the godstone?"

She weeps as her nails claw at the cold stone. He watches and waits; he still has time. She is strong, he'll give her that. Many have succumbed to his attentions much quicker than she. What is her name? He has a grudging respect for her strength of spirit, and thinks he might remember her.

No. Her name is gone, as is his own. He knows she is a sorceress - one of the old cult who worship the goddess-wife, Cinanouk. Incapacitating her was no easy feat. If any know where the godstone has been hidden, she will. And if his returning memories are real, the stone will fix whatever is broken within him.

Bored now, he asks once again, "Where is the godstone?"

The sorceress wails at him.

He approaches, fist clenched. In the other hand, he holds a rusty hook. "Where is the godstone?" He punctuates each syllable with a blow.

The night is long. For her, at least. And when it ends, with secrets whispered and death a gentle blessing, he rolls her body into a cupboard and walks away. He got what he came for - he never doubted he would. Soon, the godstone will be in his hands. He whistles as he exits the building into the moonlight, and is startled when a young lad interrupts his good mood.

"Please, Sir," the boy begs. "Please, can you spare a coin? I've not eaten in days."

High from the kill, he lashes out and boxes the boy round his ears. As the lad cowers, he spits at the wide-eyed face. Laughs when the fool runs away. That'll teach him to beg from strangers.

He resumes whistling and forgets all about the sorceress and the boy. His mind is on the godstone, and nothing will stand in his way.

HER

She kept her back straight as she waved Artur away. It wouldn't do to have him worrying about her. The old seadog deserved some peace in his latter years.

The wharf was busy with people scuttling about like beetles disturbed beneath a log. Hawkers sold their wares on every corner, and streetwalkers strode between. In the heat of the midday sun, the putrid stench of dead fish was overwhelming. Trying not to gag, she held a scented cloth to her nose and walked at a brisk pace.

It had been a long time since she'd been to Stalinoc but it seemed little had changed. The roads were the same, narrow and cobbled and lined with filth. With a sigh, she chose the one she wanted and followed it into the centre of town. The fishy smell dispersed but was replaced with the malodorous miasma of piss and body odour.

As she walked, people stepped aside to let her pass. Many stopped to look back at her once she'd gone by. Her hood was up and her cloak pulled around her body, so it wasn't her face or her shape they looked at. What drew their gaze? After watching other women, she suspected it was her confidence. She walked with a straight spine and her eyes on where she was going; they shuffled hunched over, eyes downcast as if they were afraid to draw attention. She'd known the world had changed, but seeing it in person added an extra layer of sorrow to her heart.

Ahead, the building she sought rose above the others like a heron among pigeons. Dark stone walls towered above surrounding roofs. It was eye-catching, impressive, foreboding; it seemed more like a keep than a house of parliament. She wondered if the men inside would be as pompous and bureaucratic as she remembered.

She reached the steps and arched her brow at the queue of people lined up outside the door. Pushing past them, she strode inside, glanced around, and selected the official who looked the least busy. "Where might I find the office of the Minister of State?"

The man blinked. Looked around to see who she was talking to. Realised it was him and blinked again. "You have to queue."

"No."

His cheeks reddened. "The Minister is busy."

She leaned in closer. Let him see her face. "I invoke the Edringard Treaty. Take me to see the Minister. Now."

A smug look crossed his features. "I've never heard of such a treaty, and I've worked here for fifteen years."

"Really?" She pursed her lips. "What fools do they have working here now? All should know the Edringard Treaty; every corner of the world recognises it. Or, they did."

"I'm going to have to ask you to leave." He cleared his throat, adjusted his robe, and held an arm out towards the door.

"And I'm going to have to ask you to move. If you won't show me the way to the Minister's office, I'll find it myself."

She stepped to move past him and he grabbed her arm. Making a low growl, she thrust her open hand into his throat and squeezed. She lifted him off his feet without breaking a sweat and let him see the amethyst haze roll over her eyes.

"The Minister of State," she grated between clenched teeth. "Now."

The man nodded as he gasped for breath. As soon as she set him down, he scurried along the nearest corridor, turned left at the end, and led her to a plain wooden door on the right. He knocked on the door, took one last look at her face, and hurried back to his desk.

"Come in," a voice called from the other side of the door.

With a shrug, she did as he asked. Closing the door behind her, she took stock of the room. A small window provided a modicum of light. Bright paintings decorated the walls: scenes of haunting wilderness, ancient ruins, and verdant landscapes that added colour to the drab surroundings. Along one wall was a shelving unit lined with books. A desk with a chair at each side dominated the room. Seated at the desk was a large man, more barrel than brawn, with a face made to scare small children. Ruddy cheeks glowed behind a bushy red beard and moustache so shaggy it could have homed several small mice. He looked up as she entered, brushed a crumb of cheese from his robe, and frowned.

"Who are you?"

She smiled. "That doesn't matter. Are you the Minister of State?"

"I am." He peered over her shoulder, perhaps looking for a guard.

"Then I need your help."

He pointed back down the corridor. "Have you registered? The queue is long today, I'm told."

"I am not here to queue. I invoke the Edringard Treaty."

His eyes narrowed. Widened. Almost bulged out of his head. "You *what* now?"

"Ah, so someone here has heard of it. Thank the stars!"

"Hang on." He turned to the bookshelf, ran his finger along several spines, and selected a leatherbound tome. Flipping through the pages, he found the one he was looking for and ran a finger over it, mouthing the words as he read them. He paused. Read again. Cast her a sideways glance. "Madam, that treaty is hundreds of years old."

"Yes." She let her amusement show in her voice. "And what does your book tell you?"

He glanced at it again. "That anyone who invokes the treaty should be given anything they require so long as they carry the seal shown on these pages."

In silence, she removed the glove from her hand and showed him the signet ring bearing the matching seal: a full moon encircled by flames, with the wise eyes of an owl watching from within the silver orb.

The minister's hands trembled. He put the book down. "What is your name?"

"Not important. Yours, however…"

"Gredick." He swallowed. "Minister Gredick."

"Very well, Gredick. Now we have that nonsense out of the way, I need to find someone. You and your people know, or *should* know, this city like the back of your hand. You have to help me find this man."

Gredick opened a drawer in his desk. Brought out a flask and took a long swig. He wiped his mouth with the back of his hand. "Who is he?"

"I don't know what name he goes by. He is… evil. He will draw attention to himself; he won't be able to help it. Wherever he is, you'll have reports of crimes, strange deaths, unusual malfeasance. And not just from him; the people he comes into contact with are affected, too."

"What does he look like?"

She shrugged, and a shadow passed across her eyes. "I can't tell you that, either. His appearance changes. Look at your reports; that's how you'll find him."

Gredick ran a hand through his hair, ruffling it into even wilder tufts of dishevelment. "I don't know what's going on here and I'm not sure I want to. Let me send for Barb. You'll need the best for this."

The best? She nodded, even as she wondered if the best would be enough.

LAVENDER LYLAH

"Hey, Lylah?"

She turned to the innkeeper, hand on hip. "What?"

"Keep an eye out, will ya? I'm going to check on Rulu."

Lylah nodded. The tavern was busy again and her feet screamed like banshees. She pulled a stool behind the bar and sat on it; she could see everyone and got to rest at the same time. The hubbub was usually a source of comfort to her, but something felt off these days. Tainted. Like something rotten was slowly spreading into everything else.

Loud squeals drew her attention and she watched as three male prostitutes shook their assets in the faces of a gaggle of well-dressed women. Coins exchanged hands and each man led two ladies up the stairs. Not long after, the tavern's newest belle took three rough-looking sailors up to her room. Lylah tried to ignore the noises from upstairs as much as she could. Maybe age had brought wisdom, or maybe it had just made her tired, but she grew weary of the old games.

When an older man with a thick grey moustache called her attention, she served him an ale and a smile. "How's it going, Dugal?"

"Pretty good, Lavender." He winked. "Better if you'd come upstairs with me."

She reached over to ruffle his hair. "Aww, come on, Dugal. You know I'm too old for that nonsense. You'd have a better time with Kasmin, and you know it."

He grinned behind the moustache, his cheeks pink as raspberries. "Worth a shot."

"How's your boy?" Lylah poured him another drink, knowing the first wouldn't last long.

Dugal's face darkened. "He took up with a lady over in the west side. She had a boy of her own. Well, Tobin came over last night. Told me the lady had up and killed herself after her boy ate himself to death. Tobin's distraught. He's with his mama now."

Lylah gaped as she processed what he'd said. "Ate himself to death? How in the stars does that happen?"

"I guess he suddenly started eating things he shouldn't. Tobin said the boy went out begging one night and came back changed. Started chowing down on floorboards and candles and offal in the street. Doesn't make any sense."

"I'm so sorry," Lylah said, for lack of anything better to say. Dugal downed the second drink and she poured him another; it sounded like he needed it. As an afterthought, she poured one for herself, too. What was wrong with the world these days? It seemed like everything was going crazy.

When the innkeeper returned, she went back to serving drinks, counting the hours until she could go home to Freesia. After the glum conversation with Dugal, she wanted nothing more than to hug her baby and know she was safe.

As the hour grew late and the crowd more raucous, she thought she caught a glimpse of Tonald in the doorway but when she looked again only her regular customers were there. Shrugging it off, she turned to put a mug of ale in front of Whisky Wendell. "There you go, honey."

Someone jostled her from behind, knocking the drink from her hand. She watched with a weary sense of the inevitable as it tipped all over Wendell's lap. At least it was only Wendell; she'd dry him off and they'd have a good laugh about it before he ended up face-down in his cups.

Wendell, usually a genial drunk and a friendly soul, leapt from his seat with a violent roar and landed a strong blow on Lylah's cheek.

She cried out. Stumbled back. Held her hand to her face and grabbed the back of a chair to steady herself. Her ears rang and her vision blurred for a moment. When it cleared, she saw Wendell take a swing at another customer who'd rushed to her defence. Enough was enough.

She picked up the tray she'd dropped when he hit her and swung it at the back of his head. He fell onto a table. Struggled to right himself. Without waiting, she grabbed his arm and twisted until he hollered. She frogmarched him to the door, threw him out into the gutter, and folded her arms across her chest. "Don't come back unless it's with an apology."

Goosebumps rose on her flesh. It was a cold night, and darker than the devil's heart. A full moon hovered above - a watchful, pearly eye waiting for something to happen. *Ha! You're getting fanciful in your old age, Lylah.* Snorting, she watched as Wendell scrambled out of sight, barely able to hold himself upright. She'd have to tell Tonald what had happened; he'd love hearing how she'd thrown the old drunk out of the tavern!

She turned to go back in and caught sight of the old beggar woman shivering beneath a thin cloak. She'd been there herself, once. Running inside, she grabbed a blanket and a loaf of bread from the back room and took them outside. She handed them to the woman, who took them with quivering lips.

"Be careful out here," Lylah said, squeezing the woman's hand. "If you're in need of a hot drink and a bowl of stew, come inside and ask for Lylah."

The woman grabbed her hand and held it in a vice-like grip. Her white hair hovered like morning mist in the winter sun. Folds and wrinkles danced across her face. Her eyes, blue as sapphires, pierced the darkness of the night. "Thank you."

HIM

His rage is an inferno. Around him, bodies lie strewn across the marble floor - a pretty mosaic of blood and broken flesh. The temple that once buzzed with life is now devoid of it, but he still does not have what he is looking for.

It seems the sorceress lied. And there is that grudging respect again - the bitch went to her grave without giving her secrets away. Or maybe she never knew the answer in the first place. He muses on that, even as he lashes out with his growing powers. Pots smash. Altars crumble. Walls fall beneath his onslaught. Cinanouk's temple can burn with the bodies, he decides. He breathes words of encouragement to the torches in sconces along the walls. Thrills as they burst to life, igniting curtains and tapestries and, eventually, the very stones themselves. The marble won't go up in flames but there will be enough damage to satisfy him. Priestesses will never worship here again.

His head hurts. Fragments of memory bombard him everywhere he turns. There is one face in particular... He shakes his head, trying to clear the bitterness of something half-remembered. He has to focus. So close now... He can't afford to make mistakes.

And where is the godstone? He looks down at the fake in his hand, the one he wrested from broken fingers as the women tried to deny him. It looks right. A dull sheen covers its surface, coated in layers of dust. It's hidden here for years. But why would they hide a fake godstone? Why would they protect it with their lives?

As he walks away from the flames, he wonders if something else might have happened to the stone. Gems and jewels often went missing from places of worship; perhaps something similar happened here. Perhaps someone with nifty fingers took the real stone and replaced it with this replica.

How will he find it now?

"Stop!" A crone in a red gown screams as she sees the fire. She grabs him. Tugs at his sleeve. "What have you done?"

He brushes her away like a fly, his mind already elsewhere. Where is the stone? Who could have taken it? Perhaps the answer he seeks will lie in old records... It would have taken a great thief to steal from Cinanouk's temple. Yes, that's it. He'll look through old documents; surely there'll be a record of thieves who operated in the area. He could start more recently and work his way back.

Irritation surges. Drudgery! He has better things to do than search through dusty old paperwork. But how else will he find the godstone? No, he will not be thwarted now. Not when he's so close.

With the burning temple lighting up the sky behind him, he walks to the houses of parliament to begin his search. Only time will tell what he'll find.

HER

Why couldn't he have been in the marble citadel of Sihwith? Or the floating village of Nillici? Or even Damarin, the mountainous fortress of the Ganamor? Anywhere would have been better than this foul-stenched cesspit, the woman mused.

She watched Barb as they walked, trying to get a read on the tall, stern woman Minister Gredick had lent her.

"What makes you think he's near the wharf?" she asked.

Barb lifted her shoulders. "Most of the strange shit seems to be happening 'round here."

Well, that was descriptive enough, she supposed. "You've been monitoring it?"

"Aye. When you get reports of lads eating themselves to death, best friends beating each other to a pulp, and a woman letting herself get run over by a cart because she couldn't be bothered getting up out of its way - to name a few - then you start to take notice."

"I can imagine." She assessed the area as they walked. Lots of alleyways and narrow ginnels. No torches to light the path. Plenty of dark places to hide a multitude of sins. Yes, he'd like it here. "And what are we going to see now?"

"Not sure yet." Barb scratched her ear. "Lots of witnesses. Lots of different stories. Best I can piece together is that a woman went to a party, took her dress off - a red one, as it's the only thing the witnesses seem to agree on - and threw herself at anything that moved. She got a bit too handsy with the host's daughter and he walloped her with a walking stick. Or maybe a vase. One witness said it was an ice pick. Whatever it was, she never got back up."

"Yes, I guess you would call that strange shit," she said. "Have you noticed any patterns?"

"Only that it seems to be getting worse. Happening more often. Can't find anything in common between the victims.

Or whatever they are. Probably would end up arresting a lot of them if they didn't die. What's all this got to do with the man you're looking for, anyway?"

She pursed her lips. Debated how much to say. "He's causing it."

Barb stopped in her tracks. "How?"

"Not sure. But I've traced him from Karahan to Diswelik, and everywhere in between. In all the times, in all the places, *strange shit* happens when he's there."

Spitting on the floor, Barb set off again, this time at a quicker pace. "I don't know what's going on but I know it can't be good. Let's see if this woman can give us any clues."

Before long, they reached a large building that seemed to be some sort of warehouse. The wood was a little rotten in places and the upstairs window was open to the elements. Soldiers waited outside, keeping a small crowd at bay. They recognised Barb and let them through without question.

Inside, the open space had been decorated with rich colours and ornate furniture. "Not what I expected to see."

Barb chuckled. "Don't let the outside fool you. This place used to be a warehouse until some rich doozy bought it and turned it into a club of sorts. Now it's a hive for the rich and bored to share their... eccentricities."

It took a moment to see the body, hidden among piles of soft cushions and spilled food. They studied it for a moment.

It. She was a person with hopes and dreams, and a family who cared for her. A shiver crawled up her spine. Had she seen so much in chasing him that she now looked at a body and saw an empty shell? "What was her name?"

Checking the parchment she'd written on, Barb said, "Shulia."

"Her eyes are black."

"They all have been. All the ones who died from *strange shit*."

She tilted her head. "Do you smell that?"

Barb sniffed. Lines creased her brow. "Rich. Musky. Smells like peat. It's coming from her body."

"He touched her then. One way or another."

About to reply, Barb lifted her head at the sound of grunts and cries at the back of the building. She raced to the source, throwing the back door open and surging out into a downpour that had appeared while they'd been in the warehouse.

Racing to catch up, the woman said, "What is it?"

In the alley running behind the building, a small figure danced between a handful of men, dodging blows and landing many of her own. As they both raced to intervene, the girl launched into a series of kicks and spins and tumbling blows that left the men reeling. When only one remained standing, she stalked him like a lion focused on its prey, limbs flexed and gaze fixed. He turned. Ran. She leapt on his back and brought him to the ground, finishing with a swift stamp on his face.

"If you're here to help," she said to the two women, "you're a little late."

The woman's chest was suddenly tight. She froze. Opened her mouth but struggled to push the words past her tongue. As the girl stepped into the light of a stray moonbeam, revealing an oval face and hair like onyx, the woman cried out her name, "Shah!"

LAVENDER LYLAH

"Tonald!" It wasn't Tuesday but she let him in anyway, her stomach fluttering like she was still a young girl in the first flush of love. *There you go again, Lylah - waxing poetical. Damn fool.* Still, she was allowed to feel happy when she saw him. He'd been coming around for almost a year now and she hadn't grown bored of him yet. "What are you doing here?"

He bent to kiss her. "I missed you."

Warmth filled her chest. "I missed you too. Come in and I'll pour you some tea."

She led the way into the small kitchen of her boathouse and busied herself boiling the kettle and setting out the cups. It amused her when he tipped himself into a small chair, still unaccustomed to the movement of the water.

"Freesia's out studying at a friend's house so we have the place to ourselves tonight," she said, wiggling her eyebrows.

He smiled and the light reached his eyes. "I couldn't wait until Tuesday, Lylah. I've had a difficult week and I wanted nothing more than to see your beautiful face."

She preened. "Flattery will get you everywhere, my dear. Oh! I was going to show you on Tuesday but now you're here... I've finished a new painting."

"That's wonderful." He stood - no easy feat - and wrapped her in his arms. "You're so talented. I'm sure you'll sell it in no time. One of these days, I know your work will hang in the Stalinoc Gallery."

"This one's a little different, Tonald." She bit her lip. He was always proud of her, she knew that. But she usually painted landscapes. What would he think when he saw what she'd done this time? "I've painted a portrait of someone I care for very much."

"That person must feel very honoured." He used one finger to tip her chin up and kissed her soundly. "Is it Freesia?"

"Let me show you."

She went to the back room, the one she used as a studio, and returned with a small canvas wrapped in cloth. She handed it to Tonald, who stumbled back to his chair and unwrapped it like a present. Amused anticipation warmed his face. Lylah watched and waited, nerves dancing in her stomach.

When he peeled the cloth back to reveal the detailed portrait of a man with dark hair and an open smile, he froze. His bottom lip trembled, so softly it was barely noticeable. The corner of his left eye twitched. He moved his hand to run his fingers over the image and then thought better of it. "You painted me."

"Yes." Lylah wiped the tears from her cheek. She couldn't tell how he felt about the painting. "Do you like it?"

Before he could answer, someone pounded on the door with heavy fists. Lylah jumped. Looked at Tonald, who shrugged. She hurried to the door and threw it open. Outside, the innkeeper shivered in the rain. His face was haggard, his eyes red.

"What's wrong?" she asked.

"It's Dulcie."

The ground tilted, and this time it wasn't because of the boat. "What?"

"She's dead."

Lylah gasped. Dropped to her knees as if she'd been punched in the gut. "No."

He placed a hand on her shoulder. "I'm sorry, Lylah. I wanted to tell you in person before you heard another way."

"What happened?" She wiped her eyes but found nothing there; she was too numb for tears.

"She was upset after what happened to Beckah." He took a breath. "After you took her home, it seems she never got up again. Just went to bed and stayed there until she passed."

Something in his tone broke through her numbness. She looked up. Grabbed the doorframe and pulled herself to her feet. "That's stupid. No way Dulcie would do that."

"I know. But she did. Lydi, the girl she lived with, said she tried to get her up but Dulcie just wouldn't move. Even when the doctor came, he couldn't get her up. They were going to send her to the infirmary but she died before the carriage arrived. I'm sorry, Lylah. I know you were close."

"No." Lylah shook her head. "No. I don't believe Dulcie would do that. Something else is happening here. Don't you see? All these girls... Dugal's story about the lad... What's happening? And why isn't anything being done about it?"

"I'm sorry," he repeated. "I have to get back to the tavern. I just wanted to let you know."

She thanked him and closed the door, then leaned back against it, too shocked to move. Tonald came and she thought he would comfort her, but there was a wildness in his eyes.

"I have to go," he said. "I'm sorry, I have to go. I... I'll see you soon."

Lylah gaped as he pushed past and left her sobbing in the doorway. "Tonald?"

But he didn't turn back. She watched as he faded into inky shadows and, somehow, her world seemed all the darker for it.

What just happened?

She wiped the rain from her face. Pushed the hair off her brow. Saw the old beggar woman sheltering in a doorway, blue eyes watching the shadows.

"No," she said aloud. "Something's not right."

The beggar woman looked at her.

"If no one else will do anything about it, then I will."

HIM

His rage consumes him. The records are long gone, destroyed in a fire. Why is the godstone proving so hard to find?

Sleep eludes him; every time he closes his eyes he sees the same smiling face, silken hair like a dark halo surrounding it. Who is she? Why does he yearn for her and fear her in equal measure? Sometimes, flashes of memory show him other faces, too; he tries to block them from his mind. They make him feel... soft. Warm. Ashamed. He doesn't understand. Why should he be ashamed of who he is? He is strong. Proud. Better than the fools around him - why should he not crush them beneath his feet? It is a kindness, really, to put them out of their misery. No, he wants those faces to vanish. To leave him be.

The headaches are almost constant now, driving him to swallow the white powder - mixed into honeyed mead - he took from the man on the street. It helps for a short while, driving the pain away and filling him with a sense of invincibility. It also makes him tense.

A thought springs into his mind like a lamb bounding through a meadow; he grasps it before it flits away. He remembers hearing of a woman in the marketplace... A woman who can find anything, for a price... What was her name? He ponders it as he lies on his bed, the drug stirring the aggression in his blood. He needs to move, to make use of this restless energy... Is he in the mood to fight or fuck? It's not an easy question for him to answer and he mulls over it for a moment before remembering the woman in the marketplace.

Aramas. The name settles on his tongue and he smiles. Rising quickly, he heads to the marketplace, focused on his new plan.

As he arrives at the crowded market, the drug begins to wear off and pain throbs at his temples. The busy hubbub pounds at his head and his anger builds. Pushing and shoving his way through the crowd, he snarls his fury, spittle flying from his mouth. Skin brushes skin, his breath is a miasma in the air. Gradually, people clear the path ahead of him, stepping back to avoid his wrath. He feels their eyes on his back and smiles.

Aramas proves easy to find - the irony amuses him. The main room of her shop clears when he enters and he wonders if people sense how easily he could end their lives. Aramas watches him, her hand on the hilt of a dagger at her hip. She has a square face and a double chin, and the smoothest skin he has ever seen - for a brief moment, he contemplates hanging it on his wall as a trophy.

"Can I help you?"

He turns on the charm. "I hope so. I need to find something."

She flashes a toothy grin. Moves her hand away from the dagger. "Well, you've come to the right place. What is it - a book? A magic mirror?"

"A stone."

"I –"

Aramas breaks off when her door flies open and a pair of brawling men tumble inside. She grabs a broom and runs to hit them with it, shouting curses as they roll into a vase and it shatters into tiny pieces. "What in the stars are you doing? Get out of here!"

Mid-swing, she pauses and looks out of the open doorway, her eyes widening to saucers. "Oh, my stars…"

Vexed by the interruption, he turns to see what has her so wound up. At first, he's unable to make sense of the scene outside, his mind struggling to process the chaos. After a moment, he begins to chuckle. Men, women, and children are fighting in the street, screaming and shrieking their grievances. Fists fly. Weapons swing. Teeth clamp down. Taking advantage of the mayhem, several small figures dart in and out of the crowd, stealing from pockets and market stalls alike. Three men and a woman are gorging themselves on fruit and bread, alternately stuffing food into their mouths and vomiting it back up onto the street. In the centre of the crowd, a handful of people are lying on the cobbles as others trample them underfoot; they seem to have no inclination to get back up. And, perhaps his favourite sight of the day, numerous couples - and some larger groups - are rutting against walls and tables, oblivious to the shocked stares of those still able to recognise the debauchery going on around them.

He turns back to Aramas. "I'm glad I came to you," he says. "I feel positive you can help me."

HER

She looked at the girl. Her heart surged. Her womb clenched. She repeated the name on her lips. "Shah."

"Mother? What are you doing here?"

The rain kept falling, washing away a multitude of sins. With a cry, she rushed to her daughter and held her close, making up for years of absence. "Oh, Shah."

Mouth agape, Barb watched the pair closely. "This is your daughter?"

The woman nodded. "Yes. This is Shah. Shah, this is Barb. She's helping me find your father."

Shah furrowed her brow. "I knew he was here."

She pulled back to look into her daughter's eyes. "What are *you* doing here?"

"Looking for him." Shah shrugged. "I know you told me to wait but what's the point in that? I can help!"

"I wanted to keep you safe."

"You told me nothing's safe. Not while he's out there."

She sighed. Pressed a kiss to her child's brow. "You've got me there."

Barb threw furtive glances back and forth along the alleyway. "I'm glad you two have found each other, but we should take this elsewhere."

In agreement, they followed her through ginnels and back streets until they reached a cosy tavern on the far side of the wharf. Once inside, they claimed a table at the back and ordered bowls of stew and mugs of ale. The heat of the fire warmed them. The smell of cooking lamb made their stomachs growl.

Shah turned to her mother. "Have you found Grandmother?"

"No. I... I don't know if we ever will, Shah. Your grandmother... Everything that happened hurt her badly. I don't know where she went."

The younger girl turned to her stew and ate in silence. When she'd finished, mopping the bowl clean with a slice of freshly baked bread, she said, "And what about Father? What will we do when we find him?"

Barb pretended to study her nails.

The woman sighed. "He's confused. Lost. I want to save him but... You have to be prepared for the worst, my love. I'm sorry."

"You're saying we need to kill him."

Barb's eyes shot up. Swallowing hard, she took a long swig of her ale. "I don't want to get in the middle of family business," she began.

"This goes beyond that," the woman said. "I –"

Shah shushed her. "What's happening outside, Mother?"

The three women rose to their feet and stared out of the small window. Other patrons did the same; the tavern grew quiet enough to hear a pin drop. In the soft silence, muffled screams could be heard from outside, growing louder as they came nearer. The women shared a glance.

"Shall we investigate?" Barb asked, already turning to the door.

The woman grimaced. "I suppose we must."

LAVENDER LYLAH

"I don't care what else you think you're busy doing," Lylah shouted, blood pounding in her ears. "This has gone on long enough and I demand that you do something about it."

Minister Gredick inhaled sharply. "Madam, I am already doing something about it. My best investigator is in that area as we speak. We are aware that something unusual is going on and ask for your patience while we look into it."

Lylah growled with frustration, surprising even herself. "Patience? We're dying out there while you sit here safe in your fancy office!" She straightened her spine and pushed herself to her full height. "I thought we lived in a democracy. In a place that's supposed to work for everyone, regardless of how much money they have. Are those pompous pillocks in the big houses scared for their lives? Are they looking over their shoulders while they prance about in their frippery and dine on food that would cost a year's wages for one of my girls?"

"Madam, I –"

"No. Don't you *Madam* me. Will it make a difference if I tell you I painted those pictures hanging on your wall? Will you do more then? Here." She threw a bag of coins on his desk. "Will this help?"

Gredick sighed and pushed the bag back to her. "Believe it or not, I don't care who you are or how much money you have. I like your paintings. I'm surprised such a talented artist lives and works by the wharf. But throwing money at me will not make a blind bit of difference to how much help you're offered. As I said, we are already investigating the deaths. You likely won't believe me but I do care about your friends and I have lost many nights of sleep over this. I am as confused and alarmed by it as you are. It's like nothing we've come across before." He pressed his fingers to his temple and rested an elbow on his desk.

Deflated, Lylah sank into the chair opposite him. "You really are helping already?"

"Yes."

"Oh. But…" She chewed on her bottom lip. "How do I keep my daughter safe when I don't know what I'm keeping her safe from?"

"All I can suggest right now is that you send her away until whatever this is has passed."

"I see." She thought about it. She had an aunt in Reoron; would that be far enough away to be safe? Freesia would object to being away from school but surely she could study from a distance. And yet… She couldn't send everyone away. What about her friends at the tavern? Tonald? That poor woman begging on the street? She sighed. "I pray you find answers soon."

"So do I," he said.

Lylah rose to leave, glanced out of the window, and frowned. "You need to see this."

"What?"

She watched as the courtyard around the houses of parliament filled with brawling people. Their shouts and cries resounded through the square. She clutched her bag with two hands. Wondered where Freesia was. "It's spreading."

HIM

He did this. He doesn't know how but he knows, somehow, he caused the debauchery that is erupting across Stalinoc. Everywhere he turns, people are fighting, fucking, and feasting on whatever they can lay their hands on. His amusement knows no bounds; finally, his bad mood has gone. Whatever has caused this chaos, it leaves him free to do as he pleases. When all around is mayhem, no one is looking too closely at one man meandering across town.

Aramas is looking for the godstone; he has left that search in her capable hands, for now. Yet, something still nibbles at the back of his mind. Something is missing… He feels a loss but can't put his finger on what is gone. Wanting comfort, he heads towards the wharf.

When he arrives at the brightly coloured boathouse rocking on the water, something stills within him. He knocks and hopes she will forgive him for his strange reaction to the painting; it had been strange and humbling to see his face so lovingly depicted on canvas. Did he really look like that? So kind and warm? How could she see him that way? True, she didn't know what he'd done, but surely some of that darkness should be obvious through the charm he'd always worn around her.

The door opens, but Lylah is nowhere to be seen. A young woman, wheat-gold hair braided into a loose bun atop her head, greets him from the wheeled chair she sits in. He blinks. This must be Freesia. Lylah speaks of her often but he has never met the girl before. He feels uncomfortable and regrets his decision to visit.

"Can I help you?" Freesia pushes the spectacles up her nose.

"I was looking for your mother," he mumbles.

Recognition dawns on her face. "Tonald?"

He nods.

She smiles and looks just like her mother. "She's only nipped out for a moment. I'm sure she'll be back in a minute or two. Please, come in." She grips the wheels of her chair and manoeuvres herself back into the kitchen, where a pot of tea sits in the middle of the table. "Would you like a cup?" she asks.

He nods again, wondering whether he should make his excuses and leave.

As Freesia picks up the teapot, he notices the leather strap she wears around her neck; it dangles as she leans forward to pour the tea. Hanging from it is a small stone, golden as the sun.

His hands tremble. His gut lurches. It cannot be…

"What is that?" he asks, clenching his fists to keep from grabbing at the stone.

Freesia glances down. "Oh, this." She lifts the stone and spins it in her hand. "It's a family heirloom. My mother gave it to me when I was a child. Her father gave it to her on his deathbed but she didn't want to wait that long to pass it on."

The stone catches the light and shines brighter. "Her father?"

The girl's cheeks redden. "Well, he said it was a family heirloom. Mother always wondered… He was a bit of a rogue, my grandpa. Light-fingered, and an infamous name in his day… I hope this doesn't make you think any less of Mother."

He shakes his head. All this time… All this time the godstone has been here, within his grasp. He thinks back to the moment he first saw Lylah, almost a year ago now. She'd been walking with her daughter and he'd only seen the back of them. He'd been so drawn to her, he recalls. He'd followed her to a tavern, gone inside and ordered a drink, paid an inordinate amount of coin for her extra services - and found it money well spent. Was it her he'd been drawn to or was it the stone that hung unknown around Freesia's pale neck?

"All this time…" he says aloud.

Freesia glances at him. "What?"

Thunder rings in his ears. His mind swims with a volley of thoughts and memories and wonderings. And through it all, the golden stone calls to him, mocking him with its nearness. "Give it to me."

Seeing something in his face, Freesia leans back. Puts the teapot down and moves a hand to one of the wheels of her chair.

Forgetting where he is, who he is, he stalks closer and holds out a hand. "Give the stone to me. Now."

When she recoils, he reaches out and rips it from her neck, breaking the leather strap and making Freesia cry out with fear. As soon as the stone touches his hand, it's like he's been hit by a tidal wave.

Memories. Strength. Power. All rush through him like a raging river, eroding the unnatural embankments that have restrained and diminished him for so long. His heart beat so fast he feels sure it will burst from his chest. For a moment, everything goes dark. The godstone glows. Power surges.

"Tonald?" Lylah's shaking voice breaks through the storm. "What's going on here?"

He looks at her, his eyes glazed with an inky blackness, his muscles bulging as his body returns to its former glory. In a voice as deep as the ocean, he replies, "Girathos rises."

HER

Something changed. She felt his presence in a way she hadn't in centuries. Her heart sank, knowing what that meant. "We are too late."

At her side, Shah nodded. "I feel it, too. He has the godstone."

Barb looked up from the body she was examining. "What?"

The woman took a deep breath. "We've run out of time. If we're to stop him, it has to be now. Before he grows too strong."

She threw off her cloak and ran. Her daughter followed.

Barb sighed. Mumbled curses under her breath. Took off after them. They raced through the streets, over cobbles and along shadowy alleyways. All around, the chaos worsened.

As the sun started to sink beneath the horizon, they reached a small houseboat rocking on the water. Men brawled outside the doorway. A beggar woman cowered from a shrieking streetwalker. And an inky darkness oozed from the windows and roof.

The woman gave a flick of her wrist and the door flew from its hinges. She barged inside. Followed the muffled screams through each room. Walked into a small kitchen and immediately took in the scene. A large man-shaped shadow held a woman by the throat. To the right, a girl in a wheelchair wept and wailed and threw household items at his chest. The shadow froze. Sniffed the air. Turned and smiled.

"Cinanouk," he said in a booming voice. "What did you do to me?"

She held her back straight and met his dark gaze. "Don't you remember?"

THEN

"I have to talk to you about your father, Shahla." Cinanouk *breathed through the pain and, as always, did what had to be done.*

"What is it, Mother?"

She said it quickly, knowing it would hurt either way. "He's found a way to put himself back together. He's looking for the godstone and, when he finds it, no one will be safe."

"How could he put himself back together? I don't know exactly what you did to him but I thought it was permanent."

Cinanouk shook her head. "I'm afraid not."

Shahla took her mother's hand. "I know you don't like to talk about it but I think it's time you told me what actually happened."

She took a deep breath. "Your grandmother and I..." Her nails dug into the palm of her hand. She forced her muscles to relax. "No, I need to start further back.

"Your father was a good man. A benevolent god. He adored humans; thought of them as children - a part of himself he needed to cherish and care for. He watched as they struggled with the darker parts of themselves. As wars broke out and men turned on women and murderers roamed the night. He grieved for them and searched for a way to help them overcome their baser instincts. After centuries of struggle, he finally came up with the idea of taking their sin into himself. He thought a god would find it easy to defeat human sin.

"He thought wrong. The evil of humanity was too strong, even for Girathos. He'd only taken a little of it when it overwhelmed him. He changed; his soul became gnarled and twisted, tainted by the darkness he now fought within. He hurt people and found amusement in their pain. He...

"Well, he did a lot of bad things. Your grandmother and I tried talking to him. We tried using our power to help him overcome the evil, but it was to no avail. When all else failed, and his cruelty grew to new levels, we found a way to stop him. As he slept, we took the godstone from him - cut out the eye that held it - and used its power against him.

"It was supposed to split the god from the human, but it didn't work like that. Instead, it fractured him into dozens of dark souls, *scattering them throughout the universe and into all dimensions - the force of splitting a god also split reality, creating new worlds to home his fragmented soul. Each piece was weakened as it was only a small part of the whole, but each still struggled with aspects of human sin. The piece that remained in this world woke and ran from us before we could contain it; his fury knew no bounds. He vowed to find a way to make himself whole again so he could retake the godstone and destroy everything that had left him broken. We never thought he'd find a way to do it."*

Shahla's silence was deafening. After a while, she said, "He destroyed himself, took away the father I loved, for the sake of humans?"

"They have their moments, child. There is much to love about them, if you let yourself see it. Still, he was not equipped to deal with their darkness; no one is, not even a god."

"I don't understand." Shahla's eyes flashed amethyst. "How has he put himself back together?"

Cinanouk took her daughter's hand. "All these years he's been building his strength. Experimenting to find a way to cross between worlds."

"And how do you know he succeeded?"

She waved a hand and a window appeared before them, cutting through the clouds. "I have always been able to see farther than the eye can. Watch, my darling, and see what your father has done."

An image danced across the window. Cinanouk turned away; she'd seen it all before and had no wish to view it again. Shahla watched, and her heart ached for the father she loved, and for the countless people he had hurt.

In one land, a young drummer girl battled against a man named Jyahgen - a man possessed by her father. As the girl killed him, inky shadows slipped from his body and were inhaled by Girathos. Her father took different shapes in different places but, everywhere he went, he brought death and destruction to innocent people. As a trickster god, he created chaos among tribal people until he was defeated by the spirits of their ancestors; Girathos, in the shape of a cat, licked the fragments of his soul from the black blood that oozed from the body.

Shahla wept as she watched her father drink in the misty souls of warring gods. In the guise of a small boy, he sucked the spirit from its imprisonment in a tree. The images came and went so fast she almost lost herself in them, her heart breaking as she saw the good and the bad of humanity. In a world of myth and faeries, he stole a cursed sword containing a fragment of his soul; in another land, one where women danced with the wind, he took the form of a woman and gathered broken shards of the gem housing his dark essence. When she saw the part of him that became a sleeping god in a dying world, grief gripped her anew; he remembered himself there - remembered that he had a child whom he loved deeply. Girathos took that last fragment of himself as the sleeping god died so that his world could live. He had done evil things but, beneath the bloody sheen of human sin, he was a father who loved his child. Was there no hope of him coming back to her?

Tears streamed down her cheeks. The window stilled, then vanished.

Struggling to witness the pain on her daughter's face, Cinanouk wrapped her arms around her daughter and they wept together for the fallen god they both loved. Eventually, Shahla's sobs quietened and she pulled back to meet her mother's gaze.

"Is he back here now, in this world?"

"Yes."

"And he is complete?"

Cinanouk offered a sad smile. "Almost. He still needs the godstone to return to his former glory. With that, he will be able to seal all his broken pieces back together and live as a god once more."

Shahla closed her eyes. "How long until he has it?"

"I can't answer that. I don't know where it is and, thank the stars, neither does he." She stroked her daughter's onyx hair and held her close. "I hid it after he'd gone, you see. And many years ago, another stole it from its hiding place. The thief was never discovered and none know where the godstone may be. I pray he never finds it."

"He was always good at finding things."

"Ah, but this time, he has an added disadvantage."

"What's that?" Shahla sniffed, wiping her nose on the back of her sleeve as she had when she was a child.

Cinanouk flashed her teeth. "When he returned from the last world, he didn't know that returning without the godstone would damage his mind and leave him in a state of confusion. The pieces of his soul are unsealed - they are in one form but still broken apart, and after spending so long living separately, they will not easily merge. Although he is here and almost whole, he will not know what's real and what's not. This is the one advantage we have, Shahla. If we can find him before he finds the godstone, we still have a chance to save everything."

Shahla's quiet breath echoed in the empty space. "Can we not still fight him either way?"

"No, my love. Once he has the godstone, there is only one thing he will do: destroy all life."

"Why?"

"Because his pain is greater than his ability to see past it. Isn't that why most bad people do bad things? All humans suffer, and all muddle through. What many, including your father, fail to see is that all things pass. After pain there will be joy again - in different shapes and sizes, but joy nonetheless. And after happiness there will be sorrow; it all circles round in time. But for your father, the weight of human sin is too much to bear. He believes he will never be free of it, and they will never be free of it, until the earth rises and the heavens fall and everything is crushed between. To him, ending life is a kindness. It will end suffering and bring the peace of nothingness. And he can only enact that with his full strength and the powers of godhood."

Shahla thought of the images she'd seen, of the grief and torment and brutality. Were all men capable of such darkness? How could any human bear to face another day knowing such a fate awaited them? "Is he right, Mother?"

"No." Cinanouk's voice was gentle but firm. "He is more wrong than I can say. Darling, we gods were never meant to bear human sin. Its corruption taints us - as you've seen with your father. His choice, although made with the best of intentions, brought more chaos and more cruelty to an already harsh world. He cannot see, and you have yet to truly see, the other side of humanity: they are capable of hope and kindness and love beyond measure. Their virtue lies in the very fact that they can choose goodness over evil, love over hate, despite the darkness that lies within. They are like children, still learning how to do the right thing, and it is our job to guide and protect them, even from themselves. Nothing more; nothing less."

"Then we have to find him. We have to stop him."

"Yes," Cinanouk agreed, though her heart broke anew. "Yes."

NOW

"Get out of my house!" Lylah screamed, though her lungs burned and her throat felt as if sandpaper rubbed over it with each breath. Behind her, Freesia shook and whimpered in fear. "Get away from my daughter!"

Tonald - though she now realised that was not his name - shook her until her teeth rattled and her vision blurred. With a low growl, he flung her across the room. She crashed into the wall and slid to the floor, dazed and injured by the impact. Everywhere hurt. Her foot lay at a strange angle and an awful numbness crept up her toes and into her ankle. But fear pushed the pain aside. Freesia!

He turned to Freesia and laughed as he pushed the gold stone into the gaping hole where his left eye should have been. It sunk deep into the cavity, throbbing and pulsating as its golden glow mixed and mingled with the inky blackness oozing from his body. "Foolish girl," he boomed. "All those years you carried this stone and never knew what truly hung around your neck. Now it's become the noose that will end you."

"Enough!" Cinanouk stepped between him and the girl. "You have to stop this, Girathos. You know who you are; come back to us. Please!"

He froze in place as he studied her. Anger, confusion, love rolled across his eyes until he shook his head and frowned. "I see your face in my dreams."

A tear trickled down her cheek. "I am your wife." She reached to take his hand and the shifting shadows stilled for a moment.

"Cinanouk?" He breathed her name like a prayer.

Shahla edged to his other side and took his other hand. "And I'm your daughter."

He looked back and forth between the two women. Emotions battered him. Memories haunted him. Finally, he whispered her name. "Shahla."

Freesia wheeled herself over to check on her mother and the movement drew his gaze. He gaped. Blushed. Realised what he'd done.

"Lylah?" He bowed his head. "I'm sorry."

Golden tears leaked from his left eye and inky black ones from his right. But the shadows rose within him, seeping from every orifice. Dark cracks appeared in his skin, rifts in the fabric of his being, and a golden-black light oozed from each one; light and dark fighting in the battlefield of his body. Fear filled his face. He screamed, and the black shadows burst free, surrounding him and drowning every last beam of gold.

When he looked at them again, black orbs filled the sockets of his eyes. Without a word, he pushed past them and made his way out onto the cobbles. All around, people sinned and suffered; the chaos spilling onto the street brought a cold smile to his face.

Cinanouk and the others followed him outside, calling his name.

Barb, who until then had held back and watched the situation unfold, covered her ears and screamed as Girathos raised his arms in the air and laughed. Her composure faltered; her calm disappeared. Succumbing to the power of his silent command, she rushed to the old beggar woman and lashed out with booted foot. The crone cowered and lifted her arms to protect her head.

"What's happening?" Lylah cried.

Cinanouk fought to control her growing horror. "It's human sin magnified by the divinity of a god. No one can escape it now."

Girathos laughed again. The wind whipped into a frenzy. Rain fell like arrows, sharp and inescapable. Thunder boomed above their heads. Lightning crashed. In the distance, the peak of Mount Elka cracked and toppled, plummeting down the mountain. The ground shook beneath their feet.

"Mama!" Freesia screamed, her terror audible above the raging storm.

Lylah grabbed her daughter and held her close. "I've got you," she said. "I've got you, my love."

Shahla heard a noise from the ocean and turned. Her heart jumped to her throat. "Mother."

"Yes?"

Wordlessly, she pointed at the immense wave growing larger as it rolled towards them.

Cinanouk gasped. "A tsunami."

"Is this the end?" Shahla asked. "Have we failed?"

Lylah hobbled back inside the houseboat before reappearing with something wrapped in cloth. Above the cacophony of the apocalypse, her voice called out, "Girathos! Wait!"

He looked at her but the chaos continued around him. "Why should I?"

She held up the canvas she'd painted his portrait on. Revealed his image. Pointed to the smile. "This is the man I loved. Are you really telling me you're not him? You're not the man who warmed me with kindness, who checked in on me after hard days, who came to me for comfort? You held me in your arms as I cried over the friends you killed! You wrapped me in your body and showed me what it felt like to be cherished. You picked lavender to make me smile. You listened for hours as I told you about my wonderful daughter. About how proud I am of her, and how much I love her. How can you listen to that and not see any goodness in us? How can you not see that love is worth saving?"

Girathos faltered. He watched the tears fall from her eyes and wanted to wrap her in his arms until they stopped. She'd been good to him, he remembered. She took care of her friends. Gave money to the poor. Offered kindness to anyone she met.

But he'd fucked her with the blood of her friends on his hands. He'd kissed Lylah's bare skin and forgotten all about Cinanouk, betraying them both in one fell swoop. They'd both be better off without the life that had spat vitriol at their goodness.

The cracks in his skin deepened, becoming great ravines filled with dark shadows. Agony washed over him like a wave, permeating every pore, penetrating heart and soul. He lifted his voice to the stars and cried out, "Help me!"

He saw only one way to end all suffering. Channelling his pain, he stirred the storm and the water, increasing their fury. Clouds covered the sky, hiding the light of the moon and stars. Darkness reigned within and without, and the world withered beneath its onslaught.

All around, people stopped what they were doing and watched with growing horror. By the water, Barb pulled her foot back mid-swing and recoiled from the reality of what she'd done. She looked around. Saw Girathos waving his arms to orchestrate his apocalypse. Narrowed her eyes and stepped towards him with her knife gleaming in her hand. She edged closer and raised the blade, thrusting it at his back.

Girathos spun and his emanating darkness seared Barb's body. She cried out, dropping the knife and trying to pull away. But it was too late. Laughing, Girathos took her head in his hands and pushed the shadows inside her skull.

She screamed. Kicked. Clawed at his hands.

Lightning flashed above her head and onyx blood seeped from her eyes and ears. In seconds, her feet stilled and her heart stopped. Girathos threw her body into the water and resumed his deadly work.

"No!" Cinanouk shouted. "Barb!" She rushed to tackle Girathos but he spun out of her grasp.

High on the thrill of murder, he turned to Freesia. He took one step. Then another. She trembled in her chair and met his gaze with quivering lips. "Don't be scared," he said. "There will be peace after."

"You will not touch my daughter!" Screaming her rage, Lylah dived between them. Standing before a murderous god with nothing to help her, she raised her fists and her chin, knowing she faced her own death. "You will not touch her."

His laughter shook the sky. He leaned into her, wrapping the dark fog around her body, thrilling at the scent of blood as it tore small strips of flesh from her arms and legs. When she screamed, he shuddered and rejoiced.

A blast of light knocked him away from her, Cinanouk and Shahla's power combining to force him back. Lylah fell to her knees. Whimpered and moaned. Weeping, Freesia lowered herself from her chair and sank to the ground beside her. She took her mother in her arms and stroked her hair as she waited for death to take them.

Girathos regained his feet. His jaw tightened and his eyebrows knitted together as he stood before his wife and daughter. "So you do have teeth."

Shahla ignored him and called to her mother. "How can we defeat him?"

In reply, Cinanouk raised her palm and sent a wave of light into his heart. An instant later, Shahla added her own power to the beam.

Girathos stumbled back beneath their onslaught. They pushed forward, driving him back towards the water. For a moment, it seemed to be working.

And then, he straightened his back. Dug his heels into the ground. Pushed back against their power and howled at the stars.

Darkness seemed to rush to him, swirling like a whirlwind around his body. He leeched the glow from the moon, the whistle from the wind; the sky seemed to fold in on itself, crumpling like discarded parchment as the world and everyone in it screamed. Mothers held their children close and prayed for a miracle.

Girathos closed his eyes. Cinanouk and Shahla ran to confront him and were thrown back by the force of his power. All around him, searing shadows whipped and lashed at anything that came near, flaying skin from bones and stealing the breath from lungs. Cinanouk helped her daughter to her feet and they both tried again, pushing against the power keeping them away. All their combined strength was not enough; they could not reach him.

Beside them, almost unnoticed, the old beggar woman rose to her feet. Her back straightened. The years sloughed from her body like old skin. She threw off her cloak and strode towards Girathos, silver hair glowing like moonbeams. Ignoring all else around her, she focused on the god in the centre of the dark storm and lifted her palms towards him. Rays as bright as sunlight burst from her hands as she clenched her jaw and pushed forward, breaking through the dark force surrounding him.

The cobbles shook with the effort of her exertion. Wind battered the buildings and lifted the water from the sea. The tsunami crashed around the shield of Girathos' darkness and scattered to either side, roaring down alleyways and sweeping bodies into its embrace.

Freesia clung to Lylah and closed her eyes.

The old woman kept moving. The shadows gouged at her flesh and deep cracks appeared in her skin, similar to those on Girathos, only hers glowed with the light of the sun. Her wrinkled face was a mask of agony. She gritted her teeth and pushed on. As inky claws cut and maimed her, as searing shadows burnt her from head to toe, as her bones screamed against the pressure and her eyes wept from the pain, she inched her way closer to the raging god.

"Shahla!" Cinanouk yelled above the crash of wind and water. "We have to help her!"

The two women raised their hands again and sent a rush of their own power into the darkness, throwing their added weight against the outward push of Girathos' dark energies.

Seconds passed like hours. Mountains toppled. Oceans rose. Men died and gods wept.

And the old woman, golden ichor streaming from a multitude of gashes, face so marred her features could no longer be seen amid the glow of her wounds, screamed into the void as she gave one final push and tumbled into the eye of the storm.

Watching from the outside, Cinanouk and the others saw the broken woman wrap her arms around the enraged god and cradle him like a child.

Lylah looked through eyes blurred with tears. "Who is that?"

Girathos, poised to fight, froze. Relaxed his body into the crone's embrace. Nestled his head into her shoulder and wept as he called out, "Mother."

Cinanouk took Shahla's hand, her own tears falling freely. "That is Maraebh, Mother of All. Mother of Girathos."

As the world continued to crumble, Girathos clung to his mother and said, "Why?"

She looked at him.

He lifted a hand to her face. Cupped her cheek and sobbed at the damage his darkness had done to her. "Why would you do this? Why go through so much pain to reach me? It will all be over soon anyway."

Gently, she stroked the hair from his brow. Brushed her hands over the dark cracks on his face and filled them with light. "I am your mother. Bringing you into this world caused me more pain than you can imagine, as it does every mother whose body expands and contracts and tears to give new life. I would go through any agony for you, my son."

He shook his head and dug his fingers into her arms. "To save me? I am not worth saving, and nor is anything in this world."

"Are you sure about that?" she asked, her voice as fractured as his soul.

Girathos looked at her again.

"Whatever you've done, I love you. And that love is stronger than any darkness, Girathos. You stand here and wonder why I hurt myself to reach you - don't you know any mother would break herself a thousand times over to help her child! Look around you. *Look* at the world. There is cruelty, yes. But love rises above it all.

"Look at your wife." She took his chin and gently turned it until he saw Cinanouk. "Look how, even now, she holds your daughter's hand. And your lover, Lylah - she braved your wrath to save her child, as all mothers, all *parents*, stand between their children and the encroaching dark. Think of the mothers in all the worlds you've seen. Maebh took on the fae for her daughter. Lilise fought from beyond the grave because her family needed her. Sabine instigated a miracle when her love for her child inspired a god to sacrifice himself to save the world. Love is everywhere, my boy, if you remember to look for it.

"Don't you see how much love there is in the world? How it conquers the darkness? How can you consign humanity to extinction when every mother's voice screams out in pain that she cannot save her children? How can you not see that such love is worth saving?" Tears streamed down her cheeks as she clutched him tighter. "*My* love is worth saving. I love you, Girathos. Whatever decision you make here, I love you."

As Maraebh cradled her son, Cinanouk and Shahla took advantage of his distraction and edged closer. One on each side now, they infused their power with the love they felt for him and threw it against the battlements of his darkness. Light as bright as day surrounded Maraebh and Girathos; it rolled between the shadows, writhing and tangling and fighting each pocket of bitterness and hate.

Slowly, oh, so slowly, they crept closer as the world died around them and the overwhelming chorus of screaming death roared to a crescendo.

They blocked it out. Focused on the weeping god who rocked in his mother's arms. And blanketed him in their love and light until the radiance of the sun swept through his body and washed the darkness from his veins.

Pain filled him. Horror rolled across his features as his mind awoke to the truth of all that he had done. He clutched at Maraebh. "How do I live with it all?"

She smiled. "The same way that they do. You stand up, put one foot in front of the other, and learn from your mistakes. You have to take responsibility, Girathos. There is no easy way to absolve you of your sins. Face what you've done and suffer the consequences every day until you leave the world better than you found it."

"But I want to die," he whispered.

Her mouth tightened. "No. If you die, you put another scar on the souls left behind. No, my son. You will live with what you have done and so will we."

When agony wracked him, he cried, "Mother! Mother, help me!"

Maraebh kissed his brow and lifted his chin until he met her gaze. "Let it go, Girathos. Let go of what you took from them. A god was never meant to bear the weight of human sin; it is theirs to carry, to learn from, and to overcome."

"Let it go," Cinanouk said.

Shahla repeated it. "Let it go, Father."

Girathos lifted his face to the inky sky. Opened his mouth. Bellowed to the heavens. And the darkness erupted from him like lava. Humanity's sins fell from the sky in a blanket of dark ash as Girathos' broken skin healed into scars the colour of sunlight.

TOMORROW

Time does not heal all wounds.

Girathos learned that the hard way as he watched the humans piece their world back together. Some sins were too strong to overcome; some were too cruel to forgive. And some scars never faded.

His actions had sent ripples through the world - and created others. In the wake of his chaos, whole cities had to be rebuilt and whole kingdoms restructured around a changed landscape. The mountains he'd toppled would never again tower above the clouds; the rivers would forever follow a different course. And the dead... Even he could not reach beyond that barrier. Those lost would wait in the next life to be reunited with their loved ones.

The weight of his crimes was agonising.

His mother had been right, of course - not something he'd have admitted out loud before his experience of humanity had changed him. She'd told him he'd see kindness if he looked for it, and he had. Sometimes it was obvious in grand gestures, large donations or scholarships or projects to house the homeless. At other times, however, it was the small acts that awed him, that shamed him for his failure to notice them before. The woman who gave her last loaf of bread to the children begging in the street. The young lad who helped his sister when she grazed her knees falling from a tree. The mother who loved her child no matter what.

All mothers. He saw them now, their quiet sacrifices and loud love.

Rumours had spread after the dust cleared and the gods vanished. Rumours of evil powers, terrible demons, and omniscient gods blazing to the rescue. None had it right. None but a kind painter who lived on a houseboat with her studious daughter and mourned a love that had never been real.

Guilt stabbed at his heart. What he'd done to Lylah... She'd risen above it now and he was amazed by her strength. She'd grieved for her friends and then bought her way into politics and worked to change the system from within. The goodness of her heart shone brighter than he'd ever thought possible. And somehow, she'd found it in her heart to forgive him.

Forgive.

He closed his eyes. He didn't deserve forgiveness. Didn't deserve the crowds of worshippers who once again flocked to his temples, though many more prayed to statues of the women who'd saved him with their love. He didn't deserve that, either. How could they love a monster?

He didn't know how they did it. How humans stumbled through life living with the guilt and the shame of their bad choices. He understood why many turned to drink and drugs and other escapist pursuits. Some days it took all he had to stand on shaking feet and try to do better.

He needed to find a way to atone. Every day, thoughts raced through his mind. What did the world need? *More coins? Better houses? Richer soil?* He froze. What if he could find a way to inspire people to do good in their own way? What if he sent muses to live among the humans and encourage every instance of goodness? As he wrote in a small notebook - a remnant of his memory loss meaning he now had to write everything down - Cinanouk walked behind him and lay a hand on his shoulder. He flinched and she sighed.

"You do not want me here?" she asked.

"No. I mean..." He spun to take her hand. "I'm sorry. I do want you here - more than anything. I just... How can you forgive me for what I did?"

She tilted her head to one side. "I don't know. I haven't yet."

He swallowed hard. Remembered the feeling of being inside another woman. The memory twisted a knife in his gut. "I'm so sorry, Cinanouk. I love you. My heart is yours. But I understand you may never forget my betrayal."

One side of her mouth curved. "You are lucky we have an eternity to find our way through this."

He nodded. Pressed a soft kiss to the back of her hand and was grateful she allowed it.

"Come," she said. "Shahla and your mother are waiting."

He took a deep breath to ready himself and followed his wife. In a garden bright with flowers, they waited. He ran to Shahla and pulled her close, relishing the miracle of being able to hold his child in his arms.

After a moment, he offered a hand out to Maraebh. "Mother."

She tugged him closer, held him, as he held his little one. "Girathos. It's good to see you."

He still couldn't bring himself to look at her. To see the vibrant scars crisscrossing her skin.

"Son?"

He bit his lip.

"Look at me."

Reluctantly, he lifted his chin. His eyes. Winced at the physical reminder of the pain he'd inflicted.

Maraebh chuckled. "Don't be scared of them, Girathos. My scars don't bother me so why should they bother you?"

"Because I put them there."

"Ah, sweet boy. These scars are my souvenirs. Mementoes of a time when I did the right thing. I would do it all over again with no regrets."

Although the pain still lived within him, he smiled and finally met her gaze. "The right thing?"

"The right thing," she repeated with a firm nod. "I did what any mother would have: I loved my child. After all, is there anything stronger than that?"

END

Charlotte Langtree is a poet, novelist, and writer of short fiction. Raised in West Yorkshire, she has a deep love of hills, berry-picking, and her unique accent. She has been published in several magazines and anthologies, as well as online. In September 2021, she was voted the winner of the Great Clarendon House Writing Challenge. Dragon Soul Press selected her story 'The Shadow Queen' as an Editor's Pick of 2021. You can find her online by following the links below:

Website: www.charlottelangtree.wordpress.com
Facebook: www.facebook.com/CharlotteLangtreeAuthor
Twitter: www.twitter.com/CharlotteLangt5

WHAT PEOPLE SAY ABOUT CLARENDON HOUSE

J. McCulloch, Author
Clarendon House has what the majority of other publishers lack; the personal touch. Grant Hudson draws people into his cosy library (also known as the Inner Circle Writers' Group), sits them down and works his magic. Many new writers lack confidence in their ability, so Grant fine tunes their perspective, boosts their morale and sets them up to win. I have been humbled by his untiring efforts to help us all. We are his people. He is our mentor, our eccentric English professor and our much valued friend.

D. Taylor, Author
As I was scrolling fb, and seeing all these ads from people claiming to help authors do this and do that, I thought to myself, Grant Hudson is the genuine mentor. Thanks for your solid advice.

P. O'Neil, Author
Grant is the model mentor for this new age of writing.

A. Delf, Author
The world is better with all this beautiful work seen at last.

M. Ahmed, Author
A place where good literature is nurtured.

Join the
Inner Circle Writers' Group
on Facebook!

This group is unlike most writers' groups on social media. Post ANYTHING about writing, including:
- passages from books you admire
- recommended reading
- extracts from your own work
- requests for advice or guidance about anything to do with writing

'Our little ICWG family is certainly a wonderful group full of kindness and encouragement. It's wonderful to see the growth of so many writers from the help and guidance they've received from this group alone'

Founded in 2008, this group is a thriving community, celebrating fiction of all kinds. Here you can also get a glimpse of the unique and revolutionary 'physics of fiction' as outlined in the book *How Stories Really Work* (see below) and in many articles and items.

This is not available anywhere else.

The group is free and fun.

Just go to Facebook:

https://www.facebook.com/groups/innercirclewritersgroup

Subscribe to
The Inner Circle Writers' Magazine!

A quality, downloadable pdf, available internationally, this magazine is unique, is designed to service your needs as a writer and also to entertain you in ways that right now you probably can't imagine, including with specially commissioned short stories, expert columns, interesting articles and much, much more.
- Over 100 pages each issue of expert writing advice, fantastic fiction and inspiring art
- Entry to FREE writing competitions, interviews with writers, enlightening articles
- Opportunities to see your writing in print as well as dozens of other submission opportunities
- Every issue downloaded direct to your device for only £2.00, or 12 issues for only £20.00.

Subscribe now!

https://www.clarendonhousebooks.com/magazine

HOW STORIES REALLY WORK:
Exploring the Physics of Fiction
by Grant P. Hudson

Learn:
- what a story really is
- what it is actually doing to and for you and other readers
- the things called 'plots', what they are and how they are actually made
- the four categories of the powerful force that compels readers to turn pages
- the magnetic power that attracts readers even before the introduction of any character
- what the thing called a 'character' actually is, and how to rapidly build a convincing one
- what 'protagonists' and 'antagonists' really are, and what the connection between them consists of
- the 'nuclear reactor' that drives all successful stories through to their conclusion
- how the four basic genres - Epic, Tragedy, Irony and Comedy - are
  composed and how they work to create different effects

and much, much more.

What the experts say:

As with all professionals, I too read craft books every day, to stay on top of my game. Over the last thirty years, I've read (literally) hundreds of writing books. And, lemme tell ya, the VAST majority of them are garbage. The relative few that are decent still aren't great. Writing instructors usually spend 60,000 words saying what could've been said in 60.

EXCEPT for yours, Grant. Your books are hands down, bar none, exceptional. You get down into the nitty gritty and talk about real stuff that's immediately useful. I especially like How Stories Really Work. You really nailed it with that one.

And, Grant... it's REALLY hard to impress me. But, you had me hooked from the very first sentence. In fact, I've already turned a number of my past clients onto it.

So... thank you for giving the writing world something of merit. Your book is a breath of invigorating fresh air. May it breathe new life into this great industry of ours so that writers may once again set the world on fire.

-J. C. Admore, Professional Writing Expert

An amazing book. Fascinating application of physics theory to the art of fiction writing. Presents new ways of understanding how stories work. I now look for 'vacuums' everywhere. Excellent case studies covering all genres. Thought-provoking and inspiring. I highly recommend this book to all readers and writers of fiction.

- G. Leyland (B Social Work, Grad Dip Writing, MA Creative Writing)

What the authors say:

I'm reading through How Stories Really Work. I've studied writing books for years but I've never seen anything like this!

I learned about your work after reading an article you wrote. I was intrigued by the premise, but at the time, there wasn't an Amazon review (something I must rectify when I'm finished). I decided it wouldn't hurt to read the preview. . . And promptly bought it.

This book is REVOLUTIONARY. Everything is made so simple and precise that other methods of writing seem clumsy by comparison. It's not just a way of writing, but a way of seeing.

-A. P. (Author)

It's beautiful, informative, essential reading for anyone who wants to write fiction. It's almost a responsibility point, you're committing a crime if you don't get it into peoples' hands!!!

-B.R. (Author)

Loved the book. Have used the principles in many a story. It all makes so much sense. If you want help in drawing readers in - this is the book to get.

-M W-B (Author)

This is a book every author should own. Grant P. Hudson does an outstanding job explaining story structure and the mechanics involved in creating a story or novel that readers will love. His examples are explained in an engaging manner so this book doesn't seem like reading a text book. I have already implemented many of his ideas in building a novel. This book contains great advice and I highly recommend it to all authors.
-D. T. (Author)

After reading this book, I'll never look at stories the same way. This step-by-step how-to book is full of wisdom about how classic stories are structured. You will see how to apply these principles to your own stories and novels, converting them to page-turners.

-P. V. A. (Author)

An essential purchase for anyone wishing to not only improve their writing but understand the art of story telling. You will never read a book the same way again. Nor watch a film or play without seeing the theory, that Grant so eloquently describes. Brilliant, worth every penny.

-D. S. (Author)

I have had nearly 100 short stories published and thought I knew about writing. This book taught me new ways to look at my own writing as well as other writing. Grant Hudson doesn't recycle old ways to look at the writing process, he invents new ways for a writer to examine almost every aspect of writing fiction, and provides a new vocabulary for how to do it. Very highly recommended for anyone who writes or wants to write fiction.

-A. C. (Author)

I wish I had found this book sooner. It was fascinating and insightful. I am now very annoying when watching films as I apply the techniques learned in this book, and quickly guess the twists! Very helpful in planning and forming ideas and I use this technique when writing stories.

-S. C. (Author)

I love the way Grant has approached the whole subject in this excellent book, in a very different and almost 'obvious' way compared to other books that attempt to teach the craft of writing. As a writer myself I now see in a different light what I am writing. Where was this book 35 years ago when I first started writing? One of those 'I wish I'd known that years ago' books.

-J. W. F. (Author)

I finished this book over two nights and had an epiphany. Such common sense and thought provoking ideas. This should be a mandatory text book for any serious writer. I'm excited to inject more purpose to my writing. This book will become a constant reference book for me now. Highly recommend it.

-R. C. (Author)

Your book is teaching me all the stuff that the other books don't! I can learn all about three-act structures and all that stuff elsewhere -this book is telling me exactly what to put INTO the structure! It makes writing so easy and you can immediately spot where you're going wrong! Excellent!

-L.J. (Professional)

This is an absolutely amazing achievement! I highly recommend it to anyone interested in writing fiction.

-T.R. (Student)

I was extremely impressed. This is not idle flattery.
You've done a superb job in uncovering the factors that go into making a great piece of literature.

-B.R. (Executive)

Printed in Great Britain
by Amazon